"The desire for possession is insatiable, to such
a point that it can survive even love itself."

—*Albert Camus*

To Lynne and Daniel,
with love

Acknowledgments

The author wishes to thank the following people for their ongoing help and support: Ken Atchity, friend and literary manager; Annette Rogers and Barbara Peters, my editors, as well as Robert Rosenwald, co-founder with Ms. Peters of Poisoned Pen Press. Their creative insights and unflagging encouragement make all of my books better; Suzan Baroni, Beth Deveny, Holli Roach, Michael Barson, and Raj Dayal, also at Poisoned Pen Press, for their professionalism and enthusiasm.

My friends and colleagues, too numerous to mention, but with special appreciation to Hoyt Hilsman, Fred Golan, Laurie Stevens, Jim Denova, Becky Denova, Michael Harbadin, Chi-Li Wong, Claudia Sloan, Bob Masello, Dave Congalton, Charlotte Alexander, Lolita Sapriel, Al Abramson, Richard Stayton, Dick Lochte, Peter Anthony Holder, Lynn Cullen, Thomas B. Sawyer, Bob Corn-Revere, Bill Shick, David Levy, Mark Baker, Stephen Jay Schwartz, Judy Knaiz, Doug Lyle, Mark Schorr, Jeffrey Siger, Kim Chestney, Dr. Robert Stolorow, and the late Garry Shandling.

Chapter One

Miles Davis saved my life.

I was sitting on the couch in my front room, re-reading the three-inch-thick dossier, listening to Davis' seminal album with his New Quintet. I'd slid the CD into the squat disc player minutes earlier, right after I'd poured myself a second Jack Daniels. Neat.

It was sometime after nine p.m. My broad picture window looking out on Grandview Avenue reflected an opaque darkness chilled by an earlier spring rain. As usual lately, I'd forgotten to draw the heavy drapes when I came home from work. Sometimes I even forgot to eat.

My only task, these past few nights, was to put the dossier on my lap and slowly peruse its many pages. To read yet again the police detectives' statements, peer at the crime scene photos, review the Medical Examiner's report. The hard-backed binder had become an important but cryptic artifact, the potential key to a mystery that I'd long accepted as buried in the past.

"Okay," I said aloud, to an empty room. An empty house. "Tonight I find it. Whatever the hell *it* is."

The key to a mystery. At least that's what he'd claimed it was, the man who told me about it. Who believed that hidden in the dossier's pages was an overlooked or ignored piece of evidence proving that my wife's death almost a dozen years ago hadn't been what it seemed. That the gunfire that ended Barbara's life was not the lethal result of a mugging gone wrong.

It was murder.

And the proof was in this extensive dossier that same man had once prepared at a wealthy new patient's request. Before she'd consider entering therapy. A dossier on me.

He told me all this over a week ago, as I crouched by his blood-soaked body, staring in disbelief at the man's stricken face. Moments before, he'd saved that patient's life by stepping in front of a killer's gun, taking the bullet meant for her. Although the shooter had been quickly subdued, it was too late for the wounded man.

Gasping in pain from the slug lodged in his gut, he urged me to go to his office and find his copy of the dossier. Within moments his voice had fallen to a croaked, desperate whisper as he struggled to speak, to find words, which he somehow managed to do, right before he died in my arms.

I winced now at the memory and swallowed half the whiskey, barely aware of the artful harmonics flowing from the CD player atop the nearby bureau. Denied even the meager solace I usually derived most nights from the soulful, insistent music.

Truth is, I was still pretty scarred, both physically and psychologically, from the events of the past few weeks. The kidnapping of that troubled new patient. The shocking violence and sudden, unexpected deaths that followed. The final showdown with her captors. And, throughout, my own headstrong, perhaps foolish, involvement.

God knows, I still had the bruises to prove it.

I sighed heavily. My eyes, tired after a long day seeing patients, squinted down at the blurred, Xeroxed documents arranged chronologically in the ringed binder, trying to make sense of what I was seeing. Especially the handwritten notes of the investigating detectives. As though, in the soft amber light of the table lamp, the hurriedly scrawled words had become meaningless cyphers.

Not that the police reports made up the bulk of the binder's contents. This painstakingly prepared dossier was literally the paper trail of my entire life. From birth certificate to University of Pittsburgh psychology degree, from my clinical experience to favorite bar, hospital affiliations to tax returns. My family and its many sorrows. My marriage to the former Barbara Camden, also a PhD, including our brief stint in couples counseling. My friends and colleagues, my private practice, my work as a consultant to the Pittsburgh Police. All my forty-plus years condensed into a stack of documents, copied records, data printed off the Internet. The gains and losses, both professionally and personally, that made up my life.

But it was the material pertaining to Barbara's death that drew my repeated, almost obsessive interest. Personal details were compiled by the police at the start of their investigation. Her own family's history, her noted career as a linguistics professor at Pitt, her marriage to me not long after we'd first met as graduate students. Then came the forensics from the crime scene, the futile canvas of the surrounding area. Leads that went nowhere, anonymous tips that never panned out. And finally their interview with me a month after the mugging, as I lay in the hospital bed, recovering from my own gunshot wound.

There hadn't been much I could tell them. Barbara and I had been approached coming out of a restaurant at the Point by an armed thug in a hoodie. He was about my size, I vaguely recalled, though his face was almost totally obscured by the peaked hood and the black of night. A chilled darkness barely broken by the restaurant's soft-hued exterior lamps and a single light canopied over the valet parking kiosk.

It had all happened in what seemed like moments. The guy grabbed for Barbara's purse, she resisted, and I tried to intervene. In the struggle, three shots went off, two finding my wife. I took the third to my head, putting me on the ground. Then the mugger ran off, his echoing footsteps the last thing I remembered before passing out...

He was never found.

Someone inside the restaurant called 911. But by the time

the police and an ambulance arrived, Barbara had died at the scene. I, for some reason, didn't.

I still bear the scar from the bullet that pierced my skull, evidence of my unlikely survival. My inexplicable, unearned luck.

I guess I've been trying to earn it ever since.

Despite the knot tightening in my stomach, I threw back the rest of the whiskey. It tasted as sour as I felt. Whatever clue I was supposed to discover in this dossier still eluded me, after a half-dozen careful readings on as many nights. Maybe the dying man had been wrong, and there was nothing to find.

I was just about to close the binder for the night when an old favorite track, "Just Squeeze Me," came from the CD player's speakers. Miles on trumpet, Coltrane on sax. Heart-stopping, elegant, and perfect.

Except the volume wasn't loud enough. So, favoring my still-bruised ribs, I levered myself up from the couch and went over to where the player sat on the bureau.

I never made it.

I'd just bent to turn up the volume—

Suddenly, the front window shattered behind me. A booming explosion of glass, jagged shards cascading into the room.

Frozen with shock, I felt the rush of the bullet as it whistled past me, just over my shoulder. Missing me by inches. Embedding itself in the wall.

I threw myself to the floor. Sprawled there, unmoving. Conscious only of a dull roaring in my skull. The insistent reverberation of the gunshot.

I waited, heart thudding in my chest, for the sound of another shot. Another implosion of broken glass.

A sound that never came.

Chapter Two

Still frozen where I lay, I felt cool air prickling the back of my neck. Heard the hushed rustle of the drapes.

I slowly got to my feet. A slight wind from outside, from the darkened, tree-shrouded street, wafted through the shattered window. I let out a long breath. Aware now of the sound of an angry, upraised voice, thick with drink, coming from the street.

Steadying myself, I walked carefully around the broken glass splayed at my feet and opened the front door. At first, deep shadows thrown by my porch light made it hard to see what was happening. Then, stepping from the threshold, I made out the slim form of a young woman, maybe mid-twenties, cowering behind my Mustang in the driveway. Long raven-black hair in disarray, staring out at the middle of the street.

I followed her gaze, and saw a large, thick-shouldered black man, in sneakers, tee-shirt, and sweats, waving an ugly revolver. His furious, sputtering voice cutting the moist night air like a scythe. Screaming obscenities as he raised the gun to the sky and fired again.

"Where you hidin', you fuckin' bitch? I swear to Christ, I'm gonna shoot this gun up your ass till you shit blood!"

Even in the uncertain light, I could make out his tall, muscular frame. All two hundred-eighty pounds of it. Maybe thirty, with close-cropped hair, he was strikingly handsome.

Behind him, across the street and hiding behind a car

parked at the curb, was another man. Obscured by darkness, he'd begun shouting, too. Urging the gunman to put away his weapon.

"Goddammit, Burke, put that thing away. I called the cops this time. I mean it! I've had it with your bullshit!"

The man named Burke, footing unsure, swung his head around drunkenly to peer in the direction of the man's voice.

"You want some o' this, fucker? Mind your own damn business, you racist piece o' shit."

He tried to steady his gun hand, find his new target in the dark. Alcohol fueling an inchoate rage.

By then, I'd scrambled around to the back of my car and joined the terrified girl. Even in the faint glow of the porch lamp, she seemed vaguely familiar.

"You okay?" I clutched one slender shoulder.

Her blue-green eyes stared. "Do I *look* okay, asshole?"

"I meant, are you hit?"

"Eddie can't shoot for shit, thank God. But with my luck, he'll end up killing me by accident."

I risked taking another look. Still standing uncertainly in the middle of the street, Burke had begun waving his gun again. But almost halfheartedly now. As though an engine running out of gas, his movements had slowed. Shoes scraping pavement as he stutter-stepped.

"Joy! Where the hell are you? Dammit, Joy…" His voice had grown weaker, shoulders falling. The gun now held limply at his side. "Aw, c'mon, woman…C'mon now…"

With a final, guttural sigh of resignation, he eased himself down to the pavement. Sitting with the revolver in his lap. Head lolling. Muttering to himself.

I risked getting to my feet, still at the rear of my car, while the man across the street slowly did the same. Also like me, he was reluctant to come out from behind the safety of his parked sedan. Instead, he and I merely looked at each other across the expanse of road, over Burke's slumped head.

Before either of us could move or say a word, a patrol car, lights flashing, rumbled down the empty street toward us. It braked to a stop a dozen feet from where Burke sat, unmoving, looking as forlorn as a big man with a gun in his lap can look.

I headed toward the patrol car as two cops climbed out. One was white, and on the young side. The other was older, black, with a trim mustache. Each had his service pistol drawn. As they approached Burke, whose back was toward them, I called out.

"Gun!" I pointed at the sitting man.

That was all they needed to hear. Each cop two-handed his weapon, aimed at the back of Burke's head.

"Lose the gun! *Now!*" The older uniform shouted at him. "Nice and easy. Two fingers. No sudden moves or you're toast."

"*Do* it, scumbag!" The younger cop took another step toward their suspect. "Fuckin' chooch, *do it now!*"

Burke barely stirred. Then he slowly brought his hand up, the gun dangling between thumb and forefinger. Gingerly tossed it away. The revolver traveled about six yards and skittered to a stop on the pavement. The young cop hurried to scoop it up.

"Okay. Good," the older one said to Burke. "Now don't move, all right? Hands on your head."

Burke did as he was told. Hands clasped tightly on his head, powerful arms spread like wings. Then both cops were on him, shoving him facedown, cuffing his hands behind his back. He didn't resist.

"Damn bitches, all of 'em." Burke's voice slurred, more grief than rancor. The tone of defeat. "Bitches and ho's…"

By this time, the man from across the street had come striding over to stand with me. Peering down at Burke.

The older cop craned his neck up at him. "Who are you?"

"Marv Kranski. Eddie and Joy are my next door neighbors. Eddie Burke and Joy Steadman. Lunatics, both of them."

Though he stood in the glaring strobe of the patrol car's

flashing lights, I could just make out Kranski's features. Middle-aged, with a beer belly and thick-rimmed glasses. I'd seen him, I now realized, a number of times as he drove to and from work. At least I'd assumed that was where he was going. I'd never even known his name. Unlike the old, Italian neighborhood in which I grew up, people on Grandview—at least on my stretch of street—rarely knew anything about each other.

"Were you the one who called it in?" the cop asked, as his partner hauled Burke to his feet. The big man was still muttering to himself, oblivious. Tear-blurred eyes downcast.

"Damn right, I called you guys." Marv Kranski grunted indignantly. "Him and his slut girlfriend over there are always getting into fights. Screaming at each other. Throwing shit against the walls. Real picnic living next door."

I turned to look at the pricey split-level house behind us, the one with the sedan parked in front.

"That's your house, right?" I asked him.

"And my car, yeah. Used to be a nice, quiet street. Not so much 'diversity,' if ya know what I mean. Now it's a goddam reality TV show. 'Eddie and Joy's Crib From Hell.'" He laughed at his own joke.

If the black officer took note of Kranski's comment, he gave no indication. A thick silence grew between the two men.

Finally, Kranski gave a loud cough. "Look, I figure we're done here, right? If you need anything more from me, you know where to find me."

"Dispatch has your number. Thanks for calling it in, Mr. Kranski."

He waved it off, as though suddenly bored with the whole affair. Then he trotted back toward his house.

"Speaking of Joy…" I looked past the two cops and Burke to find the young woman still motionless behind my Mustang, though she'd risen to her feet, staring distrustfully at the four men standing in the middle of the street. Even in the dim light, I could recognize the fear, the delayed panic cresting behind those angry, bitter eyes.

"Young lady." The older cop called out to her gently. "I'm Officer Pratt. Mind comin' over for a minute?"

He was practiced enough at handling domestic situations not to approach her, or ask too quickly for her side of the story. Acted as if he was just a regular guy, wanting to get to know her, giving her time to realize that the danger had passed.

But it appeared Pratt had misjudged the victim. Though she trembled slightly as she approached, her eyes remained hard. Wary. Older than her years.

As Pratt got some basic info from her, including her address—a handsome two-storied Colonial that sat at an angle across the street from my place—I suddenly grasped why she'd seemed so familiar before. I'd seen her a few times out in front of her house, retrieving her mail or getting behind the wheel of her Jaguar. She'd wave, and I'd casually wave back. Again, never having a clue as to her name or who she was.

Though now she was barefoot, wearing only jeans and a lacy, dirt-smudged top, I recalled how often she'd been stylishly dressed as she left her house. Model-stylish. Moneyed. The look and manner of casual, self-assured wealth.

Yet, appraising her pale, lovely face as she desultorily answered the cop's questions, I could make out the faint marks on her cheek from the back of someone's hand. Though he didn't say anything, I knew that Pratt had noticed it, too.

The younger cop had bundled Eddie Burke into the back of the patrol car and locked the door. He came over to where we three stood, his gaze zeroing in on Joy Steadman. Openly staring at the swell of her taut breasts in the lace top, nipples outlined against the thin fabric.

With a grimace, Joy crossed her arms across her chest. Face turning to marble.

Unfazed, the young cop turned to me, his callow smile closer to a smirk.

"I *know* you." He actually pointed at me. "You're that shrink. Dan Rinaldi."

"I'm not a shrink. I'm a clinical psychologist."

"Whatever."

"And *you* are?"

"Name's McCarthy. Yeah, lotta us blues know about you. From the news and everything. You're kinda on the job, right?"

"I consult with the Department, yes. When I'm asked."

"Or even if you ain't. Least, that's how I hear it." He chuckled knowingly. "Almost got your ass killed a couple times."

I shrugged. "You had to be there."

He rubbed the back of his neck. "Therapy, eh? That shit's for mooks and pussies."

I said nothing. He glanced over at his fellow officer.

"Want me to get the Doc's statement, too, Henry?"

The older cop shrugged. "Fine with me. He *did* get his damn window shot out."

I gave him a questioning look. "How'd you know that?"

Pratt laughed, and gestured toward my shattered front window. The wind had shifted, and was now sucking the drawn ends of my floor-length drapes to the outside.

"I figured you didn't go and shoot out your window your own self," he said. "For the hell of it."

"Point taken. But look, how about I come down to the station later and give a statement? I'm on the payroll with the Department. You can be sure I'll show up."

"Why not tell us what happened now and get it over with?"

I turned to Joy Steadman, her hands dug into her jeans pocket, eyes averted. Fooling nobody. Especially not me.

"Because I think Ms. Steadman here needs someone to sit with her for a while. Just till her nerves quiet down."

Her face came up, flushed, livid. "My nerves are fine, Doctor. I don't need anything except to be left alone."

McCarthy cleared his throat theatrically. "Not about to happen, Miss. We're definitely gonna need *your* statement. Your jagoff boyfriend was out on the street, takin' potshots and endangerin' citizens. Figures you'd know why."

"Sure I know why. Eddie and me got into a big fight, same as usual. And he was shit-faced, same as usual. Only this time he grabbed his gun and chased me out into the street. Started shooting." A shrug. "There, that's my statement."

McCarthy stiffened, about to respond. But before he could, Pratt cut him off.

"I think the Doc here's right. Let's get Eddie down to the station. Ms. Steadman can come down later and swear out a complaint—"

With this, Joy whirled and shouted over at Burke, slumped in the back of the patrol car.

"And I *will*, too, you prick! I'll see your sorry ass in jail! I hate you, I *hate* you, I—"

Suddenly she doubled over, took a half-step, and vomited onto the street. A violent, retching spasm, her arms flailing.

I raced to her side, as both uniforms instinctively backed away. McCarthy shook his head, laughing.

I looked the young cop over. Probably third-generation Irish. Classic Pittsburgh accent. Everybody was a chooch or a jagoff. Slang that you still hear sometimes, even as the Steel City continued to morph from a blue-collar, industrial town into a gentrified, white-collar hub of business and technology.

I turned my attention back to his partner. "Look, Officer Pratt, it's obvious Ms. Steadman is in no shape to give a coherent statement. She's trying like hell to fight it, but I think she's in shock. Who wouldn't be? Her boyfriend just tried to shoot her."

"So what are you suggesting?" He folded his arms wearily.

"I told you I'd come down and give a statement—though I'd like to cover up my front window first. So what if I stay with Ms. Steadman for a while tonight, then drive us both downtown tomorrow morning? We can each give our statements then."

Pratt frowned skeptically.

"Look," I went on, "call in and ask for Angela Villanova. She's the Community Liaison Officer."

"I know who she is, son."

"She'll vouch for me."

He stroked his mustache thoughtfully. "You wouldn't be tryin' to pull rank on an old beat cop, would you?"

I grinned. "Never. My dad was an old beat cop. He'd climb out of his grave and kick my ass if I ever tried that with one of Pittsburgh's finest."

The younger cop grunted. "Don't listen to him, Henry. Doc got no rank to pull. He's just a civilian, likes to see himself on TV."

Pratt turned to him. "Do me a favor, will ya, Phil? Shut your damn pie-hole."

Something in the older man's voice made McCarthy do just that. Thank Christ.

Meanwhile, Joy had straightened up, wiping her mouth with her palm. Breath coming in gasps.

"I don't need a baby-sitter." Her sour squint took in both Officer Pratt and myself.

The older man sighed. "Well, young lady, here're your options. You either come down to the station now and file a complaint against Mr. Burke, or you get a good night's sleep and let Dr. Rinaldi drive you down in the morning."

She thought it over for a few moments. Then, exhaling deeply, she finally relented.

"Well, one thing's for sure, I can't be seen looking like this. Bad for a girl's image. I just threw up on myself, and I think I peed my pants while I was hiding behind Rinaldi's car. I'll need to soak in the tub for a week."

Pratt's gaze was steady. "Maybe. But *we'll* need to see you downtown tomorrow, Ms. Steadman. Early."

She managed an offended scowl, which he ignored.

Then Pratt gestured to his partner to follow and headed back to the patrol car. As he opened the driver's side door, he peered over at me. A guarded smile.

"Now don't let anything happen to our star witness, okay, Doc?"

Chapter Three

"Why did you insist on bringing me home?"

Joy Steadman closed her front door and waved me through the elegant foyer into the living room.

"Just trying to be helpful." I offered a thin smile. "No charge for the house call."

"Bullshit. Nobody does anything for free, Doc. I learned that a long time ago."

Her frank look challenged me to disagree. So I didn't. Then she excused herself and left the room. I heard the sound of running water from a bathroom down the hall.

As I waited for her return, I glanced around the spacious, lavishly appointed room. The work of an expensive decorator, no doubt. High-end furniture, a bit too modern for my tastes. Severe lines, steel struts, black or white leather. A Rothko on one wall. Warhol silkscreen on another. The only jarring note was the sports memorabilia—plaques and trophies, a bronzed football—displayed about the room.

"That's Eddie's stuff. From when he moved in last year."

Joy had come back, her footsteps mere whispers on the plush carpet. She'd washed her face and changed into an over-sized Yale tee-shirt and yoga pants. Luxurious hair pulled back, held with a clip. For the first time, in the well-lighted room, I registered how beautiful she was.

She nodded at the photos of Eddie. "You know the story,

Doc. Rich white girl getting some jungle love to fuck with her parents. Talk about clichéd."

Joy chuckled derisively and gestured toward the trim sofa, sheened in white leather. But neither of us sat.

"If you point me toward the kitchen," I said, "I can make you some tea. Or something else, if you prefer."

She shook her head. "My maid, Maria, does that kind of thing. But she's gone for the day. Besides, I'm gonna want something stronger. Bet you do, too."

"Nothing for me, thanks."

As she poured herself a bourbon from the elaborate wet bar, I spotted a row of framed photos on the near wall. Most were from Eddie Burke's days as a college athlete, his cool good looks and muscular body accentuated by the Pitt Panthers uniform. Though one picture was different. It showed an older Burke in a Steelers hoodie and shorts, leaning against a row of lockers and cradling a football as he smiled insolently for the camera.

"That was Eddie in the Steelers' training camp," Joy said. "First day there. His dream come true."

She brought over her drink, then let herself sink into a huge leather chair. It practically swallowed her willowy form. I sat opposite on the sofa.

"What happened?"

"The front office cut him after two weeks. He gave the coaches too much lip. So much for his big career in the NFL."

"So what's he been doing since then?"

"Getting high and living off me."

She threw back her drink and got up to make herself another. I watched her carefully. Though she didn't seem shocky, there was something tentative about her movements. Deliberate. As though it was only sheer willpower, or some misguided stubbornness, holding her together. Proving something. To me?

Or to herself?

When she rejoined me, she sat forward in the chair, bare toes digging into the thick white carpet. Her gaze narrowed.

"You know, Doctor, I have my own therapist. See him twice a week. Been in therapy since I was fifteen. I used to be on Prozac, but now I'm on Wellbutrin. Or Lexapro. One of those."

Another deep swallow of bourbon.

"Why were you in treatment, if you don't mind my asking?"

"I got into trouble with this guy I was seeing. We sold dope, got into petty crimes, vandalism, that kinda thing. But he was eighteen, and super hot, and I thought I was in love. What the hell did I know? At least it was exciting. Anyway, one night we got busted by the cops. My family has money, so they were able to make it go away. But they insisted I go into therapy. 'To get your head screwed on straight,' my dad said."

She frowned at the memory. "Funny, 'cause *he* was the one who needed help. Totally lame, my old man. Feckless."

I considered this. "Not a word you hear too often."

"I know, I had to look it up. It's what my mother called him. Poor Dad thought he was an entrepreneur. Always chasing after the big score. Played the stock market. Made some stupid investments in companies that went belly-up. Like I said, lame."

She finished her drink, then let her glance take in the opulent surroundings.

"I know what you're thinking. Where the hell did all *this* come from? A trust fund, thanks to Mother. She has all the money. Tons of it. From her wealthy family in Philadelphia. But she never divorced Dad. Why give her snooty friends something to smirk about? She just had a bunch of affairs with younger men and kept Dad around for window dressing. Still does."

Joy let out a rueful sigh. "See? We both ended up with losers. Must run in the family."

I said nothing, my thoughts drifting to my shattered front window. The jagged opening exposed to the elements, including rain, should it start to shower again.

"What was the fight about? I never asked."

She unconsciously fingered the bruise on her cheek. "Same

shit me and Eddie always fight about. I accuse him of spending too much of my money and he accuses me of cheating on him."

"Either of those things true?"

"The first part, yeah. The second part is none of your damn business."

We sat in a strained silence for a long minute.

Abruptly, Joy said, "So, you work for the cops, or what?"

"No, I'm in private practice. But I consult with them sometimes. I see crime victims they send to me for therapy. People who've been assaulted, or abused. Robbed at gunpoint. Things like that. Traumatized by the violence done to them. I try to help them deal with it."

A knowing look. "If you're talking about me, Doc, forget about it. I'll be fine. After tonight, I'm kicking Eddie out. For good. Besides, like I said, I already get my head shrunk."

"I'm glad. We all need help sometimes."

"Uh-huh." She paused. "At least now I get why you were so friendly with those cops. Bit *too* friendly for my tastes."

"I caught a break. Most cops think I'm a pain in the ass."

I saw that skeptical glint in her eyes again. As if another challenge was coming. Instead, rising suddenly, she stretched. Yawned.

"Look, I appreciate your being a good neighbor and all that, but right now I just want to take a hot bath and climb under the covers."

I got to my feet as well.

"If you're sure you're ready to be alone."

"No offense, but I'm sorta looking forward to it. At least for tonight."

"I understand. Now about tomorrow morning..."

"Don't worry, I'll go downtown bright and early to give my statement. But I won't need you to drive me. I'm a big girl, in case you haven't noticed. I'll get myself down there."

"If you say so."

There was another long pause. Then she gave me a wry, half-mocking smile.

"So now what, Doc? Is this the part where we hug?"

"Not necessarily."

"Good. I hate hugs. Mother hugs." The smile melted from her face. "I trust you can see your way out."

With that, she turned and strode quickly out of the room.

Chapter Four

An hour later, I was standing in my kitchen, looking out the sliding glass door at the rain pounding my back deck. Like many other houses perched atop Mt. Washington, mine fronted Grandview Avenue at street level, while the rear sloped to the edge of a cliff. Beyond, a sharp drop down a forested hill gave me a perfect view of the glittering lights of downtown.

One very different than that of my youth. New construction had changed its contours, silver-and-glass spires replacing many of the brick-and-mortar buildings of the previous century. Pittsburgh now boasted a new, modern skyline, no longer obscured by dark plumes of soot from a hundred smokestacks.

Yet however much the city changed, it was still a patchwork of old neighborhoods and cobblestone streets—still a place where guys drank at the same bars their fathers had, played cards in the back rooms of produce stores on the Strip, got into belabored fights over football. Where ethnic pride and ethnic prejudice lived side by side.

It's a town nestled in the triangle formed by the Three Rivers, the Allegheny and Monongahela joining their flowing waters to feed the more sluggish Ohio. Though gone was the busy river traffic I remember from my youth, the parade of tug boats and barges hauling manufactured goods to points west and south from the mills and factories that had built this city.

I rubbed my eyes. It was just past eleven, yet sleep was the furthest thing from my mind. Not after tonight's events.

After being more or less dismissed by Joy Steadman, I'd hurried back to my place. A cotton-damp closeness in the air augured more rain, so I went quickly to my attached garage and rummaged through some old wood. Luckily I found a pretty good-sized piece of plywood, one that looked broad enough to cover the jagged hole in my front window. Good thing, too. The rain had already begun by the time I managed to board up the window, affixing the plywood with duct tape.

I stepped back, appraising my handiwork. Not exactly a repair worthy of *This Old House*, but at least it was keeping out the rain until tomorrow, when I could call a glazier to come and replace the entire window.

Then I crossed the room to get a closer look at the slug embedded in the wall above the CD player. By now, Officer Pratt had no doubt alerted his superiors to the incident. They'd want to send one of their forensics techs to carefully extract the bullet. I had no idea what kind of case they planned to build against Eddie Burke, if any, but the slug was definitely evidence—something I knew I shouldn't tamper with.

Of course, after that, I'd have to get the wall repaired. Fine. I'd been thinking that all the walls needed a new paint job anyway. The whole house had been showing its age lately, the result of benign neglect on my part. In my defense, I'd been pretty busy getting mixed up in things that the cops—and my friends and colleagues—kept warning me to stay out of.

I stroked my beard, wondering if what they described as my "hero complex" was true. That my involvement in some recent high-profile cases was my way of working out my survival guilt. A misguided attempt to make up for the fact that Barbara had died that fateful night and I hadn't. Not that I blamed them. It was a question I'd asked myself a hundred times over the years.

Rousing myself, I pulled the heavy drapes together to cover my makeshift repair. Then I got a broom from the closet and swept up the broken glass scattered on the hardwood floor. Finally, I scooped up the binder holding the dossier I'd been reading. It had fallen to the floor, but was undamaged.

Though wide awake, I'd wait till tomorrow to once again dig into its contents. I felt too jangly, unsettled. No surprise there. Not with that bullet still lodged in my front room wall. And, unlike Joy, I knew such a close brush with death would have a powerful effect on me. I'd been there before.

Now, as I peered through my blurred reflection in the glass door, I noted that the rain was lessening. The staccato rattle on the wooden deck replaced by a soft, rhythmic patter.

Unmindful of the drizzle, I slid open the door and stepped out onto the deck. Breathed in the storm-sweetened night air, the smell of wet earth and ancient oaks wafting up from the tree line just below.

At the same time, I thought about Joy Steadman. Her obvious unhappiness poorly masked behind her surly manner and sarcastic tongue. Moreover, her dismissive description of her parents' marriage suggested the shame and insecurities of a painful childhood. One whose echoes were revealed by her willingness to stay in a blatantly unsatisfying and abusive relationship with Eddie Burke. And God knew how many men before him.

Joy was not easy to like, but it was easy to empathize with her. At least it was for me, even as I reminded myself that she wasn't my patient. Which left me wondering what the hell her current therapist was doing to help her.

I rolled my shoulders against the rain's chill. Although it had fallen to little more than a mist, it was still wet. And cold. Especially since I was wearing the same clothes from when I'd gone out to the street after the gunshot. My usual after-work attire. Pitt sweatshirt and jeans.

I thought again about the bullet that had narrowly missed me tonight. About an angry, heartsick Eddie Burke drunkenly shooting at the ghosts of his suspicions. And about the dossier now sitting on my rolltop desk in the front room. The message within which I'd yet to decode...

Just then, the landline phone in the kitchen rang. I quickly stepped inside, sliding the glass door shut behind me, and picked up the receiver.

"Dr. Rinaldi? Phil McCarthy here."

It took me a moment to remember the name.

"Yes. Officer McCarthy. What can I do for you?"

"Listen, Doc, I'm callin' to do *you* a solid. Give you a heads-up, if ya know what I mean."

I pulled up one of my kitchen chairs and sat down at the table. The dull throb of a headache had just started. Great.

"Actually, Officer, I have no idea what you're talking about. Does it concern Eddie Burke?"

"Yep. We got him down here in lockup. Guy's a fuckin' mess. One minute he's mad as hell, shoutin' and cursin', the next he's in tears. Slobbering on and on about his girlfriend. How she's been cheatin' on him. Seein' this dude on the side."

"Yeah, so I heard. But what does that have to do with me?"

A strange, unfriendly chuckle came from the young cop.

"That's just it, Doc. Burke says this guy that Joy's been sleepin' with?...it's *you*."

Chapter Five

I stared at the phone in my hand.

"None o' my business, of course." McCarthy's voice was laced with undisguised glee. "But I sure as fuck wouldn't want this chooch mad at *me*."

"But it isn't true." Finding my own voice at last. "I'm not having an affair with—"

"I just spoke to the watch commander and he says this changes everything. Maybe Eddie wasn't firing at Joy and missed. Maybe he was tryin' to shoot *you*, inside your house."

"That's pretty unlikely."

"I was *there*, Doc. Your drapes were open. Lights were on. He coulda seen you through the window. Either way, now it's not just some domestic that went sideways. It's attempted murder. No matter who the prick wanted to kill."

"Look," I said, "even if Burke thought it was true about Joy and me, maybe he was only trying to scare me. He was falling-down drunk, out of his head with jealousy and rage. You saw him, McCarthy. He was barely aware of what he was doing."

"Not my call, Doc. Yours, neither."

"But this is crazy. I'm not sleeping with Joy Steadman. I didn't even know her name until tonight. Ask her yourself."

"We will. I mean, not me, personally. Case has moved up the food chain. They're sending one of the homicide dicks over there right now to question her."

"Who's on the floor?"

"Sergeant Polk. Why, ya know him?"

"Only too goddam well."

I sat back in my chair. I'd known Harry Polk since my involvement in the Wingfield case a couple years back. While he'd made detective at Robbery/Homicide, he was, by temperament and opinion, a cop of the old school. He'd never been comfortable with my being a psychologist, let alone my role as a consultant to Pittsburgh PD. Yet, due to unexpected circumstances, we'd ended up working together a few times. Maybe even developed a kind of grudging respect for each other. Emphasis on "grudging."

McCarthy coughed insistently. "You there, Doc?"

"Yeah. Just wondering about something. Why does Eddie Burke think I'm the guy Joy's sleeping with?"

"Why wouldn't he? She *told* him it was you."

∙ ● ● ● ∙

It took another two minutes to get off the phone with Officer McCarthy. Apparently his partner, Henry Pratt, was catching hell for not insisting that Joy Steadman come down immediately to make her statement. And that I, too, should have been formally interviewed, either downtown or in my home.

"I'm sorry to hear that Officer Pratt's in trouble." And I was. I'd liked him.

"Guys like Henry..." McCarthy clucked his tongue. "They're good cops, but sometimes they act like fuckin' social workers. Not our job, right? I'm always tellin' him that."

At the moment, I wasn't too interested in the two cops' relationship, so I thanked McCarthy for the update on Burke and hung up. Then I went into my bedroom, changed into drier clothes, and grabbed a windbreaker from the hall closet.

I wasn't about to wait until tomorrow to confront Joy Steadman. Whatever empathy I'd had for her earlier tonight was rapidly dwindling. I was cleanly pissed.

As I went out the front door, a nondescript sedan rolled to the curb in front of my house. I knew who it was before he climbed awkwardly out from behind the wheel.

"Hey, Harry. I heard you were coming."

Sergeant Harry Polk, his considerable paunch exposed by his open suit jacket, gave me his customary scowl. With thinning hair and a drinker's ruddy complexion, he had the perpetually weary countenance of a middle-aged man whose life had gotten away from him and he no longer cared. The classic example of a cop literally counting the years till retirement.

He trudged over to where I stood on the sidewalk, his hand over his eyes against the drizzle. Raindrops began spotting his wrinkled blue suit.

"I got nothin' to say to you, Rinaldi. If it wasn't for you, I wouldn'ta had to drive all the way up here in the rain."

"Come on, Harry. You don't really believe what Burke says. That I'm involved with his girlfriend."

"Don't matter what I believe. I just wanna wrap up this interview with the Steadman broad and go home."

"Home" was the dingy apartment in Wilkinsburg where Polk had been living since his divorce a few years back. It was one of those nondescript buildings where recently widowed or separated people stayed until other, more permanent, residences could be found. Harry never left.

I took a measured step toward him. "Look, let's both go talk to her. Find out what the hell's going on."

"No way. Just go back inside and let me do my goddam job."

"Forget it, Harry. I'm going with you. Nobody wants this cleared up—and fast—more than I do."

Polk sighed. "Let me guess. The more I say no, the more you're gonna keep us standing out here in the fuckin' rain."

"That'd be *my* guess, too."

He sniffed noisily. "You're lucky I feel a cold comin' on, and wanna get home to bed. Otherwise..."

Polk turned without another word and headed across the street toward Joy Steadman's house. I followed at his heels.

The lights were still on inside, so I assumed Joy hadn't gone to bed yet. In fact, she might be taking that hot bath she'd craved. Either way, given how Polk was leaning on the bell, she was going to have to open her front door.

It took a full five minutes, but she finally did. Her hair was turbaned in a towel, her slender body enveloped by a thick, thirsty robe. Skin still wet and bright pink. I'd been right about the bath.

"Ms. Steadman—" Polk began.

She ignored him, casting her eyes at me. Unwelcoming.

"Back so soon? What happened, you get lonely over there?"

I felt a quick stab of anger. "Lonely? Fuck, no, Joy. Not since you and I hooked up. It's been great."

She backstepped, blanching. Polk put a warning hand on my shoulder. Gripped hard.

"Jesus, Rinaldi—"

I shrugged him off, then got in her face. And got louder.

"Why'd you tell Eddie we were sleeping together? I mean, I don't know what kind of bullshit game you're playing, but leave me the hell out of it."

"Wait a minute—"

I cut her off. "Save it. Your goddam boyfriend could've shot me, accidentally or not, and all because you lied about us. *Why*, for Christ's sake? Why did you do that?"

Her own anger rising, Joy suddenly tried to shut the door. Polk stopped it with his foot.

She glared. "I don't wanna talk to him."

"So don't," Polk growled. "But you *do* gotta talk to me."

"Yeah? Who are you? Though you sure as shit look like a cop. You got the eyes."

He showed her his shield. "I'm Sergeant Polk, Pittsburgh PD. I need to speak to you about what happened tonight."

"Do I have a choice?"

He blew air out of his stubbly cheeks. Long past five o'clock shadow. "It's either here or downtown, lady. But it's late, I'm wet and tired, and I'd sure like to get this over with. I figger you would, too."

She frowned, but then nodded and ushered us inside. Though she pointedly avoided my gaze as I passed. Fine with me.

For the second time that night, I was led through the foyer and into the living room. At a gesture from Joy, Polk and I found seats. She picked the large leather chair again.

Polk took out his notebook. "Just to get me up to speed. Your boyfriend, Mr. Burke, lives here with you, right?"

"Yes. Every moment a little slice of heaven."

He wisely ignored that.

"We have Mr. Burke in custody, and he could be charged with attempted murder, or at least assault with a deadly weapon. Hell, maybe public intoxication, if the ADA is in a pissy mood."

"I figured he'd be looking at something like that."

Her reply was casual, assured. Trying to give the impression of bored indifference. But I noticed the anxiety pinching her eyes. A slight twitching in her fingers.

"The thing is, Ms. Steadman, Burke claims he went all bat-shit—excuse me—that he was provoked because he found out you were cheating on him. Having an affair."

"Yeah, he accuses me of that every couple weeks. It's our thing. Something we do. Up till now, I could handle it."

"But not tonight?"

"Well, gee, Sergeant, no. Tonight was different. He started waving a goddam *gun* around. I was afraid for my life."

I'd calmed myself a bit by this point, enough to keep my tone steady. Sort of.

"But Eddie believes that you and I are having an affair. He says you *told* him it was me."

Joy took a deep breath, but said nothing.

"Is this true, Ms. Steadman?" Polk stared. "Did you tell Eddie that you were sleeping with Dr. Rinaldi here?"

She closed her eyes for a moment. When she opened them, they were moist with tears. "Yes. Yes I did."

Joy turned to me, her face going pale. "I'm sorry, Dr. Rinaldi. Really. But I had to."

"Why?" As my anger slowly began to ebb.

"Because he threatened to *kill* me if I didn't tell him who it was. I was terrified. Eddie was so drunk, so crazy…And he had that gun! Then suddenly I thought about you—"

"But why me?" I asked again.

She let a small smile play on her lips.

"I don't know. I mean, you're not bad-looking, and you live right across the street. Made sense at the time."

Polk and I exchanged dubious looks.

"I know it was shitty thing to do," Joy said to me. "Really shitty. I'm ashamed of myself."

"And that's the truth?" The sergeant leaned in toward her. "You said it was Dr. Rinaldi because Eddie threatened you?"

"Yes. And then he got even crazier, yelling and cursing, and pointing the gun at me. I swear, I thought he *was* going to kill me. So I ran out the front door. But Eddie followed me and started shooting. By then I'd made it across the street and hid behind the doctor's car. I guess because it was so dark, or Eddie was so drunk, he couldn't see me. Just kept firing off his gun, shouting for me."

Polk swiveled his head to me.

"That's when one of the shots smashed your window?"

I nodded. "Luckily, it missed me. Then I went outside and saw Burke in the middle of the street. Staggering, shouting. A minute or two later, a patrol car rolled up. Officers Pratt and McCarthy came out, guns drawn. But Burke surrendered peacefully and it was over."

"That's it?" Polk said.

"That's it."

Polk considered this for a moment, then snapped shut his notebook. Scowled at Joy.

"Ya know, you coulda got the Doc here killed. Not to mention yourself."

She let her head drop.

"I know. It was stupid. Cowardly. But I was so scared…"

Again, she brought her eyes up to meet mine.

"I'm so sorry, Dr. Rinaldi. I mean it."

I looked back, at a loss. Though I was still pretty angry, there didn't seem to be anything to do about it. Nothing, at least, that I was inclined to do.

"Look, Joy," I said after a beat, "I'm not too happy about it, but I do believe you feared for your life. I guess, from your perspective, you did what you had to."

She sighed then, though whether from gratitude or relief, I couldn't be sure. Then she gathered her robe more tightly around her and got wearily to her feet.

"Are we finished, Sergeant Polk?"

The sergeant and I both rose as well, Polk grunting from the effort. Then he squinted at the young woman. "You'll still need to come downtown tomorrow and swear out a complaint."

"I will. Scout's honor."

As Polk and I made our way to the front door, I noticed Joy taking a cell phone from one of her robe's pockets.

I turned. "Are you calling your parents? Or a friend? I still think it'd be best to have someone stay with you tonight."

She pushed some buttons on the phone.

"No, I'll be fine. I'm calling my lawyer. He's used to me waking him up in the middle of the night."

Polk gave me a sidelong glance.

"It's for Eddie," she went on casually. "To get him bailed out. He can't stay in some crappy jail cell all night."

She smiled grimly at my quizzical look.

"C'mon, Doc, you've been around the block. You can't tell me you're surprised."

"Not entirely. No."

She waved a dismissive hand. "Just consider my life one of those cautionary tales you hear about, okay? Now can you two give me some privacy?"

Chapter Six

"Like I'm always sayin', women are nuts."

"I assume you mean Joy Steadman?"

Polk stood by the driver's side door of his unmarked, fumbling to light an unfiltered Camel against the push of a rising wind. I was leaning against the sedan's hood.

"Stupid broad," Polk said. "No matter what the prick did, she'll take him back. They'll fuck like bunnies, then all is forgiven. Till the next time he loses his shit."

"I've seen it before, of course. Thing is, people often accept from others what they think they deserve. And, hell, brutal attention is still attention. Some even think it's love."

"Yeah? *Crazy* people, maybe." Finally, a deep, grateful drag from the Camel. "More your line o' work, thank God."

The rain had stopped, leaving only a damp chill in the midnight air. Above, thin clouds drifted like ash-gray smoke across the arch of sky.

"By the way, Harry, most people aren't that comfortable using the word 'broad' nowadays."

He blew out a good-sized puff. "I ain't most people."

I had to give him that.

As he turned to open the car door, I put my hand on his arm. He peered at it, then at me.

"You thirsty?" I said. "I know it's late, but..."

He grinned. "You oughtta know better than that by now, Doc. You wanna throw back a few at the bar?"

By "the bar," Polk meant the Spent Cartridge, a venerable cop bar struggling to hold onto its lease—and its character—in the midst of urban gentrification. The kind of place where Iron City beer signs still sizzled in bright neon above the front door.

"No, not your usual dive, Harry. I have another place in mind. I've been meaning to take you there for a long time."

He eyed me suspiciously. Joy Steadman had been right. Polk definitely had a cop's sour squint.

"Somethin's on your mind, ain't it, Doc?"

And a cop's instincts. Because he was right.

● ● ● ● ●

"Sergeant Harry Polk, meet Noah Frye."

The latter stood behind the bar, vigorously wiping the beer-stained counter with a grimy cloth. Without stopping, he gave Polk a dark, baleful look.

"Another cop friend, Danny? What is it with you, anyway? Next thing ya know, you'll be wearin' a goddam badge and one o' them funny hats."

Predictably, Harry didn't take kindly to this. He grabbed Noah's thick forearm, pinning it to the counter. With his other hand, he pointed at Noah's broad, bearded face.

"Listen, dirtbag, I'm only here 'cause the Doc invited me. And I was stupid enough to come. So if ya don't mind, I'll be leavin' this floatin' toilet ASAP. Fuck you very much."

With a final angry squeeze, he released his grip on Noah, and then made a show of adjusting his tie. Noah, rubbing his forearm, merely grumbled something unintelligible.

"Whoa." I spread my hands. "Let's try this again, okay? You guys don't know each other well enough for this crap. Harry, chill out. And for Christ's sake, Noah, give the anti-authority bullshit a rest. It's getting old."

He scowled at me, but then nodded. Meanwhile, Polk was calming himself with some heavily labored big breaths.

"Now," I said again, "Sergeant Harry Polk, meet Noah Frye."

Grudgingly, the two big men shook hands across the bar counter. Then Polk and I took stools and ordered a couple draft Rolling Rocks. Wiping his hands on his dingy apron, Noah began pulling the taps.

While he did so, Polk watched him with obvious distaste.

Despite Noah's unruly, sweat-matted hair and ill-fitting overalls, he was clearly practiced as a bartender. His movements surprisingly adroit for a big man. Though nothing could disguise the intense, melancholic tinge in his eyes. Nor the telltale glint of madness behind them.

Noah Frye was a paranoid schizophrenic. We'd met when he was a patient and I a clinical intern at a private psychiatric clinic. A talented jazz pianist, he'd been tormented most of his adult life by persecutory hallucinations and delusions. But soon he was released from care and I left the clinic to go into private practice. Now, years later, we were friends.

Thankfully, I wasn't his only one. With the support of his long-suffering girlfriend, Charlene, who helped run the bar and lived with him in the rooms behind, Noah managed to get through most days pretty much unscarred. Of course, the psychotropic meds prescribed by his longtime shrink—and our mutual friend, Nancy Mendors—did much of the heavy lifting, sanity-wise.

"Here ya are, *gentlemen*." Noah put down two foaming mugs in front of Polk and myself. None too gently, either.

Then, with a final skeptical glance in my direction, he scuttled down to the customers at the other end of the bar. There were only a few late drinkers left before final call.

I took a pull from my beer and glanced around the room. It had been past midnight when Polk and I took his car down here to Second Avenue, to a converted coal barge called, appropriately enough, Noah's Ark. Moored at the Monongahela River's edge, the bar's interior gave no doubt as to its original purpose. Though boasting a dais for nightly jazz and new leather booths lining the walls, the spacious room still retained the old vessel's hanging tarpaper ceiling, opened portholes, and pungent river smell. What Noah blithely called its "nautical motif."

I nudged Polk, who'd already drained his glass.

"What do you think of the place?"

He wiped his mouth with a bar napkin. "Not much. Now when are ya gonna tell me why we're here?"

In answer, I gestured to Noah to bring us another couple beers. Then I led Polk over to one of the empty booths. The resident band having packed up, and with the kitchen closed for the night, we practically had the floor to ourselves.

I let Polk make it halfway through his second beer before putting down my own glass and meeting his rheumy gaze.

"Here's the thing, Harry. I need to ask you some questions about my wife's death. About what happened to Barbara."

Polk slowly lowered his glass. Considered me carefully.

"That was a long time ago, wasn't it, Doc?"

"Nearly twelve years. We were mugged down at the Point. Both of us got shot. As you know, Barbara died. For some unknown reason, I didn't."

"Yeah, but I also know how it messed you up. I read the papers. And people talk."

Then his voice grew surprisingly soft. "Look, Doc…maybe it'd be better if you left it alone. Better for you, I mean."

"I appreciate that, Harry. But I may have some new information about the case. What I'm saying is, maybe it wasn't just a mugging. Barbara might've been murdered."

"Where'd ya come up with *that* idea?"

"No need to get into that right now. I just wanted to ask you about the case. What you might remember about it."

Polk massaged his chin. "Not much. I hadn't made sergeant yet. It wasn't even my case. But I knew the cops who worked it."

So did I. "Biggs and Stanton. They interviewed me in the hospital about a month after it happened. Once I was out of ICU." A pause. "I just wanted your take on them."

"Good guys, both of 'em. Veteran detectives. Closed a lotta cases. If there was anythin' hinky about the muggin', they woulda pursued it. Believe me."

"You ever see their files on the case?"

"Why would I? Hell, you sayin' *you've* seen 'em?"

I debated my answer for a long moment. Then nodded.

Polk's brow darkened. "How the hell—? Wait a minute! Were the case files part o' that stupid dossier you wanted? From that dead guy's office?"

I nodded again. I'd promised Polk a steak dinner in exchange for getting his junior partner to retrieve a copy of the dossier. Which is how I'd ended up with it.

Polk frowned. "I thought the dossier was just about you."

"It is. Which includes my marriage, and what happened to my wife. The investigation into her death."

"So all of a sudden, you're a cold case detective? What is it with ya, anyway? Hell, even Angie Villanova thinks you're some kinda lunatic. And she's your damn cousin."

"Third cousin, once removed. Anyway—"

"Fuck it, I'm outta here." He half-rose from his seat.

"Harry, wait. Please. Listen, I wouldn't ask if it weren't important. To me. I *have* to know what happened that night. What *really* happened. Surely you can understand that?"

Polk blew air out of his cheeks.

"Well?" I met his dour gaze. "You going to help me or not?"

With a resigned shake of his head, Polk slumped back down in his seat.

"Christ, I oughtta have my head examined."

I smiled. "I can refer you to some good people."

"Yeah, right." He finished the rest of his beer. "Now, about Biggs and Stanton. What do ya wanna know?"

"Everything you do," I said.

Unfortunately, that wasn't much.

Polk's recollection about the investigation itself was pretty vague. However, despite the years since, he distinctly recalled the two detectives.

Ervin Biggs was black, college-educated, and a stickler for procedure. This didn't surprise me. Reading his notes on my wife's case in the dossier, I'd been struck by his neat, deliberate cursive. As well as his attention to detail.

"What about Biggs' partner?"

"Arthur Stanton. Artie. Divorced, I think. Or maybe not. Who the fuck cares?" Polk looked longingly at his empty glass.

"Anything else?"

"Did I mention he was the white one?" A sardonic smile.

"Very helpful. I met him, remember? Both of them."

Polk grunted. "Maybe it's this damn cold, but my mouth's kinda dry. Just sayin'."

I glanced up, hoping to catch Noah's eye over at the bar, but spotted Charlene instead. She was stacking dirty dishes onto a standing tray near the kitchen doors. Buxom and wide-hipped, her hair a tangle of red curls, she was both warm-hearted and razor-sharp. Which made her perfect for Noah.

I called her over and introduced her to Polk. Then I asked her for two more beers.

"By the way," I said, "how's Skip?"

Skip Hines, her brother, was a returned vet who'd lost a leg in the Afghan desert. We'd met a couple weeks before.

Charlene's round face darkened. "Still drinking, still living in that shitty motel. Still looking for work. But I'll tell him you asked about him."

It was clear she didn't want to say more, especially in front of a stranger. Instead, she offered a brisk, unconvincing smile and went off to get our drinks. It couldn't be easy, I thought, keeping an eye on both Noah *and* her alcoholic brother.

I brought my attention back to Polk. "About Artie Stanton. I assume he's retired by now, too?"

"Not long after Biggs did. Took early pension."

"He say why?"

A shrug. "Probably couldn't deal with the bullshit anymore. Or maybe he got restless, wanted a change. Like his partner."

I nodded. "You might be right. When Stanton and Biggs questioned me after the mugging, he seemed impatient. Distracted."

Again, this was perhaps reflected in his interview notes I'd been reading—hastily scribbled half-sentences, errors crossed out and written over. I'm no handwriting expert, but it looked like the work of a man who'd rather be doing something else.

Charlene had returned with two draft Rolling Rocks. She'd barely turned to go when Polk took a long, greedy pull from his mug.

I glanced at my watch. Noah would be closing up any minute now. Polk must have realized the same thing, finishing his beer in two long swallows. I reached for my own foaming mug, then paused. Left it untouched. I'd had enough alcohol for one night.

"Look, Harry, I appreciate your talking with me about all this. It may turn out to be nothing, but…"

"Ya want my advice, Doc? Leave it alone. Dredgin' up that old shit again, all those memories…And for what? So that the whole thing makes some kinda sense?"

"I don't know. Maybe."

"Then you're dumber than I thought you were." His boozy gaze held mine. "Let me tell ya somethin', Danny. *Nothin'* in this fucked-up world makes any sense. If you ain't learned that by now, you ain't learned nothin'."

He got awkwardly to his feet. "Now where's the little boy's room in this godawful place?"

Chapter Seven

Not surprisingly, it turned out that Harry Polk was a big fan of conservative talk radio. As he drove us up from the river, he found the station and dialed up the volume. The show's bellicose host was in full outrage mode, decrying the evils of evolution, immigration, and gun control. The usual knee-jerk litany of liberal horrors.

I groaned. "Jesus, Harry, give me a break."

"My car, my rules."

It was nearing three in the morning by the time Polk dropped me at my place. The street was silent, looking and feeling deserted. As were the houses, feeble porch lights the only indication of any life within. Overhead, obscuring the spring moon, a shroud of dark clouds promised more rain.

I stood for a long moment outside my door, chilled, though not from the cold. It was something else. Something I couldn't put my finger on. A prickling at the back of my neck. I did my best to shake it off and put the key in the lock.

Once inside, I got undressed and hit the sack. And stared at the ceiling. For almost an hour. Fatigued, but wired. My mind a jumble of chaotic images from the long night's events.

So sleep was out.

Instead, I went out to the front room, reached for the dossier and found my customary seat on the couch. Though I knew it was probably pointless, talking with Polk about the two detectives who'd worked the case prompted me to once more read their interview notes.

Between Biggs and Stanton, they'd talked to about a dozen people who'd been in or outside the restaurant when it happened. I gave the now-familiar list a cursory look: Hector Ruiz, who ran the parking kiosk, and his valets, Ed Hunter, Jack Ketch, and Sal Tulio. To this day I can recall them hustling nonstop in their red toreador jackets, either driving off to park the diners' cars in a nearby lot or speedily retrieving them.

Unfortunately, none of the valets could provide much information, though Hector was only a dozen feet away when it happened. All he saw was a guy in a hoodie approaching Barbara and myself. There was a brief struggle, he reported, followed by gunshots. Then the mugger ran off.

I flipped over some more pages. Stanton had interviewed most of the staff inside the restaurant, including our waiter, Tony Vaccaro, who said Barbara and I had "seemed like nice people." His only gripe was the meager size of his tip.

I glanced up from the dossier, smiling. Tony was right. We were still a young couple at the time. Each of us early in our careers. And each with student loans to pay off.

Then there were the two elderly people waiting for their car to be brought around. A Mr. and Mrs. Willoughby, standing to one side of the front entrance as Barbara and I exited. The very next moment, my wife and I were attacked.

According to Biggs' notes, both husband and wife were visibly distraught giving their statements, horrified by what had happened a mere yard or two away from them. But, as with Ruiz, neither could offer anything of real use. Only the sound of gunfire and the vague impression of a blurred figure running off into the night.

I let out a sigh and turned to the last page. Included in the case summary from the following day was a report from two paid informers Stanton often used to keep him abreast of any word on the street. Apparently, nobody knew anything about a mugging at the Point. Nobody was bragging about it, or flashing extra cash. Or scoring more dope than usual.

I tossed the dossier aside. As frustrated as I was, it seemed clear that Biggs and Stanton had done a pretty thorough job working the case. If there was some oversight, or even malfeasance, I sure as hell didn't see it.

Still, sleep seemed impossible. So I pulled on some sweats and headed down to the makeshift gym in my basement. Just some free weights and a bench, sandwiched between old storage boxes and yard tools. But it suited me. For the next half hour, I worked the heavy bag that hung from a ceiling beam. Grateful for the rhythmic bellows of my lungs, the sweat drenching my face and bare chest. The burn in my arms.

I'd done some amateur boxing when I was young. Golden Gloves, Pan Am Games. Maybe it was those old instincts that made me react when Barbara and I had been mugged. That made me think I should've been able to take the bastard. Save her.

I pushed the thought from my mind. Old stuff. Punishing, self-recriminating voices I told myself I'd long since banished from my psyche. And I had. Until that damn dossier...

Gasping, I stopped and looked at the cracked, grimy training tape wrapped around my knuckles. Felt the aching throb in my fists. Slowly let my breathing return to normal.

Upstairs, I showered, dressed in new sweats and a tee-shirt, and went to bed. Even as I began to doze, my mind raced. Before going to work in the morning, I'd have to call about getting the window fixed, plus find out when the CSU techs would be showing up to dig the bullet out of my wall.

Then, on literally no sleep, I faced a day full of therapy patients. A day whose beginning was only two hours away.

Just before dawn, I took an unaccustomed third mug of coffee into the front room, sank into my sofa, and put on the TV news. After some routinely disheartening reports about armed conflicts half a world away, the anchor cut to video shot at the County Courthouse just a couple hours before.

I sat up straight. The footage showed a thin, balding man in an expensive suit walking Eddie Burke out the front door. As the anchor explained, the man was Burke's attorney, having just bailed his client out of jail. The lawyer also maintained that Burke had been incapacitated by alcohol the night before, and that he hadn't meant to hurt anyone. Merely scare the woman he believed was cheating on him.

The sun hadn't yet risen when the video was shot, so the two men's faces were visible only in the glare of the camera lights. Features starkly white against the darkness. Still, now that he'd sobered up, I could see the deep anger burning in the former athlete's eyes. As well as his offended, arrogant stride. A number of on-scene reporters, mikes upraised, jostled for position to get a quote from Burke, but he brushed them aside.

Then the show cut back to the live broadcast, where the anchor reported that the DA's office was still considering whether or not to bring more serious charges against Burke.

I clicked off the screen. At least the report hadn't disclosed that Burke had shot out my window. It made a nice change not to be mentioned on the news for once. Which also meant not having to hear from various friends and colleagues chiding me about it.

After draining my coffee, I shaved, dressed for work, and made my calls. By the time I headed out the front door, another shower had started—an unseasonably cold downpour, slanted by a brisk wind. Bundling my raincoat tighter, I stepped out into it.

And froze where I stood.

Instinctively, I'd glanced across the street at Joy Steadman's house. The porch light was still on, her Jaguar parked out front.

But something was wrong.

Even through the blur of early dawn, the black-woven curtain of rain, I could see that her front door was ajar.

Until a sudden wind gust swept the street, pushed the door fully open. Sent it swinging in eerie silence against the muted roar of the storm. Banging freely against the house.

I started running.

• • ● • •

The interior of Joy's house was unlit, hushed, the only sound coming from outside. The still-banging door, the torrent of rain. I could feel the moisture dampening the back of my coat as I stood in the threshold.

Heart pounding, I went into the living room. Now, away from the opened door, there was only an oppressive silence.

As I went slowly and cautiously across the room to the adjoining hallway, I felt again that ineffable sense of dread from the night before. The foreboding that had stiffened the hairs on the back of my neck.

"Joy? Are you here?" My voice strained. Hollow. "It's Dan Rinaldi. Are you in here?"

Again, only that silence. Somehow intensified by the dimness of the rooms, the shadows crowding every corner.

But there was something else. Something about the air in this house. It was oddly, unnaturally still.

And then, suddenly, I knew what it was. Knew it as though it were a palpable fact.

It was the stillness of death.

I quickened my pace. Strode down the hall into the rooms at the back, calling out Joy's name again. Though I knew she wouldn't answer. Wouldn't be able to.

I found her on the floor of the master bedroom, as spacious and opulently furnished as I'd imagined. At its far end was a king-sized bed. Covers in disarray.

On the carpet at the foot of the bed lay Joy Steadman. On her back. Naked. Slim legs bruised, obscenely spread-eagled. Mouth agape, frozen. As though still screaming in protest.

Steeling myself, I crouched by her side. I knew enough not to disturb the body, but I did feel for a pulse. Nothing.

I stared down at her still, pale face. Those blue-green eyes, open and unseeing.

My own eyes filled with tears for this young woman I barely knew. For the pains of her shortened life, and for the way it ended. The terror of its last moments.

Because I didn't need a pathologist to confirm the cause of death. It was obvious from the ugly, indented marks on her throat where someone had placed powerful hands and squeezed…until her troubled life was over.

Joy Steadman had been murdered.

Chapter Eight

"Man, I hate bein' right all the time."

Harry Polk blew steam off the mug of black coffee I'd brought him from my house. We were sitting inside his unmarked, which was parked at my curb. Shelter from the rain that had lessened to an icy, insistent drizzle.

Not that the weather had discouraged a number of my neighbors, including Marv Kranski, from standing beyond the semi-circle of squad cars, taking videos of the scene with their cells. Just down the street was a KDKA-TV news van, a female reporter and her cameraman beside it, huddled under umbrellas.

After I'd called the police, I contacted my morning therapy patients and cancelled their appointments. I knew I'd need to be available for the next few hours to give a formal statement.

The cops soon arrived and, with practiced skill, secured the scene. The CSU team wasn't far behind. Then the medical examiner showed up and trudged through the front door. Behind him, two morgue attendants were unfolding a gurney from the back of the lab wagon. An empty body bag lay atop it, ready for use.

Now, sweat dotting my brow, I lowered the passenger side window a crack. Polk had the dash heater on, and the mixture of warm air and stale cigarette smoke was stifling.

I turned back to stare at his stoic profile. Something about the intensity of his last words had struck me.

"Looks like you *were* right, Harry. My guess is, you're pretty sure Eddie Burke killed Joy."

The veteran cop nodded. "Don't gotta guess. It hasn't hit the news yet, but it will. Happened earlier this morning."

"What happened?"

"After Burke's lawyer—guy named Reinhart—got Eddie out on bail, they were supposed to head over to some hotel. To keep Eddie under wraps till he cooled off. But once they were alone, in the parking lot, the crazy son of a bitch assaulted Reinhart and carjacked his Lincoln."

My chest tightened. "Jesus Christ…"

"Damn right. Don't take a genius to figger where Eddie went first. He came here and killed his cheatin' girlfriend. Burke didn't have a house key on him when he was processed, so that means Joy let the fucker in. Poor, stupid girl."

"Where's Burke now? Do you know?"

"In the wind. He's got wheels and knows we're after him. We got an APB out on him, and some uniforms at the airport and bus stations. But the prick could be anywhere."

I didn't say anything. The scenario was depressingly familiar, an abused woman once more agreeing to accept her abuser back. This time, at the cost of her life.

As though sensing my thoughts, Polk gave a mournful sigh. "Goddam shame about the girl," he said quietly.

"Yes. It is." I paused. "It's funny, I didn't really know her, but still…"

"Yeah. Kind of a spoiled bitch an' all, but still…"

Neither one of us had the words for what we were trying to say. So we merely fell silent.

Just then, a young plainclothes cop bundled in a raincoat came out of the house and trotted over to the car. Polk and I climbed out of our seats to meet him. After the heated interior of the sedan, I relished the feel of crisp, blustery air, though raindrops pelted my head and dripped down the back of my collar.

"M.E.'s just about through in there, Sarge. Figured you'd want to know." In his late twenties, he had a shrewd, narrow face and close-cropped black hair.

I'd first met Jerry Banks a few weeks before, though I saw him again just days ago when he dropped off the dossier at my office. The newly minted detective was a temporary replacement for Polk's longtime partner, Eleanor Lowrey, who'd taken six months' leave to help her mother raise her junkie brother's kids. The nephew of the assistant chief, Banks was the living embodiment of nepotism, displaying an unearned confidence that clearly set Polk's teeth on edge—which the sergeant did little to disguise.

Unlike Harry, Banks was unaware of my personal relationship with Eleanor. As a black, bisexual female detective in the Department, she made every effort to keep the intimate details of her life private. Especially after she'd received some well-deserved publicity (and a commendation) for her bravery during a shootout with a killer last year.

Seeing Polk's new partner again brought an unexpected stab of pain. When Eleanor had broken it off with me, unable to resolve her conflicted feelings about a former female lover, I did my best to understand. Give her the space, and time, to sort out her feelings. But occasionally, like now, I was struck by an aching sense of loss.

Which was interrupted by Banks' avid glance at my coffee mug.

"Hey, Doc, you got any more java left in the pot?"

Polk gave him a threatening look, but I held up my hand.

"It's okay, Harry. He looks cold." I gestured behind me. "Go on in my house, Detective. Door's unlocked. The coffeepot's on the kitchen counter."

A blithe grin. "I *knew* I liked you, Dr. Rinaldi."

With that, he gave his sergeant a mock salute and headed toward my front door.

Polk frowned. "Smart-ass little shit."

Before I could reply, the M.E. exited the Steadman house, opened an umbrella over his head, and joined us on the street. Dr. Rudy Bergmann was known to me as well, as he was to most people in the city. His thin, bespectacled figure was a familiar presence at press conferences and criminal courtrooms. As was his famously bad hairpiece. Nearing retirement after over thirty years in office, it was obvious he felt more than entitled to his sour view of the human race.

"Surprised to see you out here, Doc," Polk said. Given Bergmann's emeritus status, I, too, wouldn't have expected him to attend personally to what appeared to be a simple homicide.

"As am I, Sergeant. Not the kind of thing I'm normally called out for anymore. But both of my esteemed younger colleagues are working other cases, which left an old man like me to do the honors. So much for seniority, eh?"

He turned his small, perfectly round eyes on mine. "Anyway, Dr. Rinaldi, it was just as you thought. The girl was strangled. Clear finger marks, so it was done manually. Face to face."

"Any sign of sexual assault?" Polk asked.

"Oh, God, yes. From the bruising on her inner thighs, I'd say she was quite brutally raped. I'll know more when I get her on the table, but I expect to see severe vaginal tearing. Though she did put up a fight."

"How can you tell?"

"Her fingernails were manicured, but two have broken tips. Classic defensive injury. Got some epidermal matter under them, but I won't know till later whether there's enough to extract any usable forensics."

Bergmann shook his head. "It takes a great deal of rage to manually strangle someone. A great deal. I don't know what gets into people. Seriously."

He gripped the umbrella tighter, grimacing up at the constant drizzle.

"Now, as the man said, time to get out of these wet clothes and into a dry martini." A thin smile. "Just a joke, of course. Bit early in the day. Even for me. Have a good one, gentlemen."

As Bergmann walked off, Polk gave him a quizzical look. But I knew the reference. The line came from Robert Benchley, one of my late wife's favorite writers. Along with P.G. Woodhouse, Saki, and Dorothy Parker. Humorists from the twenties and thirties. Like a lot of academics, Barbara tended to specialize, even when it came to light reading or other leisure activities. I recall her telling me once about a colleague who was addicted to true-crime shows on TV. Barbara called it "murder porn."

When we got along, it was the kind of thing we used to laugh about. When we got along…

Jerry Banks, gingerly holding a steaming mug of coffee, had returned in time to watch the stoop-shouldered M.E.'s departure. He looked as though he wanted to make a comment, probably an unkind one, but his partner stopped him.

"Stay here and supervise the scene," Polk said. "I'm gonna call downtown and see how the search for Burke is goin'."

"Sure thing, Sarge. See ya, Doc."

Coffee in hand, Banks went back into Joy's house.

Polk glanced at me. "Make sure he returns your mug."

Given his obvious displeasure with being partnered with Banks, I had the feeling he was being serious.

As the M.E. wagon pulled into the street, Polk seemed ready to get back behind the wheel of his car. Then he paused.

"You, too, Doc." Polk indicated the passenger side door. "Got somethin' I need to tell ya."

Puzzled, I once again joined him inside the car. His hands on the steering wheel, he pointedly gazed out the windshield.

"Look, this ain't none o' my business, but I got a call from one o' my buddies up at State prison. He told me Lowrey's been up there to see her girlfriend."

I swallowed a breath. Eleanor's former lover was a convicted felon, doing serious time. A woman Eleanor once called the love of her life.

"Anyway," Polk went on, "this moron buddy o' mine figgered I ought to know, Lowrey bein' my partner and all.

He said it was disgustin' to see a fellow officer holdin' hands with an offender, under the glass partition. 'Didn't know your partner was a dyke,' this guy says."

Polk turned to me at last. "I told him the next time I see him, I'm gonna un-friend him. But not like on Facebook. I'm gonna use my fist. Nobody talks shit 'bout my partner but me."

I took another breath.

"Why are you telling me this?"

"I'm not tryin' to fuck with you, Rinaldi. Honest. I just figger, no sense gettin' your heart broke. So maybe you oughtta give it up about you and her. Besides, once Lowrey's back on the job, havin' you two hookin' up again is gonna be a pain in my ass. I see too goddam much of you already."

I didn't reply. Merely sipped my cooling coffee.

"I'm going back inside," I said finally. "I'll come down to the precinct in an hour or so to give my statement."

"Hey, I hope I wasn't an asshole tellin' you that."

"No. I'm okay."

Polk nodded, unconvinced. "Whatever. Anyway, I'll see ya downtown. But be careful."

"What do mean?"

"You kiddin' me? Burke just killed a girl he thought was cheatin' on him. With *you*. And he's still out there somewhere. Who the hell d'ya think he's gonna wanna kill next?"

Chapter Nine

Midday traffic at the Point was at a standstill. Which was why, even with my windows barely opened an inch, I was breathing clouds of truck exhaust. And why angry drivers all around me were relentlessly, and uselessly, honking their horns, until, finally, we started moving again. I was anxious to get to my office in Oakland in time for my one o'clock patient. It was an appointment I didn't want to miss.

It wasn't that I hadn't taken Polk's warning about Eddie Burke seriously. Though with the police scouring the county for him, I doubted whether Burke would risk staying in the vicinity. If he hadn't ditched his car, he could've already made it across the Ohio state line, or south to West Virginia. And then beyond.

I was driving up from the precinct, having just given my statement about the previous day's events. Of course, by now the news of Joy Steadman's murder had broken, as well as the continuing story of the hunt for Eddie Burke. It was further reported that his lawyer, though hospitalized, was expected to make a full recovery.

The rain had finally ceased, but the streets were still slick enough to slow the procession of cars heading down Forbes Avenue. At last I pulled into my building's parking garage, took the elevator up to the fifth floor, and unlocked my office.

I put my battered Tumi briefcase in its appointed spot next

to my marble-topped desk, and opened the shutters on the broad window overlooking Forbes Avenue and Pitt's urban campus. Lastly, I checked my phone machine for messages. Nothing urgent.

I'd just hung up my suit jacket when the signal light came on. My one o'clock was here.

It was my fourth session with Robbie Palermo, a ten-year-old student at a nearby Catholic elementary school. He had a thatch of brown hair and somber gray eyes. Every time I'd seen him, he'd worn his school uniform and high-top sneakers. A rule violation the stern nuns allowed, "due to the circumstances."

Robbie was exceedingly bright, verbal and well-mannered. Perhaps too much so. It was hard to get him to open up about his feelings, the things that troubled him. Not unusual in an adolescent boy, of course. And normally I wouldn't press a kid like him to share his emotions. Not this early in our work.

But in this case, I felt it important that he do so. His parents agreed, which was why Robbie had been referred to me.

Two weeks before, right after school, Robbie's best friend, Matthew Condon, also ten, put a gun to the side of his head and pulled the trigger. The revolver had belonged to the boy's father, a divorced city planner.

Robbie had found the body, the gun beside it sticky with blood, in the gardener's shed behind Matthew's house, where they'd planned to play video games. Robbie's parents didn't approve of the violence in his favorite games, so he couldn't play them at home. As he'd shared with me during our first session, playing them with Matthew in the rarely used shed was part of what made it exciting. It was a secret they shared.

What they'd never shared, apparently, was what Matthew had been feeling bad about lately. What might have been upsetting him. Why one day, without warning, he'd taken his own life.

Though he wouldn't talk about it, Robbie couldn't figure it out, either. Instead, he had recurring nightmares, panic attacks at school. He could barely eat, or concentrate, or show much interest in anything.

Now, sitting across from me in my consulting room, his bony arms slim and white against the chair's leather, he looked down at his sneakers. He hadn't said a word since he'd come in.

"We don't have to talk about anything if you don't want to," I said after a few minutes. "Or if you do, I'll just listen. I'm pretty good at keeping my mouth shut."

He glanced up, managed a thin smile. "Wish you'd teach that to my stupid parents."

"What makes them stupid? I mean, other than what makes most adults stupid…"

"Aw, they're okay, I guess. I just wish they wouldn't worry about me so much. It really sucks. Like I can't think things through myself."

"You're a damn smart kid, Robbie. I'm sure you do a lot of thinking. About a lot of things."

Again his head came up. Eyes narrowing a bit. "You're talking about Matthew, aren't you?"

I shrugged. "Aren't *you*?"

"I guess so." A long pause. "I mean, I've been thinking about the gaming we do. We *did*…" Voice dropping.

I let my own voice stay calm, measured. "What about those games you and Matthew played?"

"Usually they had aliens in them. You had to kill aliens. We both liked doing it." He gave me a wary look. "Does that mean anything? Like there's something wrong with me?"

"I doubt it. Might just mean you're brave. If I ever saw an alien, my first instinct would probably be to run like hell."

"I'm serious." He folded his arms. "I've been thinking a lot about the games. About how the only way to kill aliens is to shoot them in the head. Only way to snuff them."

"Head shots. Sounds reasonable."

"In this one game, every time you shoot an alien and it dies, the graphic says 'Head Wound.' Then you get points."

I wasn't sure where this was going, but I wanted to let Robbie lead me there. So I waited.

"See?" For the first time today, he stirred in his seat. "Head wounds. Maybe that's what people with something wrong with their brains have. A pain in their heads. Like wounds."

I let out a breath. Had to be careful here.

"Are you talking about Matthew again now, Robbie? That he had a head wound? Some pain in his mind?"

He nodded slowly, arms still crossed. Wanting to say more, *feel* more, but needing to stay guarded.

"Maybe that's why Matthew shot himself in the head," Robbie said quietly. "Like we did to aliens in the game."

"You mean, like maybe it was the only way he could make the pain stop?"

Another slow nod. As tears dotted the edges of his eyes.

I leaned closer, sitting forward in my chair. But not wanting to crowd him.

"It's okay to miss him, Robbie. And feel bad about how unhappy he was inside. *And* to be angry at him for what he did."

Robbie's face darkened. "But how can I feel all those things at once?"

"How could you feel any other way? I know *I* couldn't. Not about my best friend."

Another long pause. "You think that's why I'm so messed up about everything? That I got a head wound, too?"

"I think we all do, Robbie. To some degree. It's what lets us feel things. Understand the pain of others. It's what makes us humans."

His breathing slowed as he tried to take this in.

Finally, he said, "If I keep talking to you about all this, will I stop having nightmares and stuff?"

I ventured a smile. "That's the theory. We'll just have to wait and see. But I believe talking about things really helps."

He gave this some thought. Then: "No offense, Dr. Rinaldi, but you have a weird job."

Now it was my turn to nod. "Tell me about it."

The session ended soon after that, and Robbie reached for his coat and scarf. As usual, his mother had brought him for his appointment and would be out in my waiting room, reading a magazine until we were finished.

Grumbling, Robbie wrapped the scarf around his neck. Though the rain had stopped, it was still fairly brisk outside, and Mrs. Palermo had worried her son would catch a cold.

"I hate it when she treats me like a baby," he said. "You know what I mean?"

"I sure do."

Robbie didn't need to know that I could only infer what he was talking about. My own mother had been sick from the day I was born, and died when I was three. So my parenting was the responsibility of my father, a bitter, alcoholic beat cop who'd left the nurturing part to my various aunts. Until I was old enough to start training for the ring. Then he was totally, relentlessly hands-on. Sparring with me when I was still in pajamas. Teaching me to dodge, weave. Avoid the slap of his hands. And take it like a man when I didn't.

My own chance to fight back would come later, he said. Which it did, against other kids my age—other, more talented amateurs, some of whom made it to the Olympics. But in all that time, I never laid a finger on him, though I'd spent most of my teens wanting to.

Yet, when he died, I wept.

Robbie's searching look drew me out of my reverie.

"You okay, Dr. Rinaldi? Maybe you're the one getting sick."

"I'm fine. Now let's not keep your mother waiting."

Ten minutes after the last of the day's patients had left, I was heading back across town toward the Liberty Bridge with a Nina Simone CD in the dash player, filling the car with her clear, sad, righteous voice.

When I arrived at home, a pair of CSU techs—for whom I'd left the keys—were just finishing up. They had the bullet from my wall bagged and tagged, and were taking down the crime scene tape from my front door. Across the street, others from their crew were still at work in Joy Steadman's place. They'd probably be at the scene till dusk.

Alone now, I changed into jeans and a pullover sweater. Then grabbed a beer and went into the front room. To my relief, my makeshift repair of the window was still intact. I figured it should hold until the glazier arrived tomorrow.

I was just about to click on the TV news when my phone rang. It was Angie Villanova, Pittsburgh PD's community liaison officer. In her late fifties, she was a curt, no-nonsense veteran cop. Sturdy as an oak. She was also family.

"Listen up, Danny. And don't give me any shit."

"Some people just start with 'hello.'"

"Whatever. Anyway, guess what? You're invited to a cocktail party tomorrow night. The Mayor's hosting."

"A cocktail party? You've got to be kidding."

"Nope. It's a fund-raiser for His Honor's campaign. Lots of local bigwigs. Captains of industry. You'll fit right in."

"Very funny. Except I'm not going."

"Yes you are. That's a direct order from Chief Logan. So you gotta play ball. Thing is, Danny, some o' the top brass are itchin' to cancel your contract as a consultant."

"Why?"

"Why do ya think? Your behavior the last couple years has made a lotta people nervous. Gettin' your ass mixed up in high-profile investigations. Endin' up on the news for things that could embarrass the Department. Hell, I'm surprised they haven't punched your ticket long before this."

"So I have to attend this thing, whether I like it or not?"

"Yep. Logan said either you come or you're gone."

"Okay, okay. Tell me where and when."

"I'll text it to ya. Serves ya right, though. It's what you get for bein' such a media whore."

"Bite me, Angie."

"Love you, too, Danny."

We hung up. By now, the pale, uncertain light of the setting sun was painting the walls. I sat for a moment, sipping my beer, my thoughts drifting. Then my gaze fell to the dossier, open-faced on the coffee table. As if by rote, I pulled it onto my lap.

Wearily, doubting whether I'd find anything new, I flipped through the pages to the rear section, where the case files were located. Inexplicably, my eye was caught by the biographical details about my late wife that the cops had assembled. I'd read them before, of course, but for some reason found myself drawn again to the pages about Barbara's family. Particularly her bitter, widower father.

My father-in-law, Phillip Camden, died some years back, in the midst of my involvement in the Wingfield investigation. In fact, I'd been at his hospital bedside when he'd taken his last breath. A distinguished psychiatrist and clinical researcher, he'd been one of my mentors in the Pitt graduate department. Though we'd disagreed strongly about therapeutic practice, he was even more unsettled by my marriage to his daughter, and sole child, Barbara.

She'd been barely out of her teens when her mother died, so Camden was her only parent thereafter. And she'd been the only thing on this Earth that he loved. So it was no surprise that, after Barbara was killed, he blamed me for her death. For somehow allowing it. And for being the one who lived.

He died still blaming me.

I closed the dossier, throat suddenly constricted, and threw the damn thing on the floor. Feeling a sheet of shame, remorse—*something*—burning like acid on my face.

All the years came flooding back. My marriage to a woman I both loved and battled, with equal passion. My attempts to find common ground with my father-in-law while Barbara was alive, and seek some kind of solace with him after her death. But in our shared grief, there was no room for peace.

Stung by the memory, I leapt to my feet. I stared down at the dossier on the floor as though wishing I could somehow make it disappear. Make it stop pulling me back into a past it had taken me years to come to terms with. At least for the most part.

Suddenly, jarringly, the phone rang again. Harry Polk.

"Listen, Doc, I got some news. Couple joggers found that lawyer's car wrapped around a tree out past Monroeville. Looks like it skidded off the road leadin' to the turnpike on-ramp."

"What about Eddie Burke?"

"I'm lookin' right at him. Or what's left of him."

"What do you mean?"

"He's still in the car. Whole goddam front's caved in. Road crew got the Jaws o' Life tryin' to pry his dead-ass body out. They say it could take a while."

I said nothing, watching the last light fade from the room.

"That's that, then," Polk was saying. "Nice to clear a homicide so quick. Cuts down on paperwork."

"So you're convinced it was Burke who killed Joy?"

"Who the hell else could it be? We'll know for sure when we get the autopsy results. And the rape kit. Get a match for the bastard's DNA. But it was him, all right."

"And now that he's been considerate enough to die in a car crash trying to flee the state—"

Polk chuckled. "See, it even saves taxpayers the cost of a trial. A win-win all around. Right, Doc?"

According to the morning news, everyone seemed to feel the same way. The police media flack gave an on-camera statement, saying, in effect, that the case was over. Not officially, of course, but for all practical purposes.

When the station cut back to the news anchor, he added that Joy Steadman's grieving parents had arrived to accompany their daughter's body back to Philadelphia for burial.

I clicked off the TV. Suddenly, the image of her still, lifeless body flickered in my mind. Those empty blue-green eyes. I quickly pushed it away.

I swallowed the last of my coffee. Though it was just past eight, the glazier had already come and gone. It had taken over an hour to remove what was left of my front window, then replace and reset a new one. All I'd had to do was clean up the debris.

Now, heading out the door for work, the first thing that greeted me was the lilt of birdsong, normally a reassuringly familiar sound in the morning, especially after a week's worth of rain and gusting wind. But not today.

Nor was my somber mood lightened as I drove down from Grandview by the sight of a clear, startling blue sky.

"That's that," Polk had said. Perhaps he was right. Joy Steadman and Eddie Burke, two people I didn't know, had each suffered sudden, violent deaths. Summarily snuffed out of existence. Now the rest of the world, including me, was just supposed to move on.

After all, what other choice did we have?

Though it is amazing how quickly it happens. Less than twenty minutes later, I was pulling into my office garage, thinking about some of the patients I'd be seeing today. Calls and e-mails I had to return. The usual litany of everyday tasks.

Moving on.

Or so I thought.

What I didn't know—*couldn't* know—was that by the time this particular day was over, my life would be shockingly, horrifyingly, changed.

Forever.

Chapter Ten

"Danny! I'll be damned, you showed up!"

Within moments, I was enveloped in the firm embrace and insistent perfume of Angie Villanova. Having risen up the ranks to her current position in the Department, she was stout and proud, sporting a cloud of lacquered hair. Her tailored outfit as sensible as the woman herself. The only concession to the manufactured pomp of the occasion was the string of pearls she'd inherited from her mother.

"Where's Sonny?" Even standing in the foyer, I could hear the chatter of a party in full swing. "The food's free, right?"

She laughed. "Yeah, but my husband knew that if he came he'd have to talk to people. And that's somethin' neither of us wants, right? By the way, ya shoulda worn a tie."

I was in a sport coat with an opened shirt collar. Clucking her tongue, she began fiddling with it.

"Jesus, Danny, this is a fund-raiser. Wealthy folks oozin' money. What the Mayor's people call 'high-value targets.' So try to act like ya belong here, okay?"

I was about to protest when she slipped a proprietary arm in mine. "Now, c'mon, I'll introduce ya around."

I sighed. "That's what I was afraid of."

After finishing at the office, I'd just had time to hurry home, change, and head back downtown. When I stopped at a red light on Grant Street, I opened my driver's side window all the way. For the first time in a week, the night sky was clear and cloudless. An array of stars shimmered above me in the cold air. The concrete and steel towers of the urban core dusted in silver by a pale, benign moon.

Waiting for the light to change, I frowned in resentment at being forced to attend the Mayor's cocktail party. But, as Angie had warned, my position with the Department was too shaky to blow it off. So, reminding myself that there'd be liquor on the premises, I accepted my fate and set my GPS for the address.

The party was taking place at the private residence of one of the Mayor's wealthier friends, who'd just moved here to newly gentrified Lawrenceville. Once a dying small town on the outskirts of Pittsburgh, it soon became a low-rent haven for artists, musicians, and other struggling types. In recent years, however, those same colorful residents had been pushed out, unable to afford the high prices of the renovated homes and condos. Now the area boasted wealthy hedge-fund managers, software entrepreneurs, and similar movers and shakers.

My kind of crowd, without a doubt.

As Angie led me from room to room, making introductions to conspicuously dressed men and women, whose names I immediately forgot, I took in the moneyed opulence of our host's home. Soon to be featured in *Architectural Digest*, Angie whispered to me.

It wasn't until we'd reached the large, glass-domed library that I spotted a familiar face. Standing in line with people sampling exotic items from the catered buffet table was Harvey Blalock. Champagne glass in hand, he was chatting with a stunning Asian woman in a strapless dress and heels.

I'd met Blalock during the Wingfield case. President of the Pittsburgh Black Attorneys Association, he'd represented me briefly when I'd been sued for malpractice. In the years since, our professional relationship had evolved into a warm friendship. Harvey was one of my favorite people.

Angie nodded in his direction. "Go ahead and say hi to Harvey. I've gotta go find Chief Logan and the Mayor. Let 'em know you're here."

"Where are they?"

"Last I saw, they were huddled with Dr. Langstrom at the bar. Probably anglin' for a big donation to the city coffers."

She smiled at my blank look. "Langstrom's our host, Danny. Plastic surgeon to the rich and wrinkled. Lotta money in that, in case ya hadn't heard. Beats shrinkin' heads for a living."

She gave me a wink and strode off, leaving me to weave through small clusters of the rich and formerly wrinkled till I got next to Blalock. His broad face broke into a smile.

"Daniel! I hoped I'd run into you here."

As usual, Blalock looked avuncular and robust. Also as usual, his handshake was just short of crushing.

Then he turned to his companion. "Dr. Daniel Rinaldi, meet Lily Chen. One of my new hires. *Harvard Law Review*."

The beautiful woman put her slender hand in mine.

"Nice to meet you in person, Doctor. I've been following your career for years. Ever since reading about your work with that poor victim of the Handyman." She glanced at her boss. "I understand he's still on Death Row."

"Oh, yeah." Blalock gave a dark chuckle. "And he'll stay there as long as his lawyer keeps filing appeals. At this rate, Dowd will probably live to senility and die of natural causes."

Dubbed "the Handyman" by the media, Troy David Dowd was a serial killer who tortured his victims with screwdrivers, pliers, and other tools. He'd murdered and dismembered twelve people before his eventual capture and conviction.

Only two of Dowd's intended victims managed to escape. One of them, a single mother in her fifties, was sent to me for therapy. It was my treatment of her PTSD symptoms that led to my consultant's contract with the Pittsburgh Police.

I was just about to thank Ms. Chen for her kind words when her gaze was caught by another guest waving from across the room. After she excused herself, Blalock and I watched her departing form with interest.

"Has your wife met your new protégé, Harvey?"

"Wipe that smirk off your face, Doctor. Lily happens to be a brilliant litigator. Plus it's about time my shop had a little diversity, don't you think? Keep the brothers on their toes."

After having a couple drinks together, and waxing nostalgic about the blue-collar Pittsburgh of our youth, I managed to slip away from the gregarious lawyer and head across the room to where Angie was speaking to another woman. I just wanted to make sure she'd told the Mayor and Chief Logan I'd shown up, then get the hell out of there. I'd done my duty to the Department.

However, as I got closer, I realized that Angie's companion looked vaguely familiar. She was about my age, slender and elegant in a black sleeveless dress matching the color of her short, loosely curled hair. Dangling hoop earrings accentuated her high cheekbones and hooded gray eyes.

Angie took hold of my forearm. "Dan Rinaldi, meet Liz Cortland. According to the Mayor, she's his favorite cousin."

Liz shrugged. "That's only because I'll occasionally appear at these obnoxious orgies of self-promotion. Doing my bit for the extended family."

I shook her hand. Firm, unfussy grip.

"I'm sure he appreciates it. But if you don't mind my asking, have we met before? You look familiar."

"I should, Dr. Rinaldi. Though it's been over a dozen years now. We used to see each other at faculty events. I was a good friend and colleague of your late wife, Barbara."

Realization dawned at last. "Of course. Dr. Cortland. You taught Comparative Lit, right?"

"Still do. I'm even in the same office on the same floor. Three doors down from where Barbara's was. We used to grab coffee or lunch together sometimes." A pointed look. "Barbara was a brilliant linguist. A pioneer in her field."

"Yes, she was. And I hope you know how much she admired your own work. As do I. She gave me one of your papers to read."

"I trust you weren't offended. My writing was pretty strident in those days. Some people feel it still is."

I smiled. "So was Barbara's."

I could tell that Angie didn't know how to gauge the tenor of my conversation with Liz Cortland. Truth is, neither did I. Other than being aware of the tension below the surface.

Angie spoke up. "I'm so glad you two got a chance to meet again. How 'bout we all amble over to the buffet table?"

"Not for me, thanks," said Liz. "I took one look at the obscene amount of choices available and became, frankly, disgusted. This damned country. The one-percent keep living like feudal lords, while the rest of the world goes hungry."

No doubt Angie was somewhat put off by this, but she did her best to hide it. I touched her shoulder.

"I'll have to beg off, too, Angie. I had a pretty tough day. I think I better head on home."

I was about to say goodnight to Liz when she stopped me with a look. Reaching into a clutch purse, she gave me her card.

"Give me a call, will you? Now that we've run into each other, there's something I'd like to discuss with you. It concerns Barbara."

This took me aback, but I slid the card in my pocket. Then her frank gaze found mine.

"I'll look forward to hearing from you. Soon."

Dr. Langstrom had provided valet service for his party guests, but I'd bypassed it to park my car a couple blocks up the street. For one thing, the night was pleasantly cool and cloudless, and it felt good to stretch my legs. For another, I was reluctant to hand over my reconditioned '65 Mustang to some underpaid and easily distractible high school kid. My poor chariot had been dinged enough in recent years.

As I approached it, half in shadow beneath a leafy oak, I thought about my encounter with Liz Cortland. Strange running into someone from Barbara's professional life, especially now. Probably just a coincidence, but still...

I'd just unlocked my car when I was aware of two things.

First, the muffled scuff of a shoe on the pavement behind me. Then, before I could turn around, a sharp, stabbing pain at the back of my neck.

I gasped, muscles instinctively tensing. But a powerful pair of arms was already wrapped around me. Within seconds, I felt a rush of warmth course through my body. Felt my legs begin to buckle, my own arms go slack.

My vision clouded. I struggled to maintain consciousness, but my efforts were futile. Then, just before I sank into a swirling sea of darkness, I heard a cold, harsh whisper in my ear. The words unearthly, hollow. As though echoing from somewhere far away...

"I hope you've enjoyed living in your world, Danny. 'Cause from now on, you're living in mine."

Chapter Eleven

When I came to, I was staring at a large monitor screen.

A wide-eyed, frozen stare.

I tried to blink, but couldn't. The lids of both eyes had been pulled apart, and held there by some adhesive. Tape, glue. I had no idea.

As this awareness hit me, a real panic rose in my chest. Adrenaline spiking, I tried to move. But now I realized that I was strapped into a hard-backed chair of some kind. My forearms were bound to the chair arms with belt-wide leather strips, my ankles attached to the wooden legs. When I struggled against my bonds, the chair didn't budge. It was bolted to the floor.

Frantically, I tried again to blink my eyes, willing my lids to close. But whatever was holding them open didn't give.

I swallowed deep mouthfuls of air, trying to calm myself. At least enough to focus on my surroundings. To the extent that I could. I started to look around—

My head didn't move. Couldn't. It was only then that I registered the dull ache on either side of my skull. The pressure of some kind of pincers. At least that's what I imagined they were. Cold metallic discs, probably attached to the top of the chairback. Exerting enough pressure to make it impossible for me to turn my head.

Another wave of panic flowed over me as I tried to accept

the reality of the situation. Fathom its surreal, terrifying contours. That this was actually happening.

Slowly, with effort, my mind acquiesced. Accepted the facts, incomprehensible as they were. I'd been bound tightly to a chair, my eyes painfully taped open, head immobilized, so that I was forced to gaze only at what was in front of me.

But all there was to see was that blank monitor screen, hanging about four feet away from me on an otherwise featureless wall. The size of a flat-screen TV, it had been situated at my eye level. Yet all I saw was a profusion of pixels dancing across its broad face.

Using my breath once more to quell my anxiety, I finally let my aching limbs relax and stopped straining against the leather straps binding them. Tried to get my bearings.

The room itself was concrete-cold and eerily dim, its corners shrouded in shadow. What little light there was came from somewhere above me. Soft, faint. Just enough for me to gauge how small the chamber was.

Which was how it felt to me. Like some kind of chamber, or dungeon. Something out of Grimm's. Out of a lurid bedtime story.

Or a nightmare.

I swallowed again, and felt my lips part. I was almost surprised to discover that my mouth hadn't been taped shut. Or stuffed with some kind of gag.

I could speak. So I did.

At first, my words were a series of muffled croaks. Then, with each passing second, my voice grew in strength.

"Where the hell am I?" I shouted. "Who did this to me?"

Silence. Accompanied only by the multi-colored pixels gyrating in a kind of Brownian motion across the big screen.

I called out even louder.

"Dammit, who the fuck did this? Why am I—?"

A hard, raspy voice echoed off the walls. Tinny, as though from small, inlaid speakers. But unmistakably male.

"Welcome, Danny. Welcome to the rest of your life."

I fell silent. Ludicrous as I found the words, I couldn't deny the cold malice in his voice nor suppress the shiver that coursed through my arms.

"I assume it's okay to call you Danny? Since we're going to be quite intimately involved with each other."

"Who are you?" I managed to ask again.

"You know exactly who I am. Or, at least, should know."

"Trust me. No fucking idea."

His tone darkened. "Damned unpleasant attitude for a man in your position. But I don't mind. It makes what's coming all the sweeter. For me, that is. For you...well, not so much."

I strained to move my head, to look around me. Something about the acoustics in the room made it seem that the man was standing nearby. Behind me, or to one side.

It was maddening being constrained this way. Able to do nothing but stare, opened eyes going dry in the dead air, at the screen in front of me. Those erratic pixels. Dancing. Mocking me.

Steeling myself, I spoke again.

"Look, whoever the hell you are—"

"No, Danny. *You* look."

Abruptly, the pallid overhead light flickered out, plunging the room into total darkness. At the same time, a blurry image appeared on the monitor screen.

It took only a moment to realize I was looking at the view from a camera, hand-held, moving into a night-shrouded room. The person with the camera breathing hard. Short, excited breaths.

This room, I thought. *I've seen it before...*

Suddenly the camera's lens fell onto a king-size bed, and revealed a person sleeping there. Under a swath of covers, curled into a half-fetal position. Like a child's slumber.

A spray of rich dark hair cascaded onto the pillow, masking the sleeper's features.

Though I knew whose face it was.

Unthinking, with a choked cry, I tried to bolt up from my chair. To do something. But I was helpless.

As helpless as Joy Steadman, who woke with a scream as the man filming her used his free hand to roughly pull aside the covers. Naked, shrieking in terror, her hands came up, clawing at his face. But he stayed out of reach. Then, with one blow from the back of his hand, the cords of his muscled forearm thrusting into view, he knocked her back onto the bed. Her head lolled, eyes rolling up into their sockets.

She was dazed for only a few moments, but that was enough time for the man to move to the end of the bed and position the camera on some flat surface. Maybe a bureau of some kind. Now the image was static, a mute witness. Frozen in place, ready to record what was about to transpire.

The big man had aimed the camera at the carpeted floor, and for a moment I couldn't tell what was happening. Suddenly, he came into frame again, though his back was still to the camera.

He was pulling the semi-conscious girl by her hair down the length of the bed, her naked body twisting helplessly as it was dragged over the rumpled sheets. Then, roughly, he threw her onto the floor.

"Jesus Christ!" I shouted out, my voice choked with frustration and rage. "No!"

I wanted to look away. To turn my head, or close my eyes. But I could do neither. He'd seen to that.

And now I knew why.

Joy had come awake, her face white with fear as she stared up at the man looming over her. She started screaming again as the man, oblivious, pulled off his short-sleeved tee-shirt, revealing a well-muscled back covered in grotesque tattoos.

Most of the inked figures were indistinct, but one seemed to be a winged serpent. Writhing as if alive as he bent and peeled his black jeans from his body. Revealing his own naked body, coldly white, smooth. Completely shaved.

His face still hidden from view, he fell on her with a guttural howl and slammed her head back against the carpet. She struggled, but could barely move beneath his crushing weight. Could only cry out in panic as he pawed her breasts with his huge hands. A cry that turned into a gasp of pain as he entered her and began to thrust. Repeatedly, savagely.

To my horror, I watched him rape Joy Steadman.

Again, I tried to close my eyes. Look away. But I couldn't. Nor could I stop up my ears against her piteous screams, his obscene, grunting laughter.

"Shut it off, you sadistic fuck! Shut this thing off!"

A clipped laugh came from the hidden speakers, its cruel edge echoing that of the sounds from the man on-screen.

"But we're getting to the best part, Danny. I'm sure you'll enjoy it. The only thing missing is the popcorn."

It seemed to go on forever. Until Joy's cries of pain and protest had fallen to a barely audible whimper, even as her attacker reared up, ready to climax. Then, suddenly, his powerful hands were around her throat.

Joy's eyes whitened with a renewed panic, and she began to struggle again. Gasping, choking. At one point raking her nails against his shoulder. But his hands only tightened their vice-like grip, his fingers digging into the soft tissue of her throat. Squeezing the life out of her.

"Here it is, Danny." The voice from the speakers could barely contain its excitement. "The moment we've all been waiting for."

"Listen, you piece of shit—"

"There!" He shouted gleefully. "See it? Beautiful! So fucking beautiful…"

It appeared to be simultaneous. Her eyes glazing over in death at the same time her rapist emptied his hate into her.

I had no words.

"C'mon, Danny." His tone smooth, assured. "You have to admire the symmetry. Just as *I* came, *she* went."

Tears of grief edged my burning, swollen eyes as his laugh

echoed in the small, dark room. Eyes that could only watch as the man's orgasmic shudder quieted, and he slowly climbed back to his feet.

He looked impassively down at Joy's pale pink body, at what he'd wrought, and then turned to the camera lens.

For the first time I saw his face.

The shaved head. The dark green eyes, fiercely intense and yet oddly opaque. The thin, patrician nose and jutting jaw. Though his strong, handsome features were coarsened by the grin widening his cheeks.

"Recognize me, Danny?"

It wasn't a voice coming from the speakers. It was his voice. That of the man on-screen. Talking directly to me.

He took a step forward, filling the screen with his body. Beneath the sweat glistening on his hairless chest was another tattoo, directly above his heart. It was some kind of standing cup, or chalice, with rays emanating from it. The Grail…?

He leaned in closer. Smiled.

"It's me, Danny. Surely Barbara told you all about me."

Barbara? Did he mean—*could* he mean…?

"What? I don't—What are you saying?"

He didn't answer, of course. Though it took a few seconds for my fevered brain to remember the reason. I was watching a video that had been taped two days before.

"That's why this bitch here had to die," he was saying. "After I had my fun with her first. Only fair, after all."

The grin faded from his face.

"Once I learned that Joy Steadman was your lover, I knew what I had to do. What my first act would be."

Foolishly, I cried out. "But we weren't—"

As though the man on-screen could hear me. Half-crazed as I was with grief and anger. With virulent, impotent anguish.

"See how it works, Danny? You took what was mine, now I've taken what's yours. And I'm just getting started."

He flashed that arrogant, self-assured grin once more. And then the screen went blank.

The room fell dark again, leaving me encased in a numbing silence, broken only by the rasp of my quickening breaths.

Desperate, buzzing with anxiety, I tried to think. To comprehend what had just happened. And start figuring out a way to free myself, to escape. If there was one…

I'd never find out. Because even in the utter darkness I could feel the presence of someone standing behind me.

Him.

"As much fun as this has been, Danny boy, I'm afraid it's time for you to go home." "

I gasped, as once again a needle jabbed into my neck.

"But don't worry." A grim chuckle. "I'll be in touch."

Chapter Twelve

When I awoke, I was again sitting up, though this time behind the wheel of my Mustang.

In my driveway.

A harsh mid-morning sun glazed the windshield, sending needles of pain into my eyes. I blinked against the glare.

Blinked, I thought dumbly. *I can blink.*

I drew some deep, cleansing breaths. Trying to bring order to my chaotic thoughts.

Had I dreamed it all? No, because my neck still hurt from where the needle had gone in. And my eyes ached, throbbed.

Hands shaking, I reached up for the sun visor and pulled it down. Blocking the insistent light of day.

Strange, after the darkness of that room, that I'd need to protect myself from a punishing sun. Then I found out why.

Shifting in my seat, I peered up at the rearview mirror. There was deep discoloration at the edge of my eyes, the lids a raw, roughened red, as though sandpapered from where the adhesive had been applied, and then none-too-gently ripped off.

It had happened, all right. I'd seen Joy's killer, and it wasn't Eddie Burke. Dead or not, he hadn't been guilty. So, no matter what Harry Polk thought, or how convenient it was for all concerned, it wasn't "case closed" on the Joy Steadman murder.

Realizing this had the effect of abruptly snapping me back

to attention. To the present moment. I started thinking more clearly now. Putting things together.

Like the fact that he—whoever he was—must've driven me here. Which also meant that he knew where I lived.

As soon as that thought struck me, I turned around and looked through the side windows to the street. But if I'd hoped to catch sight of the man fleeing down the sidewalk, I was disappointed. Grandview Avenue looked the same way it did every bright, clear morning. Cars parked in driveways, or at intervals up and down the street. Some I recognized, some I didn't.

One thing I knew for sure. The man was long gone. Either on foot, or, perhaps, driven away by an accomplice.

No matter. The thing to do now was get in touch with Polk, let him know what happened to me last night. And that Joy Steadman's real killer was still at large. I'd seen his face clearly in the video, as well as his distinguishing tattoos. I could give the police a detailed description...

I searched my pocket for my cell. Then, ironically, I heard its familiar buzz. I hadn't noticed it had been lying on the passenger seat the whole time. I reached for it, but before I could answer, an image flickered on the screen.

It was him. The hard, chiseled face. That serene smile.

"About time you woke up, sleepyhead. And, yes, I've hacked into your cell. More like a long distance 'bot, if we're being technical. I see all, hear all. Spooky as hell, I know. How do you think I heard the cop and you talking about your affair with Joy Steadman?"

I grabbed up the cell. "But that wasn't true—"

"Right. Whatever." He massaged his chin, eyes glistening. "Listen, Danny. When you turn on the news, I'm afraid you're going to learn about another tragic death. Someone else who had the misfortune to know you."

My breath caught in my throat. Stayed there.

"Nothing so personal with this one, though." His tone easy, conversational. "I just wanted you to know how serious I am. How...what's the word?...totally *committed.*"

He seemed to relish my silence. Its shock, dismay.

"Oh, and one last thing. If you tell anyone about this… if you call the police, for instance…many more people will die. Random folks. Maybe the guy selling hot dogs on the corner. The head of the school board. The Mayor. Who the hell knows?"

A meaningful pause. "Are we clear on this point?"

I slowly nodded, assuming he could see me.

He could. "That's my boy. Let's just keep our relationship on the down-low. After all, you're a therapist. You're good at keeping secrets, right?"

Before I could respond, the image vanished from the screen.

I tossed the cell aside, then gripped the steering wheel with both hands. Hard. Using the pressure to maintain control.

Another murder? Of someone in my life. An innocent, who no doubt died suddenly, and violently, without a clue as to why.

Someone who, in his words, had the misfortune to know me. But did that make me responsible for what he'd done?

Thankfully, the irrationality of that thought struck me a moment after I had it, though the pang of guilt it caused lingered a bit longer. Then, exhaling, I roused myself, grabbed up my cell, and climbed out of the Mustang.

Another shock awaited me at the front door.

I'd just taken out my keys to unlock it when I discovered that it was already unlocked. Closed, but unlocked.

Heart pounding, I slowly opened the door and stepped into the shadowy front room. The heavy drapes were drawn, as I'd left them, blocking the noonday sun. The air was thick, turgid. Walking as carefully as I could, I moved through a swirl of dust motes toward the kitchen.

The light was on inside. And there was the distinct hum of voices. Low, conspiratorial. Two of them.

Eyes burning, still feeling spent in both mind and body, I clenched my fists and approached the open kitchen doorway.

Was it *him*? I wondered. With an accomplice? Lying in wait?

Maybe the smart move was to go back the way I'd come, retreat cautiously across the airless room and out the front door. Call the cops from the safety of my driveway.

Except that my cell phone wasn't secure. *He* would hear the call. And after what he'd said about contacting the police…his threat that he'd start indiscriminately taking lives…

I believed him.

Besides, as foolish as it seemed—and as reckless, given my weakened condition—I had to know who was on the other side of that open doorway. *Had to.*

Steeling myself, I strode into the brightly lit room.

And froze, hands still balled into fists.

As I'd surmised, there were two of them. A man and a woman. Sitting side by side at the kitchen table, their heads were huddled over a laptop, next to which were a couple of half-empty coffee mugs. The carafe bubbled on the tiled countertop behind them.

The man poked his head up, grinned.

"Jesus, Doc, you look like shit. Like one of Elliot's hollow men."

I knew him, of course. A former patient. A retired FBI profiler whom I'd treated for his debilitating night terrors.

I knew the woman as well. A current FBI Special Agent with whom I'd worked only a few weeks before.

But what the hell were Lyle Barnes and Gloria Reese doing in my kitchen?

Before I could ask the question, Barnes, wincing slightly, had risen and, using his left hand, got another mug from the cabinet above the sink. It wasn't till he'd stood up that I realized his right arm was in a sling.

Lyle Barnes had retired from the FBI after twenty long years spent profiling—and interviewing—some of the nation's most notorious serial killers. He'd spent hundreds of hours inside the heads of the likes of David Berkowitz, BTK, and the Green River Killer. And with the psychic scars to prove it.

In his late sixties, he was tall, thin and wiry, with leathered features and intense world-weary eyes. The FBI had brought Barnes and me together when, soon after retirement, he began suffering from night terrors. He'd wake from a troubled sleep screaming, clawing at his bedsheets, soaked with sweat. Having envisioned formless yet terrifying shapes, accompanied by a powerful sense of dread.

At the same time, Barnes had become a target of a ruthless assassin. However, soon after the killer was brought to justice, the tormented agent finally went into treatment with me, which concluded late last year. By then, he rarely experienced his agonizing symptoms. So off he went into a retirement that combined fly-fishing with his devout, life-long love of poetry.

Anyway, that had been the plan. Yet now, here he was in my kitchen, drinking my coffee, and with his arm in a sling. Though still keeping to his usual off-the-rack sports jacket, buttoned-up shirt, and grey slacks. Once a G-man, always a G-man.

"What happened to your arm, Lyle?" I asked.

Using his good hand, he poured me some coffee and motioned for me to sit. I did, putting my cell beside me on the table.

"I got shot." Barnes regained his own seat. "Outside my front door. Right before dawn, when I went out to get the paper. Turned out to be just a deep flesh wound, but it bled like a son of a bitch. So I lay still as a corpse, letting it pool under me. From a distance, *I* would've thought I was dead, too."

"It was a foolish risk." These were Gloria's first words since I'd entered the room. She frowned at the older man with a kind of stern affection. In turn, I looked at her.

Dark-eyed and dark-haired, Gloria was what used to be

called petite. Pretty and compact, she wore a tight sweater and jeans that revealed her slim curves. I knew from my own experience how smart and tough she was. "Small but mighty," she'd once said to describe herself. I couldn't agree more.

"Luckily," Barnes went on, "before the guy could come any closer to check me out, a truck came down the street. So the shooter decided to take off. I made sure I didn't move a muscle till he was out of sight. Besides, at my age, playing dead isn't that much of a stretch."

I stared at the two of them for a long moment.

"I still don't know what's happening," I said. "And why you're both here."

Gloria regarded Barnes. "You left out the most important part, Lyle. Better tell him."

He grunted. "Right before the guy stuck a gun out his car window and fired, he yelled 'Regards from Danny Rinaldi.'"

I said nothing for a moment, then slowly nodded.

"You don't seem surprised," Barnes said.

"He told me someone I knew had been murdered. Although I had no idea who it was till just this minute. You."

"Well, it was *supposed* to be me. I guess I did fool him, though. He thought he'd killed me."

Barnes grunted. "When I knew for sure he was gone, I wrapped a coat around my arm and drove to this doctor I know. He's a…Well, let's just say we have a history. So he wasn't going to report the gunshot wound. Last thing I needed was the Bureau's bullshit. Even though I'm retired. All the paper-work, plus follow-ups with a head-shrinker. No offense, Doc."

"None taken."

"Anyway, he dug out the bullet, which was as much fun as it sounds. Then he dressed the wound and forced me to wear this goddam sling. The only good thing to come out of it is the pain meds. Man, they've come a long way since I was in the field."

He leaned back. "Naturally, the shooter mentioning your name kinda got my attention. So after I got patched up, I drove here and invited myself in. I knocked first, of course."

"Of course." I recalled the last time Lyle Barnes had been in my house. Hiding from the killer tracking him, he'd used his considerable skills to get past the locks. Seemed like he hadn't lost his knack.

"Since you weren't here," he said, "I must admit I made myself at home. Even took a look through that dossier on the coffee table. Interesting reading."

"Jesus, Lyle—"

"No, wait." Gloria put her hand on my wrist. "Let him finish, Danny."

"Anyway," Barnes continued, "I noticed something odd in the case files concerning that mugging years ago, so I got your laptop from the desk and turned it on. To do some research. The moment I booted it up, a video started playing on the screen. Complete with audio. And nothing I did could make it stop."

I felt the blood leave my face.

"Well, *that* was something." Barnes shook his head sadly. "It showed this guy raping a young woman he called Joy Steadman. Then killing her. Then the bastard turns to the camera and delivers his little speech. To you."

"I know. I saw it." I paused. "He forced me to watch it."

As succinctly as possible, I told Barnes and Gloria what had happened the night before. And earlier this morning.

Barnes grimaced. "I figured it was something like that. And don't be surprised that he can hack your cell or control your laptop remotely. Hell, there's a reason the top brass at the Bureau—*and* the CIA—put duct tape over the camera lens on their own computers. They know what can be done nowadays."

It was then that I noticed my laptop, lid closed, on the far end of the counter. I could tell from the little light blinking next to the brand's logo that the computer was on.

I also knew without having to check that the horrific video of Joy's assault was still playing, over and over. And would probably do so endlessly.

"I watched the video a couple times," Barnes was saying, "and was pretty sure it was the same guy that ambushed me. He'd fired from his car across the street, so I didn't get a good look at him. But based on his warning to you about another murder, I see now it had to be him."

I considered this. "Though now I'm wondering how he'll react when he doesn't see a story about your murder on the morning news."

Gloria released her grip on my wrist. "I have a feeling we're going to find out. And soon."

"Which reminds me," I said to her. "I still don't know why *you're* here. How did you learn about all this?"

"Because I told her," Barnes said briskly. "The kill video was on a loop that couldn't be deleted or shut off, so your laptop was useless. Since Reese here worked that same case you and I were involved in a while back, I called her and asked her to come here. And to bring her laptop."

He gave her a wry, professional appraisal.

"Unlike most of the young morons working for the Bureau nowadays, Reese is at least mildly competent. The fact she's damned easy on the eyes doesn't hurt."

"Christ, old man." Gloria frowned. "That's just wrong on so many levels."

Ignoring her, Barnes turned back to me. "Besides, even if I could've used your computer, I knew I wouldn't get past the Bureau firewalls this time."

"You mean, like you did before. I was there, remember?"

He shrugged. "What can I say? They have better security protocols now. So I needed Agent Reese's laptop, and her security clearance, to access info on the killer."

"And I was only too happy to help." Gloria stirred in her seat. "Especially after Lyle showed me that horrendous video. I've never wanted to nail a perp so much in my life."

But my eyes stayed on Barnes.

"You're talking like you know who he is."

"Of course, son. Don't you?"

"No. But how do *you* know?"

"I told you, I read that dossier of yours. Saw right away that something was wrong. So for the past hour, Gloria and I have been digging up all we can on this guy."

"And it isn't pretty," she added, mouth tightening.

I felt my own mouth go dry as I absorbed their words. Could almost hear my heart thudding in my chest.

"Who is he?" I said at last.

Barnes hesitated, then looked over at Gloria.

Once again, she took hold of my wrist. Though this time her touch was soft, tentative.

"His name is Sebastian Maddox." Gloria's normally brash, assertive voice had gentled to a whisper. "Danny, we think he's the man who killed your wife."

Chapter Thirteen

Funny how the mind works. At that precise moment, my thoughts inexplicably went to my patients. I'd forgotten all about those who'd be coming for therapy today.

Of course, I knew immediately what had happened. Unable to process at first what Gloria had said, my brain quickly skidded over to something else. Some other concern.

Then, just as quickly, I recalled that the Mayor's cocktail party was on a Friday. Last night. The night I'd been taken.

Which meant today was Saturday. And that meant there were no patients to see.

I spotted Barnes peering at me.

"You okay, Doc?"

I rubbed my jaw. "Just trying to take it all in."

"Not to horn in on your territory, Danny," Gloria said, "but you look pretty shell-shocked. After what you've just been through, I'm not surprised."

"Me, either, Gloria. But I'll be okay soon enough. What I need now is everything you two know about this Maddox guy."

Lyle Barnes leaned across the table. "First, what can you tell me about whoever gave you the dossier?"

I told him about the dying man, and his belief that he'd found something in the dossier that proved my wife had been murdered. Something in the case notes about the mugging.

"What was his background, this guy?"

"He worked for years as a consultant for a big private security firm. The kind that provide bodyguards for celebrities and VIPs. And sets up security systems for their clients. Before that, he was in the armed forces. Did a tour in Afghanistan."

Barnes turned to Gloria. "Classic law enforcement type. Even if he never wore the badge. That's why the name jumped out at him. And why it jumped out at me when I read the case notes. We're all crime buffs when it comes to stuff like that."

She smiled her agreement. "God knows *I* am."

I was running out of patience. "C'mon, you guys. What the hell—?"

"Wait here." Barnes got up and went into the front room, returning in moments with the dossier. He opened it on the table in front of me, then hurriedly flipped through pages until he found what he was looking for. The section of the case files containing the witness statements.

"See this list of names?" He pointed at the names of the parking valets. Hector Ruiz. Ed Hunter. Jack Ketch. Sal Tulio.

"What about it?"

"The name Jack Ketch. This must've been what caught the security guy's eye. He knew right away that something was funny. So he probably did the same thing I did."

"I don't understand."

An indulgent smile. "Jack Ketch is the name of a famous British executioner who worked for King Charles II."

"I never heard of him."

"Well, you would've if you'd lived in the 1680s. He was notorious at the time for the barbarity of his executions, and for the glee he took in doing them."

Gloria spoke up. "Your security guy saw the name and instantly realized it was probably a fake. An alias the valet had given to the cops when he was interviewed that night. And given to the valet parking outfit when they hired him, I'll bet. Unlikely they would've recognized the name, either."

"Which had to make your guy wonder why. Why use a fake

name, especially that of an infamous murderer?" Barnes swiveled in his chair and pointed to Gloria's laptop. "So your late
friend did what I myself did just an hour ago. He no doubt had
buddies or former colleagues in law enforcement, and so was
able to access police data. And to search VICAP for criminals
who use or had once used the name Jack Ketch as an alias."

"That's when he found the name Sebastian Maddox?" I
asked.

Gloria nodded. "Probably. Just as we did. Sebastian Maddox.
AKA Lysander Jones, AKA Parsifal Jones, AKA Jack Ketch. You
gotta give the creep kudos for imagination."

"Real smart-ass, this guy." Barnes scowled. "Lysander was
the name of a Spartan admiral who defeated Athens. Maddox
probably thinks of himself as some kind of military genius."

"And Parsifal," I added. "A knight who pursued the Holy
Grail in the time of Arthur. Explains the tattoo on his chest.
That cup with the rays emanating from it. But what's his con-
nection to the Grail myth?"

"I may have an idea about that," Barnes said carefully.

He swung the laptop around so that I could see the screen.
On it was a digital cascade of photos, case notes, official court
documents, and other archived material he'd assembled.

"Let me give you the CliffsNotes version." Barnes folded his
arms. "Sebastian Maddox was an undergraduate at Pitt during
the same years your late wife attended—though she was still
Barbara Camden at the time."

"That's right. We didn't meet till grad school."

"Apparently, this Maddox was some kind of prodigy. Double-
major in computer science and philosophy. Came from a fairly
prominent family in the area, but a real troublemaker since he
was a teen. Vandalism, drug use, the usual rebellious crap.

"Anyway, Maddox was in one of the same classes at Pitt that
Barbara took. And became infatuated with her. According to
a statement Barbara later gave to the police, he seemed to be
obsessed. Kept asking her out, calling her, that kind of thing."

"Then he upped the ante." Gloria's eyes darkened. "Began stalking her. Showing up wherever she went. Standing outside her Oakland apartment all night long. Leaving suggestive notes in her mailbox. Scared her out of her wits."

Barnes picked up the thread. "Finally, she got a judge to put a restraining order on the scumbag. Not that it did much good. Maddox repeatedly violated it, and the cops had no choice but to pick him up. But Maddox lucked out and caught a different judge, some limp-dick who just gave him probation."

I sat forward. "What happened?"

Gloria shrugged. "Guess his parents had had enough of supporting him, not to mention his drug habit. He'd even begun dealing by then. So they yanked him out of school. The next day, he skipped town. Whereabouts unknown. Which must have been a great relief to Barbara. There's no mention in the record of her reporting any further trouble from him."

She regarded me frankly. "Barbara never told you about all this? Maddox stalking her, the restraining order?"

I shook my head. Though a part of me wasn't that surprised. Barbara had always been a private person, often reluctant to share her feelings with me. Especially difficult feelings. It was one of the things that used to frustrate me, that often stood in the way of our having true intimacy. I could see how, to her, the whole Maddox affair would be too painful to revisit.

"She probably hoped that part of her life was over," Gloria said, as though reading my thoughts. "It was all in the past, before she'd met you. Maybe she just wanted to move on."

"That sounds about right, knowing Barbara. But still...I wish I would've known about it."

Barnes chuckled. "Spoken like a true therapist. You know, Doc, some people like to keep certain things to themselves. Hell, I'm an expert at it."

I didn't respond, recalling some of the personal issues he and I had discussed during our therapeutic work together. Given all that I knew about his childhood, his broken marriage, and the psychological rigors of his job with the FBI, I was now left wondering what it was he *hadn't* shared with me.

His choice, of course, then and now. As a therapist, I've come to respect the right to privacy as much as the benefits of self-disclosure. Holding a secret isn't necessarily denial.

Keys clicking on the laptop pulled me from my reverie. Barnes had brought up another page from the Maddox case files.

"Thought you might want to see this," he said. "It's the transcript from the taped interview the cops did with Maddox after Barbara first reported him."

I leaned in and peered at the screen. Then, for some reason, found myself reading the transcript aloud.

MADDOX: I don't exactly know why I'm here, Officer. Surely Barbara's told you all about our love. The intimacies we share? The furtive glances in class, the half-smiles? Our delicious cat-and-mouse game?

DESK OFFICER: What do you mean, Mr. Maddox?

MADDOX: Oh, she played hard-to-get at first, but I knew she was only playing. Because Barbara and I are meant to be together. She knows it, too. She's always giving me these little signals of our love, our shared passion. Like when she'll take off her glasses while speaking, or whenever she wears green. Green is our special color.

DESK OFFICER: Special, eh?

MADDOX: Yes. Even when she's yelling at me to leave her alone, to stop following her. If she's wearing green, it's our secret signal that it's all an act. To fool the others. We both know that she's mine and mine alone. Just as I'm hers. That's why I don't understand why she reported me to the police. Unless it's to maintain the pretense. Or maybe even to test my love. See what obstacles I'd overcome to be with her. And I will. Make no mistake, officer. I will be with her. Forever.

DESK OFFICER: That doesn't seem to be what she wants, buddy. Do you understand that?

MADDOX: No offense, but I believe it's you who doesn't quite understand. Not that I blame you. We're talking about a level of romantic subtlety, of mutual erotic connection between a man and a woman, far beyond your ken. Isn't there a senior officer, your precinct captain, perhaps, that I could talk to?

I didn't need to read any more. I pushed the laptop away and got to my feet. Leaned with my back against the counter.

"Erotomania," I said quietly.

"What's that?" Gloria turned in her seat.

"It's a type of delusional disorder, in which a person—in this case, Sebastian Maddox—believes that another person is in love with him. Often, the person believes his or her secret admirer is sending covert signals of their mutual love. Wearing certain colors, or doing certain gestures. Some even believe they're receiving telepathic messages from their lover."

"Even if the other person denies it?" Gloria asked. "Tells them to fuck off, get out of their lives. Calls the cops?"

"Nothing dissuades them, Gloria. It's an unshakeable delusion. As a colleague of mine, George Atwood, once said, 'It's a belief whose validity is not open to discussion.'"

Barnes stirred. "That's why I wanted to show you the transcript, Doc. So you could see how screwed-up this guy is."

"It also explains the Grail tattoo over his heart," I said quietly. "And why he chose the name Parsifal as one of his aliases. He felt that Barbara was his Holy Grail, his soul's divine object of desire."

"Wow." Gloria clucked her tongue. "He really believed that he and Barbara were meant to be together."

"So you can imagine what he thought when he finally decided to come back to Pittsburgh," Barnes said. "From wherever the hell he'd been since violating the terms of his probation."

"How do you know?" I asked.

"Checked DMV. Maddox got his Pennsylvania driver's license renewed. But once he was back in town, he must've looked up Barbara Camden…and found out she'd gotten married. To you."

Suddenly I felt a chill travel up my spine. Remembering what Maddox had said to me the night before.

I hadn't understood what he meant then. I did now.

"When he had me bound in that chair, after showing me the video, Maddox said, 'You took what was mine, now I've taken what's yours.' He meant that I'd taken Barbara from him. And because he believed that Joy Steadman and I were lovers, he got his revenge all these years later by 'taking' her from me. By raping and killing her."

The room fell nearly silent, hushed except for the dull hum of the refrigerator. Outside, the sun had begun to sink toward the horizon, sending pale shafts of mid-afternoon light through the kitchen's bay window behind me.

"Now I see why you believe Maddox killed Barbara." I looked at the two of them. "Once he learned that we were married, he started stalking *us*. As he had her, years before. He'd decided that if he couldn't have her, neither could anyone else."

Barnes scratched his chin. "By this point, he probably felt that Barbara had betrayed him. His insane love for her turning into an intense, murderous hatred. For both of you."

"So he made a plan," Gloria said. "He got the job as a valet at the restaurant. He figured it was a way to kill you both, in public, disguised as a mugging gone wrong. But it wasn't. It was an execution. That's why he used the name Jack Ketch. A famously brutal executioner."

"If I were Maddox," Barnes said, "I would've applied for the valet job a few days before he knew you had reservations at the restaurant. This way he'd be familiar with the routine, get friendly with that Ruiz guy, the head valet."

He sighed. "Too bad that neither of those detectives who interviewed him after the shooting knew about the name 'Jack Ketch.' They might've held him for further questioning. Maybe even had Maddox's hands tested for gunpowder residue."

"Even so," I said, "Maddox was working hard as a valet that night. Hustling like mad. They all were. I saw them."

"I've been wondering the same thing." Gloria frowned. "I mean, I still don't know how the hell he did it—"

A thin, metallic voice cut her off.

"Really? You don't?"

Stunned into another ominous silence, the three of us turned to stare at my laptop, lid still closed, on the far end of the kitchen counter. It was Sebastian Maddox, coming from the computer's tiny speaker.

"What a shame. And you were all doing so well…"

Chapter Fourteen

"He's been listening to us the whole time," Gloria said, instinctively falling to a whisper.

"That's right." His disembodied voice eerily calm.

I slid along the counter for the laptop, then brought it back to the kitchen table. Opened the lid.

The face of Sebastian Maddox filled the computer's screen. Cold, self-possessed. Eyes glittering with malice. Other than the tops of a shirt collar, nothing else was visible. Nor was there anything to see in the background. He could be anywhere.

"That's much better. We can all see each other now."

I could feel the anger boiling up in my throat as I re-took my seat, joining Barnes and Gloria at the table. Our collective gaze riveted on the screen.

Maddox turned his head slightly.

"As for you, Mr. Barnes, I must admit I'm disappointed to find you alive. But I'll do better next time. You'll just move somewhere else in the rotation."

Then he leveled his attention on Gloria.

"And it's a real pleasure to meet *you*, Ms. Reese. It's nice to know the FBI is hiring some good-looking women. Although the quasi-feminist thing is a turnoff. But don't worry. I'll put that to one side when I'm doing you. I'm thinking oral. You blow *me*, then I blow *you*...away. How's that sound, Gloria?"

Her face hardened, and she abruptly stood up. "Fuck you, pal. They don't pay me enough to sit through this shit."

With that, she strode out of the room.

Maddox chuckled darkly. "I think she likes me."

Barnes leaned into the screen. "Listen, you sick fuck, stop waltzing us around and—"

"Are you kidding, Barnes? The dance is just beginning."

"Maddox!" My voice dagger-sharp. "Look at me!"

He did. I stared at that hard, placid face.

"I know you killed my wife, Maddox. That you tried to kill both of us that night. So why don't you leave Barnes and Agent Reese out of this? You got your revenge by killing Joy Steadman. Nobody else has to die."

"Actually, Danny, they do. But we're getting ahead of ourselves. Don't you and Barnes want to know how I did it? How, eleven long years ago, I got away with murder?"

Before I could reply, Barnes' steely grip was on my arm.

"Yeah, you piece of shit. We want to know."

I gave Barnes a sidelong look. Then saw him cast a furtive glance past my shoulder. What was he trying to tell me?

I shifted in my seat, straining to make out a barely audible sound coming from just beyond the doorway to the kitchen. It was a voice, soft but urgent. Gloria's voice.

Of course, I thought. She'd pretended to be angered by Maddox's comment so she could leave the room and use her cell. I couldn't make out the words, but I guessed that she'd contacted one of the Bureau's tech units, requesting they try to pinpoint the signal Maddox was using to 'bot my laptop. To see if they could triangulate his position.

I registered all this in less than a few seconds, my gaze never leaving Maddox's face.

"Sure, Maddox. Tell us how you did it. Since your ego is so fragile you need to be constantly reassured of your brilliance."

His eyes narrowed. "Don't try shrinking me, Danny boy. My pathetic parents spent a fortune paying guys like you to head-fuck me. All it did was piss me off. Like now."

An easy smile. "Besides, the way I've always seen it, I'm just an excitable boy. Like the Warren Zevon song. You know that song? 'Excitable Boy.' A classic. From his first album."

"Whatever. Just say what you want to say, Maddox. My guess is you've been waiting all this time to tell me."

"Good guess."

He paused, as though collecting his thoughts. As though wanting to be sure he told the story in exactly the right way.

"After I ran out on my probation, I just drifted around. Scoring dope. Selling dope. The usual junkie circle of life. But all I could think about, the whole time, was Barbara.

"Then one day—I was dealing crack in some shit-hole in Cleveland—I see a copy of the *Post-Gazette*. Months old. Somebody must've brought it from here, left it lying around. So I flip through it and what do I see? A wedding announcement. Two PhDs getting married. Met in graduate school. Romantic as fuck. Daniel Rinaldi and Barbara Camden. The son of a beat cop and the daughter of a distinguished Pitt professor. Two different worlds, etcetera. It's a goddam Hallmark movie."

Maddox paused, rubbed the side of his face. For the first time, I noticed beads of sweat on his brow. Whether from anxiety or excitement, or some combination of both, I didn't know.

"So, naturally, I come back to my beloved hometown," he began again. "And I start tracking you two. You and Barbara. Your home, your jobs. Where you went, what you did. You see, the marriage was unacceptable. You have to understand that, Danny. Utterly and completely unacceptable."

He drew a couple of calming breaths.

"Anyway, once I knew what I had to do, the rest was simple. I hacked into your home computer and saw you'd made dinner reservations at the Blue Gill restaurant for the following week. Then I applied for a job as a valet, giving my name to the head guy as Jack Ketch. I figured this mouth-breather wouldn't know who the fuck that was. And I was right.

"The night you and Barbara came for dinner, the restaurant was really crowded. That prick Ruiz had us valets running around like jackrabbits. But the whole time, I kept an eye on you two. I could see your corner table through the front entrance. So when I saw you ask for the check, I knew it was go-time.

"I parked the next guest's car in the restaurant lot, but didn't come right back. Instead, I grabbed my hoodie, gun, and shades from my own car, parked nearby. Then I ran back to the restaurant, just in time to see you and Barbara coming out.

"You know what happened next. It looked like you two were the victims of a mugging that turned violent. The plan was to kill both of you, of course. To execute Barbara for her crushing betrayal, then you, for taking what was mine. And I thought I had. Last thing I saw as I ran off was the both of you lying in pools of blood. People screaming, shouting.

"All I had to do then was return to my car to ditch the hoodie, gun, and shades. When I came back to the restaurant, I just slipped in with the other valets. Unnoticed in all the chaos. To the cops, just another stunned employee. I left feeling damned good about myself. Better than I had in years.

"Until the next day, when I see on the news that only Barbara had died, and that *you* were clinging to life in the ICU.

"It was maddening, but I knew it wasn't smart to stick around, in case you recovered and could identify me. Remember, I figured Barbara had told you all about me. Maybe even showed you my mug shot or something. So I made plans to skip town again."

"So did you?" I asked, breaking the spell of his story.

"Not exactly. I'd still been dealing, and suddenly one of my customers rolls over on me and I get busted. The fucking irony: the same day I get sentenced to ten years in prison, I hear you're being released from the hospital. Even Zeno of Citium would've been devastated."

Barnes offered a reluctant smile at my puzzlement. "The founder of Stoicism," he explained.

But Maddox wasn't smiling.

"Ten long years," he said tersely, "reading about your life. How you resumed your practice, started consulting with the cops. As the years pass, it only gets worse. Now you're getting national press about the cases you were involved with. All over the tube, giving your so-called expert opinion. On CNN, for Christ's sake. You and Wolf Blitzer, hanging. *I'm rotting in prison surrounded by low-lifes and degenerates and you're a fucking TV star.*"

I shook my head. "That's not exactly my life, Maddox. Not by a long shot."

His voice grew an edge. "Guess we'll have to agree to disagree. 'Cause now I'm out. And my only mission is to take away anyone who's close to you. Starting with that fine piece of ass, Joy Steadman. My God, they have such a tight pussy when they're young. But you'd know that."

"Look, Maddox—"

"But don't worry, Danny. Your time will come. Once I've squeezed every drop of pain out of your fucking heart, it'll be *your* turn to die. And I have something *really* special in mind for that glorious day."

Barnes grunted. "Ain't gonna happen, mister."

Maddox laughed. "Says the retired FBI man who's still afraid to fall asleep at night. Pathetic. Oh, and you can tell Agent Reese that her Bureau nerds aren't going to be able to triangulate on my location. Or ever track my IP address. I have firewalls they've never even heard of. More to the point, I'm in transit even as we speak. Here, there, and everywhere, like another cool song says."

As if on cue, Gloria reappeared, sullen.

"No luck," she announced.

But I didn't even look up, because Maddox had suddenly disappeared from the screen. In his place was a silent, grainy video image of a busy intersection. Some urban street. Hurrying pedestrians. Cars and trucks moving in and out of frame. In the corner of the image was a time stamp. 3:10 p.m.

I glanced at my watch. The current time.

"It's a live feed from a traffic security camera," Gloria said, bending to get a better look. Barnes and I both leaned in closer to do the same.

"Any idea where it is?" I asked.

"Downtown, but away from city center." Barnes pointed at the screen. "They haven't paved over the old bricks yet."

Moments later, I caught sight of an elderly man coming out of a drug store across the street. At this distance, it was hard to make out his features, except for a shock of white hair and his slightly wobbly gait.

The old man looked at his watch, then carefully threaded his way through the stream of pedestrians until he reached a free-standing bus stop sign. There he paused, peered expectantly up the street, arms folded. Waiting.

Suddenly, Maddox spoke again. No image this time, just his voice. As the traffic cam continued to stream the video.

"Recognize the old geezer, Danny? Name's Stephen Langley. Businessman, father of two. At least when you knew him. Now, in case you want to update your records, a grandfather as well."

"My records—?"

"He's hacked into your computer," Barnes said. "Probably how he found out about me."

"No," Maddox replied. "I read about you in the paper. How you and Rinaldi worked together on that case, couple years back. But you're right about my hacking the Doc's computer. All his patient files. It's how I found out about poor old Mr. Langley."

I closed my eyes, remembering him now. At the same time, I registered the sound humming in the background as Maddox spoke. Engine noise. He was in a moving vehicle. Probably driving.

My eyes snapped open, and I stared harder at the laptop screen. At the image of Stephen Langley waiting impatiently at the bus stop.

As if I could prevent what was about to happen.

"Maddox, don't!" I shouted at the screen. "It's *me* you want. I'm the one who—"

He ignored me, as if I hadn't spoken.

"Langley was your very first patient when you went into private practice, Danny. Ironically, suffering from emotional trauma after being run over by a car and barely surviving. It took months before he was able to walk on a sidewalk. Still, the old fart doesn't realize how lucky he was back then. That other driver didn't quite get it done. I will."

We heard the roar of a car engine, almost drowning out his last words. In my mind's eye I could see Maddox flooring it.

"Good God." Gloria's hands clenched into white-knuckled fists on the table.

It was like watching a nightmare. The silent, remorseless black-and-white video image. Then, suddenly, a nondescript white van appearing on the screen. Soundless as well, yet hurtling at top speed down the street toward where Langley stood on the sidewalk. Right next to the bus stop sign. The only passenger waiting there.

"No!" I jumped up from my seat.

I heard Gloria's choked cry, but kept my gaze riveted on the laptop screen.

The white van swerved as it approached the bus stop and bumped up onto the sidewalk, hitting Langley with such force that the old man went flying, limbs pinwheeling. He was thrown like a rag doll into the line of horrified pedestrians scrambling to get out of the way.

Barnes' voice was a rasp. "Jesus Christ."

The van had turned and jumped back off the curb before Langley had even hit the pavement. Now Maddox was barreling down the street again, instantly disappearing from frame.

"You fucking son of a bitch." I gaped at the laptop. The crowd gathering, people shouting, crying.

I was still staring at the image when the screen suddenly

went blank. Then that voice—*his* voice—more audible now above the engine noise as he reduced speed. Obviously making sure his van moved easily and inconspicuously into the flow of traffic.

"I know what you three are thinking. All the cops have to do is view the tape, get the van's license number, blah, blah, blah. Just like on TV. Except this little baby is stolen, and is soon going to be abandoned somewhere out in the boonies."

He didn't wait for any of us to respond.

"See, Danny, it's only going to escalate. Your punishment, I mean. Your friends, colleagues, patients. Until, as I said, I'll come for you. And finish what I started eleven years ago."

The laptop power light winked off. Maddox was gone.

Chapter Fifteen

For what must have been at least two or three minutes, I didn't say anything. After my computer had powered off, I sank back into my chair and put my head in my hands. My palms pressing against my closed eyelids as though to erase from my mind what I'd just seen. As though to make the nightmare stop.

Lyle Barnes and Gloria Reese did what they were supposed to do. Bear silent witness to my pain. My frustration.

Until the retired FBI man broke that silence.

"You didn't cause this, Doc. You didn't make Sebastian Maddox the man he is. Hell, you didn't even know he existed before today. So how can you be responsible for his actions? For *anyone's* actions, for that matter?"

I let out a long breath, seemingly exhaling for the first time since watching Langley's death.

Then I felt Gloria's small hand on my shoulder, its grip reassuringly strong.

"Barnes is right, Danny. This shit is not on you."

"I know," I said at last. "But I also know that there are people in danger, and all because their lives happened to intersect with mine."

"True enough." Barnes rubbed his narrow chin. "The question now is, what the hell are we going to do about it?"

Gloria spoke up. "First thing, we have to warn all Danny's patients. Tell them to be on alert. Make sure they're never alone if they go out. Or better yet, to stay inside."

I shook my head. "I'm not so sure about that. Most of my patients are trauma victims. Psychologically fragile. I'm afraid telling them that there's someone out there who may try to kill them will only re-traumatize them. Reinforce their worst fears about how dangerous the world is."

"Maybe," Barnes said. "But they'll be alive."

I considered this.

"Then there are your friends, colleagues," Gloria said. "If we're going to warn your patients, we should also—"

"*Warn nobody!*"

The sharp, angry voice was coming from my cell on the kitchen table, where I left it.

It was Maddox.

"You seem to have a short memory, Danny. Remember what I said? See all, hear all."

Impulsively I grabbed up the cell. Tried shutting it off.

Maddox kept talking. "Listen carefully, Danny, because I'm starting to lose my patience. Don't warn anyone, *anyone*, or all will die. This way, most of your patients and friends will live. I'm just choosing the ones I find pertinent to the mission. The mission to cause you as much personal suffering as possible."

Barnes muttered something unintelligible under his breath. I knew his own sense of powerlessness was eating away at him.

"And though I shouldn't have to reiterate this, no alerting the cops or Feds, either. Or else some poor bastard, some random victim, dies. And that'll be on you.

"Now that we've cleared that up," Maddox continued, "I gotta sign off. Places to go, people to kill. By the way, Gloria, don't think I've forgotten about you. I'm definitely looking forward to some quality face-time with you. Your face, my cock. Hell, I'm getting hard just thinking about it."

"Fuck this!" Gloria snatched the cell from my hand and began furiously pushing buttons. But I knew he'd clicked off.

I took the phone right back. "Don't bother."

Then I turned and hurled the damn thing against the kitchen wall. It shattered to pieces.

I went to do the same with my laptop, grabbing it up with both hands, but Barnes stopped me. His lean face close to mine.

"What the hell are you doing, Doc?"

All the horror, frustration, and anguish of the past twenty-four hours seemed to burble up within me.

"I've had it with this prick. I swear, I'm starting to lose it. I feel like he's in my head. Like I can't escape him."

"That's what he *wants* you to think." He offered a sad smile. "Besides, you'd never lose it, Daniel. I've worked with you long enough in therapy to realize that. God knows, you and I have been to hell and back. And thanks to you, hell lost."

"I appreciate that, Lyle. But I don't care. I just want him to shut the fuck up!"

"No, you don't. Sure, smashing that thing to bits will feel good, but that's about it. My opinion? I think you should hang on to it. I suggest you download everything important onto a flash drive, then wipe the laptop clean."

"Why?"

"Because I'd rather be in contact with that grandiose, self-satisfied asshole than go radio-silent. He's a talker, like most of the obsessed killers I've known, and the best way to stay at least on an equal footing with him is to let him talk. He needs you to be afraid, and hanging on his every word."

"He sure as hell's succeeding."

"Good. When I was with the Bureau, I never trusted a colleague who wasn't afraid. Am I right, Agent Reese? Confidence is good, up to a point, but it can dull the senses."

Calming myself, I said, "Got it."

I handed him my laptop, which he put back on the table.

Meanwhile, Gloria was busily typing at the keyboard of her own laptop. I leaned next to her shoulder to watch.

"What are you doing?"

"Trying to find the bastard." She kept her focus on the screen. "Maddox just got out of prison—he was upstate, at Buckville—so he has to have a parole officer. Who'd have a current address and phone."

"Are you going through Pittsburgh PD?"

"Nope. This guy's a computer whiz, right? Wouldn't surprise me if he had the cops' system hacked. Just in case, I'm routing my enquiry through the Bureau's interagency network."

"Another thing," Barnes offered, "if and when Maddox abandons the white van, and the cops end up finding it, they'll put a trace on the license plate and VIN number. Impound the car while they're waiting for the rightful owner to retrieve it."

"Meanwhile," Gloria said, "their forensics team will search the van for prints, hair and fiber, the works. Remember, Maddox had to have some equipment loaded into the van to 'bot Danny's cell and laptop. And to redirect the live feed from the traffic monitor camera. No matter how careful the prick was, he's sure to have left something usable behind, in terms of forensics."

"How will we know what the cops are doing? Assuming they find the car, and assuming they then find any good forensics."

"I'll keep monitoring their servers, through the Bureau interface." She smiled. "Just think of it as legal hacking by a dedicated FBI agent. Ends justifying the means, etcetera."

Barnes scowled. "On the other hand, who the hell knows where Maddox will end up dumping the van? Besides, it could take days, weeks, till someone spots it and reports it in."

Gloria turned to him. "We have to try every angle, Lyle. Otherwise, what do we do? Just sit around and—"

"And wait till he kills his next victim?" I finished for her. "Isn't there more we can do?"

Gloria nodded. "I'll have my tech team keep trying to track him. When I called them before, I told them I wanted to get a bead on a person of interest in a fraud case."

"Good thinking. We have to take Maddox's threat seriously about not calling in the cops. Or anyone else."

Her voice was rueful. "Which leaves us pretty much hand-cuffed, in terms of manpower and official sanction. Even if we do find out where this guy's holed up, we can't go bursting in without an arrest warrant. Not if we don't want him released two hours later for violating his civil rights."

Barnes scowled. "Fuck that. Let's grab the crazy son of a bitch first, then we can let the lawyers fight it out."

I nodded. "The only thing that matters is finding him. Stopping him before he selects his next target."

"If he hasn't already," Barnes said quietly.

As Barnes and Gloria followed up on her laptop, I went into the bathroom for a quick shower. I figured I needed it to help clear my head. I also wanted to scrub off the events of the past twenty-four hours, and to change into fresh clothes. I felt like burning those I'd been wearing when forced to watch both Joy's horrific murder and that of Stephen Langley.

I was just buttoning a new shirt in the bedroom when a notion struck me. A thought pricking at the edges of my mind. Something Maddox said when he had me tied in that chair.

Then, just as quickly, it was gone. Whatever it was.

When I returned to the kitchen, Gloria looked excitedly up from her screen.

"I figured I'd keep monitoring the police system, and just now saw a report about the Langley hit-and-run. The uniforms are on-scene, getting witness statements. No license number, but everyone agrees about it being a white van. Late model, no graphics or lettering on the sides. The cops have put out a BOLO for similar vehicles that might have a damaged front grille."

"We'll have to assume that Maddox knows this, too," Barnes said. "Which means he'll ditch the van as soon as possible."

I nodded. Meanwhile, Gloria sat back in her chair, rubbed her screen-blurred eyes.

"Oh, and I got the name of Maddox's parole officer from his prison file. Guy named Stanz. Just got off the phone with him."

"And?" I leaned in.

"He confirms that Maddox was released from Buckville two months ago. But after one required meeting with the P.O., he never showed up again. Stanz sent someone to check out Maddox's last known address, some group home for ex-cons till they get a job and permanent residence, but our guy wasn't there. Nobody'd seen him for weeks. And the cell number Maddox had given Stanz was a phony, too."

"So Maddox is off the grid. Could be anywhere."

Gloria gave me a resigned shrug, after which no one spoke for a full minute, Barnes roughly rubbing his beard stubble. Then, absently, he hit the side of the refrigerator with the edge of his fist. The incessant humming stopped.

"Jesus, Doc, this fridge is older than *I* am. Maybe you need to upgrade some stuff around here." He nodded toward the end of the counter, on which sat a squat, heavy microwave oven. "And don't get me started on *that* thing…"

Gloria smiled. "Yeah. I was thinking you ought to take it on *Antiques Roadshow*. Could be a collector's item."

I looked at their weary, expectant faces, appreciating their attempts to relieve the tension of the situation.

Finally, Gloria spoke again. "I know you're still thinking about your old patient, Mr. Langley. I'm so sorry, Danny."

"Yeah. So am I."

"It's weird, too. I mean, the poor guy barely survives getting hit by one car, years ago, and now—"

"That's it!"

Barnes and Gloria stared at me, both startled at the sharpness in my tone.

"It was something Maddox said last night when he made me watch Joy's rape and murder. How he loved the symmetry."

Barnes frowned. "I don't follow."

"He referred to it when narrating the moment of her death. Unless I'm wrong, trying to create or identify symmetry is one of the ways his mind attempts to order itself. He's delusional, obsessive. I think arranging things such that they appear to have symmetry aids him in feeling in control."

I quickly turned to Barnes.

"Look, how did he try to kill you, Lyle? With a revolver, out the window of a car. Similar to what that assassin had tried to do to you last year, when you were his target."

"Well, now that you mention it…"

"Then there's Stephen Langley. Traumatized years ago after being hit by a car. So how does Maddox kill him today?"

"By running him over with a vehicle," said Gloria.

"But it's more than that. What else is unique about Langley? As my patient, I mean?"

"Maddox said he was the first one you treated when you went into private practice."

"Yes. My first. If I'm Maddox, and I'm psychologically self-regulated by adhering to symmetry, who do I pick for my next victim? If Langley was the first, then—"

"Then Maddox would want to target the latest—"

"That's what I think." I took a breath. "Which means I know who Maddox is going after next. My most recent patient, whom he'd know about from having hacked into my clinical files. A twelve-year-old kid named Robbie Palermo."

Though Barnes had unscrewed the receiver and checked for bugs, I still felt uneasy about using my landline phone. Given Maddox's technical expertise, I couldn't be sure he wouldn't know how to listen remotely to my calls. In fact, I figured he probably could.

So instead, I borrowed Gloria's cell and called Mr. and Mrs. Palermo's home number.

I got their answering machine, Robbie's mother leaving a falsely cheery outgoing message. I also had my young patient's cell number, which I tried next.

And got *his* outgoing message.

"Either it's turned off or he's not answering," Gloria suggested. "He's a kid, remember."

"Let's just hope that's all it is." Barnes' face was grim. "And that Maddox hasn't got him already."

With the three of us once more gathered around the kitchen table, I turned the laptop's screen toward Gloria.

"If he does have Robbie," I said tersely, "he'll be sure to let us know. And want us to see it."

Then I kicked back from the table.

"Where are you going?" Gloria said.

"To do something about it before he does."

Chapter Sixteen

The late-afternoon sun was glazing the glass-and-steel towers of the city as I barreled across the bridge. In the post-rain clearness, the river sparkled as though bejeweled beneath me, and the distant Allegheny Mountains shrugged their aged, rounded shoulders against the blue of sky.

The irony of such a fine day being the backdrop to my urgent journey to the Palermo house wasn't lost on me, though I was thankful that it was both a Saturday and a dry day, which meant traffic on the parkway was light.

Still, it took me almost forty minutes to find the address in Verona where the Palermos lived. It was a solidly middle-class neighborhood, mostly blue-collar, whose businesses had been hit hard by the economic downturn. I remembered as I drove that Robbie attended St. Joseph's Catholic School, a venerable institution at least fifty years older than I was. One of the area's few fixed points in a changing world.

According to my dash GPS, the Palermo house was just around the next corner. I slowed as I turned onto the narrow, quiet residential street, shrouded by elms and oaks, whose leaves, still heavy with moisture, glistened in the bright sun.

As I neared the house, my heart stopped.

I spotted Robbie, in jeans and a thin jacket, standing on the sidewalk outside his house. About to step inside a van parked at the curb.

A white van.

I almost shouted as he hopped into its opened rear doors. At this distance, I couldn't see anything of its dim interior.

And then the doors were pulled closed, from the inside.

And the van pulled away from the curb.

Every instinct commanded me to floor it, to race up to the vehicle and force it to the side of the road. But I had no way of knowing who was in the back of the van with Robbie. Maddox himself? Or perhaps an accomplice, restraining the boy in some way? Unless whoever pulled the doors closed after Robbie went in was the driver himself, who then climbed back behind the wheel.

The latter scenario seemed more likely to me. Though I was only guessing, interpreting based on the slimmest of facts, my gut told me that Sebastian Maddox would be unwilling to share the grandiose delights and exquisite agonies of his delusion with someone else.

Regardless, I figured my best move was just to follow the van at a safe distance as it rumbled slowly down the street and turned onto Verona Road.

Winding along the street's tree-shrouded curves, and up and down its subtle rises, our two vehicles made their way out of Verona and into Penn Hills. Occasionally, I let a car or two get between me and the van, so as not to arouse the driver's suspicion—though by now I had some suspicions of my own.

If, as I believed, Maddox was aware of the BOLO out on any white vans matching the description given by eyewitnesses to the Langley hit-and-run, why hadn't he gotten rid of it by now? Surely, he could have easily stolen another vehicle.

Also, why did Robbie voluntarily get into the back of the van? If he'd been coerced, I didn't see it. Unless the driver had already threatened or cajoled him from inside the van, and Robbie had obeyed out of fear for his safety.

I had to know, and soon enough had my chance. The road had widened into two lanes, and as the van stopped at a red light, I slowly pulled up alongside it and risked a half-turn of my head to get a look at the driver. I knew that if he saw me, and if it was Maddox, things would go very badly, very quickly.

I don't know if I was more shocked or relieved when I registered the van's driver. She was calmly looking straight ahead, her hands at ten and two on the wheel, patiently waiting for the light to change.

The woman was in her late thirties, I guessed, and looked like what used to be called a soccer mom. The bland sound of soft jazz came from her open window.

I'd only permitted myself a moment to take this in, then turned face-front myself, so as not to alarm her.

Finally, the light still stubbornly red, I inched my Mustang forward, almost past the intersection, and craned my neck around to get a look at the van's front grille. Nothing. No dents or damage of any kind.

Just then, the light turned green and we were off. I stayed behind her again, driving more slowly in the thickening traffic, until the van pulled into a mini-mall parking lot. I found a spot a discreet distance away, from which I saw the rear doors open, and a laughing Robbie jump out. Right behind him was another kid who looked to be about the same age.

The second kid slammed the doors closed and the two boys crossed the pavement, apparently heading for a video game store.

At the same time, the mom behind the wheel gave the horn a couple quick hits, which prompted Robbie's friend to turn and offer a desultory wave. Then the van drove off, presumably to return to pick up the kids at some agreed-upon time.

I let out a long breath. Nobody else had emerged from the rear of the van, which meant it had been Robbie who'd closed the doors behind him when he climbed in the back.

Using Gloria's cell, which I'd brought with me, I called Barnes on his. He and Gloria were still back at my house, trying to run down clues as to Maddox's whereabouts.

The ex-FBI man picked up.

"False alarm," I said. "Turns out, there are a lot of white vans on the streets."

I told him how I'd followed Robbie, and what the result had been. "You were probably right, Lyle, and Maddox has ditched his van by now. You guys making any progress?"

"Not much. This guy's a goddam Mandrake root."

It took me a moment, but then I understood. "Go and catch a Mandrake root." A line from a poem by John Donne about the impossibility of attaining the unattainable. In Donne's case, he was talking about true love.

"You're lucky I'm marginally educated, Lyle. Or else I wouldn't know what the hell you're talking about half the time."

A brief, humorless laugh. "Don't flatter yourself, Doc. As I've tried to impress upon you, great poetry is man's highest aesthetic achievement. The fact that you, or anyone of your generation, can muster up a line or two from some class you were required to take doesn't mean shit. Now, unless you want me to list the various failings of our current university curricula, I suggest we end this call and let the impressive Agent Reese and myself get back to work."

"Gladly, you pedantic old coot."

We clicked off, and I settled back in my seat. I wasn't going anywhere. Although I figured Robbie was out of danger, at least for the moment, I still believed he was Maddox's next target—unless my entire assessment of the man was wrong, which was always possible.

I chided myself. Maybe my psychological interpretation of Maddox was my own way of attaining a measure of control. An attempt to gain some parity with him, if only symbolically. *His* leverage was his insane plan to kill selected people close to me. And mine, my belief that I understood him.

Of course, none of it mattered. Neither what I believed nor thought I understood. All that mattered was stopping him.

I checked in with Barnes and Gloria every so often as I waited for Soccer Mom to return for pickup. But so far, no message from Maddox. Nothing appearing, as if by dark magic, on my laptop screen. No visuals, no taunting words.

Dusk had settled around me and the few other cars in the lot. It was nearing six-thirty. Robbie and his friend had been in the store a long time. At least it seemed that way to me.

Suddenly uneasy, I was just about to climb out of my car and investigate when the same white van pulled up at the curb in front of the store. Another quick succession of horn bleats, and then the two boys were shambling out, laden with bags.

They climbed in the rear of the van, laughing and talking, and then the vehicle started to move. I did the same, and proceeded to follow it out of the lot and onto the street.

Through the quickening darkness, and in thickening traffic, we took the same route back toward the Palermo house as before. Until, about ten blocks from the mini-mall lot, the van abruptly swerved to the curb.

Half a block behind, I slammed on the brakes and peered through my headlights at the unmoving van, now cloaked in shadow by the overarching trees and the growing blackness of night.

Suddenly, one of the van's rear doors swung open and a small body was tossed out—Robbie's friend, hitting the pavement with a dull thud and then rolling over.

The rear door slammed shut and, seconds later, the van pulled quickly away from the curb. By then, I'd jumped out of my car and was running toward where the boy lay. At the same time, I hit the re-dial button on the cell.

Crouching beside the boy, I checked his vitals. He was winded, bruised, but alive, although his face was wan, and his eyes filled with terror.

When Barnes answered, I shouted into the phone.

"Lyle! Maddox has Robbie. But you need to call 911 and get an ambulance here to Plum Road and Twenty-first Street. A kid's been hurt, left alone on the sidewalk. Don't identify yourself, okay? You're just a concerned passerby, worried about the child."

"Right. Got it."

Gasping, the boy managed to squirm up to his elbows.

"Mom! Where's my mom? That man—"

I gripped his arm. "Was your mom in the van with him?"

"No, just him. What happened? Did he do something to my mom? You gotta help her—!"

"What's your name, son?"

"Benjamin Heywood. My mom's name is Dorothy."

I spoke once more into the phone. "The missing woman is named Dorothy Heywood. Make another anonymous call and have the cops check out her house. Maddox might have grabbed her when she arrived after dropping off the kids. Then taken her van."

"Or at any point between the mall and her house," Barnes said. "I just hope to Christ she's alive."

"I'm betting she is. Because her son is. Killing either of them falls outside the parameters of his 'mission.' They don't have a connection to me personally."

"Uh-huh."

Barnes sounded unconvinced, but I didn't care. I clicked off and put my face next to the fallen boy.

"I know you're scared, Benjamin. But I have to go after that van."

He nodded, tears streaming. "Robbie's still in there!"

"I know. Can you wait here till the ambulance comes? It should be here any minute. But if I don't go now…"

He sniffed, sat up straighter. "I'll be fine, just go!"

I gave him a final reassuring squeeze on his shoulder, then climbed to my feet and turned back toward him.

"Use your cell and keep calling your mom on hers. If you reach her, tell her you're okay and get her to tell you where she is. In case she's hurt and needs help."

He nodded again, clearly trying to be brave. And he was.

Back in my Mustang, I raced down to the end of the street and turned right at the corner. It was where I'd had my last glimpse of the departing van.

Now, heading up Verona Road, I was driving blind. Maddox had a good two-minute start on me. My task wasn't helped by the fact that traffic had worsened, and my eyes were stabbed by the headlights of oncoming cars.

Suppressing my panic, I called Barnes again. Told him to put Gloria on the phone. He did.

"Way ahead of you." Her voice clipped, assured. "I've linked to the Bureau's overhead feed. Air support drones. Like Google Maps on steroids. I figure a ten-mile radius, right?"

"Yeah. He couldn't be much farther away. I don't think Maddox would risk speeding. Calling attention to himself."

"Okay, hold on." A long pause. "Right, I think I got him. Looks like the top of a van. Heading South on Holbeck. If you cut through Churchill, you can catch up. Come up right behind him before he gets to the next intersection."

I was already programming my GPS. "Long as I hit nothing but green lights."

"Or else you could run all the red ones. I would."

I had to smile. *I'll bet you would.*

Neither of us spoke again as I headed in a diagonal route to intercept Maddox. We couldn't know if he'd managed by now to hack into her own cell. And we hadn't had time yet to get hold of some burner phones. So we kept communication to a minimum.

"You should be getting close," she murmured suddenly.

I peered ahead, my high beams carving bright furrows into the depths of night. Then, its own lights dimmed but visible, I spotted the white van approaching at a right angle to where I'd meet the intersection thirty yards away.

"Okay, I think I see him. I'm going to let him cross the intersection, then follow."

"Keep your distance, though, all right?" She paused again.

"I assume you're smart enough not to have your high beams on."

Instantly, I switched my headlights back to normal.

"Of course," I said.

We clicked off so I could concentrate on my driving. Which I did, following the van on surface streets all the way across town. Soon the traffic thinned, and we were heading toward the produce yards off Eleventh Street. Then, to my surprise, the van turned into one of the dark, narrow roads that crisscross the yard. At this time of night, its cavernous expanse morphs into a moonscape of weathered buildings, railroad tracks, and tin-roofed diners, warehouses and flatbed trucks and loading ramps.

It's called "the Strip" by locals. I'd worked summers here as a teen. Loading produce onto trucks. Pushing two-wheeler carts laden with crates over cobblestones embedded in the old streets. Drinking bitter coffee while listening to equally bitter men, their faces cracked and bodies bent, talk about life and its many disappointments.

The memory of that time in my youth swept over me like a curling wave, and then I was back in the here-and-now. Senses drawn tight, eyes glued to the back of the van making its slow way through the maze of weary, dun-colored buildings. Finally, it pulled to a stop beside a broken-down warehouse. Maybe three stories high. Boarded-up windows. Rusted drainpipes. A ghost.

I slowed down, about fifty feet away, and shut off my headlights. Then I pulled over to one side, my Mustang hidden under a broad slant of shadow.

For five long minutes, there wasn't any movement coming from the van. Then its lights went off.

Now the only thing threading the darkness was a single overhead lamp affixed to a top corner of the warehouse. It cast a dullish cone of light—to scare away squatters, I figured. Or druggies. Or rats. And probably doing a poor job of it.

I waited. Tired eyes squinting resolutely at the rear of the van.

Suddenly, that same single door opened, and Sebastian Maddox climbed out. Then he reached back into the van and hauled out a small, unmoving form. With an easy motion, he slung it over his shoulder. A fireman's carry.

It was Robbie. Even from fifty feet away, and in the ragged glow of the overhead, I could tell it was the body of a small boy.

My throat tightened. Was Robbie dead already, or merely unconscious? I hoped the latter, though I couldn't know for sure. I was long past knowing anything for sure.

Once I heard the sound of a door closing, its sharp creak echoing from somewhere at the rear of the warehouse, I slipped out of my car. I'd waited till Maddox had entered the building to avoid alerting him to my presence. He had Robbie with him, so I had to be cautious with my approach.

I crept along the length of the building's near side, then, in the half-light, saw the only door. Thick, sheet-metal skin. Stained with rust. The one Maddox must have used to go inside.

As quietly as I could, I pulled at the stubborn handle until the door squeaked open. I winced. No masking that sound.

I slipped inside, and made my way along a dim corridor draped with hanging spider webs. Swallowing fetid air, vision dulled by dust and darkness, I felt with my hands along its pockmarked wooden walls until I reached a second metal door.

Luckily, it looked as old and decrepit as the first one, so I gave its handle a sturdy pull.

It was locked.

Maddox had probably locked it from the inside once he'd entered the room beyond. I pulled on it again. Nothing.

My anxiety spiking, I took the risk of calling Barnes' cell again. This time Gloria picked up herself.

"Danny!" Her voice urgent, breathless. "I was just going to call you."

"What is it?"

"Your laptop. An image just came on-screen. From the looks of it, from inside some old building. Maybe a warehouse."

"It is. I'm inside myself. Or partway in. There's an inner door I can't open. What's going on? Has Maddox said anything? I know he has Robbie."

"Yes, he has him. Though the boy looks unconscious. Not dead, I can see him breathing. But he's out of it. No motor functions. Like a rag doll."

"Maddox probably used the same paralytic on Robbie that he'd used on me. What's happening?"

"He's got Robbie propped up in a chair, a metal folding chair. Bound to it by ropes. But there's something else."

"What? Tell me!"

"He has some other ropes hanging from the ceiling. But it's hard to make out what they're for. Other than some bright lights trained on Robbie, it's all pretty damned dark. But I can see something in Robbie's hand. His fingers tied around it by a thin cord…Jesus Christ, Danny, it's—"

She didn't have to say. I knew what it was.

"A gun." My voice went flat.

I took a long breath. More symmetry. Maddox was planning to replicate the event that had traumatized Robbie in the first place. The suicide by handgun of his best friend Matthew.

Only this time, it was Robbie himself who would die.

Chapter Seventeen

"Danny, wait!" Gloria's words shredded my thoughts. "Maddox just came on camera. He's talking to you…"

Maddox's voice, filtered by both my laptop's speaker and that of the cell in my hand, sounded thin, tinny. Alien.

"I have your newest patient here, Danny. Little Robbie Palermo. A *paisan*, eh? I wonder, did you ever discount your fee for fellow Italian-Americans? Nice branding opportunity you passed up there…"

I ignored him, an idea forming in my mind.

"Gloria," I whispered, my voice muffled under the drone of Maddox's ramblings. "Move away from the computer. Hurry!"

I could just make out her footsteps on the tile floor of my kitchen. At the same time, I heard Maddox ask where I was. That he needed to see me on my laptop screen.

"I have to find another way inside, Gloria," I said. "You've got to buy me some time."

"How, Danny? He's going to want you to respond. It doesn't work for him unless you do. Unless he sees you suffering."

"That's what I'm counting on. Close the laptop lid. Tell him I can't deal with what he's doing. Can't watch."

"But what if he—?"

"For Christ's sake, Gloria, just do it!"

Without waiting for her reply, I walked back down the corridor, the same way I'd come. This time moving more slowly, looking for another opening. An access door. Anything.

Meanwhile, I heard Gloria's footsteps coming over the cell. Heading back into the kitchen. Then a sudden click. She'd closed the lid of the laptop.

No sooner had she done so than I came upon a side door I'd missed on my way in. Thin and made of sheet metal, it had been hidden at first in the deep shadows crowding the dust-clouded corridor. I was just pulling it open when I heard Maddox explode in rage. Again, the journey from his camera mike to my computer speaker to the cell I was holding wrung the timbre from the growl of his words. But not the force of his anger.

"Goddam it, Danny, you gutless bastard! Now I can't see you. Which means *you* can't see the tableau I've constructed. It's a thing of beauty. As pure as one of Plato's Forms."

I stepped through the metal door into another, smaller corridor, as dim and dust-shrouded as the first. But there was a difference. At the end of this dark passageway was a narrow stone staircase, leading up.

I made my way toward it. I also knew I had to keep Maddox talking. With the laptop lid closed, I counted on his assumption that I was still there, with Barnes and Gloria—a pretense I needed to keep up till I found Robbie.

"Bullshit, Maddox." I shouted, both to infuriate him and, hopefully, to disguise the fact that I wasn't inches away from my laptop speaker. "Like you know a fucking thing about beauty. Plato, my ass. If he were here, he'd spit in your eye."

"You're debating philosophy with *me*? Hilarious."

Finally, I reached the concrete stairs and began to climb as quickly and silently as I could.

"You still there, Danny? The kid's going to die either way, so why don't you open the lid? I want to see your face when it happens. And I know you'll want to see mine."

By now, I'd reached the top of the steps, which opened onto another narrow passageway, wood-framed, cobwebbed.

Just then, I heard Gloria's faint whisper. I'd pocketed the cell, which muffled the sound. I strained to hear her voice.

"Danny...Maddox has finished with the rope thing. He's got the boy all trussed up, like some kind of marionette. Robbie's right arm's pointing at his head, the gun attached to his hand."

Her voice cracked. "My God...now Maddox is backing away from the boy, holding on to the end of the cord. The other end's tied to the trigger on the gun."

I nodded without answering. Maddox was trying to duplicate, as much as possible, the image of Robbie shooting himself in the head. As Matthew had done. If Maddox himself did it, if it was *his* finger on the trigger, the effect would be ruined.

"I need another minute," I whispered back to her. "Tell Barnes to yell at the prick."

As I crossed this smaller, tunnel-like passage, I heard an angry burst of invective. Like the roar of a lion. Loud enough to be heard from the cell in my pocket. Lyle Barnes.

"Maddox, you crazy motherfucker, I can't wait till we nail your sorry ass. When we find what dung-hole you're hiding in, I'm gonna reach down your throat and pull your rancid guts out. You hear me, you delusional piece of shit?"

"Fuck you, old man," Maddox shouted. "I wasn't talking to you, anyway. Danny? *Danny, are you there?*"

"I'm right here, Maddox." Shouting. Cell still in my pocket. "Do what you're gonna do, but I won't watch."

"I know you're just stalling for time, Rinaldi!" Maddox was livid with frustration. "But it won't work. *Open the goddam lid* and watch the kid shoot himself. Or I'll wake his ass up, I swear! *You hear me?*"

By now, I'd slipped through an opening at the end of the passageway, finding myself on a kind of catwalk with wire mesh bending below my feet.

"The little bastard's still out of it, Danny. But I promise I'll wake him up. Let him see he's about to die..."

I was moving in a crouch along the catwalk, until I came to a shadowed corner thick with dust and the smell of rotten wood and masonry. I approached and realized it was the remains of a broader, wood-planked overhang below which sprawled a huge, obviously long-abandoned storage facility.

I made the turn and stepped carefully onto the splintered wood, then peered over the edge. On the concrete floor below me were two large klieg lights, positioned on either side of a video camera attached to a tripod. The blazing light cast Robbie in an unearthly glow, his slender body bound to a folding chair. His eyes were closed, his limbs unmoving—except for his right arm, suspended by ropes and hanging perpendicular to his head. The thin white arm swayed ever so slightly in the web of ropes, causing the revolver tied to his hand to tap its barrel lightly against the side of his head.

I almost cried out, but stifled it. Because now, as Maddox spoke, his voice wasn't just coming through the cell phone in my pocket. I was hearing it in person.

Kneeling, I risked thrusting my head farther past the edge of the overhang. At last, from this angle, I could see him. Maddox, in jeans and a hooded sweatshirt, stood about six feet to the left of Robbie, the end of the cord in his fist.

Seeing Maddox in the hoodie brought an instant stab of pain. A searing recollection of that night, Barbara's screams, the roar of gunshots, the spray of blood...

I took a couple quick breaths to center myself. To focus.

Now I saw that Maddox had set up the camera at a good enough distance that it could record both his position and that of his victim. Maddox may have wanted to replicate the scenario of a boy shooting himself with a gun, but he also wanted his viewer—me—to see who'd really pulled the trigger.

"'This is your last warning!" He pointed with his free hand at the camera, still unaware that I was directly above him. "Open up the laptop and watch Robbie die. Quick and painless. At least it's humane."

I readied myself, hands gripping the jagged wooden edge of the overhang, muscles tensing.

"Or else I wake the kid up, shove the gun in his mouth and

pull the trigger. Think what his parents'll save on braces for the little shit."

In the space of a few moments, I assessed my moves. I knew I couldn't risk trying to tackle Maddox from above. Not with his hand holding fast to his end of the cord. If he fell, or was knocked off-balance, the cord would jerk back, pulling the trigger on the gun tied to Robbie's hand.

So, gathering myself, I moved to my left, three long strides past where Maddox stood below. And jumped.

My bones rattled as my feet hit the concrete, breath pushed out of me. Still moving, I fell into a roll.

Behind me, I heard Maddox gasp, momentarily stunned. But I didn't turn to see him. Instead, coming out of the roll, I ran toward Robbie, my hands outstretched.

I knew I had only seconds before Maddox would yank on that cord. Fire the gun.

With a hoarse cry, I lunged at Robbie and wrapped my arms around him. Bringing us both crashing to the floor in a twisted tangle of ropes, as the gun discharged. The bullet whistled past us, pinging off the leg of one of the tripods.

Shielding Robbie with my body, I craned my neck around in time to see Maddox, eyes black with rage, glaring at me. The muscles in his powerful neck taut and thick as bridge cables.

For the first time, I was face-to-face with Sebastian Maddox. Just six feet away from the man who'd killed my wife.

Neither one of us moved, as though frozen. Then, rousing myself, I scrambled for the gun, still tied to Robbie's hand, tangled in the ropes. If I could just wrest it free…

Maddox saw what I was doing. Without a word, he threw down the cord, turned, and ran off, disappearing within seconds into the deep darkness beyond the sizzling klieg lights, leaving behind only the echo of his running footsteps on concrete, followed by the hollow, metallic sound of a door closing.

Though we'd hit the floor hard, Robbie was still unconscious, but his breathing was regular, and he seemed otherwise unhurt.

As carefully as possible I extricated him from the tangle of ropes, pulling his limp arms and legs free. Then I untied the still-warm revolver from his hand and slipped it into my pocket.

Finally I lifted Robbie up, cradling him in both arms, and walked us slowly out of the room. I made my way through the same phalanx of shadows into which Maddox had disappeared and came to the door I'd been unable to open. As I guessed, he'd locked it from the inside after bringing Robbie in here.

Now unlocked, it opened easily to my kick and I carried Robbie down the corridor and through the exterior door. Outside, the overhead lamp offered a feeble light against the cold, flooding darkness, but it was enough to see that the Heywood woman's van was gone. I had no doubt Maddox would abandon it once he'd gotten far enough away from the Strip.

I opened my Mustang and buckled Robbie into the passenger seat. As I pulled out of the produce yard, I placed Gloria's cell in the hands-free socket and hit re-dial.

She spoke before I could.

"We saw it, Danny. All of it." An undisguised relief in her voice. "Thank God Robbie's okay."

"Is the camera still rolling?"

"No. Your laptop screen just went blank. The camera must've been set to shut itself off after a given time. The last thing we saw was Maddox running out of frame."

"He got back to the van and took off. If he hasn't ditched it somewhere by now, he will soon."

Her tone sharpened. "You know, you took a helluva chance in there going for Robbie the way you did."

"I didn't see any other way. But I know I got lucky."

"Yeah, well…" A meaningful pause. "That's the thing about luck, Danny. Sooner or later it runs out."

Chapter Eighteen

Robbie was just coming around as I carried him up the steps to the front porch of his house. Lights were on inside, and a Lexus was in the driveway. It looked like his parents were home.

I lay him on the porch and walked quickly and quietly back to where I'd parked across the street. I got behind the wheel and waited, engine and lights off, for Robbie to wake to full consciousness. The porch light was bright enough for me to see him pretty clearly.

In another few minutes, I saw him wobble to his feet, rub his eyes, and look around. Confusion clouded his features. Until, finally registering where he was, he rang the doorbell.

Suddenly the door flew open and a woman bent to scoop him up in her arms. It was Mrs. Palermo. Sobbing, frantic, clutching her son to her breast. Right behind her in the doorway was a man I took to be Robbie's father. I'd never met him before.

After they'd bustled their son inside and closed the door, I put the Mustang in gear and pulled away from the curb. As I headed for town, and home, I tried to order my thoughts.

From all appearances, it looked as if Robbie had been unconscious from the moment Maddox injected him with the paralytic. Probably right before or right after he'd thrown Benjamin Heywood out of the van. Which meant that Robbie would have no memory of being taken to the warehouse and bound to the chair, a gun tied to his hand. Nor would he remember his rescue, and our drive back to his house.

Not that the experience wouldn't be upsetting, or even re-traumatizing, but having been spared the memory of his close brush with death—especially its planned replication of the way his friend Matthew had perished—I believed it was possible the psychological effects on the boy would be diminished.

At the moment, there was no way to know. Driving across the bridge under a too-bright moon, I realized that whatever lay ahead for Robbie, his journey toward some kind of emotional equilibrium had just been made much more difficult.

I'd no sooner pulled into my driveway when Gloria came out of the front door, peering at me in the porch light.

"My God, look at you. You're all banged up."

"I'll live. Tell me, what's happening?"

"It's all over the news." We headed back inside. "Just breaking."

Lyle Barnes was standing by the sofa in the front room, TV remote in hand, watching the local news report. Gloria and I joined him.

According to the on-screen anchor, the police were investigating an attempted kidnapping this evening of two adolescent boys. After Mrs. Dorothy Heywood returned home from dropping her son and a friend off at a gaming store in Penn Hills, a male suspect approached and struck her with the butt of a gun. Leaving her unconscious on her driveway, he then used her white van to return to the store and pick up the boys. For some reason, the kidnapper soon released Mrs. Heywood's son, Benjamin, but kept his friend, a boy whose identity the police were, for now, refusing to disclose.

"A wise move," I said aloud. "Given Robbie's likely inability to recall anything about what happened to him, the cops will want to investigate further before releasing his name. Standard procedure. In case of possible sexual abuse."

"Poor kid." Barnes shook his head. "They'll probably ask to do a rape kit. Like a twelve-year-old boy wants somebody poking around in his ass."

The report went on to say that Benjamin Heywood could offer little in the way of a description of the suspect—just that he was a big man and wore a hooded jacket. Benjamin did claim that he'd been helped by a passing stranger—"a real nice man"—after he'd been ejected from the van, but couldn't recall anything about him, other than that he had a beard.

This brought a chortle from Barnes.

"You'd make a shitty criminal, Doc. A beard always sticks out to a victim as a distinguishing feature."

As for the second boy, the one held by the kidnapper, the anchor reported that he appeared unhurt, but had no memory of what transpired. He recalled seeing right away that the person driving the van wasn't Mrs. Heywood, but some man in a hoodie. Then, according to the boy, the man jabbed him with a hypodermic needle. It was the last thing he remembered before waking up on his front porch, with no idea how he'd gotten there.

"Good thing, too," Gloria said to me. "Keeps you out of the loop entirely."

I nodded, as the anchor ended his report.

"The police are unwilling to speculate this early in their investigation as to the sequence of events," the anchor said coolly. "However, sources close to the Department believe that it's possible the kidnapped boy somehow managed to escape his captor, though he's unable to recall doing so. Or perhaps the suspect lost his nerve at some point after snatching the boy and decided to dump him somewhere. After which, still dazed from the drug he'd been given, the victim simply walked home. On instinct."

The segment ended with the station displaying a phone number on the screen, with the anchor stating that the police were asking for the public's help in finding the suspect.

Barnes snorted and clicked off the TV.

"Lotsa luck. With the description the kids gave them, the cops don't have squat. And they won't find any forensics in the Heywood woman's van, either. Maddox is too goddam careful to have left his prints. Or anything else, for that matter."

"Which may not be a bad thing," I said. "This way, what's happening between Maddox and me stays contained. Just something between him and me. If it turned into a full-blown police manhunt, there's no telling how Maddox would respond. How many people he'd be willing to kill before getting taken down."

Gloria hadn't said anything during this exchange, her gaze averted. Finally she turned to me.

"I don't know, Danny. As a sworn law enforcement officer, I'm uncomfortable keeping our knowledge of Maddox to ourselves. Especially after what he's done so far. The people he's hurt or killed. Not to mention that it could end my career. Hell, I could wind up in jail."

An awkward moment of silence followed. Then Gloria stepped away from Barnes and me, arms folded, as though we were now in two different camps. And maybe we were.

Barnes spoke first. "Look, Agent Reese, I understand what you're saying. But I think our hands are tied here. Maddox is running this game. At least till we track him down."

"I know, but—"

I moved toward her, hands outspread.

"I realize this puts you in a difficult position, Gloria. And I get it. But let me ask you one question: Do you believe Sebastian Maddox will kill more people if we alert the police? Or the Bureau? Innocent people…?"

Her eyes, dark and penetrating, met my own. Then, after a long moment, she let out a breath.

"Yes," she said simply. "I believe he will."

"Then what choice do we have?"

Another pause. "None. Lives are at stake. That's the most important thing. So we have to do it Maddox's way."

I took a moment, then nodded. "Thanks, Gloria."

Barnes chuckled dryly. "Now aren't you glad I called you in on this, Agent Reese?"

Apparently, his humor was lost on her. Instead of replying, she turned on her heel and headed out of the room, calling back to me over her shoulder.

"Follow me, will you, Danny?"

"Wait a minute."

I'd just remembered that I still had Maddox's revolver in my pocket. The one he'd tied to Robbie's hand. Using my thumb and forefinger, I held it out for Barnes. He, in turn, used a handkerchief to take it from me, but gave it a sour squint.

"We both know there won't be any prints on it." He wrapped it in the white cloth and put it on the coffee table. "Maddox probably wiped it before tying it to the boy's hand."

Gloria nodded ruefully, after which she asked me again to follow her. She led me to the bathroom and waited while I took a quick shower, then wrapped myself in a thick towel before coming out. Smiling, she ordered me to sit on the edge of the tub. Finding swabs and antiseptic in the medicine cabinet, she went to work tending my old bruises, as well as a few new ones.

Finally, she stood, yawning. "By the way, you have a good-sized welt on the back of your neck. Probably from where Maddox injected the paralytic."

"Yeah. He jabbed it in pretty hard. Hurts like hell."

"I'll bet. Anyway, I'm looking forward to a shower myself. But not at home. I'll just swing by, pick up some clothes, and check into a hotel. And get some sleep. But if that whack-job contacts you again—"

I interrupted her. "Good idea, Gloria. About the hotel. With Maddox, we can't be too careful. Now that he knows you and Barnes are working with me. By now he's probably tracked down where you each live—"

"That's what Lyle and I think, too. The old man's getting a room, too, but in a different hotel. Neither of us will know where the other is. Just in case."

"I agree. I don't want to know where you two are staying, either. It's safer that way. For all of us."

"Plus, Lyle's picking up some throwaway cells for us to use from now on. Untraceable." She paused. "Speaking of hotels, it wouldn't be a bad idea if you made yourself scarce, too."

I said okay, though the thought of Maddox forcing me to flee from my own home rankled me.

Her face softening, Gloria touched my forearm. "Hang in there, okay, Danny? You're not alone."

I nodded my appreciation, which brought a second, firmer squeeze of my arm. Then, with a half-smile, she leaned up and kissed me on the cheek, giving me a whiff of her subtle perfume.

Without another word, we returned to the front room after a quick stop in the kitchen to retrieve her laptop. Remembering that I still had her cell, I returned that to her as well. Then Gloria said good-bye to Barnes and me, and left.

"Great girl. A bit on the skinny side for my tastes, but with a superb ass." Barnes settled down on the sofa. "And by the way, Doc, you're an idiot."

"What do you mean?"

"While you were out, Gloria told me she made a move on you a couple weeks back. After that case you were both involved in wrapped up. She said you told her about still carrying a torch for some other woman who's broken it off with you."

"It's complicated. And none of your goddam business."

"Suit yourself, Doc. But you're not getting any younger."

Bristling, I stared at him. "I'm going to try to get some sleep. At least until the next time Maddox surfaces. I figure you can see your way out."

Maybe it was fatigue, or the stress of the past two days, but I wasn't in the mood for Barnes' Neanderthal views of women. Nor his opinions about my personal life. Not that he'd been any less truculent or confrontational during our clinical work together. At the time, I'd seen it as classic resistance, especially since he'd been required to receive therapy from a younger man. And a civilian, to boot.

But now, in a sense, we were working together. In a kind of covert partnership necessitated by Sebastian Maddox's demands. Along with Gloria Reese, he was my ally in my battle against a madman, which changed the dynamic of our relationship. Like it or not, we were no longer merely therapist and patient.

I also realized that whatever we were now would take some getting used to.

I went into my bedroom and pulled on a pair of sweats and a Pitt jersey. Then I sat on the edge of the bed and reached for my landline.

Maybe Maddox was listening, maybe not. At this point, I didn't give a damn. There was nothing I was going to say on the phone that would give the game away.

Stifling a yawn, I called the Palermo house. After a half-dozen rings, Robbie's father answered. I introduced myself.

"Yes, Doctor. My son…he's spoken very highly of you…"

Despite his best efforts, his voice had a quaver in it. The man still trying to process what had happened to his boy.

"I just wanted to call and see how Robbie's doing. I saw on the news about—"

"Yes. Everybody keeps calling. Family and friends. The press…" A heavy sigh. "Somehow his name leaked out…"

"I can't even imagine what you and Mrs. Palermo are going through, let alone Robbie. I know it's quite late, but if you need me to come by…"

"No, thanks. Robbie's pediatrician sent over some pills to help him sleep, and it looks like they finally worked. My son's upstairs, lying next to his mother in our bed."

"Probably the thing he needs most."

It was the kind of platitude I rarely expressed, but at the moment all I wanted to do was offer comfort, reassure him that his son would eventually come out on the other side of this.

"Look, Dr. Rinaldi, we're grateful for all you've done for Robbie since Matthew's death, but with this new…thing…" He swallowed a breath. "Anyway, my wife is going to take Robbie out of school, get him away from here. Go stay with her mother in California. I have to remain in town for work, but—"

"Not a bad idea. How long will they be away?"

"For as long as it takes for my boy to heal. I mean, how much more can the poor kid take?"

Before hanging up, I told him that Robbie could always call me, even from the West Coast, if he needed to talk, and that, of course, I would be available to continue treatment with him when he came back to town.

If he came back, I thought.

I was glad Robbie's family was taking him three thousand miles away. As long as Sebastian Maddox was at large, there was every reason to believe he'd try again to take the boy's life. That's why, as a precaution in case Maddox *was* able to listen in on my landline, I didn't ask Mr. Palermo to specify exactly where in California Robbie and his mother were heading.

The only other call I made was to my office voice mail, which I suddenly realized I'd neglected to check even once today. Luckily, there were no new messages from patients. No one in crisis who needed to speak to me.

The only message was from Noah Frye. From the sounds in the background, I could tell he was calling from his bar.

"Hey, Danny, it's me. It's weird leavin' a message on your office voice mail, but you're a hard man to reach. I tried your

cell but didn't get an answer. When I tried your landline, I got a
busy signal. I swear, if I wasn't standin' here lookin' at your bar
tab, I'd think I've been hallucinatin' you all these years. Which
would kinda suck.

"Anyway, you should get your ass down here tonight 'cause
I'm sittin' in with the trio. Remember my old band, Flat Affect?
Some o' the same guys'll be playin'. We're all on our meds, so it
oughtta be a real tight set. Oh, and Charlene says hi."

Given recent events, hearing Noah's slightly manic voice
was a welcome balm. And a part of me yearned to take him up
on his invitation. But now, with every passing hour, it felt as if
I'd entered some alternate reality, not my own. As Maddox had
predicted, I was in *his* world now.

But it wasn't about me anymore. It was about the obscene
death of Joy Steadman. And Stephen Langley. Even that of
Eddie Burke. Despite his abusive treatment of his girlfriend,
he didn't deserve to die in a horrible car crash fleeing from a
murder charge of which he was actually innocent. Then there
was Robbie's family, whose lives were abruptly upended as a
result of Maddox's actions.

No, despite Maddox's desire to inflict pain on me, it wasn't
about me any longer. It was about what had happened to his
victims that fueled my deepening grief and outrage.

With a heavy sigh, I rose stiffly from the bed and padded
down the hallway to the kitchen. It was nearing midnight, and
my body was craving sleep, but I wanted to fill the coffeemaker
so it would be ready first thing in the morning. Although I
couldn't foresee what would happen tomorrow, I knew damn
well it wouldn't be good.

Preoccupied with that thought, it wasn't until I'd turned
from the counter that I noticed my laptop wasn't on the kitchen
table, where I'd last seen it.

Puzzled, I glanced into the front room. There I spotted Lyle
Barnes, in a cotton tee-shirt, boxer shorts, and socks, sleeping
fitfully on the sofa. He lay on his back, his long, lean form tak-

ing up the entire length of the cushions. On his stomach, rising and falling with his every breath, was my laptop, resting in the crook of his arm in its sling.

I smiled to myself. At least Gloria had been right about one thing. I wasn't alone.

Chapter Nineteen

I slept pretty fitfully myself, until roused at dawn by Lyle Barnes, in his same street clothes from yesterday, standing at my bedside, backlit by pale morning light streaming through my bedroom shutters.

"You got company." He jerked his thumb over his shoulder. "Pittsburgh PD knocking at your door."

Blinking into wakefulness, I climbed out of bed.

"Who is it?"

"Your buddy, Sergeant Polk. From his knock, I'm guessing he's not exactly a morning person."

I shrugged. "He's pretty miserable any time of day. Listen, you better make yourself scarce. Maybe down in the basement. Your presence here will just invite a lot of questions, none of which we can risk answering."

"True enough."

We left my bedroom together, Barnes heading for the steps to the basement while I padded barefoot to the front door. Slowly. Buying myself a few extra seconds to clear my head.

I opened the door while Polk was in mid-knock, his fist mere inches from my face. I smiled at it.

"Jesus, Harry, you know what time it is?"

He grunted unhappily. "Yeah, it's time for you to put on your big-boy shoes and socks and come with me."

"Where are we going?"

"Downtown. That's where we usually interrogate suspects."

"I'm afraid you've lost me."

"Hey, don't blame me. Personally, I think Biegler's nuts, but he wants you brought in on the Joy Steadman murder."

"You can't be serious."

"I told ya, I'm not. But Biegler is. Now are ya comin' easy or do I have to get out the cuffs? Not that I'd mind doin' it."

I groaned. "Give me a minute."

True to my word, it only took about that long to change into jeans, Polo shirt, and jacket. But before rejoining Polk, I stopped in the kitchen and wrote a short note to Barnes, explaining my absence. I left it right next to my laptop, which he'd already brought back to the table. I also noticed he'd turned on the coffeemaker I'd prepped the night before.

Now, glancing at the near-empty carafe sizzling on its grate, I wondered how long Barnes had been up. Had he gotten any real sleep at all? Or had his former symptoms recurred, his slumber once more invaded by night terrors and the cascade of fearsome, demonic images, the horrifying yet illusive shapes. And then the haunting, inexplicable dread when wrenched awake. Sweat-soaked, heart pounding…

"Yo, Doc! We ain't got all day!"

Polk's belligerent voice ended my ruminations, at least for the time being. But I'd have to address it with Barnes at some point, and sooner rather than later. Despite the present crisis we were dealing with, my clinical obligation to him remained.

I hurried back to join Polk, then followed him to where his unmarked was parked at the curb.

It was another bright, clean-shaven morning, downtown nearly deserted on a Sunday. I couldn't remember if there was a Pirates game today, in which case city-strangling traffic would soon materialize as though summoned by the baseball gods. But for now, the drive to the main precinct was an easy sprint along empty streets and through long, dawn-birthed shadows.

As we neared the Old County Building, I regarded Polk's stolid profile, an unlit Camel balanced between his lips.

Neither of us had said much on the drive down from my place.

"Are you going to tell me what's going on, Harry? Why Stu Biegler has such a hard-on for me all of a sudden?"

His beefy hands turned the wheel, guiding us into the parking lot. "What are ya talkin' about? The Lieutenant's hated your guts for years."

"I see your point. What I *don't* see is how Biegler can think I had anything to do with Joy's death."

He found a spot near the building entrance and shut off the engine. But instead of getting out of the car, he turned in his seat, facing me. Cigarette bobbing up and down as he spoke.

"It's 'cause of the forensics."

"From Joy's autopsy? What about them?"

"That's just it, Doc. There ain't any. No hair, fibers, nothin'. No DNA, either. The M.E. says the perp swabbed her with somethin' like rubbing alcohol afterwards. Even douched her."

I didn't reply, thinking back to the video of the assault Maddox had shown me. His naked body was hairless, completely shaved. And I figured he'd been careful enough not to leave fingerprints on anything in the girl's bedroom. Nor to come unprepared for covering his tracks afterwards.

I also realized what this meant to the police.

"I get it," I said at last. "The working theory is that Joy's death was unplanned, the impulsive act of her angry, jealous boyfriend. Meaning that if Eddie Burke jacked his lawyer's car and went straight back home to kill Joy, it's unlikely he'd have prepared any of these precautions. Or taken the time after the murder to swab any traces from her body."

Polk nodded. "That's what Biegler figures. Besides, nobody who knew Burke thinks he was smart enough to do all that shit. Not to mention the fact that no rubbing alcohol was found in the house, no swabs an' stuff, which meant the perp took it all with him afterwards. Except nothin' like that was in the lawyer's car when it was found. Nothin' but what was left o' Eddie Burke."

I nodded reflectively, at the same time fully aware of how disingenuous it was to be discussing the case with Polk while secretly knowing the actual identity of Joy Steadman's killer.

"So," I said, hoping my voice didn't betray my thoughts, "how does this suddenly make me Joy's killer?"

"Well, first off, there's your affair with the girl—"

"I told you, that wasn't true. Hell, you were sitting right next to Joy when she admitted she'd made it up."

"Maybe she was lyin' to protect you. Maybe *you* was lyin' when you told me it was all bullshit." His eyes narrowed. "You ain't always played straight with the Department, ya know."

"C'mon, Harry. I wouldn't lie about something like that. You *know* me, right? At least I hope so."

He shrugged. "Maybe I do, maybe I don't. I mean, sure, I think Biegler's off his head likin' you for this, but whoever the killer was, he was fuckin' smart. Smarter than a coke-head like Eddie Burke. But not smarter than *you*, Doc."

With that, he opened the driver's side door and climbed out. After a long moment, I did the same.

• ● ● ● •

As we passed through the lobby on our way to the bank of elevators, a uniformed desk clerk—old, bored, gone to fat—called over to me.

"Hey, Dr. Rinaldi. You got a call a few minutes ago. Some female, asking for you. She left her number."

Polk glowered at me. "You're fuckin' kiddin' me..."

I suspected it was Gloria Reese.

"Might be important, Harry. I'll meet you in the conference room in five minutes."

"Look, Doc, just 'cause you're some bullshit consultant..."

"Which means I'm hardly a flight risk. Five minutes?"

I could hear his disgruntled sigh over the hum of the fluorescents above us. I also thought I spotted the heavyset cop behind the desk trying to hide a smile.

"Five goddam minutes," Polk growled, "and then I come down here and haul your ass upstairs."

Snatching the unlit cigarette from his mouth and shoving it in his jacket breast pocket, he strode off toward the elevators.

The desk jockey pointed with a sausage-like forefinger.

"You can use the lobby phone over there. She said you had her number."

There were a couple faux-leather, pea-green chairs facing a small plastic table in an alcove at the far end of the lobby. On top of the table was a landline phone, circa 1990s.

I dialed Gloria's cell. She picked up after one ring.

"Are you at the station?" she said without preamble.

"Just now. You've met Polk's boss, right? Weasel named Biegler. He thinks I look good for Joy's murder. And before you say anything, yes, the irony isn't lost on me. If that son of a bitch Maddox finds out I'm a suspect, he'll laugh his ass off."

"To hell with that prick. How are *you* doing?"

"Sleep-deprived, but otherwise okay. Where are you?"

"At your place. I must've just missed you. Lyle showed me the note you left. That's how I knew where to call."

"Has Maddox made contact? On my laptop, or some other way?"

"Not yet." A pause. "Christ, I think it's worse *not* hearing from him. Not knowing what he'll do next."

I considered this. "I feel the same way. But it's part of the game of nerves he's playing. Making me wonder whose death will come next. And when."

There was another, longer pause on the phone.

"Listen, Danny," she said finally. "I'm calling from your bedroom. With the door closed. For privacy."

"Okay…" Keeping my voice steady. What was going on?

"I mean, it's no big deal. Not in the middle of this shit-storm. And I shouldn't even have mentioned it. But Barnes and I were talking about you, and…"

I heard her take a breath, as though preparing herself.

"Look, it's embarrassing as hell, but I told Lyle about that time last month when I made a fool of myself. Coming on to you, I mean. Totally balls-out. And I'm sorry, it wasn't—"

"Are you kidding? The only fool I remember from that night was me."

"Well, I don't know…"

I chose my next words carefully.

"Believe me, Gloria. You're not the kind of woman a man wants to disappoint. And at the time…well, there was someone else's feelings to consider."

Her voice grew soft. "And now…?"

"I don't know. She—look, maybe being on a break from each other means just that…that we're taking a break."

Gloria fell silent. Then, as if suddenly uncomfortable, as if she'd disclosed too much, her tone lightened.

"Well, for what it's worth, Lyle thinks you were an idiot for not hooking up with me."

"I know. He told me. Those were his exact words, in fact."

"No shit? A wise man, that Lyle Barnes."

Now I found myself smiling. "You know, in my clinical opinion this a crazy conversation. Under the circumstances."

"I couldn't agree more, Doctor. But in some psych course I took once, I learned that levity is a great stress-reliever. So maybe that's what we're doing. Relieving stress."

"I concur, Agent Reese. Now I better go up and see Lieutenant Biegler before the cops put out an APB on me."

"Yeah, go ahead. Like you don't have enough to worry about. Meanwhile, Barnes and I will keep trying to get a fix on Maddox's whereabouts. He's got to be holed up somewhere."

"Great, thanks. And if you could, it might help to learn everything we can about his life. His past, his background."

"Got it. A psych profile. Right up Lyle's alley."

I was about to say good-bye when she spoke again.

"And by the way, Danny. If you're ever interested, I can think of another way to relieve stress."

She hung up without another word.

• ● ● ● •

I got off the elevator on the fifth floor and strode down to the conference room. Most of the desks lining the corridor were empty, though a few detectives had surrendered their Sundays, apparently to catch up on paperwork. I knew a number of them by sight, if not always by name, and received halfhearted waves in response to my own casual greetings.

Like Polk, most cops in the Department had, at best, mixed feelings about my involvement in some of its more high-profile cases—especially given the media attention that often resulted. Nevertheless, over the years, I'd managed to develop decent relationships with a number of them. Though this was probably due as much to the fact that I was the son of a cop as to any affinity they had with me. And for these few men and women, the fact that I was a psychologist made them uncomfortable.

As I neared the shiny double doors of the conference room, I heard querulous voices coming from within. I couldn't make out all the words, but it was clear the argument was about me.

I knocked, heard Biegler's thin voice call out "Come in!" and opened the door.

There were only three of them, Lieutenant Biegler sitting at the head of the conference table, Polk and Jerry Banks on either side. When I entered, Biegler made an imperious gesture toward one of the empty chairs. I sat.

Over the years, Stu Biegler, head of Robbery/Homicide, had shown even less patience with me—and my consultant's position with the Department—than Harry Polk. Just past forty, yet with the callow face and slim body of a much younger man, Biegler's career ambitions always seemed to trump any real interest in law enforcement. Which didn't exactly endear him to the cops under his command. Especially one Harry Polk.

"I heard you guys arguing in here." I figured I might as well start the ball rolling. "About me, right?"

"We were *discussing* the Steadman case, Doctor." Biegler tried on a smile. "Out of deference to your position with the Department, Sergeant Polk feels we should conduct our interview with you in here. Like colleagues. And not in some grimy interrogation room."

I turned to Polk. "Why, Harry? You guys have grilled me before in interrogation rooms. Plenty of times."

Biegler gave a short laugh. "That hardly speaks well of your character, does it? Which means it shouldn't come as much of a surprise that I've had you brought in today."

I sat forward in my chair.

"Hell, I can't say I'm not impressed. Two of Pittsburgh PD's finest, pulling duty on a Sunday. What happened, did you lose a bet or something?"

Jerry Banks started to chuckle, but wisely stifled it after a warning look from Polk.

Unlike the young detective, Biegler was not amused.

"As you well know, Rinaldi, the victim's family are quite prominent people. Good friends of both the Mayor and District Attorney Sinclair."

"And campaign contributors to both those fine public servants," I said. "So since you guys aren't happy with the case against Eddie Burke—convenient as it was—you have to work up an alternative theory of the crime. That's where I come in."

I'll give Biegler this much. He didn't flinch.

"That's because I think you're good for it, Doctor. At the very least, I consider you a person of interest."

"Based on what? Other than your animus toward me."

"Based on the facts. The alleged affair with the Steadman girl, who happened to live right across the street from you. A girl whose dead body you were the first to find. And whose autopsy revealed the hand of a clever, sophisticated killer." He spread his own hands on the top of the polished table. "And based on the fact you're a wise-ass who thinks he's smarter than everyone else. See, I'm not some stupid cop from the sticks, Rinaldi. I know what 'animus' means."

"Good for you, Biegler. But you left out a motive. Why the hell would I want to kill Joy Steadman?"

Polk cleared his throat. "I gotta admit, Lieutenant, I've been wonderin' 'bout that myself."

After glancing coolly in Polk's direction, Biegler returned his officious gaze at me.

"Motive is easy. You're a noted psychologist, a consultant with the Department. And for some reason I can't fathom, sort of a media darling. An affair with a young, vulnerable woman half your age wouldn't do much for your image. Especially as part of a romantic triangle with a known drug addict. And a black man, to boot. From the slums of Homewood."

Before I could respond, he held up a slender hand.

"And, no, I'm not being racist. I just know how the public thinks. How people really think when they're not talking to pollsters. Besides, maybe the motive is even simpler. You wanted to end things with the girl and she didn't. So you killed her."

"And raped her first?"

"What better way to make it look like the work of someone else? Eddie Burke, for instance."

I turned from him to Polk. "You know this is bullshit, right, Harry? There was no affair, and I didn't kill anyone."

He shrugged his thick shoulders. "Not my call, Doc."

I'd had enough. I kicked back my chair and stood up.

"Fuck you, Biegler. You have nothing and you know it. Man, you're so happy at the thought of jamming me up, it's pathetic. Now either charge me, in which case I'll call Harvey Blalock—"

"That's his lawyer," Polk said helpfully.

Biegler's jaw set. "I know who he is, Sergeant."

"Either charge me," I said again, "or let me get the hell out of here."

The Lieutenant got up from his seat as well, so that now we were eye-to-eye. His pale face reddening.

"Listen, you arrogant bastard—"

"I'd rather not. I get to *choose* who I listen to, Biegler, and you're not on the list. You want to talk to somebody, I'm happy to make a referral. I know a couple shrinks who specialize in assholes. I'm sure one of them can fit you in."

Out of the corner of my eye I saw Polk shake his head. Both of us knew I'd crossed the line, and that I'd better make myself scarce. And fast.

So I did.

Chapter Twenty

Back down in the lobby, the desk cop told me that Polk had called him to arrange for a uniform to drive me home.

"No, thanks." I headed out the door. "I'll figure something else out."

I was still roiling with anger from my encounter with Biegler. What was really maddening was defending myself from his ridiculous accusations while knowing who Joy's real killer was.

But it wasn't just that. The brown-nosing little prick had been trying to undermine my position with the Department for years, and I was tired of it. Tired, too, of our familiar verbal jousting. What I'd really wanted to do up there was lay him out.

I get like that sometimes. Sue me.

Standing outside the precinct, jangly, still fuming, it occurred to me what I needed to do. I needed to hit something. The mid-morning sun pouring down, people coming and going around me, but it was all I could think about.

It wasn't because of Biegler. He was a minor irritant. It was the specter of Sebastian Maddox, and my frustration and anger in the face of his campaign of terror, of death. Knowing he would strike again.

And soon.

• • ● • •

That was the thing about being a paid consultant to the Pittsburgh Police. On the one hand, I sometimes had to deal with cretins like Stu Biegler. On the other, I had access to the Department's new health club, a handsome sandstone building abutting the main precinct. Unlike the old Police Athletic League gyms of my youth, this new complex boasted state-of-the-art equipment, a lap pool, and air conditioning. Also, in contrast to the VFW halls and community centers in which I'd fought, there was a boxing ring with ropes that weren't frayed and leather turnbuckles that weren't cracked.

I pushed through the club's gleaming glass doors. As I'd hoped, the place was nearly deserted on a Sunday. Even the few cops lifting weights or using the machines seemed impelled more by rote routine than a desire for a real workout.

As I walked past the racks of free weights, I remembered that the last time I was here was with Eleanor Lowrey. We'd agreed to meet and work out together, which led to that first night in her apartment. The beginning of our relationship.

Now, at her insistence, we were on a "break," something that was beginning to seem pretty permanent. Especially after what Polk told me about her visits to her former lover up in state prison.

Then there was Gloria Reese, and whatever the hell was going on with that…

I kept a set of gym clothes in the locker room, so I changed quickly, geared up with training tape and gloves, and went out on the floor. For a good twenty minutes, I worked the speed bag. Hard.

Then, the sting of healthy sweat in my eyes, I climbed up into the ring and started shadow-boxing. Throwing combinations at invisible opponents. Bobbing and weaving, though not as steadily or cleanly as usual, due to fatigue, probably. And the distraction of unwanted thoughts was dulling my reflexes, playing havoc with my concentration.

I was just about to call it quits when a young voice shouted at me from outside the ring. Gasping, I walked to the ropes and looked down at a muscular guy in his mid-twenties, in sweat shorts and sleeveless Steelers tee-shirt. He also wore a boyish grin that belied his formidable appearance.

"Ya wanna spar some, mister?"

"I don't know. You look pretty tough."

He laughed dismissively. "C'mon, I'm talkin' about some light sparrin' here. Just foolin' around."

Still, I hesitated.

He took another step closer to the ring. "Look, I'm goin' nuts just hittin' the bag. Know what I mean?"

"Yeah, I guess I do."

Now my reluctance felt unwarranted. So, finally, I nodded. "Okay, sure. Maybe for a couple minutes."

"Great, thanks!"

I watched him climb up between the ropes. He outweighed me by about thirty pounds, all of it muscle, and the way he tapped his gloves together confirmed that he probably knew his way around a ring. It also seemed more aggressive than necessary.

But what bothered me the most was the abrupt change in his demeanor—the look of grim determination on his face.

"What's your name, son?" I said as we touched gloves.

"Don't matter. We ain't gonna be friends."

Before I could react to the sudden malice in his tone, he threw a right cross to my jaw that nearly knocked me on my ass. I staggered back, eyes blurring from the impact. Hands coming up in front of me for protection. Blocking his next series of blows with my forearms.

What the hell—?

He tried another right to my head, but telegraphed it enough that I could duck under it.

Then, surprisingly light on his feet, he danced away.

"Whoa…" My voice choked, shaky. "We're just sparring, for Christ's sake. Take it easy."

"Fuck you, man." Bouncing on the balls of his feet. Throwing a few air-punches. Enjoying himself.

Gulping air, I kept my distance from him, my mind quickly hitting the reset button. Because we sure as hell weren't sparring. For some reason, I'd been suckered into a real fight.

I ignored the pain shooting up the side of my face and went on offense. I knew I had no choice. Meanwhile, my bruised ribs were screaming in pain. Because he was younger and stronger than me, my only chance was to try to put him away fast. Or else get hammered.

So I went in quick and hard. A solid jab that took him by surprise, then another, even as I felt the pain in my ribs worsening, my legs starting to wobble.

Gasping, sweat pouring down my face, I risked it all and went with an uppercut. It missed by inches, and my momentum behind the swing threw me off-balance.

That was all the kid needed. He drove his right fist into my gut, pushing the air out of me, bringing a hoarse cry I didn't even recognize from the deepest part of me.

I crumpled to the canvas, heaving, my whole body shuddering from the pain, sweat dripping from my forehead in thick drops.

My head down, eyes lidded, I didn't even see the kid standing over me. But I could hear his heavy breathing, smell the sweat sheening his face and exposed arms.

Unlike what you see in the movies, a blow to the *solar plexus* can be paralyzing. You fight for every breath and against waves of nausea. And I was doing both.

When I finally managed to raise my head, I saw the kid looking off, past the ropes. Wincing, I shifted position enough to follow his gaze.

There was a man in gray slacks and a collared shirt sitting on a bench at the far wall. It wasn't until he got to his feet, his intense, knowing eyes meeting mine, that I recognized him.

"Thanks, kid," said Sebastian Maddox. "Nice work."

"Easiest hundred bucks I ever made, mister." The young guy broke into a grin. Not so boyish this time.

He gave me one last condescending look and climbed out of the ring. I was still crouched on the canvas, trying to catch my breath, to will myself to get up, when Maddox took a small step forward. Hands in his pockets.

"Tell you the truth, Danny, I thought you'd put up more of a fight."

"Happy to have a re-match sometime," I managed to say between labored gasps. "With *you*."

He shook his head gravely. "And here I thought this little attitude adjustment would help you to see things more clearly."

I gulped more air. "What the hell are you talking about?"

"You don't know? This was payback for ruining my plans with the Palermo kid. I don't take that kind of thing lightly."

"But how…how…?"

"How did I know where you were? I'm afraid I did it the old-fashioned way. I was watching your house since early this morning. When you drove away with that cop, I followed. Then when you came in here, so did I. Watching you work out from that corner back there."

I took a quick glance around the gym, hoping someone might be seeing this. Listening. But the boxing ring was in a back corner, away from the maze of equipment. Moreover, by now it was lunchtime, leaving only a few guys in the place, lifting free weights on the other side of the room. Far out of earshot.

Despite the pain radiating from my gut, I tried to bring a measured rhythm to my breathing.

"And the kid…?" I said. "My sparring partner…?"

Maddox shrugged. "I never got his name, though he told me his dad was a cop. That's why he gets to use this gym. Anyway, when I offered him a hundred in cash to teach you a lesson, he jumped at the chance. Greedy bastard didn't even ask why. I swear, I don't understand young people today."

By now, I'd recovered enough to get to my feet, gloved hands pulling me up on the ropes. Maddox was so close. All I had to do was get down from the ring, then—

Maddox smiled when he saw this and turned away, heading for the nearby exit door. Then he stopped for a moment, looking back at me over his shoulder.

"By the way, Danny, I hope this proves how easy it is for me to get to you. Anytime, anywhere. But not now. And not soon. Your end will come when it suits me, and not before."

The feeling had returned to my limbs, and I began to climb awkwardly out between the ropes. To my horror, my bruised body moved as slowly as if made of concrete.

He paused, enjoying my struggle. His hand on the door-knob.

"Oh, I almost forgot. The next one? Won't be a patient. Someone a lot closer to home. Just to mix things up a bit."

By the time I'd made it down from the ring, he'd gone out the door. I crossed the room as quickly as I could and followed him out into the noonday sun.

I looked up and the down the street.

Maddox had disappeared, as though he'd never been.

• • ● • •

A few minutes later, I was standing under a steaming shower in the gym. Everything hurt like hell, the stinging pain a seeming rebuke for my foolhardiness in agreeing to spar with that smiling young ape in the first place.

Back in my street clothes, I used the gym's phone to call for an Uber. It arrived in a matter of minutes, and I slid into the backseat. As we headed across town for the Liberty Bridge and home, I closed my eyes and tried to calibrate my breathing. Slow, deep inhalations, followed by equally slow exhalations. Though I doubted it would do much good.

I was right. Before too long, I could feel my tired limbs stiffen, my muscles aching under the skin. My body's expected response to the punishment I'd taken in the ring.

As the dull throb of insistent, deep-tissue pain coursed

through me, I found myself wondering if I had any analgesic meds back at the house. I'd gotten a prescription some time back, but couldn't remember now if there were any pills left.

As my driver made his way up to Grandview, I replayed my conversation with Maddox in the gym. His boast about how easy it was to get to me. Any time he wanted. As always, his goal was to mess with my head, to feed a growing sense of powerlessness.

Mine was not to let him.

The moment I came through the front door I was met by both Gloria Reese and Lyle Barnes, sharing the same anxious look.

"Where the hell have you been?" Gloria said sharply. "We figured you'd be back long before now—"

She stopped abruptly, having registered my bruised face, my careful gait. Instead, Barnes spoke next.

"What happened to you downtown, son? Unless Pittsburgh PD's got some secret goon squad I don't know about…"

I explained quickly, including the last thing Maddox said to me. His threat that the next victim would be closer to home.

"Yes, but what does that mean?" Gloria sat on an arm of the sofa. "A friend, a colleague?"

"No idea." I could tell my brain was still clouded, as though drugged. Which reminded me.

"I'm going to see what I have in the bathroom." I headed for the hallway. "For the pain."

"You'll also need to attend to those bruises," Gloria said.

Barnes rubbed his chin. "If you don't mind, Agent Reese, how about playing nurse again while I keep monitoring the Doc's laptop? Plus, I'm just starting to make some headway pulling data on this Maddox creep."

Gloria smiled her agreement and went with me once again into the bathroom. I resumed my previous position on the edge of the tub while she rummaged through my medicine cabinet. Within moments she found what she was looking for.

"Okay, Rinaldi." Gloria turned, laden with swabs, tubes of cream, and small brown bottles. "Off with your shirt. And don't worry, I'll try to control myself."

I gingerly slipped out of my jacket and peeled off my shirt, each movement sending shivers of pain through my arms and torso. Glancing in the mirror over the sink, I saw a patchwork of gray, angry bruises and splotches of reddened skin.

"Don't tell me," she said, beginning to apply one of the creams. "I should see the other guy."

"Nope. Truth is, the other guy looks fine. I pretty much got clobbered."

"Serves you right, Danny. It was a dumb thing to do."

I was too tired to argue with her, especially since I knew she was right. Sparring with that guy was dumb. Besides, as Barnes had pointed out, I wasn't getting any younger.

She'd returned to the medicine cabinet and found some surgical tape and adhesive, and was now carefully bandaging my ribs. Other than her bemused murmurs of disapproval and my occasional wince of pain when she touched a particularly tender area, the whole procedure was pretty much wordless.

Finally, she sat back to observe her handiwork.

"It could be worse. If I hadn't run out of bandages, you'd be a spitting image of the Mummy."

"Hilarious." I nodded at the medicine cabinet. "You didn't happen to find any pain meds in there?"

"Just Motrin. I'd take a few and try to get some sleep."

She handed me the bottle. "I'm serious, Danny. You took a helluva beating. If you weren't in such great shape, you'd be in much worse shape." A warm smile. "If you know what I mean."

I nodded, and slowly climbed to my feet.

"Thanks, Gloria," I said quietly. "I mean, for everything. This thing with Maddox...helping me the way you are. It's... well, just know how much I appreciate it."

Her smile broadened. "Your tax dollars at work."

She put her palm against my bare chest, letting it linger there for a long moment. Then, without another word, she turned and left the room.

Chapter Twenty-one

Suddenly famished, I went into the kitchen to make myself something to eat. That's when I saw Lyle Barnes through the sliding glass door leading to my rear deck. His back to me, he was leaning against the pinewood railing.

He turned when I joined him there, a half-eaten sandwich in his hand. Obviously, we'd had the same idea.

"I've always liked this deck you got here, Doc." He chewed reflectively. "Good place for a man to think."

"About Sebastian Maddox?"

He nodded, then squinted out at the sun-drenched day. A vault of blue sky backed a meager threading of clouds, offering the hope of more dry days ahead. Not always the norm for a Pittsburgh spring. But at least for today, the Three Rivers sparkled below us as though requisitioned by the chamber of commerce. And the array of new office buildings at the Point, polished to a sheen by the recent rains, glistened in the sun.

"He's out there somewhere." Barnes lay his unfinished sandwich on the railing, then brushed crumbs from his shirt.

"And I'm stuck here with my head up my ass, wondering where. Just as I used to wonder about the serial killers the Bureau was after. I'd profile the unknown suspect, based on the usual psych parameters and historic data, but I still knew most of it was guesswork. While our agents in the field were flying blind. All of us aware that with every passing day we were giving the sick bastard another opportunity to act."

"At least we know who the guy is."

"Yeah. With Maddox, it isn't about profiling, it's about research. Learning everything we can about him to help us try to anticipate his next move. And unlike a serial, he's not killing indiscriminately. He's targeting specific people in your life."

"And *getting* to them…"

Barnes grunted. "We'll find the bastard, I promise."

"Maybe. But that's what I'm worried about, Lyle. If we do find him, if he's cornered…I can't say why, but I get the feeling he'd want to go out in a blaze of glory. That he'd never be willing to go back to prison. This time, maybe on Death Row."

The other man managed a wry smile. "Funny you should say that. I've had the same vibe for a while now. This whole thing has 'end game' written all over it. I knew perps like that. Guys who'd never allow themselves to be apprehended. And if it looked like they *were* going down, they'd take as many people with them as possible."

"Christ, this just gets better and better."

We lapsed into a long silence, both of us distractedly watching as a flock of birds crossed the sky. Until Barnes stifled a yawn.

I saw my opening. "You get any sleep last night, Lyle?"

"Define your terms."

"You know what I mean. Are you having symptoms?"

"On and off, the past couple weeks. But nothing I can't handle. It's not like before."

I stared at the side of his angular face till he turned.

"I'm telling the truth, Doc. Your patient is doing fine. A satisfied customer." An unconvincing smile. "I'd be happy to recommend you to all the screwed-up ex-agents I know. Which is pretty much all of them."

His smile faded as he put a hand on my forearm.

"Let's face it, Daniel. We have bigger fish to fry, as my old man used to say."

"I know. I just—"

"Besides," he went on, "*I'm* not the one who looks all beat to shit. If anyone needs sleep…"

"Yeah, I know that, too. Maybe I'll try to grab a few hours… as long as you or Gloria keep monitoring my laptop. Maddox is going to make his next move soon. I can feel it."

"Don't worry, Agent Reese and I are all over this. Though before you sack out, I think you should cancel tomorrow's patients. Maybe even for the whole week."

"I already considered that. Probably a good idea. Nobody's in a particular crisis at the moment…"

Barnes gave me a frank look. "You mean, besides you?"

I returned the look. "Point taken."

I pushed off from the railing and was about to go back inside when another thought occurred to me.

"I just realized, Gloria will have to return to the office tomorrow. She's a senior field agent, and the Bureau's probably working its usual load of cases—"

"Then it'll just have to get along without her for a while. She told me she took some overdue vacation time."

I frowned. "Hardly a vacation."

He offered me an enigmatic shrug, then turned once again to stare out at the uncommonly peaceful day.

Using the landline again, I called all of the upcoming week's patients and cancelled their appointments. Then, after staving off my hunger with a simple ham sandwich, I padded into the bedroom. The afternoon sun streamed through the window, so I drew the shutters, plunging the room into soothing darkness.

I stripped and climbed under the sheets. Gratefully closing my eyes, and hoping that my wired brain would at least let me rest…

It was the last thing I remember thinking, until the sound of the shutters opening roused me from sleep. At first, I covered my eyes, expecting the room to be flooded with light.

But, instead, it was as dark as before, if not more so. When I glanced at the window, I saw that night had fallen. I realized I must have been asleep for hours. The rest of the day, in fact.

Still groggy, I pulled myself up to my elbows. It was only then that I turned my head, and noticed that I wasn't alone in the bed.

As my eyes adjusted to the dark, I made out Gloria's oval face. Her searching gaze offset by a wry, beautiful smile.

Even partially concealed under the covers, I could tell that she was naked.

"Somebody needed his beauty sleep." Her voice softly mocking. She stirred then, pushing the covers away. The smooth curves of her body barely visible in the dimness.

Before I could form words, she put her finger to my lips.

"Keep it down, okay? The door's locked and the old man is in the front room, but he isn't deaf."

"But...I mean, Maddox...Has he—?"

"Nothing, Danny. Not a peep. I watched the laptop the whole time you were asleep."

I shook my head to clear it. "I had no idea I'd sleep so long... Must've been more wrecked than I thought."

"Yeah..." Her voice changed, lowered. "Must've been..."

She moved stealthily on the bed, until her body was on top of mine. I felt the pressure of her small breasts against me, the languorous touch of her legs scissoring mine. Then her full lips pressing down, a hungry kiss that was like a jolt to my heart. Despite myself, I melted into it. Savored it.

I took hold of her shoulders—like the rest of her, slender but strong—and gently pushed her up.

"Look..." My words a weary rasp. "I'm pretty banged up...I mean, I don't know if I can..."

Suddenly I felt her hand encircle my urgent erection.

"You don't, eh?" she whispered. "Looks like your cock didn't get the memo."

With that, she slid down and took me in her mouth.

My thoughts shredded, fell away as I lay back and let myself become lost in the sensation...

And then she reared up, face near to mine. We kissed again, harder this time. And then I was inside her, all of me, deep, reveling in her moist warmth. Her muffled gasps as we fell naturally, wordlessly, into a rolling, measured rhythm.

It was strangely exhilarating, the exquisite charge of our lovemaking blending with the sharp twinges of pain as my body's bruises protested. Our hearts pounding even as we kept our voices constrained. Our urgent cries muted.

We clung to each other, seeking solace in our entwined bodies, a barrier of flesh and desire against the horrors we'd faced. And those that lay ahead.

Afterwards, I cradled her in my arms, enveloped by the comforting darkness. I wanted to stay that way forever. I said as much. Gloria murmured her agreement, and snuggled in closer.

I closed my eyes. For once, I wasn't thinking like a therapist. Assessing, interpreting. Wondering how this had happened. So suddenly, unexpectedly. Yet maybe there was nothing to wonder about. Sometimes the body has its own wisdom.

But what did this mean for Eleanor Lowrey and me? If anything? At this point, I didn't know whether what we had now could even be called a relationship anymore. Especially given her renewed feelings for her former lover.

Putting these thoughts aside, I turned and kissed Gloria.

"Delicious," she whispered. "And I wouldn't mind going another round, but..."

"Yeah, I know. Reality's on the other side of that door, and, like it or not, it's waiting for us."

She nodded ruefully. But before stirring, she returned my kiss with a long, slow one of her own.

Then, as we started to climb out of bed, I winced.

"Jesus." I gingerly rubbed my bandaged ribs. "It's not like I wasn't sore enough before…"

"What did I tell you?" A knowing wink. "Small but mighty."

We each dressed quickly and went down the hall to the front room. Now in a sweater, slacks, and loafers, Barnes was leaning forward on the sofa, staring at my laptop on the coffee table. His arm in its sling propped on one bony knee.

"Interesting career track, our Mr. Maddox." Other than a brief nod to acknowledge our presence, he didn't move a muscle. "From age seven or so. Makes for fascinating reading."

Gloria planted herself on the cushions next to him. "I'd settle for the CliffsNotes version again."

Not me. I wanted as much history as I could get. There might be something in Maddox's past that could help us. Give us a way into his psyche. Or at least reveal repetitive patterns of behavior. *Anything.*

But before I could make my case, the landline on my rolltop desk rang.

Equally startled, we three exchanged worried looks. Then I strode to the desk and looked at the phone display.

It was Noah Frye. I picked up. His frantic, breathy voice was barely intelligible.

"Danny, it's me! Have you seen Charlene?"

"What? Noah, slow down—"

"It's my Charlene! She never came home after having dinner with her brother tonight. I called Skip and he said she left hours ago."

"Have you tried calling her?"

"Yes! YES! I'm crazy, not stupid. But there's no answer from her cell…Danny, she'd never—"

I could hardly speak myself, dread choking my throat. It was Maddox. It had to be.

"Oh, Jesus…Oh, Christ…" Noah was almost babbling now. "What happened to Charlene, Danny? Where the hell is she?"

Chapter Twenty-two

A half-hour later I was weaving down the hill from Grandview Avenue, my high beams poking twin holes in the resolute darkness. The twinkling lights moving slowly across the bridge below revealed much more traffic than I would have expected for a Sunday night. Not good.

After I'd hung up with Noah, I hurriedly checked my office voice mail for some message from Maddox, informing me that he had Charlene Hines, and what he intended to do with her. But there was nothing. Meanwhile, Barnes and Gloria were peering anxiously at my laptop, which remained silent, its screen blank.

"Check your cells," I said. "Just in case he's identified them and hacked in."

They each flipped through their respective phones. Again, nothing. No images or audio.

"Doesn't mean anything." Gloria pocketed her cell. "Maddox might still be setting up the scenario for her death. After what happened with the Palermo kid, he's not gonna take any chances."

"I agree," said Barnes. "The prick won't get in touch till he's good and ready."

I nodded. "Then call me when he does."

I grabbed up one of the prepaid cell phones that Barnes had brought, pulled on my jacket, and headed for the door.

"Where the hell are you going?" he said.

"Down to the bar in case Noah freaks out and does something stupid. I mean, to himself. He's tried it before."

Gloria frowned. "Yeah, what's the story with this guy Noah? I've been wondering."

"Years ago he was a patient at Ten Oaks, the clinic where I interned. He's a paranoid schizophrenic, suffering from persecutory delusions. Once, during a psychotic episode, he got a hammer and some nails from a construction site and went around asking people to please crucify him."

She stared. "So he's obsessed with…crucifixion?"

"Among other things. But he's been stable for years, thanks to his meds, and I want to make sure he stays that way."

Barnes took hold of my arm. "Understood. But you're taking your damn car?"

At my puzzled look, he released his grip, but kept the grim determination in his voice.

"Maddox said he followed you this morning when he saw you and Polk get in the unmarked, right?"

"Yeah. Tailed us to the precinct, then followed me after that to the police gym."

"But how could he have known Polk was coming to pick you up today? That the cops wanted to question you about the Steadman girl's murder?"

Gloria spoke up. "Maybe I was right and Maddox *has* hacked into the Pittsburgh PD system."

"He probably has. And maybe that's why he was parked across the street at the crack of dawn. Lucky for him, he got here in time to see you and Polk head out. But if I'm right, he was outside the house bright and early this morning for *another* reason. To put a tracking device on your car. If I was Maddox, that's what I'd do. Remember who we're dealing with, Doc."

I'd no sooner voiced my agreement than Gloria was striding for the door.

"Try the wheel wells first, Reese," Barnes called after her.

"Plus he could've jimmied his way inside and planted it under the dashboard."

"I've done this before, old man," she said over her shoulder. Then, to herself, but for our benefit: "Jesus."

I quickly followed her outside, my porch light the only illumination in the deepening darkness. Gloria had just gotten a heavy-duty flashlight from her own car at the curb and was trotting back to my Mustang in the driveway.

As I watched, she bent and aimed the flashlight beam under the left rear wheel. Then, with unhurried and practiced skill, she checked each wheel well. After that, she rolled on her back and shone her light up at the car's undercarriage. Inching her way along the length of the chassis. Satisfied, she got to her feet again and held out her hand to me.

"Keys?"

I got them out of my jacket pocket and tossed them over. Without another word, she opened the driver's side door and began examining the Mustang's cramped interior. Five minutes later, she poked her head out of the car and smiled. In her hand was a small metallic device with a miniature antenna.

"GPS tracker. State-of-the-art." She climbed back out of the car. "It was hidden under the passenger side seat. I've left it turned on, so Maddox won't know we found it. He'll think your car's still sitting in your driveway."

I squinted at the device in her palm. "Thanks, Gloria."

"Thank the old man. Because he's right, Danny. We can't afford to underestimate Maddox." Her eyes grew solemn. "The fucker's determined."

All I could do was nod. Then, with a somber smile, Gloria gave me back my keys. But before I got behind the wheel, she squeezed my arm. Same place that Barnes had, but it felt a helluva lot different.

"Do I have to tell you to be careful, Doctor?"

"Never hurts to be reminded." I bent so that our foreheads touched. "Just make sure you call me if you hear from Maddox."

• ● ● ● •

Noah closed up at midnight on Sunday nights, so there was still an hour to go when I pulled to the curb twenty feet from the entrance. But coming through the door, I noticed only two tables in use and a half-dozen drinkers at the bar.

What surprised me more was Noah himself, in his usual spot behind it. Calmly working the taps, chatting with a pair of boisterous customers as he filled their steins.

I crossed the room, about to call out to him, when I was met with an even bigger surprise. Charlene Hines, arms laden with a tray of drinks and burgers, bumping through the kitchen swinging doors with her generous hips. She gave me a friendly wink, then went on to serve a young couple at one of the tables.

My initial relief quickly gave way to anger. In two long strides, I reached the bar and slammed my hand down on its polished surface. Noah, startled, almost dropped the beer steins. His two customers had pretty much the same reaction.

I ignored them and gazed at my friend's perplexed face.

"What the fuck's going on, Noah? I thought—"

"What do ya mean, Danny?" Then, as realization dawned in his deep-set eyes, he broke into a grin. "Oh, yeah. That."

He kept the grin intact for his rattled customers.

"Nothin' to worry about, folks. Just a misunderstandin' between friends. Beers are on me."

Noah placed the mugs in front of the pair before moving down the length of the bar to where the stools were unoccupied. I followed him, then leaned across and gripped his shirt collar in both fists. Still steaming.

"Jesus, Noah, you scared the shit out of me. When you called and said Charlene was missing—"

"But that's just it, man. Turns out, she *wasn't* missin'. She's fine. After she left her brother's place, her car broke down. Plus her cell was outta juice. So she hadda flag somebody down— not as easy as you'd think, times bein' what they are, everybody all suspicious and weird nowadays—"

"Noah, goddam it…"

"Anyway, she used the guy's phone to call for help, and it took forever for the tow truck to come. When they got to the repair place, she called to let me know what happened. Man, was I relieved when I heard she was okay and everything was fine."

"You and me both, Noah." By now, I was starting to feel foolish, so I released my hold on his collar. "But why the hell didn't you call me back? Let me know Charlene was safe?"

"Oh." Another grin, more sheepish this time. "I guess I sorta forgot."

"You forgot?"

"Hey, dude, we got super busy in here and Charlene was AWOL. I had to hold down the fort all by myself. And as you know, I'm not real good at multi-taskin'."

I sat back on a stool, a long exhalation escaping me like air out of a tire. Though my temples still pounded.

"Now let me ask *you* a question, Danny." Noah made a point of looking appropriately offended as he adjusted his shirt. "What's got into you? *I'm* the one supposed to freak out on a regular basis, not you. *I'm* the fuckin' paranoid, remember? What the hell's *your* excuse?"

I had one, of course, but not something I could reveal.

"I'm sorry, man. You're right." I rubbed my forehead. "When I got your panicked phone call, I guess I overreacted."

"Ya think? Maybe you need one o' them chill pills they got nowadays. Before ya stroke out or somethin'. It's the silent killer, ya know. That or heart disease. I forget which."

"I hear you, Noah."

He sniffed loudly, apparently mollified, and stepped over to one of the taps. He put a foaming mug of Iron City in front of me, patted my shoulder solicitously, and ambled back down the bar to rejoin his customers. From their loud, slurred voices it was clear they'd already forgotten the previous incident. Drinks on the house are pretty good mollifiers, too.

Sipping my beer, I felt my pulse slowly return to normal. I didn't blame Noah for his confusion about my behavior. After all, he couldn't know why I'd reacted the way I did. That I'd thought Charlene's life was in danger.

I drained my beer and went around the counter to tap the keg for a refill. I remained behind the bar, sipping my beer, letting my thoughts drift.

Maddox had said his next target wouldn't be one of my patients. Rather, it would be someone "closer to home." That's why I responded so quickly when Noah called about Charlene. To my mind, she fit the bill.

Which meant Maddox had yet to claim his new victim. Or, if he had, he hadn't revealed who it was. At least, not yet.

I finished my second beer and went back to my seat on the stool. For the first time in twenty minutes or so, I looked up and noticed my surroundings. The two tables in the middle of the room were now empty, and the last few customers at the bar were paying their tabs. The place was finally closing up.

I spotted Charlene busing one of the tables, so I went over. She looked up from the stack of dishes and smiled.

"I'm glad you're okay," I said. "Noah was worried."

She chuckled. "Tell me about it. He practically hugged me to death when I finally showed up. But I'm sorry he worried you, too, Danny."

"Only added a few more gray hairs to the beard. You can't even notice."

"Truth is, he just now told me he never called you back to let you know I was okay. Classic Noah, the crazy S.O.B. But with Mr. Schizo, you gotta take the good with the bad. I figure you know that as well as anybody, right?"

I sighed. "Right."

She gave me a rueful look and shuffled off with her fully loaded tray toward the kitchen.

I was about to leave when I saw Noah again, alone on a bar stool, sipping a beer, the night's work over. I apologized again for my angry outburst earlier, then told him I had to go.

"Fine with me, man. I'm just sittin' here, shootin' the shit with Satan and his minions. See 'em? Two stools over."

I started, which brought out a booming laugh.

"Jesus, Danny, I'm fuckin' with ya. Don't worry, I told ya, I'm takin' my meds every day like a good boy. In fact, Dr. Nancy just sent over my refills."

"Yeah, well, make sure you take them."

He was still chuckling as I went out the door.

I hadn't driven two miles from Noah's place, heading east along the river on Second, when the burner cell rang. Taking a breath, I scooped it up and placed it in the dash holder. Pushed the button. Gloria answered.

"It's Maddox," she said simply. "Hold on."

Not knowing what to expect, I pulled the Mustang to the curb and killed the engine. With my anxiety spiking, I didn't want to have to focus on driving.

Gloria's terse voice came from the cell's speaker again.

"He's streaming a live image onto your laptop screen. I'm forwarding it to you now."

I bent toward the dash to better see the playing-card-sized image on the cell. Maddox's chiseled face, lips upturned in a self-assured grin, filled the entire screen.

"Hope you're still awake, Danny. 'Cause it's show-time. Ready for some Midnight Madness?"

My chest tightened, capturing my breath. Holding it there.

Suddenly, Maddox vanished from the screen, to be replaced by a somewhat grainy black-and-white image similar to the traffic camera image from the city street where Stephen Langley had been killed.

I leaned forward, eyes not five inches from the tiny cell screen. I was right, it was a live streaming image from a static security camera mounted high enough to capture a wide swath

of some shadowy, concrete interior. A parking garage, the lens'
angle revealing about a half-dozen vehicles in prominently
labeled spaces. High-end cars and SUVs, their skins buffed to a
proud gloss by the harsh fluorescent lights overhead.

For four or five long minutes, nothing happened. Then, in a
far corner, a set of elevator doors opened and two people came
out. A heavily built black man with a briefcase and a younger,
more slender woman.

It wasn't until the pair began walking toward the line of
parked cars that I recognized them. At the same time, Maddox's
voice crackled from the cell's speaker, narrating the scene in a
strange, stilted cadence.

After a moment, I got it. He was doing a bad impression of
Rod Serling, from the old *Twilight Zone* TV show.

"Witness, if you will," he intoned, "two of our city's finest
lawyers. Harvey Blalock, president of the Pittsburgh Black
Attorneys Association, and good friend of one Daniel Rinaldi,
psychologist and blatant self-promoter. Accompanying Mr.
Blalock is his new protégé, Lily Chen."

"Christ, no!" As though Maddox could hear me. But I knew
he couldn't, since I was getting picture and sound relayed from
my laptop. Which he probably assumed I was home watching.

And that was all I *could* do. Watch. Helpless, impotent.
Unable to intervene. Just as before.

"Rumored to be having an affair," Maddox droned on in
that horrible clipped voice, "Blalock and Chen have been
working late in the office tonight. Attending to important legal
matters, of course. Sharing briefs, if you get my drift."

Onscreen, Harvey and Lily exchanged a warm embrace
before separating to head for their respective cars. It was then
that I recognized Harvey's silver Lexus parked less than a dozen
yards away. And the lawyer was wasting no time walking
toward it.

I quickly reduced the image and tapped in Gloria's number.
She answered immediately. "Yes, we're seeing this, and—"

I interrupted her. "Listen, Gloria. You've got to call Blalock on his cell. Warn him."

"What's his number?"

I went to check my cell's contact list, but then remembered this wasn't my phone. It was one of the throwaway cells Barnes had bought. None of my usual numbers were programmed into it.

"I..." Trying to think. To remember Harvey's cell number. But I drew a blank. Having always used speed-dial to call him, I'd let the number slip from my memory.

"Wait a minute," I said to her. "Where's my cell? The one I smashed?"

"Still in pieces in the corner, where you swept it. I'm in the kitchen, looking at it now."

"Go check to see if the memory card is intact. If it is—"

"Right. I can put it in one of the prepaids here, pull up the number."

"Yes! Hurry!"

I restored the image from the parking garage security cam. By now, Harvey was approaching his car, arm outstretched, thumb tapping something in his hand, obviously using his remote to unlock the Lexus. At the same time, in the opposite corner of the streaming image, I could make out Lily Chen standing next to a dark Toyota Highlander, searching her purse for her keys.

Again, all this was occurring without sound, like an old silent movie. A particularly eerie silence that somehow enhanced the horror of the moment, my growing sense of dread.

A silence broken only by Maddox's cartoonish impression of Serling's voice, continuing on. Something about how Blalock's affair with the much-younger female lawyer mirrored my own relationship with Joy Steadman.

There it was, I thought. Like an Old Testament God, Maddox took delight in punishing sinners whose supposed transgressions were similar. Again, his disordered mind using symmetry as a form of self-regulation. Reifying his sense of mastery, control.

I couldn't bear to listen to him anymore, so I reduced the image again. Still in contact with Gloria's cell.

Waiting.

"Okay, Danny," she said at last. "I switched memory cards and got the number."

She gave it to me and I clicked off, going back to the streaming image. Blalock stood at the driver's side door, reaching for the handle.

I quickly dialed his cell, and saw him glance down at his suit jacket's pocket. Obviously where his cell had started ringing. He drew it from his pocket, answered.

"Harvey, it's Daniel. You're in danger. You—"

"Danger?" He chortled. "Hell, man, that's my middle name. Besides, since when—?"

He opened his car door and got behind the wheel.

"Look," I said, "I don't know what he's got planned, but—"

"Who're we talking about, Danny?"

Through his windshield, I saw him reach to turn the key in the ignition.

Suddenly, Maddox's voice bellowed from my cell's speaker.

"Too late, Danny boy. Enjoy the fireworks."

I shouted into the phone. "Harvey, no! Don't—"

Blalock started his car.

Chapter Twenty-three

The explosion, terrible in its silence, had such acoustic force that the camera image jiggled for a moment. Then the Lexus was engulfed in flames, an angry blood-red fireball that sent spiraling ribbons of intense heat toward the roof.

"Oh, Christ, no!" My voice a croak, splintered like glass as I gazed in disbelief at the nightmarish image.

Suddenly, from the other side of the garage, Lily Chen came running toward the flaming car. Brushed back by the searing heat, she fell to her knees on the concrete floor, mouth wide in a silent scream. Her hands to her face.

"Hey, Danny." Maddox had abruptly reappeared on-screen, replacing the video feed. Eyes as bright and incendiary as the carnage I'd just witnessed. "This one turned out so well, I might just post it on YouTube. What do you think? Too much?"

He burst into a loud, shrill laugh, then vanished from the screen. Leaving me to stare at a small rectangle of gray.

Like a dam breaking, an intolerable rage flowed over me. I cried out in frustration and started pounding the steering wheel with my fist, ignoring the pain from my fight in the gym shooting up my arm, radiating across my bruised ribs.

Harvey Blalock was dead. A friend of mine killed simply for the crime of *being* my friend.

I finally quieted, gasping, my throbbing hand resting on the wheel. Harvey Blalock had always been so *alive*, so full of the juice of life. And now, suddenly, he was gone.

How many more victims would Maddox claim? Friends of mine. Patients, past or present. Colleagues.

I leaned back in the seat, feeling the blood leave my face. I kept picturing Harvey. His easy laugh. His wry, uncompromising intelligence. The respect he'd worked so hard to attain. The wife and children he'd left behind.

For a fleeting moment, I couldn't believe he was really dead. That what I'd seen had actually happened.

But it had.

Closing my eyes, filled with an aching despair, I prayed to the God I no longer believed in. For help. For solace.

And got the answer I expected.

I was still parked at the curb on Second Avenue when Gloria called again.

"I'm so sorry about your friend." Her voice low, tentative. "I won't pretend to know what you're going through."

"I appreciate that, Gloria. What's Barnes doing?"

"Poring over his research on Maddox's life. Collating all the salient material."

I nodded to myself. Knowing Lyle Barnes, I figured that the only way he knew how to deal with his own sense of helplessness was to keep busy. Keep working the problem.

"Are you heading back home?" Gloria asked.

"In a while. But let me know—"

"Don't worry, I will."

After we hung up, I sat for a few minutes, simply staring out my windshield. Then I opened the car door and stepped out under a cold, star-swept arch of sky. To my left, on the other side of Second Avenue, the Monongahela River flowed gently, ceaselessly, as it has since before the first settlers came.

I crossed the street and stood at its bank, atop the slope of grass that met a set of timbers inlaid in the soil. Tar-spackled and weathered by a half-century of rain and sun, the old black wood braced itself in terraced steps against the implacable push of the river.

Across its width was the newly gentrified South Side, most of its lights dimmed, businesses closed for the night. Forty years ago, it was the site of Jones & Laughlin, a seventeen-mile-long stretch of steel mills whose smokestacks funneled coal dust and blast furnace exhaust into Pittsburgh's leaden skies. Today it boasted trendy shops and restaurants, clubs catering to students from Pitt and CMU, and much cleaner air.

Now, the Steel City almost seemed more defined by what was gone than by what had been. Progress, of a kind, no doubt.

Hugging myself against the wind and the night's chill, I watched the luminous eddies formed by moonlight in the sluggish waters. Breathed in the oily river smells. Heard the urgent cries of the night birds.

These sights and sounds seemed to ground me. Anchor my mind against its desire to drift, to spin away, to embrace a futile denial. Instead, I tried to make sense of the sequence of events of the past days. How what started as an attempt to decipher the meaning hidden in the case notes of my wife's death years ago had turned into a relentless cat-and-mouse game with her killer.

As a therapist, I was quite familiar with the idea of the past invading the present. But in the case of Sebastian Maddox, it had taken on a tangible and horrific reality. And, as I'd believed was true for Lyle Barnes, I now realized that my only respite from the anguish of that reality was action.

To do that, I'd have to get inside Maddox's head, the way he'd gotten into mine. Before the number of deaths escalated.

The guttural sound of an engine out on the water suddenly drew my attention. As the small cruiser approached, its blinding spotlight and illuminated Departmental insignia identified it as a Pittsburgh River Police boat.

Pinned within a blazing white circle of light, I squinted at the man standing on the craft's forward deck. I could just make out enough to register that he was squinting back.

"Hey, buddy! Not for nothin', but watcha doin' there, eh?" Those flat Pittsburgh vowels. Third-generation, at least.

"Just looking at the river, Officer." My voice upraised against the motor's idling roar.

The boat's pilot, invisible behind the cabin windows, cut the engine. Bobbing slightly, the cruiser floated closer to the shoreline. The surefooted officer swayed along with it.

"Ya don't hafta stand so close to look at the goddam river, mister." As the boat drifted toward me, the cop's face and body became more distinct. Both were full, fleshy. "That grass there is real slippy. Ya could fall right in, and ya don't wanna do that. River's cold as ice, night like tonight."

"Look, my name's Daniel Rinaldi, and I—"

"Never heard o' ya."

"I mean, I work with the—"

"Hell, I don't care what your story is. I just want your ass back up on the road and away from my river. Got it?"

"Got it, Officer."

I turned and worked my way carefully up from the mound of grass and onto the berm of the road. As if asserting its authority, the cruiser emitted a couple of short horn blasts.

Offering a quick wave in return, I walked back across the street and got behind the wheel of my car. Strapping on my seat belt, I felt another spasm of pain from my ribs. And my hand still throbbed from when I'd pounded the steering wheel.

There was no getting around it. Each one of my forty-plus years rebelled against the punishment I'd taken from that young punk in the ring. But, unlike the psychic pain dished out by Maddox, eating at my soul like battery acid, at least I could do something about the physical kind.

Putting the car in gear, I headed back along Second, but didn't turn onto the bridge. Instead, I drove downtown, straight to Pittsburgh Memorial, where there was a guy I knew...

● ● ● ● ●

His name was Marone, a doctor about ten years my senior who worked in the ER. A fellow Pitt grad I'd met some time ago at an alumni function, he had sunken cheeks and wounded, evasive eyes. I didn't know much about him, other than he was twice-divorced.

As I'd hoped, he was on duty, even at two in the morning. Pulling double shifts, he'd once explained, to cover the brutal alimony and child-support checks. Without asking any questions, he prescribed some pain meds, which I got filled at the all-night pharmacy next door. More surprisingly, he didn't give me the standard lecture about my apparent inability to stay the hell out of harm's way. Probably because the place was too busy. Or else, like a number of my other acquaintances, he'd given up on me long ago.

It was nearing three a.m. when I finally got home. As expected, Lyle Barnes was on Gloria's laptop at the kitchen table, empty mug beside him. The equally empty carafe in the coffeemaker on the counter testified to how much caffeine the ex-FBI man had consumed.

I understood. For a person still struggling with night terrors, awake was always better.

"I'll have a pretty complete picture of our guy ready for you by morning." Barnes barely looked up from the screen. "Meanwhile, you and Agent Reese oughtta get some sleep."

As if to emphasize his point, Gloria came down the hall from the bathroom, rubbing her eyes. Barefoot, in jeans and a Penguins tee-shirt, and with her hair pulled back in a ponytail, she looked much younger than her thirty years.

When she saw me, her face softened.

"I keep thinking about Harvey Blalock. It was so…"

"I know. I'm still in shock. Harvey was a good guy. This'll kill his family." I shook my head.

She and I just stood there, a few feet apart. Neither of us moving toward the other. As though frozen in sorrow. At a loss.

Finally, head still buried in his work, Barnes spoke sharply. "For Christ's sake, go ahead and hug each other or some damned thing. I'm not an idiot."

Gloria and I exchanged wan smiles, and then did as Lyle had suggested. It felt good having her in my arms again.

At last, Barnes looked up from the laptop. The creases on his lined face seeming to have deepened.

"I'm sorry about your friend, too, Doc. But at least he died quick. Instantly."

"It's cold comfort."

"In this life, sometimes that's the only comfort you get."

I said nothing. Just gave Gloria a quick squeeze, after which she drifted from my embrace. Both of us aware of Barnes' steady, noncommittal gaze.

He broke the silence with a feigned irritation in his voice. "Now will you two both get out of here so I can work in peace? I'll let you know if—"

He leveled a baleful look at my laptop, which he'd placed next to Gloria's on the table. She and I joined him in gazing at its opened lid.

Barnes cleared his throat. "That is, *when* he makes contact again. After what he did to Blalock, he might want to savor what he imagines Danny's reaction to be. Let us sweat it out a little before calling again."

"That's just it." Gloria took a seat next to Barnes. "It could be hours, it could be days. Jesus, it's the not knowing that makes me crazy. I'm not good at waiting for the next bad thing to happen. I'm better at facing it right now and doing something about it."

I nodded. "That's what he's counting on, Gloria. If he keeps us in the dark as to when and where he'll strike next, it ratchets up our anxiety. Our sense of vulnerability. It's like an inversion of what behavior psychologists call 'intermittent reinforcement.'"

"Which means what…?"

"By staying silent for varying amounts of time, Maddox has gotten us hooked. We have to wait, but we don't know for how long. Yet we have no choice. Because if we do miss his next message, we miss learning the identity of his next victim. As well as any chance to prevent the death."

A sullen silence fell over the three of us. Gloria slumped in her chair, while Barnes just keep tugging at his chin. Too wired to sit, I turned to the counter and reached for the coffee carafe before remembering that it was empty.

Instead, I got a glass of water from the sink and tossed a couple of the prescription pain meds in my mouth. Maybe not the best idea when I was already so exhausted, and had three beers in me as well, but I realized Barnes had probably been right. Sleep might be just what my battered body—and mind—needed at the moment.

The older man gave me a wry smile.

"With any luck, those things'll knock you out for a while. Meanwhile, I've still got biographical research on the tricky bastard I want to organize and collate."

I considered this. "Maybe you ought to finish that up back at your motel. You, too, Gloria. Time for both of you to get out of here. At least till morning. Which brings up something I've been thinking about."

Arms folded, I regarded them both carefully.

"Listen, when it comes down to it, this is between Maddox and me. I mean, I really appreciate all you two have done to help, but I can't ask you to…well…After all, you do have lives, and I've got no right to ask you to—"

Barnes bristled. "Do me a favor, will ya, Doc? Shut the hell up and go to bed."

I turned and gave Gloria a quizzical look.

"I agree with the old man," she said. "I'm here for the duration."

I let out a long breath.

"I…both of you…I don't know how to thank you."

"We'll figure something out," Barnes said. "Personally, I wouldn't mind a tasteful gift basket. But not till after we nail the crazy prick. Now scoot!"

Five minutes later, I'd stripped and was buried under the covers. Gloria came into the bedroom moments later, stepped out of her own clothes, and curled up next to me.

"I thought you were going back to your hotel," I said.

"I am. In a minute. Or five."

A long beat of silence.

"Funny." She stifled a yawn. "We barely know each other, really, and yet...well, here we are..."

I nodded. "Here we are."

She took my hand and brought it around her body, cupping her breast. Holding it there.

Despite my deep, lingering sorrow about Blalock, I felt the stirrings of arousal.

"Damn thing has a mind of its own," I said.

"They usually do. But you're not there, are you?"

"Not really. I keep thinking about...everything. Especially Harvey. I'm sorry, but would you take a rain check?"

She snuggled closer. "I was just going to ask you the same thing. I'm pretty beat, and..."

Her nipple stiffened against my palm. Then, abruptly, we were kissing. Hungrily, urgently. My lips tracing a path from between her breasts down to her smooth, hard belly, and then lower. Taking my time until I heard her gasp, and felt her deep, convulsive shudder.

I entered her then. Our bodies now welded together, finding a charged, undulating rhythm. The sudden, wordless lovemaking fueled by grief, the ache of loss.

Finally, spent, we lay in each other's arms. After a long moment, her sleepy eyes found mine.

"You know, I'm starting to wonder what *non*-crisis sex with you would be like."

I smiled a reply, as she yawned again. Gloria said nothing more, and within a matter of seconds had dozed off.

I knew I should have woken her, sent her on her way. Instead, I merely listened to the soothing cadence of her breathing, as the potent medication began to ease my aching muscles. Not long after that, it lulled me to sleep.

Thankfully, even my psyche cooperated. If I *was* visited by nightmares, by a parade of horrific images spawned by the past days' events, I didn't remember them the next morning.

Although, when I awoke, I was alone.

Chapter Twenty-four

When I padded into the kitchen, I found that Lyle Barnes had made a full carafe of coffee before leaving. As I poured myself a steaming mug, squinting at the light glazing the bay window above the sink, my burner cell in the front room rang.

Coffee in hand, I went to answer it. Suddenly I was aware of how empty the house felt without the two of them. Shaking it off, I swallowed half the mug and picked up the cell.

"Where are you?" said Gloria.

"Home." I took a seat on the sofa.

"Listen, Barnes just called me from his motel room. Turn on the morning news. But stay on the phone."

I did as requested.

As expected, the lead story was about the violent death of Harvey Blalock, described by the anchor as "the noted Pittsburgh attorney and community leader." The reporter on-scene relayed what details were available about the tragedy in a somber voice as CSU techs, a platoon of cops, and various medical personnel trudged around behind her.

In a far corner, cordoned off by crime scene tape, were the twisted remains of the victim's Lexus. No doubt the station had been refused permission to show the security camera footage of the explosion itself, though that didn't mean a pirated copy of the parking garage video wouldn't find its way to the Internet.

After a brief retelling of Blalock's rise to prominence,

accompanied by stock footage of Harvey at various civic functions and still photos of his wife and children, the anchor added that the police were currently questioning a Ms. Lily Chen. A new young lawyer recently hired by the firm, she was the object of speculation concerning a possible affair with the deceased. When reached by the station, Chen, through her own attorney, refused to comment on "these spurious accusations." Nor would the Blalock family, who, through a spokesman, asked for privacy during this difficult time.

"Jesus," I said into the phone. "Poor Harvey."

"It'll be worse online." Gloria clucked her tongue. "That's where the gloves really come off. Where the trolls rule."

Just then, one of the other prepaid cells we'd left on the coffee table rang. It was Lyle Barnes. I put it on speaker.

"You watching this, Doc?"

"Yeah. And thanks for the coffee."

The TV station had cut to a live shot of the assistant chief, who described himself as a friend of the murdered man, and who reminded viewers and the press that the investigation into the bombing was in its early stages.

"While we just sit here, unable to render assistance." Barnes' voice was weary with disgust. "Knowing what we know, knowing who the bastard is, but…"

His words trailed off. Neither Gloria nor I said anything. Because there wasn't anything to say.

The station then ran a follow-up story about Robbie Palermo's kidnapping, including the breaking news that the family's stolen white van had been found. Some city workers had stumbled across it earlier this morning in a vast dump miles east of downtown. According to police sources, the vehicle had been torched, with gasoline the probable accelerant, eliminating the possibility of retrieving any useable evidence.

"Maddox isn't a fool," Barnes said. "If any forensics *had* been found, the cops might have been able to ID the prick. He's in the system."

"But what about the other white van?" I asked. "The one used in the Langley hit-and-run?"

I scooped up the remote and clicked around to some other local stations, but found no mention of that crime.

"Probably because there's nothing *to* report." Barnes grunted. "After a couple days, hit-and-runs kinda drop off the radar screen."

"Wait a minute," I said. "Here's something about it."

I turned up the volume on a report airing on an independent local channel. The female anchor was sharing the screen with a head shot of my late former patient.

"In other news, police sources confirm that the stolen van purportedly used in the hit-and-run death of Stephen Langley has been found in a junkyard in Braddock. The van has been impounded and the owner notified. However, preliminary reports indicate that whoever stole the van used some kind of bleach or solvent to clean the vehicle's interior. Which leaves investigators very little to go on. "

Gloria gave a short laugh. "What a surprise."

"When questioned by reporters," the anchor went on, "a police spokesman acknowledged that the van was similar to that used in the kidnapping of young Robbie Palermo. However, he stressed that they'd ruled out any connection between the two crimes, other than the coincidental use of stolen white vans. He also emphasized that experts estimate there are over thirty thousand white vans of various makes and models registered to drivers in Allegheny County alone."

I clicked off the TV.

"That's not just spin for the media," said Barnes. "I'm sure detectives have already questioned the families of both victims. Robbie's parents and whoever Langley leaves behind. My guess is, both parties are total strangers to each other. As far as the cops are concerned, there *isn't* a connection."

"Let's hope it stays that way." I got to my feet again. "If Maddox has even the suspicion that we've fed anything about him to the cops, God knows what he'll do. Maybe another bomb, maybe this time at the Mayor's office. Or a college campus."

Gloria sighed. "Part of me still thinks he's going to try something like that. Something big. In the end."

"But not till after I'm dead," I reminded her. "If nothing else, we can count on that."

I'd no sooner hung up from both calls when my landline rang. It was Angie Villanova, her usually gruff voice choked with grief.

"Jesus, Danny, have you seen the news? About Harvey?"

"Yes, I was just watching it. I'm stunned."

"It's…unbelievable. I mean, him and me weren't super close, but I sure as hell liked him. A tough son of a bitch, but he always played fair with the Department. Blalock was one of the good guys in a town not exactly overrun with 'em."

"I hear you."

"God forgive me, but I can't wait till they find the fucker who did this and stick a needle in his arm."

"That'd be too good for him." And I meant it.

I heard her swallow a couple of deep breaths, calming herself.

"Listen," she said finally, "while I got you on the phone. Did you really mouth off the other day to Biegler? Call him an asshole or somethin'? I just found out he's registered a formal complaint about you to Chief Logan."

"C'mon, the guy's a total dick."

"Not the point, Danny. And after all I went through to get you back on Logan's good side."

"I know, and I appreciate it."

"My ass. Look, I'll try to smooth things over downtown. But I can't make any promises."

"Thanks, Angie. See why you're my favorite relative?"

"And you're a bullshit artist. Anyway, come for dinner this Sunday. I'm making baked ziti. My mother's recipe."

I gave an inward sigh. Dinner at Angie's meant breaking bread with her bitter, bigoted husband, Sonny.

"I'll try, Angie, but—"

"Just be there, will ya, for Christ's sake?" Her tone softened again. "We'll drink a toast to absent friends. Like Harvey Blalock."

"I'll be there," I said.

For the first time in days, an ominous string of gray clouds stretched across the sky from the west, filtering the morning sun. Having just driven down from Grandview, I sat in Monday commuter traffic on the Liberty Bridge. A hastily packed travel bag lay across my backseat, alongside my laptop, though there hadn't been any contact by Maddox since Blalock's death. No doubt the sadistic prick was enjoying making me sweat.

Before hanging up on our group call earlier this morning, Barnes had given Gloria and me an address in Wilkinsburg, asking us to meet him there in three hours.

"I'll need at least that long to get it ready. Useable."

"What is it?" Gloria asked.

"An abandoned FBI safe house. Probably from before your time, Agent Reese."

"Why abandoned? Was its location breached?"

"Yeah." He chuckled. "By a crack team of rats. The four-legged kind. See you guys there."

After which, I quickly dressed, threw some clothes in the bag, grabbed my laptop, and locked up the house. But before pulling out of the driveway, I repeated the search of the Mustang I'd seen Gloria do. Inside and out. And found nothing.

Now, as the traffic finally lessened, I headed down the ramp toward the parkway. Placing the prepaid cell in the dashboard cradle, I dialed my office voice mail. Though I'd canceled my patient appointments for the week, I still needed to check my messages, in case anyone was in crisis.

To my surprise, the only message was from Liz Cortland, Barbara's former colleague at Pitt with whom I'd spoken at the Mayor's cocktail party.

"Dr. Rinaldi, this is Liz Cortland. I hope you check your office machine soon. I'm calling because I'm in my office this morning, grading papers. I was hoping you might be free to stop by. I should be here till noon, when I have to teach a class. Just come on up."

By "up" she meant her office on the faculty-only fifth floor of the Cathedral of Learning, the most iconic building on the Pitt campus. The office she'd mentioned was three doors down from where my late wife's had been. Of course, I'd been in Barbara's office many times when she was alive, though never, as I recalled, in Liz Cortland's.

Stopped at a light, I debated what to do. As preoccupied as I was with Sebastian Maddox, I couldn't help thinking about her message. At the Mayor's party, Liz had said she wanted to talk to me about something that concerned Barbara. Was that what this sudden invitation was about?

I glanced at my watch. I still had plenty of time before I was supposed to meet up with Barnes and Gloria at the safe house. Besides, there was a question I'd been wanting to ask Liz Cortland myself. One that had been nagging me since this whole nightmare began.

My mind made up, I angled around the Point and crisscrossed the clogged city streets until I was headed down Fifth Avenue. Traffic in Oakland was its usual headache, but I managed to find a parking space in the metered lot across from Hillman Library.

The looming spire of the Cathedral of Learning looked as regal and timeless as ever against the gloomy sky. Inside was even more impressive, especially to a former student like me. The ponderous, chilled embrace of Medieval-style masonry, the broad ground-floor expanse, framed by recessed alcoves and dotted with study tables. Side corridors led to the various Nationality Rooms, each decorated in the style befitting its specific country. And, throughout, the familiar sharp tap of student footsteps echoed on the stone floors.

I took the elevator up to the fifth floor, passing a number of offices, including the one Barbara had occupied. I'd never bothered to find out who'd been assigned it after her death.

Finally, I found Liz Cortland, her office door open. She was in a collared shirt and jeans, sitting at her desk with some exam papers. Her pen moving hurriedly and somewhat furiously over the one in front of her. I didn't envy that student.

At the sound of my footstep on the threshold, she looked up. The determined set of her lips quickly turning to a smile.

"Good, you got my message. Come on in, Dr. Rinaldi."

I did, as she rose to shake hands. Then she motioned to the only other chair in the cramped office and invited me to sit.

"Thanks. And please call me Dan. Or Danny."

"Yes." She settled back in her seat. "Danny. That's what Barbara always called you. And, of course, I'm Liz."

An awkward moment of silence followed.

"You know," she said suddenly, "I've never put much stock in the so-called sisterhood to which women in the Humanities are supposed to respond as a matter of course. But it was different with Barbara and me. We actually liked each other."

"I know. She really valued your friendship. She always said that she could confide in you. Talk about anything."

"We certainly did that. Which is one of the reasons I wanted you to come by. Because the thing she talked about the most was you. Or should I say, your marriage."

I took a breath, which she registered.

"Anyway, Dan, in case you weren't sure, Barbara did love you. She said you were smart, generous, and could always make her laugh. She also said you were a good lay." A brief smile.

"On the other hand, she made it damn clear that you were no day at the beach. Stubborn as hell. Quick to anger. She often said she wasn't sure the marriage would last."

"Neither was I. If she was that candid with you, you're probably aware of how much we fought. How we'd even sought couples counseling. Though I'm not sure it helped."

"Yes, she spoke about the fights. But it was more than that. Though Barbara considered herself a feminist, she hated having displeased her father by marrying you." She paused, looking off. "No matter what, it never changes. Fathers and their daughters. Christ. Probably explains the problems in both of *my* former marriages."

Another long beat of silence. Obviously, this wasn't a subject on which she wanted to elaborate.

"Look," she said at last, rising from her chair. "There *is* a reason I wanted to see you. I have something of Barbara's that I think you ought to have."

She moved some books aside on the near shelf and withdrew a bound manuscript. About a hundred pages, it looked like. She handed it to me.

"It's a book Barbara was working on. On linguistics, of course. She hoped it would break new ground."

"A book? I didn't even know…"

"She didn't want to tell you—or anyone, really—until she was sure it was any good. She only told me about it because I happened to come into her office once and found her working on it. Though I could tell she was glad to be able to share her excitement about it with someone."

I felt a sharp sting at her words. Wishing, out of pure ego and hurt pride, that Barbara had felt comfortable enough to tell *me*. That she would've wanted to.

Liz must have guessed my thoughts.

"Open the first page. The dedication."

I flipped to the front and read the words written there.

"To Daniel. My husband, my partner, my love. Barbara"

I swallowed hard, let the manuscript drop to my lap.

Liz folded her arms. "Most people wait till the book's finished to worry about a dedication. But Barbara told me it helped motivate her to write it first. To you. So she could imagine you reading the final product. And being proud of her."

I just sat there, moved beyond words. Ashamed of my initial, self-centered response.

"I've made a copy for myself," Liz went on, "but I always wanted to give you the original. Even unfinished, anyone reading it can see how remarkable her work was. How unique and seminal her thinking. What a great book it would be."

"Would've been." My eyes lifted to hers. "Why didn't you get in touch with me after her death? Show it to me then?"

A pause. "I don't know, really. Somehow the timing never seemed right. Then, after a while, it felt like too much time had gone by. Your life had moved on, and I worried that all I'd do is dredge up old, painful memories."

"But when we saw each other at the party..."

"I realize it doesn't make sense, but somehow it felt like a sign. That the time was right to give you her manuscript." She ran a hand through her short hair. "Pretty touchy-feely for a hard-ass like me, I know. But there it is."

I nodded, and thanked her for her time. And the manuscript. But I paused before getting up to leave.

"If you don't mind, Liz, I'd like to ask you a question. You and Barbara were so close, such good friends...I just wondered if she ever mentioned a man named Maddox? Sebastian Maddox. They were in a class together as undergrads, and—"

Her face paled. Then she slowly re-took her seat.

"Yes. Maddox. I know all about that. One time, when we'd had a few drinks after work, she told me the whole story."

I nodded, but said nothing.

"She also revealed that she'd never told you about it. Even after you two were married. And even though it had all happened years before she'd ever met you."

"I know. I've only just learned about him. What can you tell me about it?"

"Only what Barbara told me. They were both sophomores, both taking an art history class. She because of her genuine interest, and Maddox because it was one of those humanities courses that the tech students were required to take. Apparently, he was some kind of computer genius."

"Yes. A double-major with philosophy."

"Real Brainiac, it seems. But not like what you'd expect. He was considered a total hunk. Handsome, athletic..." She hesitated a moment. "The truth is, Barbara was quite attracted to Maddox. So they started dating, and—"

My mouth went dry. This was something I hadn't expected to hear. Or, more honestly, never wanted to learn.

"How serious was it?" I managed to say.

"Not serious at all. Barbara said that after a couple dates, just dinner and drinks, she began to get a weird vibe off him. That he really creeped her out. So she stopped seeing him."

"That's when his obsession with her took over."

Liz nodded. "He kept insisting they were in love, that they were soulmates. Fated to be together. He began stalking her, becoming more and more threatening. Until she literally feared for her life. Thank God she finally went to the cops. That must have scared him off. She never saw him again. Turns out, he left school soon after."

"One last question, Liz. Did Barbara ever say why she'd never told me about Maddox?"

"To her, it was all in the past. A horrible period in her life that she didn't want to relive. Or burden you with. Truth is, if she hadn't had so much to drink that night, I doubt she'd ever have told me. Especially since she came to me the next day and asked that I never repeat the story to anyone else. And particularly not to you." A thick pause. "I hope it was okay that I told you now."

I shrugged. "Well, I'm the one who asked."

Tucking Barbara's manuscript under my arm, I thanked Liz again and stood up. We exchanged a brief, awkward hug. And then I left.

• • ● • •

Walking back to my car under grayish clouds pouting with the promise of new rain, all I could think about was the bound manuscript under my arm. Stunned and saddened that I'd been unaware of such a crucial part of Barbara's life during those last months.

Was her reluctance to tell me about it really due to her concern as to its worth, or was it merely another sign of the growing distance between us? Yet, if that were the case, how did I explain the book's dedication to me?

I realized then that it was symbolic of our whole marriage. Triggering images in my mind of the unique, challenging woman I remembered. Her solemn gaze, her stern humor, how her voice faltered when speaking to her father. The endless fights, the prolonged silences. That barely discernible fragrance she wore, which I loved but that always made me sneeze. Certain sounds she made in bed. Her bitter laugh. Her hidden, conflicted love.

How, even toward the end, I both knew her and didn't know her…

I made my way slowly across Forbes Avenue, unmindful of the students hurrying past me, eyes glued to their cells—some bundled into thick sweaters, others wearing spring jackets zipped up against the cooling, damp-cotton air.

Maybe, I thought, the manuscript was just another example of the conflicted nature of our marriage. How we each yearned for connection and yet distrusted intimacy.

Proven by what I'd just learned from Liz Cortland. I knew I'd need time to process the news that Barbara had actually dated Maddox. Not out of any jealousy—she and I hadn't even met yet—but due to my lingering regret that she'd never told me about her experience. Her growing terror at being stalked, her having to resort to a restraining order. This was a significant, no doubt traumatic, event in her life, and I'd never even known about it.

Not to mention the cruel irony. Two casual dates with him, and yet it was the genesis of an erotic obsession that would end up, many years later, costing Barbara her life...

I'd no sooner stepped up onto the curb when a few droplets of rain began to fall. By now, the parking lot outside Hillman Library had filled, but I had no trouble finding my Mustang.

Still burdened by thoughts of the past, I distractedly opened it up and placed Barbara's manuscript on the backseat.

And froze.

The travel bag was still there, where I'd left it. But my laptop was gone.

Straightening, I glanced at the passenger side seat in the front. The laptop was sitting on top of it. Lid open, the screen completely filled with the face of Sebastian Maddox. A still photo, like an actor's head shot.

As I stared at the piercing eyes and cruel, self-satisfied smile, I suddenly heard his voice crackle from the laptop's speaker. Cool. Darkly gleeful.

"Afternoon, Danny. I thought you could use a new screen-saver. Your old one sucks. Luckily, I take a nice picture."

Chapter Twenty-five

"I looked all around the lot, but there was no sign of him." I took the cold beer Barnes handed me. "Yet Maddox couldn't have been that far away. He'd had time to get into my car and move my laptop to the front seat. I *know* it was in the back when I left the house."

"The bastard's gaslighting you, Doc." Barnes' lean frame was propped against the refrigerator door. "Trying to mess with your head."

"I realize that, Lyle. Just as I know he probably tracked me using the laptop. I should have left it at home."

On a stool at the other end of the tiled kitchen island, Gloria shook her head, her ponytail bobbing behind it.

"Maddox couldn't track you that way, Danny. Not unless he installed a special app in your laptop. Or had its ID number and registered it with the manufacturer. And I doubt he's had that kind of access to it. Besides, Danny, the idea is to make it *easy* for Maddox to contact us. So we know what he's doing. With your cell in pieces, it's the laptop or nothing."

I sipped my beer. "Unless he's managed to hack into *your* cell by now. Or Lyle's."

"Doesn't matter," said Barnes. "Before we vacated your place, I broke apart both Agent Reese's cell and my own. Just to be on the safe side. Then I tossed them off your rear deck. We're all using the throwaway phones now."

She gave him a bemused look. "Isn't it about time for you to start calling me 'Gloria'?"

"Nope. But I'll let you know when it is."

By the time I'd arrived at the former Bureau safe house, Lyle and Gloria were already there. The address Barnes had given us was of an abandoned movie theater off the main drag in Wilkinsburg. Most of the light bulbs arrayed on its weathered marquee had long since been shattered, either by thrown rocks or, I suspected, more than a few bullets. Target practice by gangsta wannabes. Old posters from the last film to play there—*Rocky IV*—hung in tatters next to the boarded-up entrance.

I found my way in through the exit door at the rear, its rusting lock recently broken. By Barnes, obviously. Inside the darkened passageway behind the empty, dust-covered concession stand was another door, so embedded and flush with the wall, it was nearly invisible.

Or would have been, had Barnes not also left it open, revealing the lights coming from within.

Going through the door and down a flight of steps, I found myself in the first of a series of cinderblock rooms, just below ground level. Some were bedrooms, the rest merely windowless spaces with a few old upholstered couches as furniture.

I heard Barnes' voice echoing from a room somewhere to my left, and went through a surprisingly well-lit corridor to the safe house's spare kitchen. There I found him talking with Gloria, both of them holding fresh beers.

I also realized why Barnes had needed some time before letting us join him here. I'd heard the hum of the generator coming from one of the side rooms as I headed for the kitchen. He'd had to replace all the bulbs down here, bring in a portable generator, and stock the refrigerator with drinks and takeout. Given his precise nature, I was sure he'd also swept and tidied up a few of the rooms. Especially since a young lady would be among those in attendance.

"Nice job," was the first thing I'd said to him when I joined them. I pulled up a stool at the tiled island counter that smelled of ammonia and cleanser.

Barnes waved his hand dismissively. "We might be here for a while. Place has to be livable. That said, I can't guarantee how secure it is. So we can't stay permanently. But we should be all right for the time being."

Gloria sat forward on her stool. "What about the rats?"

"Cleared out for greener pastures, I guess. At least I haven't seen any sign of them. But let's not leave any crumbs around, okay? You never know."

The two laptops were side by side on the conference table in one of the side rooms. Mine with the lid closed on Maddox's photo we were unable to delete, Gloria's open and facing out to where the three of us sat. It was after five, and though we could hear the rain coming down outside, we couldn't see it. No windows here in the basement safe house.

We'd just had Chinese takeout that Barnes had brought with him earlier and reheated in the microwave. Now, all evidence of the meal cleared away, Gloria and I gazed at her laptop screen as Lyle began showing us the data he'd assembled about Sebastian Maddox. Starting with photos and videos of an adolescent Maddox and his distressed-looking parents, from various occasions at the family's home in Blackridge. The obviously forced frivolity of holidays and birthdays was almost painful to watch.

Barnes tapped a few more keys and a complete listing of Maddox's exemplary middle school grades and awards for science projects marched across the screen. Juxtaposed with it were truancy reports, a record of frequent disciplinary actions for anti-social behavior, and prescribed visits to various child psychologists. His diagnoses ranged from oppositional disorder to borderline personality to outright sociopathy, depending on the therapist. By his late teens, and after two arrests for drug possession, some petty theft, and a DUI, Sebastian was fairly well-known both to high school authorities and the police.

Gloria chuckled without humor. "Shit. What did Maddox call himself? An excitable boy? *There's* an understatement."

"It was only his parents' money and position in their community that kept Maddox out of juvenile hall," said Barnes. "Though even with his background, he was accepted at a number of colleges. Apparently, most counselors were willing to ascribe his past to 'youthful indiscretions.' In fact, I found a report from one university's admissions officer stating that— here it is—'we must accept the fact that the gifted are often unburdened by the dictates of conventional morality.' Asshole."

"Maybe," I agreed. "But it's a pretty common assessment of brilliant students like Maddox. Especially if the college underestimates the extent of the kid's transgressions. A few drug busts or behavioral complaints aren't that big a deal if your main goal is recruiting top candidates. Future alumni that will reflect well on your school. *And* donate to it."

Gloria pointed at a photo of Maddox's parents, standing stiffly with their sullen son at his high school graduation.

"What about his family?"

"Sebastian was their only child. Father a noted research scientist, mother a fancy lawyer. The father's family came from old money, which seems to have carried a lot of weight in Blackridge. Their kid must've been a helluva embarrassment."

I nodded. "That's probably why the restraining order Barbara took out on Maddox led to his parents yanking him out of Pitt. It was the last straw. Their patience had run out."

"What happened to Mom and Dad?" Gloria said.

"Dad died of a heart attack a year after Maddox had to leave college. Mom swallowed a bottle of pills a month later. Left a suicide note blaming their son for ruining her life."

"Jesus…"

"The house in Blackridge was bought by some rich investor soon after and razed to the ground, replaced by a McMansion. Wouldn't surprise me if they salted the earth first."

Barnes sipped from a cup of recently brewed coffee, his eyes burning as though flooded with caffeine. He'd drunk over half the carafe already.

"Meanwhile, back to the benighted son…"

Another quick tapping on the keyboard brought up a mug shot of Sebastian Maddox. Scowling insolently at the camera, he was wearing the familiar prison orange.

"Remember what he told us? The day after he shot you and your wife, and before he could skip town, Maddox was busted for dealing. Court records show he had to cool his heels in county jail, awaiting trial."

"While I was in Pittsburgh Memorial," I said, "recovering from my gunshot wound from that night."

"Right. Then, a couple months later, Maddox gets convicted and sent up to Buckville maximum security. The exact same day you're finally released from the hospital."

I considered this. "Wait, I get it now. *He* goes in, *I* get out. There's that goddam symmetry. Probably where the concept first lodged in his mind. If there's a seeming order to events, an underlying pattern, then his mission of revenge against me is somehow sanctioned. Practically ordained. The perfect delusional rationale in support of his emotional self-regulation."

Barnes tried not to roll his eyes. "You don't know when to quit, do ya, Doc? I don't care what's in this nut-case's head. I just want to take the bastard down."

"So do I, Lyle. We just use different tools to do it."

"Uh-huh." His catch-all retort when unconvinced.

"It's funny," Gloria said quietly. "Crazy or not, Maddox has been completely honest about his past. His obsession with Barbara. His reasons for wanting Danny dead. Even his decade in prison. But why? Unless he gets off on trying to make us see how much he's suffered for love."

I glanced at her. "That's a good point, Gloria. In fact, it might be something we can use."

Barnes grunted. "Well, not to break up this little clinical conference, but our Mr. Maddox hasn't been *totally* honest. Check this out."

The ex-agent gestured toward a series of files popping up on-screen. Prison records, police reports, newspaper articles.

"About halfway through his ten-year-stretch, prison officials found out about something Maddox had been doing. I mean, besides building hard-time muscle in the rec yard and playing nice with the Aryan Brotherhood."

Gloria and I peered at the screen.

"Given his college studies," Barnes continued, "Maddox was assigned work duty in the prison electronics shop. Turns out there were a lot of discarded computer parts laying around. So guess what the boy genius did?"

He didn't wait for an answer. "He designed and built an elaborate computer system that he hid in the shop room ceiling. A system he used to hack into the prison's servers and program them to access systems out here in the civilian world."

"Are you kidding?" Gloria stared.

"Nope. This enabled him to stay on top of all the latest IT developments. Probably when he first started keeping track of the Doc's life, too. By the time he was found out, he'd built his own elaborate, sophisticated network. The authorities couldn't prove it, but they suspected he'd used it to steal funds from hundreds of bank accounts and credit cards. Money that they were never able to trace."

"Which Maddox could retrieve once he was released from prison," I said. "Money that's funding everything he's doing now. But why didn't he get more jail time for what he did?"

Barnes laughed. "His attorney cut a deal with the local DA. No additional hard time in exchange for Maddox showing the authorities how he did it. From what I could read between the lines, the prison warden just wanted to put the whole thing behind him. Maddox had made them look like fools."

I thought this was all that Barnes had to show us, but he pulled up one more image. A colorful, beautifully rendered painting whose subject I recognized immediately.

"That's like the tattoo Maddox has on his back. I saw it on the video he showed me of Joy's assault. A snake with wings."

"To be more accurate, it's described in the primary source literature as a 'feathered serpent.' This old painting is one of the many depictions of Quetzalcoatl, the patron god of the Aztec priesthood. Representing learning and knowledge."

Gloria frowned. "Figures. Ego much, this guy?"

"It looks like a prison tat," Barnes went on, "but no way an Aryan brother did it for him. Maddox must've done a favor for some talented Chicano up in Buckville, too. Got him drugs or cash. Isn't much you can't get hold of in—"

Suddenly, Barnes was interrupted by a burst of static coming from Gloria's laptop. The painting vanished, replaced by a live-streaming image of Sebastian Maddox. Shirtless, hands clasped behind his shaved head, he was sitting comfortably in a big leather chair. The harsh lighting accentuating the sharp planes of his face, the rock-like contours of his biceps. And the vivid tattoo of the Grail on his bare chest.

We three sat, stunned once again into silence. Maddox seemed pleased by our surprise.

"I know your laptop is Bureau issue, Agent Reese, but how long did you think it would take for me to hack into it? By the way, I also took a cyber-tour of your personal computer at home. Really, Gloria? Match.com? I figured a babe like you would have no trouble hooking up with one of your fellow G-Men. Or should I say, G-Persons?"

Gloria glared at Maddox's image on-screen, her voice steady.

"Fuck you, Maddox. Twice."

"It's a date, hon. Meanwhile, Danny, it's time for you and me to go for a little ride."

I got my face close to the screen. "What do you mean?"

"I mean I'm gonna let you see the next victim die right in front of your eyes. Up close and personal, as they say."

My hands involuntarily closed into fists.

"Damn you, Maddox! Who? Who is it?"

His eyes narrowed, all mirth gone. "Just make sure you come alone. Or there'll be consequences. For a lot of people."

"Come where?"

"Clock's ticking, Danny boy. It's not a long drive, but you better get started. See you there."

He disappeared from the screen.

"Where?" I shouted at the empty gray window. "Maddox! Where am I supposed to—?"

Barnes gripped my shoulder.

"He said it's a drive. That means you need to get in your car. *Now*. He'll let you know where to go."

I gaped at him, anxiety squeezing my throat like a vice.

"How can you be sure?"

"I can't. But you got a better idea?"

Chapter Twenty-six

Though it was still early evening, the sky was a patchwork of purplish-gray clouds that cloaked the setting sun. The rain had slowed to a soft drizzle, but I barely noticed the moisture beading on the back of my neck. Running to where I'd parked my Mustang a block down from the entrance to the movie theater, I was behind the wheel in less than a minute. Engine revved, wipers on, I pulled away from the curb.

But to go where? Before I even had time to ponder the question, my dashboard GPS came on. A detailed street map of the surrounding area was accompanied by the device's familiar female voice. Cool, unhurried, definitive.

"Go straight along Wilkins Avenue until you arrive at the intersection…"

My eyes flitting back and forth from the GPS screen to the mist-shrouded road, I followed the directions toward downtown and the Point with no idea where I was going.

At least now I knew what was happening. Sebastian Maddox was controlling the GPS signal remotely, so while the directions were voiced by the instrument's built-in software, the data was being input by Maddox, determinedly leading me to my unknown destination.

As I drove alongside the Ohio River, as directed, I remembered having read somewhere that government security experts were concerned about the possible hacking of GPS equipment.

A terrorist or some other of our country's enemies remotely sending directions to planes, trains, or cars, which was what Maddox was doing with me.

By now, the measured female voice had guided me along the main road leading to McKees Rocks, about five miles east of downtown. My eyes straining to see through the dampened fog beyond my windshield, I was soon past the main thoroughfare and heading toward one of Pittsburgh's shipping ports on the Ohio.

The throwaway cell I'd brought with me vibrated on the passenger seat beside me. I scooped it up. Gloria.

"What's going on, Danny? Where are you?"

"Just outside McKees Rocks. Looks like Maddox is steering me toward the river port."

The digital GPS voice spoke again, and I turned as directed onto a long dockside stretch of old wooden warehouses, raindrops dripping from roofs and gutters. Dozens of sodium lamps on regularly spaced poles glowed against the drizzle, the sizzling lights mere blurs in the growing darkness. Beyond, a row of cargo ships flanked the dock, their weathered hulls ghostly in the unending mist. Beside them stood towering heavy-duty cranes with huge metal container pods suspended beneath them.

Despite the inclement weather, man and machine were hard at work doing the dock's business. Flatbed trucks, headlights blazing, laden with sheet rock. Forklifts piled high with large sacks of grain or gravel. Men and women in rain gear and hard hats scurrying to assist in the busy port's ceaseless rounds of loading and unloading.

"Put me on speaker." Gloria's voice was brisk. "Lyle and I want to stay connected with you."

I did as asked, slipping the cell into my jacket pocket.

Following the GPS instructions, I wound my way past the main dock and through a maze of smaller buildings till I came upon a second group of cranes. As I slowed my car, peering through the wet gloom, I realized that the area seemed deserted.

No workers moving about. No rolling trucks. The loading cranes were still, and no container pods hung by chains below them. Silent and unmoving, they were like tall sentinels long since frozen at their posts.

Just then, my invisible female companion spoke for the last time. "You have reached your destination."

The GPS map flickered for a moment, then went black.

At first, I stayed in the car, hands gripping the wheel.

Though the drizzle had finally stopped, the night beyond my windshield was dark and draped in misty, diaphanous folds.

I rolled down my window. Outside, all was silent, except for the gentle lapping of the river and the muffled creaking of the old dock's pillars. The air was cold, damp.

"I don't see him," I said aloud, for Gloria's benefit. "I don't see anyone. I'm getting out of the car."

"For Christ's sake, be careful!"

Without answering, I opened the door and stepped out onto the thick wooden planks of the dock. The wet darkness shrouded me almost instantly, and I involuntarily shuddered against the night's chill.

Looking to my left and right, I started walking toward the base of one of the loading cranes. I'd seen what looked like a flash of light just behind it, on the side facing the river.

As the Ohio's pungent, oily smell wafted up to meet me, I was brought up short by a sudden, rasping sound. A metallic whine, like that of a buzz saw.

Coming from somewhere above my head.

I stopped, swallowing hard, and looked up. It floated about a dozen feet overhead. The size and shape of a car tire, it was a beetle-like thing with a pair of lights for eyes, shining down on me. Four thin struts extended from its sides, propellers whirling at the ends.

Quelling the panic that had risen in my chest, I realized what it was. A drone.

Gloria's muffled voice came from the cell.

"Jesus, what's that—?"

"A goddam drone!" I shouted back. "Somehow he's—"

Another voice boomed down from above me.

"Hi ya, Danny." *His* voice. Tinny and unearthly, like aluminum foil crinkling, it echoed from the drone's speaker. Obviously, the drone also featured a camera lens.

I squinted up at the pair of blinding lights but didn't reply. I instinctively backstepped, unnerved.

"I know how much you like standing by a river," Maddox said. "So you should appreciate what's in store for you. The death of someone even closer to home than poor Harvey."

The drone rose unsteadily a few more feet in the air, buzzing like a great angry insect, and swept toward the river. Then banked and turned back, to hover overhead again.

"Come on, Danny! Hurry, or you'll miss it!"

At first, still stunned by the otherworldly sound of Maddox's voice, I stood rooted to the spot. My eyes tracing the drone's lazy circles in the damp, night-shrouded sky.

Finally, when the drone swooped off again in the direction of the river, I roused myself and followed along below. Maddox was leading me toward the base of that silent crane, behind which I'd seen the flicker of light. Though as far as I could see peering up ahead, now there was only unremitting darkness.

It wasn't until the drone paused and hovered high above the base of the crane that I realized *it* must have been the source of the light I'd seen. The crane stood well back from where the dock jutted out over the river, and suddenly the drone's searing high beams were sweeping the waters below it.

I hurried around the boulder-sized, steel-plated base and found myself at the dock's weathered edge, feeling those same unwavering high beams pouring down on me like a shower of cold light.

"Here we are." Maddox spoke from high above me with an austere authority, as though from the heavens themselves. "Just like I promised. Up close and personal."

By now, I was squinting past the harsh overhead lights into the black waters below me. But it was hard to see anything. With the splintered dock planks creaking beneath my feet, I stepped to the very edge to get a closer look.

It was then that I heard something—some*one*—splashing in the water. A frantic, sputtering voice piercing the mist.

A voice I thought I recognized.

Maddox's rattling laugh rained down on me. "Time to say your good-byes, Danny!"

Suddenly, the drone's powerful lights, as though having been draped there, lifted from my shoulders and skimmed along the river's surface until they came to a dock pillar, long ravished by a century's immersion in the flowing waters. A thick, weary stanchion buried deep into the riverbed.

In the blazing light, I could see there was someone lashed to the pillar with heavy ropes. Head lolling, shoulders slumped, drained by fatigue, and growing weaker by the second. From her jerky movements in the swirling water, I could tell she was listlessly kicking with her legs. Desperately trying to keep her head above the brackish, oily-green water, even as it spooned slowly, remorselessly, into the woman's mouth…

The woman was Angie Villanova.

Before I could react, I heard the rasp of the drone as it lowered toward me. Then Maddox's sonorous voice.

"As Socrates said, 'Doing philosophy is practicing for death.' Think of all the practice I'm giving *you* lately—"

He was still talking when I dove into the water.

Maddox had mistimed it. He'd led me here to witness Angie's death by drowning, but I'd arrived while she was still clinging to life. Fighting for every last breath.

As I knew she would.

I also knew she only had seconds left. The Ohio River's

depth was regulated by a series of locks, but with the recent rains could swell to thirty feet, rising like an ocean's tide.

Swimming hard against the pull of the river, I'd covered half the distance to where Maddox had bound her when the drone's blazing lights suddenly cut out, plunging Angie and me into a watery darkness.

With visibility removed, I pushed myself toward the ancient pillar, guided only by the sound of Angie's anguished cries.

Maddox's voice was a mechanic rasp, laced with rage, sounding again like an angry Old Testament God, railing from above.

"You're too late, Danny! The old bitch dies tonight!"

I closed my ears against his words. I had to.

Moments before jumping into the river, I'd grabbed my cell out of my pocket. Put it to my lips.

"Ambulance!" Then I tossed the phone to the dock.

I had to hope that Gloria had heard me, and was notifying the Port Authority, and that help was on its way.

My eyes stinging, ribs screaming in pain, I plowed through the filthy water as fast as I could. Angie's voice had grown faint. Choked with water. And resignation.

I reached her at last and threw my arms around her stout form, hoisting her head above the waterline. By now I'd grown accustomed enough to the dark to see her slackened face, her stark white eyes. She'd stopped pumping her legs, and it took all my strength to keep her airways cleared of the water.

"I'm here, Angie! I've got you—"

She didn't respond or give any sign of recognition.

I shifted position until I had her supported with one arm, while I snaked my other one around the side of the pillar. Fingers anxiously searching for the ropes binding her to it.

Luckily, between their time in the water and her frantic struggles, the ropes had been loosened enough for me to work my fingers against the knots. Pulling, stretching.

As I did, I kept shouting her name. Trying to rouse her. But her only reply was the involuntary sputtering of her lips against the roiling waters. Her heaving, choking gasps.

Finally, I felt the knots pull apart enough for me to wriggle Angie's body free. Crying out from the effort, I put both arms around her again and lifted her out of the circle of ropes and onto my shoulders. Then, turning us both in the direction of the dock, I began pulling us toward it. Swimming with one hand, my progress was slow but steady.

As the contours of the dock emerged from the mist carpeting the black waters, I made out a thin wooden ladder hung from just below its weathered edge. Emboldened, I swam harder, kicking my legs even more.

Only a few more yards…only a few…

My labored gasps were now the only ones I could hear. Angie, unmoving in my grasp, had ceased to make a sound.

Finally reaching the ladder, I pulled Angie's seemingly lifeless body up onto my shoulders and took hold of the first rung. Grunting under the strain, I managed to climb all the way to the lip of the dock. With a last explosive burst of effort, I hauled us both up and onto the damp planks.

I lay Angie on her back, then scrabbled anxiously on the dock around me, trying to locate the cell I'd tossed aside. I'd just managed to find it when I heard the approach of the drone, returning to hover about twenty feet above.

And then its searing lights flared to life, flooding the area around Angie and me. Exposing us to the drone's lens.

"Still playing the big hero, eh, Danny?"

I ignored him, and instead used the sudden bright lights to scan Angie's face and torso. To my horror, her mouth drooped on one side, and her body shuddered as though convulsing. Then her left arm seemed to stiffen.

I knew what was happening to her. I'd seen it before.

A stroke.

I barely registered Maddox's mocking tone.

"She isn't gonna make it, Danny. You failed. I love it."

Crouching beside her, I knew I should try to keep her warm until medical help arrived. But all I had was my own jacket, as soaked with river water as were her own clothes.

Absurdly, I found myself cataloguing them. Though she'd lost her shoes, I noted her no-nonsense sweater and slacks. The gold crucifix given her by her mother, wound by its chain around her neck. Her everyday watch with its simple black band.

As though it mattered, I realized that these were the kinds of things she wore at the office. Which meant that Maddox had somehow spirited her away after work today, perhaps injecting her with a powerful paralytic as she bent to open her car door.

Which meant, too, that Maddox had become even bolder, more reckless. And unusually lucky. Assaulting and kidnapping a high-level police officer in the Department's own parking lot. Unless there *had* been a witness to the crime, and even now Pittsburgh PD was searching the city for one of their own…

All these thoughts flooded my mind in a matter of seconds, probably as a way to distance myself from the reality of Angie's condition. A kind of self-protective dissociation.

Which, I also realized, I couldn't afford. Not now. Despite my concern for Angie, my palpable grief, I had to stay focused. Think clearly. A madman's mechanized avatar floated above me.

"Time for you to go, Danny. And for her to die…"

I rose to my feet and stared up at the drone. As though its blinding lights were in fact his own intense eyes.

"No. I'm not leaving till an ambulance gets here."

"Think again, Doctor. If you're here when it arrives, and you tell what you know about me—"

"Fuck you, Maddox! I'm staying right here."

"Goddammit, I'm warning you—"

His voice was cut off by the whine of an approaching siren. I turned where I stood and saw the red flashing lights of what looked like an ambulance. As I'd hoped, Gloria had alerted the Port Authority, which has emergency medical staff standing by in case of accidents on the loading docks.

The drone suddenly dropped to within a dozen feet of me.

"Remember, Danny, this stays between you and me till *I* decide to end it. Or else many more people will die. Random people whose blood will be on your hands!"

Then, as easily as it had descended, the drone rose again. Flying quickly over the length of the deserted dock until it vanished from sight.

The ambulance was less than a hundred feet away, the racing vehicle's twin high beams now replacing the bright lights of the drone. I knew that, in a few seconds, the driver would be able to see Angie and me.

Which meant I had no choice. With a last look down at her still form, I started running toward my car. Though draped in darkness, I could see the glint of its front grille in the passing headlights of the ambulance.

Cloaked now by that same darkness, I got behind the wheel and hurriedly drove off in the opposite direction. In my rearview mirror, I saw that the ambulance had reached where Angie lay, and two EMTs were scrambling toward her.

I tried reaching Gloria again, but by now my cell's battery was dead. All right with me. I wasn't up to talking.

Heading out of the port and back along the main road into McKees Rocks, I felt a sickening mix of guilt and fear. I knew I had to take Maddox's threat seriously, but it was wrenching to leave Angie like that with only the hope that the medical team could get her to a hospital in time.

In minutes, I was back in the city. Wet and cold, my spent body wracked with pain, I made my way past the glittering lights of the Point and headed to the safe house.

Though the rain had fully stopped, the clouds over the city rolled like flat, black waves toward the hills. An undulating shroud over the silver and glass heart of the new Pittsburgh.

Meanwhile, I kept replaying Maddox's words to me as I'd peered down at Angie's body on the old, deserted dock.

"You failed," he'd said. "I love it."

Because he was right. On both counts.

Chapter Twenty-seven

Fortunately, the ever-resourceful Lyle Barnes had opened the pipes and re-lit the water heater after breaking into the abandoned safe house.

Standing under the steaming hot shower, I vigorously scrubbed off what felt like a slimy, full-body film of river water. Then I let the nozzle's jets play along my aching back, the heat and pressure soothing the stressed muscles.

Nothing, though, could soothe my concern about Angie, and the bitter knowledge that yet another person close to me had been victimized by Sebastian Maddox.

Then, by some weird mental alchemy, my thoughts turned to young Robbie Palermo, and our conversation about head wounds. In a way, it's exactly what Maddox was doing to me. Delivering repeated wounds to my mind, my psyche…

When I shut off the shower and stepped through the glass door, I found Gloria Reese standing there in the small bathroom. In one hand was a towel, in the other a roll of bandages. While her eyes shone with excitement.

"Gloria? What are you—?"

"Hurry up and dry off." She handed me the towel, then reached past me to turn on the shower again.

"To muffle our voices," she explained. "Just in case. Bastard's made me paranoid."

I quickly toweled off, after which she began wrapping the bandages around my ribs. Also quickly.

"Has something happened?"

"Yeah, we got a break. When you told me you were at the river port, I called my tech guys downtown and asked for an aerial recon of the area. Remember, they still think they're helping me track a person of interest on another case."

"And—?"

"The recon picked up a scattering of signals, and they just now analyzed the data. One was a bi-directional transmission from what turned out to be a drone."

She finished taping the bandages, then straightened, hands clasping my shoulders.

"Danny, they traced the signal back to a location in Swissvale. Maddox was operating the drone from there. We *got* the son of a bitch!"

I threw on some clothes from my travel bag—jeans, a sweater, and fresh sneakers—and went out to the main lounge area. There I found Barnes and Gloria in the midst of a heated discussion about whether or not to bring in the authorities to deal with Maddox.

"I'm a sworn Federal agent," Gloria was saying. "Now that we know where he is, I should notify the Bureau's tactical team. And, to be honest, Pittsburgh PD, too."

Barnes shook his head. "And tell them what? That we've been conducting a rogue investigation of some crazy bastard who's off the grid? Meanwhile, wasting valuable hours explaining what's been happening, securing a warrant…"

I stepped between them.

"Lyle is right, Gloria. Remember, this is Maddox we're dealing with. He could have his Swissvale place booby-trapped. Hell, he could have bombs planted all over the city. Explosives he might activate remotely if he's cornered. I don't think we can take that chance."

Barnes grunted. "Yeah, and every minute we delay…"

Gloria held her hands up in mock surrender. "Okay, I get it. Besides, I agree that we don't have time for debate. Just remind me about this later, when I get kicked out of the Bureau."

"If you do, I'll take you fly-fishing. You'll love it," Barnes said.

Gloria gave him a skeptical look, but said nothing.

Barnes grinned, then started checking a Glock handgun he'd brought with him. Given his arm sling, his movements were alarmingly awkward. I kept that observation to myself. I also took note of the fatigue pinching his red-rimmed eyes— the brutal cost of going days without proper sleep.

If Gloria noticed this, she gave no indication. She just slammed a fresh chamber into her own regulation automatic and thrust it in her back pocket.

Barnes frowned at me. "If the Bureau hadn't cleaned out the armory station when they abandoned this place, I'd have a weapon for you. Maybe that means you should sit this one out."

"Yeah. Like *that's* gonna happen."

Gloria arched an eyebrow at Barnes. "Told ya, Lyle."

He shrugged. "Well, that's another argument we don't have time for. We gotta get going. But remember, Doc, if you get your ass killed, I'll have to find another goddam therapist. And just when I finally got you broken in."

The FBI techs had tracked the drone signal's location to an apartment building just west of Swissvale. It was a squat, ugly, three-story structure, circa mid-1950s, that shared the modest suburban street with small family homes and a mini-mart at the corner. Modest being the operative word with Swissvale.

It was nearing ten when we pulled up to the curb in Lyle's late-model Buick, which he parked about a block away from the building. The street was empty, quiet.

We three got out of the car without a word.

With the deep cloud cover, the night was black as wet ink, the darkness broken only by lights from within the houses, as well as from some of the apartments overlooking the street.

As we neared the building's front entrance, Gloria pointed up at the row of lighted windows. "But which one is Maddox's?"

Barnes indicated a sign next to the entry door.

"Building manager's in Number One. A Mr. Abrams. Why don't we wake the poor bastard up and ask him?"

After a series of knocks, the door of Number One opened to reveal a smallish, balding older man in pajamas. Taking a step across the threshold, his sour face registered his annoyance at the intrusion. Until Gloria flashed her Bureau ID.

"Are you the manager? Special Agent Gloria Reese, FBI."

He started, then drew himself up and rubbed his eyes.

"Yes, Officer?...I mean, Agent...?"

"We're looking for a man named Sebastian Maddox. Though he may not be using that name. He's forty-ish but looks younger. Shaved head, muscular frame. Does he rent a place here?"

Abrams squinted. "I think you mean Mr. Mudgett. Herman Mudgett. He's in Number Four."

Barnes gave a sour laugh. "That's him. Mudgett was the real name of H.H. Holmes."

"Who?"

Gloria sighed. "One of the first documented serial killers. Over a hundred years ago. Another of Maddox's inside jokes."

"Yeah," I said. "Guy's a million laughs."

Abrams rubbed his brow. "What? I don't understand... Look, I don't want any trouble. Truth is, I haven't seen Mr. Mudgett since he took the apartment."

"And when was that?"

"Two months ago. But he paid me in advance for three."

Gloria turned to Barnes. "Two months...according to his parole officer, that's when he was released from Buckville."

The building manager stared. "Buckville? The prison…?"

"I commend you, Mr. Abrams," said Barnes. "Not many people would rent a place to a convicted felon."

"But…but I didn't know. Like I said, I never see him. I haven't even been inside the apartment since he…Oh, my God…"

He suddenly looked pretty shaky on his feet.

"Just give me the master key." Gloria held out her hand. Abrams gulped nervously, disappeared for a moment into his apartment, then returned with the key. Pocketing it, Gloria used her palm to push Abrams back inside the door.

"Stay inside, okay, Mr. Abrams? And don't come out."

The little man quickly shut the door.

We took the elevator to the second floor, where apartments Three and Four were located. As we approached Maddox's door at the end of the narrow, wallpapered hallway, Barnes and Gloria each drew their weapons.

Once again, as the sole current Bureau agent, Gloria did the honors, pounding on the door.

"FBI, Maddox. Open up, then step back, hands on your head."

Nothing. Not a sound from the other side of the door.

She knocked again, announced herself again, and waited. Two-handing her weapon, chest high. Behind her, Barnes held his gun in his good hand, barrel pointing up at the ceiling.

After another long pause without a response, Gloria took out the master key and unlocked the door. Using her foot, she slowly and cautiously pushed it open. Gloria entered first, followed by Barnes, and then me.

To my surprise, the small, wood-paneled entranceway was well-lit by an overhead lamp. As we made our way into the main living area, we were met with another surprise.

"I guess these places are rented unfurnished," Barnes said dryly. "Unless Maddox has *really* simple tastes."

Still brandishing her weapon, Gloria went down the hall to her left. Moments later, she reported that the bedroom and bath were in the same inexplicable condition.

The room we stood in—like the rest of the apartment—was completely empty. No furniture, no TV or radio, not a single table or lamp. The only illumination in the square, carpeted living area came from a high-wattage ceiling light.

Completely empty, that is, except for a laptop computer, its lid open, sitting on the carpet in the middle of the room.

The computer screen was blank.

Barnes sniffed. "What the hell—?"

He took a few steps into the room, toward the laptop. Suddenly its screen lit up, flickering to life.

"Shit," Gloria gasped.

"Must be motion-activated." Barnes froze where he stood. "I was a damned fool not to think of that."

I took a step closer myself and peered down at the screen. It revealed a live-streaming image of Sebastian Maddox, his smiling face taking up the entire frame.

When he spoke, he pitched his voice to sound like a parody of a pompous TV announcer. Deep and self-important.

"Lady and gentlemen, LIVE from somewhere else, it's *me!*"

Barnes practically spat. "Christ!"

Maddox laughed, and resumed his usual mocking tone.

"You guys look surprised. I mean, sure, the apartment's a bit Spartan. In fact, I bet you were expecting something really dramatic. Like pictures of Barbara plastered all over the walls. Maybe even a little shrine to her memory, complete with candles and incense. If so, you've seen way too many movies."

I kept my own voice even. "Listen, Maddox…"

But his face had grown serious, almost stern. "Do you really think I'd do something like that, Danny? Something so obvious, so gauche? What Barbara and I had was rare and fine. And real. Or was, until you bewitched her away from me."

I didn't bite. "Cut the crap, Maddox. Where the hell are you?"

He sat back from the camera lens, thick arms crossed on his bare chest. "At a secure, undisclosed location. As they say."

Gloria spoke up. "But we tracked the transmission signal from your drone to this place."

"Of course you did. I figured even those brainless losers you call tech support would latch onto that signal sooner or later. So I re-routed it from my actual location to this charming building in Swissvale. A kid I knew in grade school lived just down the block. I used to steal his lunch money."

"Yeah," I said. "You're a real bad-ass."

"Got you and the Scooby Gang running in circles, don't I? By the way, how's Angie? I mean, she's only your third cousin or something, so maybe you don't care that much. But she looked pretty bad last time I saw her. Kind of on the dead side."

I didn't answer. Wouldn't.

Then, abruptly, his tone changed. Sharpened. "But here's the thing, guys. I thought I made it quite clear what would happen if one of you alerted the authorities. But Special Agent Reese *had* to keep her tech friends at the Bureau on my ass. Tracking the signal from my drone. Which I think any judge in the land would consider a breach of our verbal contract."

Gloria went white, panic edging her words. "But, wait! You re-routed the signal. Got us up to this empty apartment. I admit you outsmarted us, Maddox. We still don't know where you are."

He shook his head mournfully. "Not good enough, Gloria. I mean, it's the principle of the thing. I *told* you to keep law enforcement out of it and you didn't…"

"But—!"

"Oh, good. Here it is." He glanced over at something beside him. "I've been watching the local news. Figured the story would break any minute now…"

Barnes growled. "What the hell are you talking about?"

Maddox merely smiled. "Don't worry, I'll patch it right in for you."

Suddenly, his face disappeared from the screen, to be replaced by a live broadcast from one of the local news stations.

It showed a sleepy side street, now clustered with police units, EMTs and an ambulance. A zippered body bag was being lifted from a gurney into the back of the M.E.'s wagon.

A graphic along the bottom of the screen read: "Breaking News. Drive-By Shooting in Blawnox."

From the corner of my eye, I saw Gloria lean back against a wall, head in her hands. But I couldn't tear my gaze from the screen, even though I knew what was coming.

"According to police," the on-scene reporter told his viewers, "a local Blawnox man was shot and killed while eating dinner with his family in their home. Witnesses report that a car with blackened windows came down the street and stopped in front of the man's house. Then the driver, holding a handgun of some kind, leaned out and fired twice into the dining room window. The victim, Howard Lister, forty-five, a husband and father of two, was pronounced dead at the scene."

Then the image from the TV station vanished, and Maddox appeared once more. Reflectively stroking his chin.

"So *that's* who I shot." As though to himself. "I didn't know his name. I just picked a house at random, saw the happy family eating dinner, and squeezed off a couple."

His eyes glinted out at us from the screen.

"Poor Howard. Never even got dessert. And bear in mind, his death is on you guys. We had an understanding, and... Well, if you do it again, I won't be responsible for what happens. How many *more* innocent people will pay the price."

The bastard actually smiled.

Suddenly, with a growl of frustration and rage, Lyle Barnes raised his Glock and pointed it at the screen. "Fuck this."

Gloria whirled to face him. "Lyle! No!"

He didn't even turn his head to reply. "I can't take this goddam shit anymore." He took a further step toward the laptop. "Hear me, Maddox? *You hear me? Die,* you son of a bitch! *Die!*"

Before either Gloria or I could stop him, Barnes fired, the booming sound echoing like thunder in the small room. The laptop screen exploded into pieces, as the force of the shot knocked the computer back. Until, hopping across the carpet, it slammed up against the far wall.

I grabbed at Barnes' gun arm, pushed it down.

"Jesus Christ, Lyle! He might've *told* us something. Named his next target—"

His jaw set. "That prick wasn't gonna tell us anything. Not now. Not tonight."

Gloria turned as well to confront him, her face livid.

"How the hell do you *know* that, old man? From all your years on the job, which you keep throwing in my face? Or maybe you're just losing your shit, since you haven't slept a wink since this nightmare started. Face it, Barnes! You fucked up!"

The stark silence that followed seemed almost as deafening as the gunshot.

Finally, shoving his Glock in his belt, Barnes strode out of the room. Gloria and I exchanged chagrined looks, and then followed him down the hall.

None of us said much on the drive back to the safe house. I could tell that Gloria was consumed with guilt about the death of Howard Lister. I also knew enough to give her the space to process it in her own way, and in her own time. Until she'd come to realize where the blame for Maddox's horrific crime actually lay.

Then there was Barnes' impulsive, frustration-driven reaction. Blasting apart the laptop. Given Maddox's fragile narcissism, his self-appointed grandiosity, I feared he'd be unable to resist a further retaliation of some kind.

I was right.

● ● ● ● ●

It wasn't until we'd turned onto the side street in Wilkinsburg that we saw the flashing lights of the fire trucks and police units. They formed a grim semi-circle, facing what had once been the deserted movie theater.

As we drew closer, I could see the blasted, smoking remains of the abandoned building. Most of its walls had collapsed, behind which danced a few small licks of flame. Firefighters in protective gear, wielding hoses, sprayed powerful streams of water at these last active fires in the charred structure.

Gazing out the window, Gloria could only manage a stunned whisper. "Holy shit…"

Barnes pulled to the curb a good hundred yards from the scene and we scrambled out. As we headed toward the fire line and the various clusters of first responders, I noticed that both my Mustang and Gloria's hatchback were parked far enough down the block to have been spared any damage.

The acrid smell of black smoke, hissing metal, and smoldering wood hit my nostrils as we approached. At first glance, it appeared that the entire above-ground structure had been flattened. More significantly, a huge, crater-like hole revealed severe damage to the FBI's abandoned facility beneath.

"Maddox." This murmured word was the first one Barnes had uttered since we'd left Swissvale.

A tall black man turned at our approach, his weary features reflected in the glow of the flashing lights. He wore the same protective gear as everyone else from his fire company, but without the hard hat. His name tag read "Capt. Morris T. Welch."

Before he could question us, Gloria flashed her badge.

"We were just passing by," she explained, "pursuant to a local case, when we saw the trucks and cruisers."

Welch nodded at the three of us, then indicated the growing throng of people being held behind a police line. Neighbors from the block, I figured, many armed with cell phones whose cameras were directed at the smoking debris.

"Gawkers shootin' video to sell to the news channels," the captain said. "Or to put up on YouTube. People like that really tick me off."

I nodded. "I can imagine, Captain. Any idea what happened? Anybody see anything?"

"Well, right now we just want to keep this thing contained. Which is pretty much done, far as I can see. I'll know more when my guys down in those underground rooms report back. Gotta make sure they're no dead or wounded down there."

For the first time, Welch seemed to register Barnes' arm sling. His eyes narrowed suspiciously, bringing a hasty response from the ex-agent.

"Fell down chasing a perp last week." Barnes offered a sheepish smile. "I think I'm getting too old for this job."

Welch smiled back, though his look remained guarded. "You and me both, mister."

Quickly, Gloria reframed my question. "Any witnesses?"

"Just one. Guy across the street was out walkin' his dog, said he saw somethin' come outta the sky and fly right into the theater. Looked like a big bug with headlights for eyes."

She spoke carefully. "Sounds like a drone to me."

"That's what we figger, too. Won't know for sure till the tech guys show up, but my money's on some kinda drone packed with explosives. C-4 or somethin' like that."

Welch had no sooner finished speaking when a camera truck from KDKA-TV came rumbling down the street, stopping right behind the crowd of chattering bystanders.

"Great." Welch heaved a sigh. "My favorite part o' the job. Dealin' with the media."

Gloria gave him an encouraging pat on the arm. "Then we better get out of your way and leave you to it."

Chapter Twenty-eight

As we walked away, Gloria turned to Barnes.

"You know what this was, right, Lyle? Payback for what you did in Swissvale, shooting up Maddox's laptop in the middle of his taunting victory speech. A guy with that ego? It's like he's saying, you screw with me, I'll do the same to you."

"Maybe. But how the hell did he know where the safe house was? And that we'd been using it?"

"Who knows?" Gloria's anger grew. "We're just lucky we weren't inside when it happened. We could've been killed."

I shook my head. "No, I don't think so. I mean, I'm sure you're right about Maddox sending that drone in response to what happened in the apartment. But I also think he timed it so that it would strike before we got back."

By then, we'd reached Barnes' car. I leaned against it.

"Remember, he's spent a long time planning his revenge on me. Seeking out victims close to me. Building up to the last act: my own death. There's no way he won't want to be there in person to see it."

Barnes stroked his chin. "I think you're right, Doc. Killing all three of us, long-distance?…It just doesn't fit."

I turned to Gloria. "Are you okay? I mean, about that man getting shot? Remember, his death is on Maddox, *not* you."

"I know." Her chin lowered. "But still, it's hard…"

Then, rubbing her eyes, she looked up. Let out a long

breath, and gave Barnes and me a brave smile. Letting us know she'd be all right.

And I knew she would be. As much as anyone could.

● ● **●** ● ●

Still standing by Barnes' car, we discussed where we might set up what he called our next command post.

"Maybe a tugboat out on the Allegheny?" I suggested, only half-kidding. "Or a hot air balloon?"

"I was thinking more along the lines of a chain motel," Barnes said. "I'm staying in one now. Out past GreenTree."

"God knows what it's like." Gloria folded her arms. "I got dibs on the room without the bedbugs."

He regarded her. "I'm frugal, Gloria, but not unhygienic. Besides, how long are you going to stay mad at me?"

"I haven't decided yet. But at least you finally called me 'Gloria.'"

His eyes gleamed mischievously. "Old profiler trick. Seek rapport with your adversary. Build intimacy and trust."

"No kidding? Well, you've still got a ways to go, buddy."

He shrugged. "In the meantime, we still have a problem. Both of your computers were down in the safe house. They're probably toast."

"Along with all that data you collected," said Gloria.

"Not exactly. Before we left there, I copied all the docs to your personal computer. As a precaution."

She started. "You mean, back at my place? The one that Maddox hacked? *You* did, too?"

"It wasn't that hard. Frankly, Gloria, you really need to get some better spyware on that thing."

Gloria's lips tightened. "Guess you're still not clear on that 'intimacy and trust' thing, eh, Lyle?"

"Let's say it's a work in progress."

I saw her make the effort to calm down. To consider the pros and cons of the situation. I also saw that it wasn't easy.

But finally the professional in her prevailed.

"Okay. It's good that you backed everything up." She fished her keys out of her pocket. "I'll just swing by my apartment and pick up my laptop. Then meet you guys at the motel."

"You think that's smart?" I said. "Maddox could have eyes on your place, you know."

"Fuck him. I don't care who he is, he can't be watching everything and everyone at once. I'm sure I can get in and out of my place without his knowing."

She frowned at my skeptical look. "And we *need* a computer, Danny. Access to those files Barnes assembled, police reports. Whatever. Plus a way for Maddox to contact us. I said it before: if he stops talking to us, we're *really* in the dark."

"Then I'm going with you."

"No, you're not. You're going to start checking the hospitals for news about Angie. I know how worried you are."

"You mean, like I am for you?"

Her look was steady. "That's sweet, Danny. But I can take care of myself. In fact, I insist on it. If you don't agree, we have a real problem."

Our eyes locked. And I knew she wasn't going to budge.

Meanwhile, Lyle Barnes looked from one of us to the other. He was either amused or exasperated. I couldn't tell which.

Finally, he said, "I think she's talking about respect, Doc."

Without turning, Gloria pointed a finger at him. "*You* stay out of this! I'm still trying to get over being pissed at you."

I kept my gaze fixed on hers. And saw that Lyle was right. "Okay, Gloria," I said at last. "Message received."

She managed a slight, crooked smile.

"Now if you two don't mind, I'd like to leave this sausage party and get on the road. Lyle, text me the address of the motel in GreenTree and let's meet there in the morning."

"Sounds like a plan."

With that, she nodded at the two of us, then trotted off in the direction of where her hatchback was parked.

"I like her," Barnes said simply, before opening his car door and getting behind the wheel.

"Me, too."

I watched him pull away from the curb. Walking toward my own car, I glanced up the street at the scene of the fire. It looked as though most of it had been contained, though plumes of smoke rose up against the opaque sky. By now, a second TV news truck had arrived, even as some of the responders were beginning to pack up their gear.

Back inside my Mustang, I took a moment to glance at the rear seat. Thankfully, unlike my laptop and travel bag, I'd left Barbara's unfinished manuscript in the car. Otherwise, it would probably have been destroyed in the fire.

Instinctively, I reached over the seat back and placed the bound manuscript next to me on the passenger side. It wasn't something I wanted to risk losing.

With a stroke, time is of the essence. The EMTs who attended to Angie obviously knew that as well, so I used my throwaway cell to get the number of a hospital in or near McKees Rocks. The closest one to the river port was Mercy General, so I called there, identified myself as both a police consultant and the patient's relative, and persuaded the duty nurse to confirm that Angie had been admitted.

It was nearing three a.m., and the rain had still held off, so I was able to drive to the low-slung, white-brick hospital complex fairly quickly. The open-air lot wasn't even half-full, and I had no trouble finding a parking spot near the entrance. My guess was that after being rushed to the ER, Angie had been taken up to the ICU. So I went into the main entrance.

My police consultant's ID seemed to have more weight with the receptionist than my blood connection to the victim, so I was directed to the elevators and told Intensive Care was on the third floor.

When I arrived in Angie's room, I was met by two people standing vigilantly by her bed. One was a doctor whose name tag read "Robert Hilvers, M.D." The other was Sergeant Harry Polk.

The latter was the first to speak.

"Jesus Christ, Rinaldi. I mighta known you'd show up. How the hell did you find out about this?"

I didn't reply. Other than giving each man an acknowledging nod, my gaze went directly to Angie, bundled under a swath of sheets in the hospital bed. An IV drip fed into one of her doughy forearms, while a series of leads fed into a rack of monitors at her side. Their steady, ominous beeping was like the echo of a sluggish, beating heart.

The doctor—young, slender, wearing wire rims and a smug expression—turned toward me. His voice laced with asperity.

"You're related to the patient, Mister—?"

"Doctor. Daniel Rinaldi. Yes. Related by blood and a long history. How is she?"

He fingered the stethoscope coiled around his neck. "Given the trauma she's undergone, I'd say as well as can be hoped."

"What does that mean?"

"I'm afraid it's too soon to tell, Doctor. It was a fairly significant event…the stroke, I mean. No doubt caused by the shock of what happened to her. We're keeping her stable, but as to its long-term physiological or cognitive effects…" Hilvers took a mournful pause. "This is one of those cases for which the only treatment is tincture of time."

Polk stirred, eyes narrowing. I could tell he didn't much care for Robert Hilvers, M.D. But whatever he'd thought about saying, he apparently decided not to say it.

The doctor glanced at the opened doorway. "I'll be back to check on Ms. Villanova in a few minutes. Till then, I'll send in one of our floor nurses."

"Thanks, Doctor." I surprised him by reaching out to shake his hand, figuring it was smart to stay on this pompous jerk's good side. At least for now.

I'd guessed right. He returned my handshake with a broad, appreciative smile. Then, having been accorded the proper respect and deference, he strode from the room.

As I took a position across the bed from where Polk stood, he leveled his heavy gaze on me.

"Real piece o' work, that guy. Couple times, I wanted to shove that stethoscope down his throat." Harry rubbed his beard stubble. "So what do *you* know about all this?"

"I was going to ask you the same question."

"There ain't much. Somebody grabbed her right outside the precinct, gettin' into her car after work. We only know 'cause some uniform happened to see it go down from across the lot. But the fuckin' balls, takin' her right outside our own house."

"But what happened to her?"

As before, I had to maintain a disingenuous ignorance of events I'd actually witnessed. It wasn't the first time in my career with them that I'd had to lie to the police, but I was never comfortable doing it.

Polk paused, looking down at Angie's chalk-white face, her closed eyelids. The slackened mouth, lips slightly cracked.

"Looks like the perp knocked her out—probably with some kinda drug, the doc says, though we won't know till the blood tests come back. Then he ties her to one of the pillars down at the McKees Rocks port. Tryin' to drown her, looks like. But that sure ain't the easiest way to do it. Or the fastest, the sadistic son of a bitch. Funny thing. We still don't know how the hell she got free o' the ropes and outta the water."

I shrugged. "Angie's a fighter, Harry. You know that as well as I do. But I think you're right about the perp…Sounds like he *wanted* to terrify her. Make her suffer."

"Yeah, that's what Chief Logan says, too. Biegler woke him outta bed a couple hours ago to tell him about it. And to the Chief's credit, he wants every available cop brought into this. From senior detectives down to traffic control. He really wants to nail the bastard who did this to her."

"I'm not surprised. Angie and Logan go way back." I gently touched her shoulder. "So do we. From the old neighborhood."

"Yeah, I know." For the first time, he offered me a look of commiseration. "I figger this is pretty tough on you, Doc."

"Not as tough as on her. Or her husband, for that matter. Where *is* Sonny, by the way?"

"Ya just missed him. He's been here since Angie was brought in. Right before you showed up, Doc sent him down to the lounge to grab a couple hours' sleep."

"Just as well. I'm not one of Sonny's favorite people."

"Yeah." Polk failed to suppress a smile. "Seems like ya have that effect on a lotta folks. By the way, ya never answered my question. How come ya knew Angie was here?"

"I happened to be here in the hospital, helping to admit a patient of mine in crisis."

"At three in the mornin'?"

"Psychotic episodes don't keep banker's hours, Harry. Anyway, while I was conferring with the staff shrink on call, I heard one of the nurses talking about a patient named Villanova being brought up to ICU."

It sounded plausible, so Polk bought it. At least it looked that way.

Then, for a long moment, he and I merely stood on either side of the bed, watching Angie's slow, measured breathing.

"Any leads on the perp?" I asked Polk at last. "Or ideas about motive?"

"Well, whatever the prick's reasons, this was goddam personal. Nobody does somethin' this fucked up unless it is. Like you said, he wanted her to suffer."

"Hopefully, Angie can give you more to go on when she wakes up...recovers enough to talk..."

"*If* she can talk." Polk's face darkened. "Doc said earlier there was a good chance she might not be able to. Ever."

Though the possibility of this had crossed my mind already, it was still a shock to hear it put into words, to contemplate the possible permanent effects of the stroke. For all the years I'd known her, Angie had been like a force of nature. Funny and combative, yet with a boundless love for her family and friends. Now to have that energy, that vitality, stilled forever…

Just then, one of the unit nurses came in. She was a tall, strong-looking black woman whose face registered both competence and compassion. A veteran caregiver who, I suspected, had zero tolerance for any nonsense from patients, visitors, or doctors.

"Gentlemen." Giving us a cursory glance, she said her name was Rosalind, then began checking the monitors and the IV tube. I stepped away from the bed to give her room to work.

Abruptly, she looked up from her duties to stare at Polk.

"Are you the police?"

"Detective Sergeant Polk, ma'am."

"Then tell me something, Detective Sergeant." With heavy emphasis on those last two words. "I heard what happened to this poor woman. Tied up in the river and left to drown. So tell me: who could do such a thing?"

"That's what we're gonna find out. Way I see it, there are three kinds o' people in this world: good, bad, and worse. The man who did this—"

She interrupted him. "There's no mystery here. The man who did this has the devil in him. That's all you need to know."

Before he could respond, Rosalind went back to attending to her patient. I looked over at Polk, who stood uneasily, as if he didn't know what to do with his hands.

"I better go," I said. "I'm just in everyone's way. Harry?"

"I gotta stay. Biegler and Chief Logan are due here any minute. They wanna see how she's bein' treated."

"They also probably want to figure out how to spin this for the press. As the Department's Community Liaison Officer, Angie is pretty well known throughout the city. Speaking of which, have her kids been notified?"

"Sonny already called 'em. They're on their way in, too." A heavy sigh. "Gonna be damned crowded in here pretty soon."

Rosalind had just finished with Angie when I turned to leave. Suddenly, she tapped me on the shoulder.

"Hey, mister. What's that welt doing on your neck? If that's from a needle stick, somebody did a lousy job of it."

Instinctively, I felt the back of my neck where Maddox had plunged in the hypo loaded with the paralytic. To my surprise, the raised puncture site was still quite pronounced.

"I think it's some kind of insect bite," I said lamely.

She grunted, unconvinced. "Whatever. Want my advice, have that thing looked at."

With that, she hustled out of the room. Right afterwards, promising to check in with Polk later, in case there were any new developments, I, too, made my exit. Then I found Rosalind at the nurses' station and asked for her card.

"If you don't mind," I said, "I'd rather get progress reports on Ms. Villanova from you than from Dr. Hilvers."

She gave me a wry smile. "I don't blame ya, mister."

I wasn't halfway down the ICU's main corridor when it struck me. The answer to a question that had been nagging me since earlier tonight at the river port.

Yet, though I was in a hospital, the perfect place to deal with it, I knew I couldn't. Not here, not with doctors I didn't know. Who'd ask questions. Who'd feel duty-bound to report it to the cops.

No, the only two people I could trust were Lyle Barnes and Gloria Reese.

I just had to hope that one of them knew how to handle a scalpel.

Chapter Twenty-nine

Gloria held the small scalpel up to the light of the bedside lamp.

"Where the hell did you get this, Danny?"

"Mercy General. On my way out, I snuck into one of the service closets and got it out of a discard bin."

"Great. So it's not exactly sterile."

"No, but it's not exactly brain surgery we're talking about, either."

Sitting next to her on the motel bed, I pulled my sweater off over my head. Even that minor effort brought a spasm of pain to my bruised ribs.

Lyle Barnes stood a few feet away, rubbing the underside of his arm sling. "If I didn't have this damned thing, Doc, I'd be happy to do it."

I managed a grin. "That's what I was afraid of, Lyle. Truth is, I trust Gloria's reluctance and general disapproval. It means she'll be slow and careful."

"Thanks," she said. "I think."

We were in Gloria's room at the motel on the outskirts of GreenTree, right next to the one I'd be sharing with Barnes.

I'd come straight from the hospital, and though the sun hadn't yet risen, an accident on the parkway had traffic backed up for miles. When I finally pulled into the motel's lot, I was surprised to find that it wasn't as bad as Gloria had feared. With its garishly colored sign proclaiming free cable TV and complimentary Continental breakfast, it was like most other chain motels built in the mid-1960s.

I'd seen more than my share of places like it when I was a teenager, traveling to amateur boxing matches around the tri-state area with my dad. In that way, it was like coming home.

But, seeing Gloria's car parked next to Lyle's, my primary feeling was one of relief. As she'd promised, she'd obviously managed to retrieve her laptop from her apartment and make it here to the motel. Once inside her room, and seeing it on a little desk in the corner, I received further assurance that Maddox hadn't seen her or followed her.

"Give me some credit, will ya, Danny? I know when I'm being tailed. And when I'm not."

Still, the laptop itself represented potential danger, so she'd not only closed the lid but buried it under a couple of the room's pillows. And a bedsheet.

"Harder for him to hear us," she'd explained. "If he's even listening. I mean, Christ, even *he* has to rest sometimes. Eat. Go to the bathroom. Right?"

"Right." Wishing I'd sounded more convincing.

Now, while Lyle ran steaming hot water over the scalpel in the bathroom sink, I lay on my stomach on some towels that Gloria had spread on the bed.

With a deep exhalation, she bent over me and gingerly touched the welt on the back of my neck. I could smell the last traces of her subtle perfume. I found it oddly calming.

"Now that I'm looking for it, I can feel it," she said. "The chip Maddox embedded under the skin."

"Yeah. I realize now it must've been when he'd given me the second injection. Right after showing me the video that night, when I was still tied to the chair. After the drug took effect, he implanted the tracking chip."

"No wonder it still hurt like hell. But how did you figure it out?"

"I didn't. Not till that nurse mentioned it. That's when I put it together with something Maddox had said at the port. He said he knew how much I liked looking at a river."

"I don't understand."

"He was referring to the other night, right after Harvey's death. Remember? I was too rattled by it to come right back, so I stood at the Mon's riverbank. Just thinking. Trying to come to terms with what happened to Harvey. Until I got chased out of there by some river cop."

I raised my head to turn toward her, but she gently guided it back down on my crossed forearms on the bed.

"I wondered about that," I went on. "How could Maddox know I'd walked down to the river? Even if he'd somehow managed to track me by my laptop, that didn't apply in this case. It wasn't in my car. It was back at my house."

"But we'd always assumed he'd tracked your movements using the GPS we found in your car."

"You mean the one we were *supposed* to find...that Maddox wanted us to find. To throw us off. Make us think he couldn't track me anymore."

I heard Gloria cluck her tongue. "Now I get it. That's also how he knew about the safe house. At least its location."

"Right. When I showed up there, I'd inadvertently led him right to us. This whole time, he's had me belled like a cat."

"Well, not for long."

It was Barnes, coming out from the bathroom. Holding the scalpel by its slim handle, he gave it to Gloria.

"Let the butchery begin."

She must have been too nervous to come up with a snappy comeback. Instead, she patted me on the shoulder and took a number of fairly audible deep breaths.

Lyle Barnes bent his tall frame and peered sideways at me.

"Want a shot of whiskey? For the pain? I always keep a flask in the car. For medicinal purposes such as this."

"No, I'm good. I just want the damned thing out."

"Suit yourself." Barnes reached behind him and pulled one

of the motel's thin washcloths from his back pocket. "At least you oughtta bite down on this."

He rolled it up and inserted it between my teeth. As instructed, I bit down. Hard.

At the same time, I felt a cold liquid splash on the back of my neck. From the smell, I knew that Barnes had found another use for the whiskey. A makeshift antiseptic.

"Here goes," Gloria whispered.

· ● ● ● ·

It was the longest ten minutes of my life.

Then, finally: "Got it," she said.

The pain had been considerable, but biting down on the rolled-up washcloth did indeed help. Though not much. Especially when I felt Gloria digging around the edges of the incision, to work the scalpel's tip deep enough to get under the chip.

I let the washcloth fall from my mouth, but stayed on my stomach as Gloria bandaged the wound. Luckily, along with the flask, Barnes had a first aid kit in his car. I can't say that this surprised me. In many ways, he was a combination of a hardened, world-weary Federal agent and overgrown Boy Scout.

Another tap on the shoulder was my signal to get up to a sitting position. The back of my neck throbbed with pain, and the towels beneath me were spackled with my blood. But I seemed to have come through the procedure in one piece.

Barnes and Gloria were both looking at me expectantly, even as she daubed at the sweat on her forehead with her sleeve. Her eyes still wide and brimming with apprehension.

"Thank you, Gloria." I tried on a smile.

Somewhat speechless, she could only nod. Meanwhile, Barnes was examining the bloodied metallic chip in the palm of his hand. Poking it with a long forefinger.

"Looks like an RFID transponder," he said. "Nifty little gizmo. Long-range transmission. Very nifty, indeed."

I frowned at him. "Well, I'm glad you're impressed, Lyle. I'd hate to see you disappointed."

"It's always good to know your enemy, Doc. It's even better to show him the proper respect. Later on, it can save your ass."

He showed the chip to Gloria. Slowly coming out of her post-op trance, she took a moment to examine it.

"Pretty advanced subdermal implant. Encased in silicate glass. I've seen one before." She looked up at us. "We have to assume it's still functioning. So now the question is, what do we do with it?"

"Good point." I stirred slightly, sending a shaft of pain up the back of my skull. "If we destroy it, Maddox will know we've found it."

Barnes considered this. "Then let him go on thinking it's still where he put it. This way he keeps getting its signal."

"Which means we get to lead *him* around by the nose." Gloria gave a weak smile. "Instead of the other way around."

I nodded. "I like *that*."

"Speaking of other way around," Barnes said. "I think it's time for me to tell you to get some sleep, Doc. You look pretty damned done-in."

"Not yet." I slowly stood up from the bed. "Not before I see if the story broke about Angie, and what the police are saying about it. If they're saying anything."

Despite their half-hearted protests, I scooped up the TV remote on the bedside table and clicked on the set bolted to the wall across the room. In moments, I found the early morning news. The assault on Angie was the lead story.

"According to a police spokesman," the bland anchor said, "there has been an attempt on the life of a high-ranking member of the Department's administration. While the name of the victim has yet to be released, Chief Logan confirms, through that same spokesman, that the crime happened last night, and that the well-regarded member of his staff is in critical condition."

"They're keeping things pretty close to the vest." Barnes was watching from his seat on the edge of the bed. "Like I expected. Especially given how little they actually know."

"At least until Angie wakes up and can talk." I quickly corrected myself. "*If* she can talk. Even so, I'm sure Maddox was too careful to let her get a look at him. Just in case."

Gloria murmured her agreement.

The news anchor then switched to another segment, detailing the police department's admission that there was little progress in its ongoing investigation into the death of Harvey Blalock. The piece ended with a video of a press conference the day before, at which the new acting-president of the Pittsburgh Black Attorneys Association promised she would continue to pressure law enforcement, and the Mayor himself, until the cowardly killer had been apprehended.

Finally, there was a shorter piece about last night's fire at the abandoned movie theater in Wilkinsburg, including some aerial footage shot by the station's news chopper. When they cut to an on-scene reporter, he explained that the building had been deserted for years. Further, that Captain Welch of Fire Company 27 had confirmed there'd been no loss of life. As to the cause of the explosion, it was still under investigation.

I clicked around to other news channels, but they all relayed pretty much the same information about the various crimes. However, I was struck by the fact that no mention was made of the hit-and-run death of Stephen Langley.

"That's *old* news," Lyle said bitterly. "Concerning an old guy that nobody gives a damn about."

Something in his wan countenance suggested to me that he was implicitly referring to himself. But whatever I thought I saw there, it quickly faded from his face.

Meanwhile, Gloria was still holding the tracking chip between her slender fingers. Brow knitted in thought.

"Guys, if we're right in assuming this thing's still working, Maddox now knows where we are. And that means—"

"We have to move again," I said.

• ● ● ● •

Which we did, after Barnes used his throwaway cell to book two rooms in another motel, about four miles south of Pittsburgh International Airport.

Each in our separate cars, we drove through the pale dawn light to a motel that was practically a duplicate of the one we'd just left. As part of the same nationwide chain, the only difference was that the L-shaped building was smaller, and located in a much more sparsely populated area.

Though before I joined Barnes and Gloria there, I got off at a nearby exit ramp and searched the near-rural roads for a vacant lot. Finding one not too far from the parkway, I pulled up beside it and tossed the tracking chip into a clump of weeds.

With any luck, Maddox would think this was the location where the three of us had holed up next.

Not that our luck had been so great up till then.

Chapter Thirty

Sitting on one of the twin beds in the motel room, hazy morning light streaming through the shutters, I swallowed two of my pain meds. Not that I'd need much help getting to sleep. Barnes had been right. I was physically and emotionally spent.

As at the previous motel in GreenTree, Lyle had gotten a room for the two men and a second for Gloria. It was ludicrous on the face of it, but something about the arrangement soothed Barnes' sense of propriety. He'd also pointed out that renting one room for the three of us would attract the desk clerk's notice, which was something we certainly didn't want.

Regardless, Gloria had spent the past few minutes in here, making sure I was really going to go to bed. Which I dutifully did, pulling the threadbare covers over me.

"And don't worry," she said now, closing the shutters against the light. "I won't climb in later and molest you."

Gloria gave me a smile somewhat brighter than our situation warranted, bent and kissed my forehead, and then left the room.

Despite the images from the past days' events swirling in my mind, and the persistent pain at the back of my neck, I fell almost instantly into a deep, enveloping sleep.

I woke up at three in the afternoon, both reasonably well-rested and ravenously hungry. As I'd expected, the room's other bed hadn't been slept in. Pulling on the same clothes I'd stripped out of to sleep, I went over to the shutters and let in the somber half-light. Another gloomy, overcast day. But at least it wasn't raining again.

I found Barnes and Gloria in her room, on facing chairs at the writing desk, a tray of empty paper plates and Styrofoam coffee cups between them. Next to the tray was another paper plate, covered in plastic wrap. They'd gotten me a toasted BLT and fries, with a lidded coffee cup to one side.

"Good, you're up." Gloria nodded at the covered plate. "I was just about to split that with Lyle."

Balancing the plate on my knees, I sat on the edge of the bed. After two huge bites of the sandwich, I started to come back to life. More or less.

"Before you ask, Doc," said Barnes, turning in his seat toward me, "there's been no contact from Maddox."

Instinctively, I glanced over at Gloria's laptop, uncovered and with its lid open on the bedside table. The screen blank.

"We'll see how long that lasts." I sipped the strong black coffee. "Until then, I better check my office voice mail. I don't like spending so much time out of touch with my patients."

Gloria stirred. "About your voice mail…You realize we can't assume it's secure. Maybe it's not something you should keep using."

"Hell, Gloria, I've never assumed Maddox hasn't hacked it. But my patients have to have access to me, even now. Besides, it's not as though he doesn't know who they are. Or all about them. From the files in my laptop."

Barnes weighed in. "We should also assume he's broken into your house by now and bugged your landline phone. The one connected to an answering machine. Remember, he opened the lock on your Mustang without leaving a trace, and I've already proven—twice—how easy it is to get into your house."

I frowned. "Thanks for reminding me. And you're probably right about my home phone. But, frankly, I'm starting not to care. I'm tired of giving him that psychological edge."

"What do you mean?" Gloria sat up in her seat.

"One of the ways Maddox keeps spooking us is by seeming to be omnipresent. All-seeing, all-knowing. Which in turn makes us tentative, reactive. Always playing defense."

Barnes scowled. "That's because it's his game, so he gets to make the rules. Whether we like it or not."

"But that's my point. It'll stay that way until we figure out a way to *change* the rules."

Gloria folded her arms. "Well, I'm open to suggestions."

"I'm working on it," I said.

And I was.

At Gloria's insistence, I finished my meal. Then I used my throwaway cell to check my voice mail. Two messages. One was from a long-time colleague, following up on our plans to have drinks together soon. The other was from Noah Frye.

After listening to his anxious, rambling message, I hung up and regarded Barnes and Gloria.

"Noah called me. He said he was just watching the news and heard about Angie."

"So they've released her identity," Gloria said. "I'm kinda surprised they didn't withhold it longer."

"Me, too. Though it's probably to get out in front of the media. I know from experience that it's better that her name comes from Pittsburgh PD than the press. This way, they can take some control of the narrative."

Barnes grunted. "Son, you've been hanging around with the Department brass way too long. You're starting to sound like one of those lame-ass suits."

"Maybe. But wasn't it *you* who said something about knowing your enemy?"

I swallowed the rest of my coffee and stood up.

"I'd better return Noah's call. Give me a couple minutes."

However, the first thing I did when I got back to my own room was check the TV news. As Noah said, the police had released Angie's name, and a vague description of what had happened to her. Omitting, of course, any specific details. They also confirmed that she was still listed in critical condition.

Clicking off the TV, I used my throwaway cell to phone Noah at the bar. If memory served, there was still a little time before Happy Hour, when he'd be too busy to talk.

Noah picked up on the third ring.

"Sorry to hear about that Angie lady, Danny. Ain't she your cousin or somethin'?"

"Or something. Hard to keep track of all the branches on the family tree. But I've known her since I was a kid."

"Right. But promise me that don't mean you're gonna play amateur detective and try to do somethin' about it?"

"Don't worry, Noah. Never entered my mind."

"Right," he said again, voice thick with doubt. "Ya know, Danny, it ain't always easy bein' your best friend. Havin' to worry all the time about what you're gettin' yourself into."

"Believe me, I know the feeling."

"Whatever. By the way, forget about comin' to see the old trio back in action. Rufus, my bass player, just split for Atlantic City. Says he got a better gig with some sax player he knows from when they were in rehab. What a douche."

I didn't mention that I'd forgotten all about it.

"'Course, I shouldn't be surprised," he went on, oblivious. "Rufus is just like everyone else. Christ, I hear it every day at the bar. Guys get hammered, then start bitchin' and moanin'. Sayin' how they shoulda done this, coulda done that. If only *this* would happen. That's the trouble with people, Danny."

"What do you mean?"

"I mean, nobody's happy. And ya know why? 'Cause everybody thinks the party's happenin' somewhere else."

I was still digesting his words when I heard a rapid knock on the door. Then Gloria's urgent voice.

"It's Maddox, Danny. And it's bad."

• • ● • •

Back in her room, the three of us gathered at the bedside table, our eyes riveted to her laptop's screen.

Sebastian Maddox, in a collared denim shirt, glared out at us. Livid.

"*Now* you've done it, Danny. You fucked with me and my plans, which means I'm going to have to fuck you back."

I'd never seen his normally mocking, self-possessed face this dark with anger. His green eyes narrowed to icy points.

"What are you talking about?" I leaned in to the screen.

"The chip I implanted, as you damn well know. It's not there anymore." He shook his head. "Jesus, are you that clueless? Did you think I wouldn't know? Wouldn't find out?"

Barnes couldn't help himself. "How, dammit?"

"The wonders of nanotechnology, Lyle old boy. I improved on the transponder by adding software I designed myself. I coded it to send me a digital signal if the chip's core temp changes from 98.6, plus or minus five degrees. I gave it a little range in case Danny here got a fever or caught a chill. Just to cover all contingencies. Sweet, eh?"

For a brief moment, he permitted himself a smile.

"I don't know where you hid it, dropped it, or threw it, but it's sent me the warning signal. So I know you and the chip have parted company, Danny. And after I went to all the trouble of planting the GPS tracker in your car where you'd find it."

"Yeah," Gloria said coolly. "We figured that out already."

Ignoring her, he aimed those merciless eyes at me.

"Like I said, since you messed with me, I'm going to do the same to you. Change things up a bit. Raise the stakes. I'm sure there's a philosophical pretext for doing so, but as Aristotle said, 'It is unbecoming for young men to utter maxims.'"

Barnes looked as though he wanted to respond, but suddenly Maddox disappeared from the screen. Instead, we only heard his voice, returned somewhat to its didactic tone.

"As you know, Danny, I've spent a good deal of time and energy compiling the names of those who are close to you. A pool of people from which I can select my victims. My kill list, so to speak. And while I trust you can guess who they might be, I always think visual aids make a much deeper impression."

The screen flickered for a moment, and then a still photo of Sergeant Harry Polk appeared. Some recent candid shot, taken on a city street in daylight.

"For example, Sergeant Polk. Maybe not someone you'd want to have for a sleep-over, but an intimate acquaintance."

Another picture appeared. An image on a press badge.

"Then there's Sam Weiss, feature writer for the *Post-Gazette.* Your friendship with him began when you treated his younger sister after she'd been raped and disfigured. Swastikas carved on her tits. To be honest, I'm not sure whether I want to kill him or the little sister who got sliced and diced."

I felt anger spike in my chest. "Stop this, dammit—"

"But we're not finished yet." A meaningful pause. "And if I were you, I'd shut up and pay attention."

Gloria gave my arm a warning tap. I calmed myself.

"Next," Maddox continued, "we have Lieutenant Stu Biegler."

A posed photo of the head of Robbery/Homicide filled the screen. He stood in his dress blues, the American flag and the flag of Pennsylvania displayed on the wall behind him.

"I think Biegler's probably safe, since killing him would be doing you a favor. Though his position in the Department, and his overall obnoxiousness, make him a tempting target."

Next came another posed picture. Leland Sinclair.

"Here's the city's illustrious District Attorney, with whom you've had more than a few run-ins. Based on some e-mails hacked from both of your personal accounts, and doing a little cross-referencing, it looks like at one point you were both sleeping with the same woman. Geez, that must've been awkward."

I heard Gloria's small intake of breath, and when I glanced at her she averted her eyes.

Barnes reached out suddenly with his good arm and gripped the top of the computer's lid. He was going to shut it.

"That would be a mistake, Lyle." Maddox's voice tightened. "I suggest you trust me on that point. Danny?"

I took Barnes' arm and gently disengaged it from the lid.

"No, Lyle. Don't."

"Very wise, Daniel." Maddox gave a dark chuckle. "Because you need to hear this—and see it—all the way to the end. But don't worry, we're almost done."

Even as I released my grip on Barnes' arm, another photo appeared on the laptop screen. An official picture from a corporate personnel file.

"Next we have Nancy Mendors, Clinical Director at Ten Oaks, the private psych hospital where you were an intern years ago. At the time, she was a staff shrink going through a painful divorce and you were a recent widower…"

"Thanks to you," I said bitterly.

"Not relevant. What matters is that you two found mutual solace by having a brief affair. However, you've remained friends, since you're invited to her upcoming wedding to that pediatric surgeon. Apparently she had no trouble moving on."

I gave Gloria a sidelong glance, but her expression was unreadable. Which was also the case when Maddox showed us the next—and last—photo. Another candid shot, from another day on a busy city sidewalk. In her jeans and sleeveless shirt.

"Last, we have the delectable and annoyingly bisexual Eleanor Lowrey. You and she were going pretty hot and heavy for a while there, Danny, you dog, you. But now things are somewhat up in the air. Good news for you, Gloria, I think."

Her voice was deadly quiet. "Fuck you, Maddox."

We heard his weary laugh over the laptop's speaker. "You're going to have to come up with another retort, Agent Reese. I'm afraid you're wearing that one out."

With that, Maddox abruptly reappeared on-screen.

"Now I want Lyle and Gloria to back away from the screen a bit, okay? Give Danny and me some personal face-time."

At a nod from me, Barnes and Gloria moved off to one side, though each kept their eyes trained on the screen. Steeling myself, I again leaned in close.

"Here's the thing, Danny boy," he said, almost amiably. "One of these fine folks I showed you is going to die at midnight tonight. I'm not saying which one, mainly because I haven't decided yet. But—"

"For Christ's sake, Maddox—"

"Hold on. Let me finish. One of them's going to get extremely dead...*unless you do exactly what I say.* If you do, then they all make it through the night. Blissfully unaware of the bullet they just dodged—literally."

"Are you serious?"

"Deadly serious. Yet it's more than fair on my part, don't you think? You do something for me, and I do something for you. *Quid pro quo*, in the time-honored lingo."

"What do I have to do?"

"Take a drive across town, to the Bassmore Cemetery. Be there by ten o'clock tonight. You'll find the security guard in his little kiosk by the entrance. He'll provide your next instructions."

"Bassmore Cemetery?" My throat was going dry.

"Yes. And, as before, make sure you come alone." Maddox smiled pleasantly, showing a row of perfectly white teeth. "I assume you know the address?"

I knew the address. I'd been there before.

Chapter Thirty-one

The wind had risen with the deepening night, and as I drove out of the motel parking lot, the surrounding trees bent like stoop-shouldered old men. Pale stars shone only intermittently behind the lumbering, ash-gray clouds. And when I crossed the interchange, bypassing downtown Pittsburgh, the sleek new skyline's sparkling lights seemed equally cold, remote.

I knew what was happening. It wasn't just fear, or the slow-welling dread that had seized me from the moment Maddox vanished from the laptop screen.

It was as though I was estranged from the rest of the world. Caught in some surrealistic landscape outside of everyday experience. Everything that had made up my life till now seemed stripped away, reduced down to this struggle with Maddox.

I also knew something else. That whatever it took, and regardless of what awaited me in the hours ahead, I had to survive this night.

An hour before, as Maddox's last words faded along with his self-satisfied smile, it was Gloria who'd reached past me this time to shut the laptop lid. I didn't stop her.

Meanwhile, Barnes had begun to pace. Uncommonly agitated.

"You can't do this, Doc. A goddam cemetery? It's obviously a trap of some kind."

"I don't have a choice, Lyle. You heard what he said. If I don't, one of those people will die tonight."

Then I turned to Gloria. "And look, I'm sorry about what you just saw…or if what you heard—"

Her look was pointed. "No worries, Danny. I'm a big girl. And like I said before, you and me…? Probably just crisis sex. Though usually when I hook up with a guy, I don't see a slide-show presentation of his former lovers."

I took another step toward her, but she held up a hand.

"Besides, none of that matters right now. *Nothing* does, except figuring out our next move with Maddox."

"Gloria's right," said Barnes, no doubt happy the subject had changed.

"*We* don't have another move," I said. "But I do. He said to come alone, so that's what I'm going to do."

"Then at least stay in contact with us by phone."

I agreed, and we all checked the battery charge on our respective prepaid cells, to be on the safe side.

Before leaving, I went out to my car in the motel lot and retrieved Barbara's unfinished manuscript. Then I brought it back to the room I shared with Barnes. He was there alone, his sling undone, bending and stretching his wounded arm.

"What the hell are you doing, Lyle?"

"Testing my range of motion. You never know when I might have need of both arms sometime soon."

"Yeah, well, until then, get your injured one back in the sling. And do something else for me, will you?" I showed him the bound manuscript. "Keep this here in the room with you. Just in case things go sideways later tonight. I want to make sure it never gets into Maddox's hands."

He asked me what it was, so I told him.

"And you never knew she was writing it?" he said.

I shook my head. He merely shrugged, and took it from me.

Then Barnes and I went back to Gloria's room, to find that she'd re-opened her computer's lid. As he'd done with my own laptop, Maddox had replaced her scenic screen-saver image with that of his smiling face.

"We'll monitor this." Gloria indicated the screen. "And call you if he gets in contact again."

"He won't." I looked from one of them to the other. "This is just about me tonight. For my eyes only. Whatever it is."

● ● ● ● ●

Despite its ongoing gentrification, Pittsburgh proper still boasted a large percentage of wooded, undeveloped land. One of which was the Beechwood community's Hidden Greenway, a broad, hilly expanse of trees crisscrossed by primitive trails. The occasional deep gully was carved into the wild landscape, along which ran a few rusting, long-unused railroad tracks.

Bassmore Cemetery lay in the crook of this unclaimed, forested patch of terrain. Built over a hundred years ago, it had eluded renovation due to a combination of civic nostalgia and corporate disinterest. Dotted by thick, spreading oaks and bordered by rows of weary hedges, Bassmore was a sprawling graveyard of faded headstones and moss-covered mausoleums.

Taking an off-ramp from Highway 51, and following a lonely road that wound under interlaced branches sawing each other noisily in the brisk wind, I spotted the cemetery's mournful silhouette up ahead. The shanks of its low knolls and jagged outlines of its lofty trees were displayed in stark relief against the somber sky, like a Dickensian woodcut.

Damn him to hell, I thought, my hands tightening on the steering wheel. Of course Maddox would know about Bassmore. What it meant to me. The additional soupçon of pain it would bring.

As I pulled into the empty gravel lot just beyond the gated entrance, I reflected on how many years it had been since I'd walked its lonely fields and sloping hills.

My late wife, Barbara, was buried here, alongside her father, and for a long while after her death I made regular visits. Especially on her birthday, or the anniversary of our marriage.

Then, over time, the visits became less frequent. My busy life soon occupied by more pressing issues, significant demands on my time, people in the here-and-now who needed me.

At least that's what I told myself, then and now.

Climbing out of my car, it also occurred to me that my previous visits had always been in daylight. When the sun shone warmly through the tangled tree branches and across the grass-carpeted fields, and when there were usually other mourners attending to the graves of loved ones.

Stepping into a cold night blanketed by dour, rolling clouds, the empty parking lot felt peculiarly desolate. Whether it was the sound of my shoes scraping the gravel, or the way the wind flailed angrily at the trees beyond, I felt enveloped by a sense of foreboding.

It took every ounce of will to keep myself centered, to focus on following Maddox's instructions. I remembered from previous visits that the security guard's kiosk was just outside the entrance gate, whose ornate iron-wrought arch soon loomed up ahead. There was a single light on in the little shack.

As I approached, I slowed my step on the gravel so as not to startle the guard. I could see him clearly now through the kiosk's open doorway. He was a stout, gray-haired man sitting with his broad back toward me on a swivel chair, a Steelers thermos beside him on his cluttered desk.

Unmoving, he seemed riveted by the desktop security monitor screen before him. Even from where I stood I could make out the checkerboard of real-time images on the screen, showing various areas in the tree-shadowed cemetery beyond.

I'd just stepped across the doorway's threshold, about to speak, when I abruptly stopped. Adrenaline shot through me, and I felt the heat rise in my chest.

Because suddenly I knew. Recognized that pungent, coppery smell.

Fresh blood.

Steeling myself, I took another step into the small shack and reached for the back of the guard's chair. Turning it slowly on its swivel.

He was dead, of course.

To be sure, I checked his vitals. No pulse, no breath. No life. A knife of some kind was buried to the hilt in his chest, blood from the wound slowly spreading in rivulets down the front of his shirt.

Except for the blood seeping around the edges of an iPad, which hung from a lanyard looped around the knife's hilt. A few crimson drops speckled the device's blank screen.

It suddenly flickered on, revealing Maddox's face.

At the same time, I remembered what he'd said back at the motel. That my next instructions would be provided by the security guard. This is what he meant.

Maddox's voice echoed in the cramped kiosk.

"I'm impressed, Danny. Right on time. Even a bit early."

"Dammit, Maddox, why did this man have to die? I don't know him. He's not part of your mission."

"True. But, frankly, I didn't see how I'd persuade him to wait patiently in his chair for you, holding the iPad on his lap. Or else maybe it was because I've never killed someone with a knife and wanted to give it a try."

"Or maybe just because you're a murdering lunatic."

"Really, Doctor. Your pathetic attempts to bait me are growing tiresome. Meanwhile, I have some news that I think you'll find of interest. I've decided who I'm going to kill tonight at midnight. That is, *if* you fail to do as I say."

I swallowed my anger, and kept my voice measured.

"Who is it, Maddox? At least tell me that."

"So you can warn the lucky winner? I hardly think so. That's not how the game is played."

I stared at his smug face on the iPad, as a single drop of blood meandered down the middle of the screen.

"But first," he continued, "show me that prepaid cell phone you brought with you. Come on, I know you must have one."

Reluctantly, I withdrew the cell from my pocket. Held it up to the iPad so he could see it.

"Good. Now stomp on it. Break it into pieces. Right now, and then show them to me."

When I hesitated, his face darkened.

"I mean it, Danny. *Do it or everything stops right now.* Which means someone dies tonight…"

Quickly, I dropped the cell to the concrete floor of the kiosk and brought my foot down hard. Then harder. Finally the plastic shattered, pieces calving off.

I gathered them up and held them before the iPad screen.

"Good. But don't worry, you're about to trade up. Look on the guard's desk, right next to his thermos. See the smartphone? Put it in your pocket."

I saw it, and did as he asked.

"Next, turn to your left and you'll see a shovel standing in the corner. Brand new, too. I got it on sale at Walmart."

I took hold of the shovel. It was heavier than that used for yard work. I'd seen ones like it at construction sites.

"Now here's what you're going to do next. And don't try to fool me, because I'll be watching. Through the laser sight of a sniper rifle, if you must know. But I'd really hate for things to end that way, Danny. Not after all we've been through together. And certainly not yet."

I leaned in toward the blood-spattered screen.

"Jesus, Maddox, don't you ever get tired of hearing yourself talk? I sure as fuck do."

The self-assured smile twisted up into something malignant. And the green of his eyes turned icy. As did his voice.

"You have until midnight. Do *exactly* what I say, or—"

This time I didn't hesitate. "What do I have to do?"

"Take that shovel and the smartphone and go to burial plot J-191. You know where it is."

My heart stopped. "Maddox, no…"

"Oh, yes. Go to J-191 and start digging as though the life of someone you care about depends on it. Because it does."

His smile returned. All teeth.

"You're going to dig till you reach the coffin, and then you're going to open it. And then, Danny boy, you're going to use that smartphone to take a selfie of yourself and what's in the coffin. Or should I say, what's *left* in the coffin."

My nerves twisted in my gut, and again I had to push down my rising panic. Try to hold onto myself.

"There's a number pre-programmed into the smartphone," he went on. "Once you've taken the picture of you with the dearly departed's remains, you'll send the photo to me."

I had no words. No thoughts.

"Do you understand, Rinaldi? Say something! At least nod your stupid head. Now! *Make me know you understand!*"

Finally, after an eternity, I slowly, dumbly, nodded.

Plot J-191 was Barbara's grave.

Chapter Thirty-two

I was in hell.

Gripping the shovel with one hand, I staggered out of the kiosk in a kind of trance and headed up the main access road to where the plots were laid out. The recent rains had churned the road's dirt into uneven scallops of mud that had then dried in the sun. This left treacherous ridges and unexpected troughs practically impossible to see in the yawning darkness.

Although I'd thought to bring a flashlight with me from the car, its pale light bobbing up ahead on the road somehow made my path seem even more harrowing. Like a chiaroscuro landscape, with flickering, distorted images leaping out of the night.

Daunted by the road's rising elevation, I was reminded of the physical toll my body had taken recently. My ribs ached, and my legs felt stiff and cramped. Every step was an effort.

At the top of the first hill, gasping, I stopped to catch my breath. Though the biting wind chilled the air around me, I could feel sweat sheening my forehead. Not from the exertion alone, but from the feverish intoxication of fear.

My every nerve rebelled at the thought of the unspeakable task ahead. The desecration demanded of me. Made even more horrific by the creaking of tree branches in the ceaseless wind. By night shadows clinging like webs to every jagged rock and spindly bush, under a leaden sky swept clean of stars. It was as though my very surroundings had become a palpable manifestation of Maddox's twisted mind.

Get a grip, I thought. *This is what he wants. Don't give it to him…*

Steeling myself, I deliberately straightened, despite the pull of bruised muscles. Then I swung the flashlight beam across the hedgerow marking the end of the main road, aiming it toward the side path I recalled from former visits. Although the wooden sign at its head was weathered and hard to read, it confirmed that the J-designated plots lay in that direction.

This narrower, sloping trail was overhung with unruly branches and pockmarked with mud holes stiff as hardened clay, evidence of how poorly the cemetery was now maintained. With every other step, my foot caught, nearly sending me stumbling to the ground while sharp twigs and nettles scraped my face.

As I trudged on, the tree canopy became thicker, obvious from the abrupt change in terrain beneath my feet. The sudden gluey softness of the mud. Little sunlight had penetrated the foliage above after the rains, and the ground was still sodden.

It was slow going, and I began to worry about the time. A quick glance at my watch revealed that there was still a good ninety minutes before midnight.

Permitting myself a moment's rest, I stopped to wipe the sweat from my forehead with my sleeve.

Just then, the smartphone rang. I picked up. Maddox.

"You're doing fine, Danny. But it must be lonely as hell up there in those woods. So how about I entertain you with some interesting factoids?"

I didn't reply, just stared at the phone in my hand. Then I slipped it back in my breast pocket.

I continued clambering up the muddy path, guiding myself by flashlight through wiry brush and under low-hanging branches. With Maddox's voice a muffled-though-insistent rasp.

"Do you know what happens to a body after twelve years in a coffin? Fascinating, really. Of course, rates of decomposition vary, but it all starts pretty much right after death."

I told myself not to listen. To somehow stop up my ears.

"Since the blood's no longer circulating, the body starts changing color. Usually it looks kind of ashen. Like David Bowie after his Ziggy Stardust period."

Losing focus for a moment, I almost slipped in the dark on a patch of viscous mud.

Fuck him, I thought. *Don't answer. Don't say anything.*

"But, Danny, here's where it really gets weird. Soon after death, blood settles in those parts of the body that are closest to the ground. The top part turns a waxy, grayish white, while the underside darkens. Yuck, eh?"

My foot slipped again and I fell to one knee, immediately soaking my pant leg in soft mud. Using the shovel for leverage, I pulled myself up again.

"Then, over the weeks and months following death, all these microorganisms in the intestines go to work. They're sorta like Scrubbing Bubbles, you know? Ever see that commercial? Anyway, from the corpse's standpoint, things go from bad to worse."

The words tore from my lips.

"*Shut the fuck up, Maddox!*"

"Hey, man, I studied up on this, and I hate to think of all that time wasted. Anyway, first the bacteria starts chewing through the gut, and then putrefaction spreads down to the chest and thighs. This produces gases that push the intestines out through the rectum, while fluid from the lungs oozes out of the mouth and nostrils—"

"I'm not listening…"

"Suit yourself. But, hey, you know what's crazy? They even categorize this stuff. You start with your garden-variety putrefaction, right? Where the body is swollen with gases and has this godawful odor. Then we level up to black putrefaction, when the skin turns—you guessed it—black, and the corpse collapses as gases escape. Then comes fermentation…"

"I'll smash this phone, Maddox. I swear. And then you won't get your fucking picture."

"True. But then *you* end up reading about one of your pals in the obits."

I stopped again, pounding my palm against my forehead. As though his voice was in my skull, in the marrow of my psyche, and I was trying to force it out.

"Besides, I didn't get to tell you about that last stage. The one with the really strong odors and the surface mold—"

With a guttural cry, I grabbed the smartphone out of my pocket and threw it to the ground. It stuck in the mud.

Eerily, his voice floated up at me from the phone.

"Did you just get rid of the phone? I thought I heard something like a thud. Did you throw it, Danny? Because if you did…Whoa, look at the time! And you're not even there yet—"

"Okay, dammit!" I shouted. "All right…I'll pick it up…"

Using my flashlight, I quickly retrieved the phone, wiped off some splotches of mud, and put it back in my breast pocket.

"I…I've got it again, Maddox."

By now, I barely recognized my own voice. It was ragged, hoarse. Stretched as tightly as my nerves.

"Good." Maddox went on, oblivious. "Because now we fast-forward through the years, during which the bacteria are joined by an army of insects. All kinds of creepy-crawlies. Hungry little bastards, too."

Gripping the shovel by its handle, I swung it over my shoulder and began moving as fast as I could up the path. I no longer cared if I stumbled, or if a spiky branch whipped across my face. I just had to keep moving.

"Until, after a dozen years, we come to today." His tone sharpened. "To this very moment. When you get to be reunited with your late wife, the woman whose betrayal pierced my heart. Ruined my life. As Boethius said, 'The worst sort of misery is to have once been happy.'"

I pushed my way past a hanging tangle of branches and found myself standing before a grassy field. An open expanse like a smooth, unfurled flag, stretching to the horizon. Even without much of a moon, I could make out row upon row of headstones.

Gathering myself, I walked stiffly toward plot J-191. Barbara's grave. Her father was buried next to her.

Against the noise of the blood pounding in my temples, Maddox's voice had fallen to a low, droning buzz. Though as I approached Barbara's burial site, and its simple, unadorned headstone, I could just make out his final words.

"Here you are, Danny. Thanks to me, you'll get to see Barbara again. Though I don't think she'll look quite like what you remember. After twelve long years, she'll be—how does that phrase go again?—I doubt she'll be much more than a rag, a bone, and a hank of hair."

Standing beside the grave, I loosed the shovel from my shoulders and angrily drove its metal nose into the dirt. Holding it upright by the handle with both hands.

I couldn't seem to move.

"What are you waiting for, Danny boy? It's nearly ten-thirty. You better start digging."

Still I couldn't move. My head throbbing as though about to explode. My arms and legs stiff as marble.

"Not much time left, and a pretty big hole to dig." A cold malice edging his words. All amusement gone.

"Or else somebody you care about dies…Tick-tock, Rinaldi. Like the bad guys say in the movies. Tick-fucking-tock."

It was without thought. Without feeling.

It was sheer, mindless will.

I began to dig.

It must have been the recent rains, because the dirt was surprisingly loose and easy to dislodge.

I'd thrown off my jacket and was sweating through my shirt, the bandages around my ribs coming away from the skin. Back muscles protesting as I bent to my task. Pulling shovelfuls of earth up and tossing them aside. Without checking my watch, I guessed that I'd been digging for about twenty minutes.

And had scooped out a sizeable rectangular hole about three feet deep. That's when I realized I might not make it.

Gasping, winded, I pulled the smartphone from my pocket. "Maddox, I can't! There's not enough time—"

For once, there was no caustic response from my tormentor. No mocking quote from the ancients. His only answer was silence.

I went back to digging.

Tick-tock, he'd said. Words I'd begun to silently repeat to myself. Feeling them form on my dry, cracked lips as I dug.

After a while, as the thrown dirt piled up beside me, and the wind whistled restlessly through the trees, and my hands grew raw from their grip on the shovel's handle, I lost all track of time. No longer imagined the clock ticking away in my head. Was aware of nothing but my numbing, panic-driven labors.

And then, so suddenly that it shook me out of my mental stupor, the tip of the shovel sliced through a layer of dirt and hit something solid. From the dull thud, it sounded like wood.

Glancing at the illuminated dial on my watch, I saw that I still had fifteen minutes. Still had time to get the coffin open by midnight. And prevent a murder.

Furiously now, I scraped away the final layers of dirt on the wooden lid, then dug a sort of trench around the sides of the coffin. Heart banging in my chest, breath coming in hoarse gasps, sweat literally pouring from my brow.

Yet the faster I went, I realized with a sharp inward pang, the sooner I'd have to pry the damned thing open.

And see what lay within.

Finally, the lid was totally exposed. Another glance at my watch. Mere minutes to go.

Half out of my mind with grief and rage, my body spent and wracked with pain, I took the smartphone from my pocket.

"Maddox! Are you there, you son of a bitch? I made it."

This time, he answered.

"Not yet, Danny. Not till you open the lid."

"I know, I..."

My voice faltered. I let it. Why not? I didn't have the words to alter what was about to happen. What I had to do.

The phone fell from my hand.

With agonizing slowness, as though in a dream, I reached for the flashlight from where I'd positioned it on the edge of the opened grave. Then, shovel in my other hand, I slipped down into the narrow space I'd dug beside the coffin.

Breathing hard, I let the flashlight beam play along the dirt-streaked sides of the coffin until it rested on a bolted hasp. Solid brass, it looked like, and intricately carved.

Pushing the butt of the flashlight into the soft dirt wall behind me, I aimed its harsh white beam directly at the hasp.

Then I gripped the shovel with both hands, held it above my head, and brought it down with all the strength I had left.

The hasp made a startling, pinging sound as it broke.

I wrestled it free from its brackets.

I threw the shovel down.

Then I put both hands on the lid, and, with an anguished cry, pulled it open.

Chapter Thirty-three

It was Barbara.

Unchanged. Whole.

Her long black hair, her glasses, the Pitt jacket...

Stunned, I stumbled backwards, falling against the dirt wall. Feeling with trembling hands behind me for the flashlight I'd embedded there.

It couldn't be, it—

It wasn't.

Leaning forward, I shone the light directly into the coffin. And saw what it was. What he'd done.

The wig, styled as she'd worn her hair when I first met her in grad school. Same with the glasses. And the Pitt jacket, still sold at the campus store today.

He'd even gotten the outfit right. The simple sweater and skinny jeans. The Kate Spade sandals.

I gripped the edge of the coffin, staring at the manikin.

Until I heard his dry chuckle coming from above me. From where I'd dropped the smartphone.

"Congratulations, Danny. You made it with two minutes to spare. Eleanor Lowrey lives to eat pussy another day."

The last vestige of energy drained out of me, and my chin fell to my chest. Still holding fast to the coffin's sides, I fought against a sudden, rubber-legged swaying.

Somehow I found the words. "I...I haven't taken the photo yet. You said you wanted—"

"Aw, to hell with that. Who cares? What I wanted was to see your reaction when you opened the coffin. And let me tell you, dude, you didn't disappoint."

"You...you saw me...?" Finally steadying myself. "How?"

"I watched you on the monitor. As it happens, I've been here in the security kiosk for the past half hour. The guard doesn't seem to mind. He's busy being dead."

I looked up, squinting in the darkness at the skein of tree branches. Then I saw it. One of the cemetery's security cameras, aimed at this row of burial plots.

My head clearing, I also realized something else. Why the gravesite was so relatively easy to dig. It wasn't due to the rain. It was because Maddox had been here earlier, maybe days before, and had already dug down to the coffin. So he could substitute the manikin for—

I scrambled up the side of the opened grave and snatched the smartphone from the dirt. Glaring at his gleeful face.

"Where is she, Maddox? Where're Barbara's remains?"

"Where they belong."

"Goddammit, tell me—"

"No! *I'm* the one who tells, who says what to do. *You're* the one who does it."

I shook my head at him. "No more."

"Brave words, but, under the circumstances, meaningless. There are still plenty of targets on my list. But don't worry, I'll let the Lowrey bitch live tonight, because a deal's a deal. After all, what is a man if he has not honor?"

"Which Greek said that?"

"Not a clue. Coulda been Jimmy the Greek, for all I know. But enough chit-chat. You still have some work to do."

"What work?"

"I want you to toss that phone into the coffin with the manikin and close the lid. I can't let you take it with you, so you and your FBI buddies can scour it for forensics. I mean, I think I was careful, but why take chances?

"After that, you need to fill the grave back in. Including covering it with the grassy sod, just the way I did. I'm sure you want it to look nice for Barbara."

I didn't move.

"I'm waiting, Danny. Remember, I'm watching you right now on the monitor. I can see whether or not you do as you're told."

I let out a long, dispirited sigh, and threw the smartphone into the coffin. Then I climbed back down into the opened grave, closed the coffin lid, and retrieved the shovel and my flashlight. I wearily levered myself back up.

Maddox had fallen silent again, but I could almost feel him watching through the security cam as I began shoveling the soft dirt back into the grave.

In maybe an hour I'd re-covered the coffin and filled in the rest of the hole with the dirt I'd removed. Then I lay the sod across its surface, tamping it down with my foot.

It was hard to tell, judging only by the flashlight, but I thought the grave looked all right. Like when I'd come upon it.

Shouldering my shovel, I took a moment to shine a light on Barbara's headstone. Wondering again what Maddox had done with her remains. Though some of the possible answers I came up with sent bile burbling in my gut.

I started back down to the cemetery entrance.

As expected, when I reached the kiosk, Sebastian Maddox was gone. So was the iPad that had hung from the knife still buried in the security guard's chest. By now, the blood on his shirt-front had congealed somewhat, though droplets occasionally fell to the floor beneath him. Like the slow drip of a leaky faucet.

Using some scrap paper from his desk to hold the kiosk phone's receiver, I dialed Gloria's cell back at the motel.

"Christ, Danny, what the hell happened? Lyle and I were just about to try and find you—"

"I'm fine, but I'll explain later. Now listen. You need to make an anonymous call to the police. There's been a murder at the Bassmore Cemetery in Beechwood. The security guard."

"The guard? But—"

I hung up on her. Then balled up the scrap paper and shoved it in my pocket, to be disposed of later. I also scooped up the broken pieces of the throwaway cell, and used my sleeve to wipe the back of the guard's chair from when I'd turned it around. I was sure Maddox hadn't left any fingerprints on the knife, nor anywhere else here in the kiosk. I didn't plan to, either.

Before I left, I took a moment to actually look at the dead man in the swivel chair. The sagging mottled face, with the spittle of red-tinged foam on his fleshy lips. Rheumy eyes. I guessed his age as late sixties.

For the first time, too, I noticed his hands, resting lifelessly on his lap. Rough workman's hands. Whatever he did before becoming a security guard here at Bassmore involved physical labor. Perhaps this was one of those part-time jobs that some people take after retiring.

Then there was the plain gold ring on his finger. Maybe his wife was still alive, maybe not. I remembered that I'd worn my own wedding ring for a good while after Barbara's death.

I sighed heavily. If the guard's wife *was* still alive, she'd soon receive terrible news. From which point her life would never be the same.

Sebastian Maddox had made another widow.

It was almost three a.m. by the time I got back to the motel, assured Barnes and Gloria that I was all right, and showered. I'd promised them the full story of tonight's events, but not till I'd cleaned up, taken two pain pills, and put on fresh clothes.

Which I had, thanks to Barnes. On his way to that first motel in GreenTree, he'd had the foresight to stop at a clothing store and buy some for me. Jeans, shirts, a thick sweater. He'd done a pretty good job guessing my sizes, too.

"Always be prepared," he'd replied when I thanked him.

Like I said, Boy Scout.

After my shower, I stood in new jeans at the bathroom sink, scrubbing dirt and mud off my shoes. Shirtless, I couldn't avoid looking at myself in the mirror. The ugly bruises, the still-raw redness of my ribs. Then there were the numerous cuts and scratches on my face from my trudge up to the gravesites. Not to mention the shadow of fatigue crowding my eyes.

"Talk about the walking wounded."

It was Gloria, standing in the bathroom doorway, in sweats and a tee-shirt. Holding a roll of bandages.

As before, she quickly re-bandaged my ribs, then applied some arnica cream to my arms and shoulders. Another wise purchase by Lyle Barnes.

When she'd finished, I gingerly slipped into one of the new shirts and followed Gloria out of the bathroom. Barnes was waiting for us, sitting at the writing desk, resting his arm sling on its faded blotter. Next to it was a whiskey bottle and three plastic glasses. Motel issue.

He poured us each a drink, then I sat back on the edge of the bed and told them everything that had happened. After which, Barnes wearily shook his head.

"You're lucky he didn't kill you right there. Toss your body into the coffin with the manikin and re-bury the thing."

"That actually occurred to me as I was driving back here. Which means he has something even better planned for me."

"It's weird, though," said Gloria. "David Bowie, Warren Zevon. Christ, *Scrubbing Bubbles*?…Maddox sure loves his pop culture references. Mixed in with all that high-brow philosophy stuff. Probably thinks it makes him seem cool. Disarming."

"Whatever." Barnes turned to me. "By the way, what did you do with the shovel? Might be some useable forensics on it."

"I figured the same thing, Lyle. It's in the trunk of my car, wrapped in some plastic bags to preserve any evidence that might be lifted from it. Though Maddox said he bought it new."

Gloria shrugged. "It probably doesn't matter. He's too smart to have left any traces on it."

Barnes thumbed his chin. "That still leaves the question of your late wife's remains. What he did with them."

We exchanged sober looks. Given his many years profiling serial murderers and the like, I knew he'd seen and heard dozens of horrific stories about what happened to victims' remains. Everything from the killers having sex with them, to eating them, to using them to fertilize their gardens...

Which was probably why he stayed silent now. To spare me any more images than my imagination had already given rise to.

I finished my drink and got shakily to my feet. The meds were doing their best to numb my physical pain, and my mind wanted to follow suit. After what I'd been through tonight, I craved nothing so much as numbness.

• ● ● ● •

At her insistence, Gloria led me into her room, where I stripped down and climbed under the sheets. She did the same.

Holding me in her arms, she whispered, "I'm so sorry for what Maddox is doing to you, Danny. I wish I could help."

"You've been wonderful," I said. "I mean, I'm grateful for all that Lyle's done, but you...I can't even put into words what it's meant having you here."

She smiled warmly. "I bet you say that to all the female FBI agents."

"Nope, you're the first." My eyes met hers. "And this isn't just crisis sex. Not for me. And you know it."

"Yeah, I know." A shrug. "How about that old standby, 'friends with benefits?'"

"What did I just say about not putting it into words?"

I gave her a brief kiss, then leaned my head back against the pillow. I could feel that sleep, blessed sleep, was coming.

She snuggled closer.

"By the way," she said casually, "did I tell you my ex is getting married again?"

"No, but I remember you telling me about that guy. Sounded like a complete jerk. How do you know?"

"I saw it on his Facebook page a couple weeks ago. Lots of photos of him and the bride-to-be, on a beach somewhere. Blonde with big boobs. What a surprise."

"Well, after being with you, he's marrying down. Once a dick, always a dick. And that's my clinical opinion."

A fuller smile. "See, I *knew* there was a reason I liked you, other than your oral sex skills."

I was too tired to manage a witty response, and within moments I'd drifted off to sleep.

And dreamed of that manikin in the coffin, dressed to look like Barbara. I was standing there, about to close the lid, when it sat up and spoke to me.

Yet when I awoke, around noon the next day, I couldn't remember a word she'd said.

I mean, *it* said...

Chapter Thirty-four

While Gloria was in the shower, I went next door to Lyle's room, where I found him sitting upright on the bed, reading from a thick paperback. *Collected Poems of Pablo Neruda.*

On the writing desk were a half-dozen Styrofoam cups.

"I did a coffee run," he said, not looking up from his book. "If you're hungry, the motel diner isn't bad."

"Thanks." I pulled out a chair at the desk and sat. Lifted one of the coffee lids, blew steam off the hot contents.

"I've been thinking about your experience last night at the cemetery. Imagining what you must be thinking and feeling."

"I'm still trying to sort that out myself." I sipped the strong black coffee. "I keep landing somewhere between grief and rage. Which, I suppose, is exactly where Maddox wants me."

Barnes gave me a sad smile. "I think Neruda has something to say about what you went through." He flipped a page in the book. "Here it is: 'The great roots of night grow suddenly from your soul, and the things that hide in you come out again.'"

I absorbed the words. "Sounds about right."

We sat in silence for a few minutes, until my gaze fell upon Gloria's laptop. The lid was open, still displaying Maddox's grinning head shot.

Barnes noticed me noticing it.

"Gloria brought it over after you fell asleep. She knew I'd probably be up, so I'd be able to keep an eye on it in case Maddox made contact."

"I didn't think he would," I said. "Not after the cemetery. Gloria's right about one thing: even he has to sleep. Speaking of which, Lyle..."

He put down his book.

"Don't worry, Doc. I take little cat naps. Not much REM, but better than nothing."

"How are your symptoms?"

"Fine, thanks. How are yours?"

"I'm serious, dammit. If you're relapsing, if the night terrors are increasing, you'll need to—"

"All I need is to take down Sebastian Maddox. After that, I promise, I'll sleep for a week, night terrors be damned. But no meds, and no clinical intervention from my favorite psychologist till then, *capice?*"

I shook my head. "I'm beginning to think that's the only Italian word you know. Maybe I should teach you another one. Like *capa tosta.*"

"What's that mean?"

"It's slang for hardheaded. Stubborn."

"Bet your father used that one a lot on you growing up."

"Only on his good days. The rest of the time..."

I swallowed the last of my coffee. Despite how beat-up my body still was, and how stinging the cuts on my face, that nine hours of sleep had been remarkably restorative. At least I felt more or less human again.

"Listen, I'm going to call the hospital about Angie..."

"Good idea," Barnes said. "I checked all the news channels an hour ago. There weren't any additional details. At least nothing that Pittsburgh PD is willing to release."

I fished in my pocket for Rosalind's card, hoping that the nurse was on duty. I'd liked her immediately, and trusted I'd get the straight dope about Angie's condition from her.

Using another of the prepaid cells, I called Mercy General and was transferred to the nurses' station on the ICU ward. I was pleased when it was Rosalind herself who picked up.

"I thought I'd hear from you, Dr. Rinaldi. Seems like everyone else from the Mayor on down has come by to see the poor woman. Her husband and kids, too."

"I'll try to make it in today myself. But how is she?"

"The good news is she's conscious and her vitals are good. But as of now, there's extensive paralysis, I'm afraid."

"Can she talk?"

"That's the same thing every cop who's been in here keeps asking. I mean, shoot, I hate to sound like Dr. Hilvers, but the answer is, not yet. We'll just have to wait and see."

I took a moment to digest this.

"I appreciate your being candid with me, Rosalind."

"And I appreciate your respect. Not a lotta that going on around here, if you're a lowly nurse. And yet—"

"Don't worry, I know what keeps a hospital going. And the patients thriving."

A wry chuckle. "Now you're just tryin' to blow smoke up this black girl's behind."

I got some information about visiting hours, and when Dr. Hilvers would be making his rounds on the ward, then hung up.

As I did, there was a brisk knock on the door, then Gloria let herself into the room. Both she and Barnes were practiced at using credit cards to jimmy open the locked motel room doors. But in Lyle's case, it didn't matter, since he'd used duct tape to cover the locking bolt on his door. The way he'd explained it, since Gloria and I would be coming in and out, why bother? As for security, by the time anyone would be able to pick the lock or break in, he'd be more than happy to shoot them.

Gloria, in sweats and a sleeveless tee, her wet hair bundled up in a towel, came to sit next to me at the desk.

"I just heard that last part. How's Angie doing?"

"Conscious, at least, but it's too soon to know how much her movement or speech has been affected."

She reached up and stroked my cheek. Fingers playing lightly on the scratches there.

"And how are *you* feeling?"

"Better than I look, at least. But not by much." I picked up the cell again. "Meanwhile, it's time I checked in with my voice mail again."

Gloria took that as her cue to get up and go sit next to Barnes on the bed. When she saw the book in his hand, she leaned closer and started reading over his shoulder.

There were only three messages on my voice mail. The first was from an old patient wanting to schedule an appointment. He said he "needed to make a pit stop." The next call was from a journal editor I knew, asking if I'd like to contribute a paper for the fall edition. The last, to my surprise, was from Jerry Banks, Harry Polk's temporary partner.

"Hey, Doc, this is Detective Banks. Me and the Sarge are trying to get a hold of you. We've been to your house and to your office, but you weren't at either place. I hope you're not outta town or something, 'cause Lieutenant Biegler wants us to interview you about this Angie Villanova thing. Since you're a close relative, he figures you might have some idea about who'd want to harm her. It's just routine. But between you and me, the Lieutenant wasn't too happy when we said we couldn't find you. So give us a call when you get this, okay? Then we can set something up."

When I relayed the message to Barnes and Gloria, neither supported the idea of my going down to the precinct.

"What if Maddox is watching the place?" Gloria said. "We already know he's probably hacked the PD's system."

Barnes agreed. "Which means he might know if you call downtown and arrange a time to meet with the cops. He could be waiting for you when you go in."

"At police headquarters? I doubt it."

"He's done it already, Doc. When he grabbed Angie right outside the precinct."

"I know that, Lyle. But she wasn't on the lookout for anyone. *I* will be. Plus, if I don't get back to them, it'll look suspicious.

Biegler's already pissed. It's a weekday, and they know I'm usually seeing patients now. If I'm not home sick, then where the hell am I?"

I could see that my argument made sense to the two of them. But it didn't make them happy.

Not that I was too thrilled with the idea, either.

• ● ● ● ●

An hour later, I was sitting in Lieutenant Stu Biegler's office. Not the conference room, nor an interview room. His own office, facing him across his desk, where he sat stiffly in front of a wall plastered with framed photos of civic events he'd attended. Shaking hands with the Mayor, the DA, the president of the Pittsburgh Chamber of Commerce. Plus a visiting movie star or two, from one of the many film productions that the city now attracts.

It was all very impressive, if you're impressed by that sort of thing.

Joining us was Sergeant Harry Polk and Detective Jerry Banks, the former on the chair next to me, the latter leaning against a wall to our left, arms folded.

"Let me be blunt, Rinaldi." Biegler said this as though he'd ever been otherwise when it came to me. "We've had two significant crimes in the past few days, and you've figured in both of them."

"I guess you weren't blunt enough, Stu. I don't get what you're saying."

"First of all, it's 'Lieutenant Biegler.' I don't recall giving you permission to use my Christian name."

"That's okay, I don't recall asking for it."

Harry elbowed me in the ribs, sending a sharp stab of pain up my side. Though I made sure not to show it.

"Your sarcasm isn't helping you, Doctor." Biegler sat forward, hands clasped on his desk blotter. "What I'm referring to is the rape and murder of Joy Steadman, as well as the attempted murder of Angela Villanova."

"What about them? We've already gone over the Steadman crime, and established I had nothing to do with it. As for Angie, I've known her since I was a kid, we're related, and I love her. Why the hell would I want to hurt her?"

He proffered a thin smile. "People kill their loved ones all the time, Rinaldi. In fact, they're usually the prime suspects in homicides. And usually guilty."

"If they have a motive. What's mine?"

"At this point, we don't know. But that doesn't mean there isn't one."

I gave Polk a sidelong glance, then gazed again at Biegler.

"You know this is bullshit, right? Even *you* don't believe I'm involved. You're just busting my balls because you resent the hell out of me."

Biegler laughed. "I'm not one of your pathetic patients, Doctor. So spare me your analysis. I have no agenda here, other than pointing out that you're a common factor in both these crimes. Which is unusual, if nothing else. Beyond coincidental, some might say."

Jerry Banks spoke up from his position against the wall.

"Plus we couldn't find you. Where the hell have you been all morning, eh?"

I didn't bother turning, but gave my answer to Biegler.

"Since neither crime occurred this morning, I don't need an alibi for my whereabouts today. Aside from that, it's none of the Department's business where I was."

Biegler's face darkened. "You're a goddam paid consultant, Rinaldi! If we want to know where you were, you sure as hell better tell us."

"Nope. Unless it's in the fine print somewhere, I don't remember seeing anything like that in the contract I signed."

Polk grunted loudly. "For Christ's sake, Doc! Give us a break here and tell us where you were."

"Yeah." Banks again, also louder. "You say you're on our side, one of the team. Fuckin' *act* like it!"

Both Biegler and Polk stared icily at the young detective, who instantly shrank back against the wall as though wishing he could disappear into it.

"If you guys must know," I said stiffly, "I was down at the Strip, getting some fresh fruits and vegetables. I used to work there when I was young, and I bumped into a couple guys who—"

Biegler held up his hands. "Okay, okay. Like I give a shit about your life story. But even you have to admit, you're a common element in both these cases. How do you explain that?"

"Bad luck? Karma? Maybe I'm cursed."

"Laugh all you want, Rinaldi." Biegler's tone deepened. "But we only have your word for it that you *weren't* involved with Joy Steadman. And with neither she nor her boyfriend, Eddie Burke, around to corroborate that claim, I still think you're a possible suspect in her death."

Polk stirred heavily in his chair. "Jeez, Lieutenant, I really don't think—"

Biegler ignored him. "As for Ms. Villanova, who knows what we'll find when we explore each of your financials, or your working history? We'll question people close to both of you, friends and extended relations. We're sitting down later today with her husband, as well as her co-workers. If there was any bad blood between you and her, any personal or professional squabbles, contested inheritances or things of that nature, we'll find out. Trust me, Doctor, we'll find out."

I sat up straighter. Keeping my own tone equally measured.

"Nice speech, Stu. And I'm glad you're so excited about spending the Department's limited resources on a wild goose chase. But it wouldn't be the first time you've done that, and I bet it won't be the last."

With that, I stood up. "If you want to speak with me further, let me give you the name of—"

The words caught in my throat.

"Your lawyer?" Biegler grinned. "If you mean Harvey Blalock, I'm afraid he's no longer in practice. Given your track record, though, you better find another one fast. I hear his former mistress, that Asian hottie, is pretty good…"

The Lieutenant and I both got lucky. Harry Polk, moving surprisingly fast for a man of his size, had his big arms wrapped around me before I was halfway out of my chair. Fists clenched, I was just about to vault over Biegler's desk and punch the officious creep's lights out.

At the same time, Jerry Banks had launched himself from his position against the wall and placed two hands on my shoulders. Unnecessary, since I'd already begun resuming my seat. But I guess he figured it'd look good to his Lieutenant if he mucked in to help Polk.

Meanwhile, Biegler had reeled back in panic, using his feet to propel his wheeled chair back from his desk. Hitting the wall behind him with such force that a couple of the framed photos fell to the floor, glass breaking on impact.

Literally shaking with rage, Biegler jumped to his feet, pointing a thin forefinger at me.

"Assaulting a police officer! You son of a bitch, Rinaldi, you've done it now! You arrogant, grandstanding piece of shit, you're spending tonight in a cell! Sergeant, cuff him!"

"Aw, c'mon, Lieutenant." Polk released me, then motioned for Banks to back away, too. "Things got outta hand, that's all. You know the Doc here's a hothead. You and me laugh about it all the time, right? 'Bout what a loose cannon the bastard is?"

"Which is why I want him arrested, Polk, goddammit!"

"Go ahead and arrest me," I said, with a bravado I didn't quite feel. "But I didn't assault you, Biegler. I merely stood up forcefully, on my way to storming out of here."

"That's crap—"

"No it isn't. Nobody in here saw me take a swing at you. You don't have a mark on you, either. So go ahead and arrest me.

I'll sue you, and the Department, for false arrest, slander, and emotional distress. And I'll sell it to any jury in the city."

"Listen, you…"

But Biegler had already lost a good deal of his bluster. Like many—but certainly not all—bullies, he was easily cowed when challenged.

A tense silence settled on the room for half a minute.

Finally, Polk looked at his boss and spread his hands.

"So, Lieutenant, what do ya want me to do with this mook?"

Biegler took a number of deep breaths, then settled back into his chair. Hands folded serenely on his thin chest.

"Show Dr. Rinaldi to the door, Sergeant." Studiously avoiding eye contact with me. "And make sure he knows that we expect him to be available for further questioning at any time."

"I'll be sure to tell him, sir."

And he did, once we were out in the hall. As he gripped my shirt collar in his meaty fists.

"See what you almost did, you lunatic? You coulda ended up in a cell."

"Biegler's never going to cut me some slack, Harry. Why should I give him any?"

"'Cause we're the goddam law and you're not! Why can't you just sit in your office like a good little shrink and steal your patients' money? It's a cake job, there ain't no heavy liftin', and people think you're a fuckin' saint."

"I'm a psychologist, not a shrink. We've been over this."

With a gale-like sigh of disgust, he released my shirt. But from the look on his face, I could tell this wasn't just Polk's usual bombast. He was clearly angry.

I tried another tack. No snark.

"Look, Harry, we've been through a lot together these past few years. Not, I admit, that you were always happy about it. But I'm damned grateful, because you're one of the best cops on the force. Believe me, I know. I've been around cops all my life, including my old man."

"So? What's your fuckin' point?"

"My point is, we *know* each other. Hell, we've saved each other's lives. How many guys can say that? And one other thing: we both know what a weasel Biegler is. You think *he'd* ever have your back when the shit goes down?"

Polk chortled. "Biegler? Not for a second."

"Well, then, fuck him. You *have* to kiss his ass because he's your boss, I *don't* have to because he isn't mine. I'm not saying it's fair, but it's the way it is. That's no reason for it to mess with our relationship."

"I hate to tell ya, Doc, we ain't *got* a relationship."

It was my turn to smile. "I hate to tell *you*, Harry, but yes we do. So we might as well make the best of it."

He gave me one of his favored scowls, but I wasn't having any. I turned and headed down the corridor to the elevator.

Polk called out to me.

"I don't care what you said to Biegler, I know somethin's goin' on with you, Doc. I can feel it in my gut. Soon as I dope out what it is, you and me are gonna have another chat..."

I believed him.

Chapter Thirty-five

On my way out of downtown, I called Gloria on my new throwaway cell and filled her in on the meeting with Biegler.

"Shit, Danny, you're lucky I'm not on my way down there to bail you out of jail. I know guys like Biegler. They may not seem so smart, but they can be damn savvy. With great survival instincts. Pricks like him often end up running things."

"True enough. Any word from our favorite psychopath?"

"No. Radio silence, as Lyle likes to call it."

"By the way, don't tell him, but I'm going to swing by Noah's Ark and get Lyle a good bottle of bourbon. He's been picking up the tab for the liquor since this thing started."

She was quiet for a few moments.

"Are you sure you're all right, Danny? I mean, with all the stress and everything? Especially last night?"

"Why?"

"You sound…I don't know…almost euphoric. Like you're overcompensating for how upsetting last night was. Like you're trying to prove you're still on top of your game."

My first instinct was to react defensively, but I quickly tamped it down.

"Look, I understand what you're saying. In fact, I've been wondering since I left the precinct if I didn't lose it up there *because* of all the stress. Acting out my aggression against Biegler because I'm unable to do so with Maddox."

Stopped at a light, I gave myself another few moments to collect my thoughts.

"And it's also possible that what happened last night at the cemetery was more traumatic than I think. Or allow myself to accept. Which is pretty ironic, considering what I do for a living. The patients I treat."

"Then why don't you give yourself a break?"

"Because if I let myself sink into despair, then I'm useless. To you and Barnes. And especially to myself."

"What do you mean?"

"No matter what's churning inside me, Gloria, I have to live with it. At least for now. Or else Maddox wins. And I can't let him win."

"I get that, Danny. But please be careful. Just because you want to be on top of your game doesn't mean you are."

"Duly noted. And just as an observation: I'm afraid you've been hanging out with me too long. Some of that psych lingo you were using had an oddly familiar ring to it."

She laughed. "Yeah, I'm starting to worry about that, too. Maybe we should just stick to the sex, and leave all the deep-dish talk to old shamans like Lyle."

"Works for me."

After we hung up, I swung onto Second Avenue. Afternoon traffic in and out of the city had thickened, made even worse by a light sprinkling of rain. The clouds to the left promised more in the hours, and maybe days, ahead, so I checked with the all-news radio station. My own personal forecast was confirmed.

As always when it rains, the Monongahela had turned gun-metal gray, its surface pock-marked by the falling drops. With my windows slightly open for the air, the familiar river smells wafted into the car. Along with that of burnt, oily smoke from the few passing tugs and barges.

It was nearing four when I parked at the curb about a block from Noah's Ark. The wind had kicked up, so the raindrops pelted me at an angle as I made the short walk to the bar.

Inside, professional drinkers and office workers who'd finished early for the day occupied most of the tables and booths, though there were still a couple of stools free at the bar. I took one.

To my surprise, Charlene was working the taps.

"Where's Noah?"

She shrugged. "For some reason, he keeps coming in and out of the kitchen. But with the place gettin' busy, I'm gonna need his sorry ass behind the bar full-time."

"Is he okay?"

An indulgent sigh. "I think he's having one of his bad days, ya know? Shuffling around, mumbling."

"Is he taking his meds?"

"Every day. I make him take them in front of me."

"What does Nancy say?"

"I left a message for Dr. Mendors, but she's out of town because of what happened at the clinic…"

"Oh, that's right. I forgot."

I'd seen on the news the week before that Ten Oaks had suffered water damage when a main line broke, so the staff and patients had been temporarily relocated to a wing of a nearby hospital. "According to Clinic Director Dr. Nancy Mendors," the anchor had said, "repairs would probably take a month."

Charlene did little to hide her irritation. "Yeah, she and her fiancé are on some kind of pre-wedding honeymoon trip. And the shrink she has covering for her is a jerk."

"Knowing Nancy, I'm sure he's competent. But, okay, if she doesn't get back to you soon, and you're still worried about Noah, here's a number where you can reach me."

I gave her the number of my prepaid cell, which she eyed suspiciously. But she didn't ask, so I didn't tell.

Just then, Noah came out of the kitchen, munching on a huge salami sandwich. Other than his hair being more disheveled than usual, he looked about the same to me.

After he took over for Charlene, who hustled off to see to

the customers at the booths, I made a point of staring at his eyes. Checking for any telltale signs.

To which he responded with a laugh. "Just the usual crazy, Danny. Not too little, not too much. So what can I get you?"

"Whatever's on tap. I'll also need one of your best bottles of bourbon. To go."

"No shit? You plannin' a big night?"

"It's for a friend. Going through hard times," I added, hoping it gave a touch of verisimilitude to my story.

"I got just the thing."

He poured me an Iron City from a keg, then went down to the end of the bar and came back with a bottle of Wild Turkey.

"Your friend'll like this," he said. "I call it 'Milk of Amnesia.' Good for whatever's buggin' you."

As I examined the label, he turned and clicked on the bar's wide-screen TV, which was already set to one of the local news channels. The anchor was midway through a report about the death of the cemetery security guard.

"Other than confirming that Mr. Lawlor's death was a homicide, the police are releasing no information about the case. However, sources within the Department report that there was little evidence at the scene and no eyewitnesses. Beechwood officers were alerted to the crime by an anonymous tip. Any viewers with information that could aid in the investigation are asked to contact their local police."

Though I hadn't expected to be connected to last night's events, I still found myself breathing a sigh of relief. As for Sebastian Maddox, he continued, like a ghost, to precipitate one horror after another, yet remained unseen. Unknown.

Except to me. And, of course, Barnes and Gloria.

Thinking of them, a worrisome notion occurred to me. While I was up at Barbara's gravesite, Maddox would have had plenty of time to plant another tracking device on my car in the lot.

Maybe he'd figured, after our having found the one he'd

wanted us to find, we'd have our guards down. Not expecting him to plant another. It's what I would assume, if I were him.

Finishing my beer, I paid Noah for the bourbon and got up from the stool. More customers had come in, and he was busily moving back and forth behind the bar. Mumbling to himself.

"You sure you're okay?" Catching him between taking orders.

He grinned. "I *will* be."

With that, he swiveled awkwardly, clicked off the TV news, and turned on the bar's sound system. The muscular harmonics of Ornette Coleman's alto sax wafted through the air.

Noah jerked his thumb over his shoulder at the TV.

"See? No more bad news. Best medicine in the world."

Before getting into my car again, I duplicated the search for a tracking device that I'd seen Gloria perform. Finding nothing outside the Mustang, I climbed inside, put the bottle on the seat next to me, and repeated the interior search.

Again, nothing. Though I was glad I checked. At this point, I no longer knew whether I was being paranoid or merely careful. The difference was now lost on me.

However, as I headed up Second Avenue toward the bridge, I called Barnes on his burner cell and relayed my concerns. To my chagrin, he quickly confirmed them.

"I'm sure you did an adequate job checking for the GPS." Trying not to sound condescending. "But Maddox may have planted it in such a way as to make it impossible to find."

"Assuming that's true, then I'll lead him right to where we are as soon as I return to the motel."

"If he doesn't *already* know. Which means we have to change locations again. Just to be safe, once you get back here, we'll leave your car in the lot. You can ride with Gloria or me."

"I don't like the idea of leaving my car unattended for who knows how long."

"Uh-huh." Which was Barnes' way of allowing me enough time to realize we had little choice.

"Okay, Lyle," I said. "I'll be there soon."

As I drove up the parkway toward the motel, it occurred to me that Maddox wasn't the only ghost haunting the Steel City. Lyle Barnes, Gloria Reese, and I had also become rootless, invisible spirits, without a tangible presence in our own lives. Cut off from family, friends, and colleagues. Engaged in a duel to the death of which everyone around us was unaware. With an enemy about whom no one knew.

The rain had dwindled to a fine mist, but between that and the bank of purplish clouds stretching to the horizon, it already felt like night. I switched on my headlights.

Suddenly, less than five miles from the motel, my dashboard GPS came on. Automatically. The same authoritative female voice emanating from its speaker.

"Take the next exit and make a left under the highway."

Stunned, I almost drove off the road, fish-tailing on the slick surface. Working the steering wheel and pumping the brakes, I managed to right myself. Stay in the lane.

"Look for the entrance ramp for I-376 East," the voice continued, "and get back on the highway."

I stiffened, my breath coming in staccato bursts.

It was Maddox. Like before, he'd hacked my GPS. And was sending me back the way I'd just come.

My cell still in its dash cradle, I called Barnes again. It rang a dozen times.

He didn't pick up.

Heart racing, I tried Gloria's throwaway cell.

Again, no answer.

Thoughts tumbled wildly in my brain, like thrown dice. Barnes had been right. Maddox must know we were staying in the motel. As I feared, he'd put a tracker on my car while it was unguarded last night in the cemetery lot. So when I'd returned to our rooms afterwards, he found out our location.

But where had he planted the tracker? I'd searched for some sign of it, both inside the car and out. Maybe, due to the misting rain, I'd somehow missed it under the chassis...

Then, staring at the dashboard GPS, the answer came to me. My jaw tightened. Talk about hiding in plain sight.

One hand on the wheel, I reached with the other and felt around behind the GPS device. There was a small, nodule-like bulge in the back. With a quick tug, I pulled it from the magnetic strip holding it to the plastic sheath. And held the dime-sized tracker between my thumb and forefinger.

Son of a bitch!

I angrily threw it to the floor, then realized that the exit ramp I'd been instructed to take was up ahead.

I debated what to do. One part of me wanted to ignore it, and continue on to the motel. Maybe Barnes and Gloria were in danger there, and needed help.

On the other hand, what if Maddox had already taken them, and was using the dash GPS to direct me to where they were?

Because I knew one thing for sure. If he *was* planning to torture or kill them, he'd certainly want me to witness it.

●　●　●　●　●　●

As instructed by the GPS, I made a right turn just before the tunnel, and then up the hill to Grandview Avenue.

Maddox was leading me back to my house.

It was nearing six, and my neighbors along both sides of the street had already turned on their porch lights. Although the rain had stopped, a chilled dampness hung in the air, above which ominous clouds scudded across the sky.

As the GPS voice announced that I'd reached my destination, I pulled into my driveway. No other vehicles were parked at the curb for a half-block in either direction.

My porch light was unlit, leaving my house shrouded in darkness, its front entrance hidden within a bowl of shadows. The heavy drapes were closed behind the recently installed new picture window, and, shrouded by trees crowding the roof, the house looked desolate, long-deserted. A dead thing.

Taking my flashlight with me, I got out of the Mustang and went up the walk to the front door. Reached for my keys—

The door was ajar.

Gathering myself, I slowly pushed it open and stepped into the pitch-black front room. A quick sweep with the flashlight told me that nothing had been touched. At least as far as I could tell.

Cautiously, I made my way across the room to where it met the hallway, also unlit. Then continued on through to the dark kitchen, silent except for the hum of the refrigerator, the muffled ticking of the wall clock.

I was about to turn toward the hall again, to check out my bedroom, when a cold breeze stroked my cheek. Guided by my flashlight, I moved carefully through the kitchen, fingers tracing along the tiled countertop, until I reached the sliding glass door that led to my rear deck.

It was open. The source of the breeze.

Though it wasn't until I'd brought my light up and shown it on the deck itself that I saw them. Lyle and Gloria.

They were sitting back-to-back on chairs positioned next to the deck's rear railing. They seemed unharmed, though both were bound and gagged. Their hands awkwardly roped behind them, their ankles firmly tied as well.

When they felt my light on their faces, they both turned. Gloria more slowly, head lolling as though coming out of a drug-induced fog. While Barnes' brow was creased, his eyes narrowed to slits. The grimace of a man in great pain.

I instantly knew why. Maddox had removed his arm sling so that he could tie the ex-agent's hands behind his back.

Opening one of the counter drawers, I shone my light inside till I saw the glint of a steak knife. Grabbed it up.

"Hold on, I'll cut you loose," I called out to them.

As I stepped across the sliding door's threshold.

And heard a sharp click.

Instinctively, I looked down at my right foot. It was standing on a strip of metal about three inches wide that spanned the threshold. I'd felt it give a little when I heard the clicking sound, and my heart sank as I guessed what it was.

At the same time, I heard the voice of Sebastian Maddox. It was coming from somewhere to my right.

"Oops, Danny boy. *Now* you've done it."

His mocking chuckle filled the room, and, knowing not to move my foot, I sought out its source with the flashlight. And found it.

It was a cell phone, set on speaker mode, and placed on the top shelf of the open pantry, propped up by some cans and an old bottle of cooking oil. Looking absurdly out of place.

"FYI," Maddox went on, "there's been a change of plans. To be exact, I'm moving the timetable up a bit."

"What are you saying, Maddox?"

"Well, to be honest, my original plan was to kill the old man, then sex it up with the FBI bitch before whacking her, too. Problem is, Barnes kinda bores me, and the girl's too goddam mouthy for me. So I figured, fuck it, let's get rid of both of them so we can move on to the grand finale."

I'd carefully shifted position so that I was facing the rear deck again, my flashlight beam shining on Barnes and Gloria. My foot still firmly planted on the metal strip.

Maddox continued in the same conversational tone.

"Now you might be wondering why I brought you all here. Back to your house. Unless you want to try and guess."

"That's easy. Symmetry. Your belief that adhering to it somehow sanctions your acts. This house is where Lyle, Gloria, and I first met up in response to your attempt on Barnes' life."

"Exactly. This is where the Three Musketeers got together, so this is where they finish up. *Two* of them, anyway. As I promised, I'm saving the last dance for just you and me."

"I'm looking forward to it."

"I doubt it, Danny."

"Oh, you have no fucking idea, *Sebastian*."

By now, I'd played the flashlight beam along the wooden deck beneath where Barnes and Gloria were bound. There it was. Barely the size of a brick, wrapped in brown paper and hard to make out in the dark space below and between the two chairs.

A bomb.

"I see what you've got planned for them." Keeping my eyes glued to the device, and its tiny blinking light.

Another wry chuckle. "It's a little *bon voyage* gift I made especially for them. Packed with C-4. And, as you've probably figured out by now, you're standing on a dead-man's switch. A bit low-tech, I admit, but still cool. As long as you keep standing on it, your friends are safe. The moment your foot rises from that metal strip...Boom!"

"*Now* who's seen too many movies?"

"There you go again, Doctor. Trying to bait me. Haven't you realized yet that it just doesn't work?"

"Guess I'm a slow learner."

"Enough with the false bravado, too. We both know you can't stand on that thing forever. The good news is, once you step off it, *you'll* be fine. Maybe get hit with some blood spatter, bits of brain and bone. But that's all. See, I packed just enough explosives to blow up the deck...and take your friends along with it."

Maddox took a long, meaningful pause.

"And then, finally, it'll just be you and me."

Chapter Thirty-six

"I can see you standing there, Danny. Trying to think of some way to save your friends. But it's been over five minutes."

I didn't respond, my fist tightening on the handle of the steak knife. Turning my head, I stared at the little green light of the camera on his cell phone. As if I could see him through the same lens with which he was seeing me.

"I'll be honest," he went on. "I thought it'd be fun watching you sweat, your face all scrunched up as you tried to figure a way out. But now it's just sad. So, c'mon, man. Step off the damn thing and put us both out of our misery."

"You don't want to watch anymore? I can fix that."

Careful to keep my foot where it was, I shone my light on the cell phone and hurled the knife at it. But my aim was off, and the knife missed the target, instead knocking over a soup can on the pantry shelf.

Yet I'd gotten lucky. It had been one of the cans propping up Maddox's cell, and when it fell off the shelf, the phone went with it. Landing screen-side-down on the kitchen floor.

The cell's speaker, also face-down, reduced Maddox's howl of protest to a muffled rasp.

Ignoring it, I turned toward the rear deck, letting Barnes and Gloria see my light again.

"I think I have an idea." Hoping my voice sounded more confident than I felt. "But I need the light."

I swung the beam back again, once more plunging the deck—and Barnes and Gloria—into a cold, clammy darkness.

I put the back end of the flashlight in my mouth and clamped down hard, the metallic taste making me wince. I knew I wouldn't be able to keep it between my teeth for too long.

Turning to my left this time, which directed the flashlight beam onto the tiled countertop, I took a moment to debate with myself about the feasibility of my plan. But since it was the only one I had, I had to embrace it.

Just as I had to hope that it could actually work.

Planting my right foot more firmly on the metal strip, I put out my left as far as it would go on the kitchen floor. I'd need it for balance.

Exhaling deeply, I stretched my arms out toward the end of the counter, where, by the flashlight's beam, I could make out the contours of the microwave oven.

It was big and it was heavy and it was the only thing I could think of.

So I reached for it, extending my arms as far as I could. Imagining them being wrenched from their sockets. My fingers were splayed, desperately feeling for some kind of purchase on the squat appliance. And grasping nothing but air.

Sweat dotted my forehead, and, once again, the bandages began pulling away from my ribs. Pain sliced at my sides, and crawled like saw's teeth up my back.

Reach a bit farther…just a little bit more…

I struggled to calm that urging voice in my head. I knew that the more I stretched out my hands, the more risk there was of my foot slipping off the dead-man's switch.

I took the risk.

My teeth aching from their hold on the flashlight, I forced myself to reach past the cone of light it threw and lunge for the heavy oven outlined within it.

My fingers touched the microwave's sharp metal edges, then

slipped off. I tried again, this time able to slap my palms on its broad sides. Straining, I pressed my hands hard against the plastic casing and began to pull it toward me, its flat bottom scraping along the countertop tile.

In moments, I'd dragged it close enough for me to wrap my arms around and so lift it from the counter. Then, once more using the flashlight beam as a guide, I carefully lowered it down to the floor.

Okay, I thought. *Nice and easy…*

I bent again and heaved the microwave oven up a few inches from the floor. Then, as carefully as I could, I set it down directly on the thin metal strip. At the same time, I slowly lifted my foot off, hoping the oven's weight would be enough to compensate for my own.

And prevent the switch from triggering the explosion.

It was.

I took the flashlight out of my mouth and aimed it at the bomb beneath Barnes and Gloria.

Nothing. Its pale light still blinking.

With a grateful sigh of relief, I stepped back, and more or less collapsed against the kitchen counter.

Giving myself only a few seconds to catch my breath, I went over to where the steak knife had fallen and retrieved it. On the floor nearby was Maddox's cell.

I scooped it up and looked at the screen. Blank.

His fun spoiled, Maddox was long gone.

"I'll be damned." Lyle Barnes used his good hand to sip from a beer bottle. "Using a microwave as a counter-weight."

I shrugged. "Like they say, it seemed like a good idea at the time. Hell, it was my only idea."

His arm once more in its sling, which Maddox had tossed on the deck, Barnes stood with me and Gloria in the kitchen, looking down at the microwave oven. It still rested on the deadly metal strip at the sliding door's threshold, the three of us careful not to jostle it when stepping in and out.

After picking up Maddox's cell, I'd used the flashlight to find the kitchen wall switch. First I turned on the overhead lights, then did the same for the rear deck's exterior lamps, which were in wall niches on either side of the glass door. The deck was suddenly flooded with light.

With the threat of the bomb neutralized, at least for the moment, I went out and used the steak knife to cut Barnes and Gloria loose from their bonds. Then I helped each of them into the kitchen and onto a chair at the table.

They were both still groggy, although from how quickly they were recovering, it was clear Maddox had used a different drug than he had on Robbie Palermo and me. Probably so that his victims would be awake enough at the end to see what was about to happen to them.

I'd offered each of them a bottled water to help clear the lingering effects of the drug, but Barnes insisted on a frosty Iron City. Gloria settled for fresh black coffee.

Meanwhile, through the opened sliding glass door, I could see that night had finally fallen. Cold, cloudy, and damp.

Soon enough, Barnes and Gloria seemed clear-headed enough to get up, and now the three of us found ourselves staring down at the microwave oven.

"You two have to admit," Barnes said at last. "There's a certain surrealistic quality to this. Our lives saved by a kitchen appliance."

I nodded. "I get that, Lyle, but it can't stay there forever."

"Doesn't have to," said Gloria.

She abruptly stepped over it and went out on the deck, Barnes and I on her heels. Watching as she pushed the two chairs apart and bent to carefully examine the bomb.

"Pretty simple." Her fingers gingerly traced a wire that wound around the paper-wrapped package. "Low-tech, all right. I guess sometimes our guy really likes old school."

Barnes took another pull on his beer. "Meaning what?"

"When the dead-man's switch is released, it completes a connection that sends an electrical impulse here to this receiver. The bomb-maker knows the thing's locked and loaded by this little blinking light."

"So what do we do?" I asked.

"Disconnect the wire to the receiver."

Barnes cleared his throat. "I assume you've done this before, Agent Ree—I mean, Gloria..."

"Took a class at Quantico once. Got an A. Though I think the instructor had a crush on me."

Gloria pulled out the wire.

Then she climbed to her feet, the brick-sized package under her arm, and smiled at our disconcerted faces.

"See, guys? No boom. But just to be on the safe side..."

Gloria took the inert bomb into the bathroom, from which we could hear water running in the tub. After about five minutes, she returned to the kitchen, wiping her hands on a towel.

"I weighted it down and put it in a full tub. I doubt this kind of device transmits through water, so even if I'm wrong about the wire I disconnected, we should be fine."

Barnes gave me a wary look, but without a word, we bent on either side of the microwave and lifted it off the metal strip.

Gloria smiled. "See? Again, no boom."

I let out a breath. "I never doubted you."

After Barnes got another cold brew from the fridge, he joined Gloria and me at the table. With the bomb deactivated, they felt ready to tell me what had happened back at the motel.

"He caught us with our pants down, simple as that." Barnes toyed with his beer bottle's label. "That diner I told you about is connected to the motel by this little covered passageway. When I went out to get some coffees to-go, Maddox slipped up behind me and stuck me with a hypo."

Gloria nodded mournfully. "When Lyle didn't come back after a while, I left the room to look for him. I didn't get five steps from the door when I felt the jab of a needle in the back of my neck. He'd been waiting right outside the room."

"And nobody at the motel saw this?" I asked.

"Guess not," said Barnes. "It was cold, wet, and dark outside, so whoever had rooms there were probably staying in them. Having a drink and watching TV. Or screwing. Nobody checks into a motel to enjoy the outdoor sights."

"But how did Maddox get you guys here? A stolen van, like before? The trunk of a car?"

Gloria shook her head. "No idea. I'd barely come to, when I felt my hands tied behind my back."

"Same here." Barnes took a healthy swig of beer. "I don't even remember him taking off my sling. Just how much it hurt when I woke up and realized my hands were bound."

I reached behind me for Maddox's cell, which I'd placed on a paper towel on the kitchen counter.

"Any chance this can help us find him?" Using the towel to protect possible forensic evidence, I lay the cell on the table. "Maybe trace the signal off a cell tower, get a bead on his whereabouts? What do you two think?"

Barnes leaned over and squinted at the phone.

"Not a chance, Doc. Another throwaway, like ours. Plus it wouldn't surprise me if Maddox could remotely send a destruct signal from wherever he was calling from. Fry the damn thing from the inside."

Soon afterwards, as Gloria was re-doing my bandages in the bathroom, she mentioned the bottle of Wild Turkey I'd bought for Barnes. I'd forgotten all about it.

Patched up again, I went outside to get the bourbon out of my car. It was where I'd left it, on the passenger seat. As I reached for it, I remembered that this was where I'd placed Barbara's manuscript the day before.

The image of those bound pages flickered in my mind, and I told myself that the first thing I'd do when this was all over was read her unfinished book.

It was then that the idea occurred to me.

●●●●●

When I presented the bourbon to Lyle Barnes, he smiled gratefully, then placed it on the kitchen counter.

"We'll open it after we nail the bastard. To celebrate."

Gloria smiled. "I like the sound of that."

While the two of them debated the risks involved in returning to the motel to get their cars, I left and went down the steps to my basement gym. What I sought was somewhere amid the clutter of cardboard boxes piled behind my workout bench and free weights. Moving my equipment to one side, I began reading the handwritten labels scrawled on masking tape on each box.

In a few minutes I found what I was looking for. A dust-covered box containing some of Barbara's old notebooks from her days as an undergraduate at Pitt. Sitting on the cold basement floor, I opened it up and fished through the contents till I spotted a notebook marked—in her careful, slightly cramped handwriting—"History of Renaissance Art, Survey Class."

As I flipped through the pages filled with handwritten notes she'd taken during each class, I remembered a time early in our relationship when she'd laughingly showed me one of her notebooks. She had a habit, she'd explained, carried over from her teens, of adding side comments to her notes whenever her mind wandered during class lectures. Or when something was on her mind, especially if it was bothering her. Short, dashed-off notes to herself. Concerning her thoughts, her worries.

This history class at Pitt was the one that both she and Sebastian Maddox had attended. As Liz Cortland suggested, it was probably one of the Humanities classes that science undergrads like Maddox were required to take.

As I went back to the beginning pages and read more carefully, I was able to witness in truncated form the progress of Barbara's connection to Maddox. She must have noticed him during the second class, having written "that Sebastian guy is hot" in one of the margins. Then, a few pages later during that same class, "hunk keeps staring at me."

To say my feelings were mixed as I scanned these pages would be an understatement. Though, to my surprise, I wasn't as jealous or angry as I'd expected. Mostly, in the knowledge of what Maddox would ultimately do, I felt a growing anxiety as I read her offhand remarks.

By the third class, she'd written, "if he asks me out, I'm going." But it wasn't two weeks later before she wrote "he still stares at me, though I ended it. Weird."

Week six: "He took a seat closer to me. Had a fight with him yesterday on street. He follows me places."

Week seven: "Guy creeps me out. I called him 'Mad Maddox' in cafeteria. Everybody laughed. Now I'm one of those mean girls."

Week ten: "He's not in class, but left me gross note. I keep looking over at his empty chair. Scared. Silly bitch!"

Week eleven: "Really scared. He watches through my window. Can't sleep. Need better locks for door."

On the last page of week twelve, there was just a phone number scribbled in the margin and repeatedly circled with her pen. Beside it was one word: "Cops!!"

There were two more classes, but she only records her notes from the instructor's lectures. There were no more asides.

I returned the notebook to the box and closed it up again. Based on the timeline suggested by her comments, and then the lack of any notations in the final two classes, that circled phone number must indicate that she was finally going to report Maddox to the police. To request and then be granted a restraining order against him. After which, he soon left Pitt.

I put the box back where I'd found it, shoved my workout equipment into its usual position, and climbed up the stairs. I found Lyle Barnes and Gloria Reese, still seated at the kitchen table.

Good. A plan had begun formulating in my mind, and I wanted to run it by them. Especially Gloria.

Because it wouldn't work without her.

Chapter Thirty-seven

Dr. Hilvers lowered his wire rims to meet my gaze.

"There's no predictable arc of progression, in either a positive or negative direction."

"I'm not asking you to consult a crystal ball," I said. "Just give me your best professional guess."

What I was really asking for was his gut feeling, but I'd come to suspect he rarely had one. Or if he did, he probably wouldn't trust it.

The young physician and I were standing in a corner at the rear of Mercy General's ICU ward. I'd hoped to get a sense of Angie's prognosis before visiting her in her room.

It was nearing noon, the day outside the ward's windows as gray and cloudy as the one before. Perhaps a bit cooler.

After I'd explained my plan to Barnes and Gloria, I'd driven them back to the motel to retrieve whatever they needed from their respective rooms. Then we each drove in our own cars to three separate motels—one on the South Side, one near PNC Park, and one in Oakland. Given the announcement by Maddox that he was stepping up his timetable, we decided it was safer to split up and stay in contact via our throwaway cells.

I spent the morning in my room in the Oakland motel doing the preliminary work on the plan I'd outlined to them. Then, after showering and changing into jeans, Polo shirt, and jacket, I headed over to McKees Rocks and Mercy General.

Now, in view of Hilvers' reluctance to advance an opinion, I had to settle for a description of Angie's current symptoms.

He folded his arms. "At present, she displays significant paralysis on her left side. Her cognitive status is unclear, though she's awake and knows she's in a hospital."

"What about her speech?"

"She can manage the occasional word, with effort. In terms of the permanence of this condition, as I just explained—"

"Yeah. No predictable arc."

I'd gotten as much from him as I was likely to get, so I thanked him and strode down the corridor to Angie's room.

As before, I found Harry Polk standing by her bedside. Only this time, he was accompanied by Jerry Banks.

Polk's eyebrows lifted at my approach.

"I'll be damned, Rinaldi. Once again, ya got perfect timin'. Ya just missed Sonny and the kids. They're downstairs gettin' lunch."

Banks, leaning against the far wall, spoke up then.

"Speaking of lunch, Sarge…"

Everything about his body language proclaimed his discomfort with being in a hospital sick room. Hands in his pockets, shoe tapping the linoleum floor. Eyes averted.

"Sure, Jerry." Polk indicated the door. "Go on and grab somethin' to eat. But make it fast."

The younger detective nodded gratefully, gave me a wary glance, and hustled out of the room.

I smiled at Polk. "I don't think he gets me."

"Who the fuck does?"

I kept my smile intact and went to stand on the other side of Angie's bed. She was still hooked up to monitors, and the IV tube was still gurgling. But her eyes, while filmy, were open.

Leaning over the bedrails, I took her hand. Squeezed.

"Angie, it's me. Danny."

She didn't squeeze back, though I watched as her slackened lips slowly formed a word.

"Danny..."

Polk spoke in a hoarse whisper. "Hilvers says she can't move her whole left side. Can't feel nothin' there."

I didn't lift my eyes off Angie.

"But that can change, Harry. It's way too early to speculate about her motor functions. Or her speech, for that matter. Hilvers just confirmed that, too."

"Meanin' what, exactly? We just...wait...?"

"If *she* has to, I guess that's the least *we* can do." I stroked her forehead. "Has she said anything about what happened to her? Anything at all?"

He shook his head. "Nothin' much. When Chief Logan was here, we tried tellin' her what we knew. That she was taken by force by some unknown perp. And that she was tied up down in the river, and somehow got free before she drowned."

"What was her reaction?"

"She just nodded. But real slow. Like maybe she could understand, but maybe she couldn't. Like her mind was a million miles away." He scowled. "Christ, I hate seein' her this way."

"Me, too."

I turned my attention back to her pallid, unmoving face.

"Do you know who I am?" I said softly.

Again, her lips moving awkwardly to form the words.

"Yes...Un...for...un...for..."

I grinned. "'Unfortunately?'"

Angie managed a slow nod, along with a crooked smile. Though that effort brought a bubble of spittle to the side of her mouth. I took a Kleenex from its box on the bedside table and gently wiped it off.

Polk placed his hands on the opposite bedrail.

"Goddammit, she's still in there." Grinning.

I squeezed her hand again. "She sure as hell is."

This time, she squeezed back. And I saw that her eyes had sought out mine. She wanted to communicate something.

"Yes, Angie?" I bent lower, my face near hers. "You want to tell me something?"

Again, her rubbery lips struggled to wrap themselves around the words. Which came in barely a whisper.

"Thank...you..."

Exhausted from the effort, her eyes closed with a flutter. And she quickly dozed off.

When I straightened, Polk gave me a quizzical look.

"What did she say?"

I shrugged. "I don't know. I couldn't make it out..."

Out in the hospital parking lot, Polk leaned against the hood of his unmarked and lit a Camel. I stood next to him, peering up at the thickening clouds.

"Yep." Polk blew a ribbon of smoke into the damp air. "It's gonna rain some more, that's for sure."

He was waiting for Jerry Banks, who'd finished lunch and come up to Angie's room just as Polk and I were leaving. Then Harry had sent the kid back down to the cafeteria with orders to get him a takeout coffee and bring it to the car.

I eyed him carefully. "I get the feeling you want to say something, Harry. Before Banks comes back. Is it about Biegler? What happened up in his office?"

Polk nodded. "He's gonna try again to get your Department contract cancelled. Plus, he's got an eyewitness who'll confirm ya almost took a poke at him."

"Young Jerry Banks, I assume?" His silence was my answer. "And whose side will you be on, if this thing goes forward?"

"Yours, I guess." Looking pained. "Way I see it, I got no choice, now that Angie's outta commission. She's the one usually hauls your ass outta the fire when it comes to the brass."

"That's for damn sure."

He angrily tossed the cigarette. "Christ, Rinaldi, why the

fuck didja have to put me in this position? Eh? Like I need this shit in my life!"

Abruptly, he jerked open the driver's side door and got behind the wheel. Face front, scowling at the windshield.

Meanwhile, Jerry Banks had strolled out of the hospital's front entrance, a steaming Styrofoam cup of coffee in each hand. As he approached Polk's vehicle, Banks gave me a quick, guarded look, which I didn't return.

After watching them pull out of the lot, I got into my own car. I hadn't driven a mile from the hospital when it hit me.

● ● ● ● ●

It was after four when I strode into Noah's Ark, the bar just starting to fill with its regulars, a classic Sarah Vaughn ballad coming from the room's speakers.

As before, I found Charlene working behind the bar. At the same time, I noticed a young woman who looked barely legal taking customer orders at the tables. She wore nose and lip studs, streaked hair, and an apron that was too big for her.

Charlene jerked a thumb in the girl's direction as I slid up to the bar. Her oval face clouded with worry.

"That's my niece Sally. Helps out around here sometimes. Like now, when Noah—" The words caught in her throat.

"That's why I'm here, Charlene."

I indicated the end of the bar, whose stools were as yet unoccupied. Where it was relatively private.

When she joined me there, the full weight of her concern brought tears to her eyes.

"I'm so glad you came, Danny. I'm really worried about Noah. He's been more and more agitated today. Mumbling to himself. Snapping at me."

"Where is he?"

"That's just it, I don't know." It was rare to hear such panic in Charlene's usually wry, knowing voice. "Given his behavior,

I shouldn't have let him take the truck, but—"

"He took the truck?"

"I tried to stop him…and usually he listens to me. But he just got more belligerent…"

"Charlene, wait. Remember when we talked the other day? About Noah's meds?"

"He's been taking them, Danny. I swear. He swallows them right in front of me…"

I gazed at her anxious, perplexed face and chastised myself for having taken so long to figure it out. Not until twenty minutes before, as I was leaving Mercy General's parking lot.

But now it made sense. Something that had been bothering me since the night Maddox showed those photos of the people on his kill list. The people close to me, one of whom would die if I didn't get to Bassmore Cemetery in time.

There was one person who *should* have been on that list, but wasn't. Noah Frye. Because Maddox had already selected him as the victim who'd be the bait for his final trap. When, at long last, he'd get to exact his revenge on me.

But that still didn't explain Noah's recent behavior. Unless…

"Charlene, go get the bottle of meds. Noah said that Nancy Mendors had sent over the refills."

"Yes, she did. Though I was surprised, because he still had some pills left from his former prescription. But I figured, since she was gonna be out of town, she just went ahead and—"

"Who brought the refills?"

"Someone from the pharmacy delivered the pills. A new guy."

"What did this guy look like?" Though I already knew.

"Good-looking, maybe forty. Shaved head, lots of muscles. He had the pharmacy logo on his shirt."

A tight ball formed in the center of my chest.

"Go and get the pills, Charlene. Hurry!"

Suddenly, two businessmen types at the other end of the bar shouted down to where we stood. Red-faced, ties undone.

"Hey, can we get a coupla more brewskis here?"

Charlene gave them a steely glare, but I grabbed her arm.

"Go take care of them. But tell me where the pills are."

"Kitchen. Top shelf, above the fridge."

As she went to attend to her unruly customers, I walked in the opposite direction and through the swinging doors to the small, cramped kitchen. As she'd described, there was a series of shelves built above the refrigerator. The top shelf was cluttered with both prescription bottles and over-the-counter meds. Still, it only took a few moments to find the bottle I was looking for.

The pharmacy label was legitimate, one I recognized from seeing other meds from the place. I'd have expected no less from Maddox. It wouldn't have been difficult for him to steal one while distracting some intern pharmacist.

The medication and its dosage were also accurate. With access to my records, and the fact that Nancy Mendors always cc'd me about her outpatient treatment of our mutual friend Noah, Maddox knew exactly what meds were prescribed.

Already knowing what I'd find, I poured a couple of the capsules into my palm. Right look, right colors. Neither Charlene nor Noah would've suspected a thing.

Turning to the counter opposite the fridge, I cracked open one of the capsules and poured out its contents. Then I dipped a finger into the soft white mound and tasted it.

Sweet. Probably powdered sugar.

Then, cursing Maddox aloud, I angrily swept the useless stuff onto the floor.

Noah had been without his psychotropic meds for days, which explained his sudden mood change. But that wasn't the problem. Soon he'd be in the grip of powerful, self-recriminating delusions. Vivid and excruciating. If he wasn't already.

Pushing through the swinging doors, I hurried once more out to the bar, where a flustered, distracted Charlene was trying to keep up with her customers' demands.

I leaned across the bar, got her attention.

"Where's the truck parked? Out on the street?"

"Yeah. Around the corner. Usually. But—"

"Did you see Noah drive off in it? Did you hear anything?"

"No, but he said he was going to—"

I didn't stay to hear the rest, and instead moved quickly through the thickening crowd to the front entrance. Then out to the street, under a darkening sky at war with the sinking sun.

I quickly looked up and down the street in front of the bar, then ran to the corner and made the turn. There, about two car-lengths down the block, was Noah's truck.

Before I got close enough to check, I already knew that it would be empty. But I still placed my palm on the hood. Cold. The engine had never been started.

I felt a stab of grief, of anger.

Poor Noah. He'd be terrified, in a near-psychotic state by now. Bewildered and totally vulnerable.

And he was in Maddox's hands.

Chapter Thirty-eight

I went back into the bar and found Charlene standing behind the polished counter, head down, hands gripping the brass edges, her face hidden by the cascade of her flowing red curls. She looked on the verge of collapsing.

Meanwhile, those same two customers were berating her, demanding another refill. One louder than the other.

"You got people waiting, lady! Thirsty people! What the hell's wrong with you?"

I'd had enough. Jostling my way next to them at the bar, I grabbed this boisterous clown by the forearm.

"Here's the deal, pal." I didn't have to manufacture my anger. "You and your buddy pay your tab and get the hell outta here—*now*! Or I'll throw you out…"

"Hey!" The guy squirmed against my grasp. "You can't—"

"Yeah? Watch me…"

His friend had the good sense to toss some twenties on the bar and take hold of the guy's other arm.

"C'mon, man, let's go. C'mon, fuck this guy…"

It took a couple more tugs on the complaining guy's sleeve, but the more practical of the two headed them out of the bar.

Then I indicated to Charlene that she should follow me into the kitchen. Luckily, the other patrons at the bar were either too confused or too alarmed to squawk as she walked away from her post.

In the kitchen, I took hold of both of her hands. And told her what I'd discovered about the refills. She turned pale.

"Then Noah *hasn't* been taking his meds…"

"No. I'm so sorry. It was a trick."

"But without his medication…" Her voice dropped.

"I know, Charlene. That's why I have to find him. And I will. I promise."

"Shouldn't we…should we call the police?"

"He hasn't been missing long enough. Given his history, they'll say he just wandered off. Left voluntarily. Besides, I'd rather be the one to find him. We don't know what kind of shape he'll be in, and some scared cop might overreact."

"Christ, no! I've always been afraid of something like that happening if Noah…I mean, if he ever…"

"I told you, I'll find him." Maddox would see to it.

"But, wait…" Her eyes narrowed. "These fake pills…who did this? Was it that pharmacy guy? What's going on?"

I tightened my grip on her hands.

"There isn't time to explain, Charlene. Noah's in real danger, and I—"

"Has someone taken him? That guy?—"

"Sorry, Charlene. I've gotta go. Now!"

"But…"

"Listen, I think you and Sally should kick everybody else out of here and close up for the night. Just say it's a family emergency. Something like that."

She stared at me for a long moment, breathing deeply. Then she glanced down at her hands, still clamped between mine. I let them go. Watched her struggle to calm herself.

"You're right," she said at last. "I should close up. God knows I'm useless out there."

I brought my gaze up to match hers.

"I'll get him back, Charlene."

She sniffed loudly, her shoulders straightening. As though willing herself to stay strong. Eyes boring into mine.

"You see that you do. You see that you bring him home."

Up ahead, beyond the snarl of traffic, I caught sight of Gloria's motel near PNC Park. A more upscale version of the motel chain Lyle had booked us into, it had two floors, a pool, and a decent-looking restaurant next door.

It was also perched at the top of a sloping hill. A paved road wound lazily from street level up to the motel entrance.

I'd already called Gloria from the car to fill her in about Noah and get her room number. Now, having finally navigated the clogged intersection, I drove up the curving road, parked in the near-empty lot, and knocked on her door. But it was Lyle Barnes who answered it.

"He has Noah," I said.

"I know. Gloria called and told me."

I followed him across the standard-issue motel room to the queen-sized bed where Gloria sat, glancing occasionally at her laptop on the side table. Its screen-saver was still the posed photo of Sebastian Maddox.

"Nothing yet." She gave me a quick nod as I sat next to her on the bed. Briefly clasped my hand.

"Maddox is enjoying making us wait," said Barnes.

"Won't be a long wait," I replied. "I can feel it."

Barnes remained standing, looking down at the two of us. Lined face grim. Eyes puffy with fatigue.

"I don't know about this idea of yours, Doc. Or even whether we can pull it off."

"I don't either, Lyle. I'm just guessing, based on my read of Maddox."

"Great. That's a load off my mind."

With that, Barnes began pacing back and forth, clucking his tongue. He was worse at waiting than Gloria.

Luckily, though, I'd been right about one thing.

Maddox didn't make us wait long.

He was wearing that same black hoodie.

As soon as the screen-saver disappeared on Gloria's laptop, it was replaced by a live-streaming image of Maddox. He'd tilted his camera lens so that we'd see him from the waist up, his face framed by the jacket's hood. The background was too vague to offer any clues as to his whereabouts.

I bristled involuntarily. Seeing him dressed that way—exactly as he'd been the night of Barbara's death—brought a familiar shard of pain. As he no doubt assumed it would.

"Good to see you again, Danny. Ready for the last act?"

Unlike on the night of the mugging, his dark green eyes weren't hidden in shadow. They were lit as though from an inner fire, somehow burning both hot and cold as he glared out from the screen.

The predator's blood lust. Incarnate.

Barnes had come to join Gloria and me sitting at bedside, his righteous outrage palpable. But before the ex-FBI man could say anything, I stopped him with a gesture. Spoke to the screen.

"Where's Noah, Maddox? What have you done with him?"

"Nothing...yet. But I have some big plans for your crazy friend. Which I'm sure you'll find fascinating. Illuminating, even. From a clinical standpoint, that is."

"What are you saying?"

"Now, now, let's not get ahead of ourselves. I think you and I both deserve the chance to savor this final moment. The culmination of our shared journey. Especially the way it's coming together. We should revel in its...wait, what's the word I'm looking for?..."

I paused. "Symmetry."

"Ah, you know me so well. Because you're right about the symmetry. See, Danny boy, tonight everything comes full circle. It ends where it all began. At least, for you and Noah."

"Ends where it began...?"

Gloria stirred. "What's he talking about?"

But I kept my eyes on the computer screen.

"You're at Ten Oaks, aren't you, Maddox? The clinic where Noah and I first met."

"Yes. A touching meet-cute, right out of a buddy movie. Noah, the poor schizophrenic patient; you, the untested but caring psych intern. Then he goes his way, you go yours. Until, years later, you meet again. And that, as Bogart might say, was the beginning of a beautiful friendship."

Next to me, Barnes whispered under his breath. "Isn't that place undergoing repairs?"

Maddox laughed. "Your *sotto voce* needs a little work, Lyle. But, yes, at the moment Noah and I have the place to ourselves. The workmen left about an hour ago, and the two security guards are otherwise engaged."

Gloria's tone was flat. "Meaning they're dead."

"Collateral damage, unfortunately." He spread his hands. "But it was all in a good cause. *My* cause."

I leaned forward, gaze meeting his.

"Again, two people with no connection to me have died. Very sloppy, Sebastian. Far outside the parameters of your so-called mission. In the military, they call this 'mission creep.'"

His knowing smile melted from his face.

"I don't like this new attitude I'm getting from you, Daniel. And it certainly won't help your friend Noah."

Barnes and Gloria both gave me worried, perplexed looks, which I studiously ignored. As I hardened my voice.

"We're not talking about me, Maddox. Or Noah. We're talking about *you*…and how you're starting to lose it."

His cold eyes narrowed. "Careful, Danny…"

"Fuck you, Maddox. I'm done being careful. All it's done is get people killed. And now that I know where you are, I'm coming after you. Tonight's the end, all right…for you!"

Then, without another word, I slammed the laptop lid shut.

"Jesus Christ!" Gloria gaped. "What are you doing? He has Noah, remember, and he might—"

I rose to my feet. "He won't do anything to Noah. Not until I'm there to see it. Which is my only chance to stop it."

Barnes shook his head. "I don't get it, Doc. You *know* who we're dealing with…"

"Yeah. Someone who's committed to seeing this thing through to the end. We have to count on that."

Gloria got up as well, pulling on a jacket. "Are we still sticking with your plan?"

I nodded. "I think it may even work better now that we know where he is. That is, *if* Ten Oaks still has power."

"Why?"

"You'll see." I headed for the door. "I just hope I got Maddox mad enough to mess with his head. If only for a little while. He's most dangerous when he thinks he's in control. So I tried to take that away from him. Gives us an edge."

As it turned out, I was wrong.

Chapter Thirty-nine

The cold night threw a starless shroud over the bedroom community of Penn Hills, its rolling contours obscured behind the misting rain. To the west, angry thunder rumbled.

Ten Oaks Psychiatric Hospital was located just within the town limits. With only a few lights glowing behind its many windows, nestled in the bank of trees that inspired its name, it loomed forbiddingly as I drove through its iron-wrought front gates. Surrounded by acres of landscaped lawns and gardens, it was a sprawling, gable-roofed building that had been—over a hundred years ago—the opulent home of one of Pittsburgh's earliest industrialists. Now it served the clinical needs of the most severely disturbed grandchildren and great-grandchildren of those same wealthy families.

Nearing the massive double front doors, I blinked against the harsh klieg lights buried in the rain-churned mud, trained on the temporary sheds, trucks, and construction equipment being used for the building's repairs. Though it wasn't until I'd parked on the empty gravel lot and trudged around the eerily silent vehicles and stacks of copper tubing that I saw the security guards' shack. It was larger than the kiosk at Bassmore Cemetery, but its single interior light and forlorn look in the black rain prompted a similar shudder of dread.

Taking my flashlight from my pocket, I forced myself to approach its opened doorway. I was less than a dozen feet away when I shone my light inside and saw the bodies.

Two men, of indeterminate age, both in the uniform of a well-known security company, lay next to each other, limbs intertwined. Blood still pooling beneath them from the gunshot wounds to their heads.

At least, what was left of them. Which wasn't much. Their skulls were shattered, caved in, bits of brain and pulpy flesh splattered against the shack's walls. Clinging in fat drops to a file cabinet, a *Playboy* calendar, a framed photo on the desk.

Involuntarily blinking against the horrific sight, I forced myself to keep thinking clearly. To process what I saw. Even in the diffused glow of my flashlight, I could tell each man had fallen victim to a high-powered weapon. Maybe a rifle, fired from a distance. Maddox had claimed to have one up at Bassmore.

I shook my head, as if to literally dislodge the abhorrent, blood-draped image from my mind, then started moving again. Veering past the guard shack, and guided by my flashlight, I slowly crept to the building's entrance. The gilt-edged doors were barely discernable in the darkness, but I was able to find one of the large handles and turn it.

Unsurprisingly, the door swung open easily. An invitation from Sebastian Maddox.

For a moment, I hesitated. I'd told Barnes and Gloria, who'd followed me here, to wait out on the street till I contacted them. I knew that Maddox would be watching my approach from somewhere within the building, and that if he saw I wasn't alone there'd be no predicting how he might react.

I stole my hand into my pocket, assuring myself that the throwaway cell was still there. Then I pushed open the entrance door and stepped inside.

In the dark, the spacious reception area seemed even more expansive than in daylight. I swung my flashlight beam around the room, giving me mere glimpses of the familiar high-end furnishings, wall prints, and admission desk. Then I aimed the light up at the huge circular skylight, its glass dome opaque against the night, rattling as raindrops pounded down on it.

It felt strange, being alone in the broad, unlit space that I'd once crossed daily on my way to the patient quarters and therapy rooms beyond. The extensive main body of the clinic was separated from the bright, welcoming reception area by a series of locked, heavily reinforced doors whose primary purpose was to muffle the anguished cries of the broken souls within.

Making my way slowly along the polished hardwood floor, swinging my flashlight beam waist-high in front of me, I looked for some sign from Maddox. Some indication of where I was supposed to go.

I found it. The doors to the patient wards were at the rear of the reception area, so it wasn't till I'd gotten close enough to shine my light on them that I saw that one was wide open.

This time I didn't hesitate but went straight through into the corridor, one of the main arteries linking the patient rooms and staff offices. My flashlight beam bobbing ahead of me, I headed down the narrow, shadowy hall, past the closed doors of the staff lounge, medical bay, and exercise rooms.

At the end of the corridor was the service elevator, its doors standing open as well, its starkly lit interior disconcerting in the relentless dark of the hall.

When I stepped inside the elevator cab, I noticed that the "Stop" button had been pushed, which accounted for the doors being locked in position. I also noticed that the only lighted button on the array above it read "Roof." Three floors up.

Again, my hand slipped into my pocket for the cell. But I knew better and didn't withdraw it. There was every chance that Maddox could, if not see me, at least have bugged the service elevator so that he could hear me.

A chance I couldn't take.

So I depressed the elevator's holding button, and the scratched, paint-flecked doors slowly rumbled closed. Then I pressed myself back against one of the elevator's walls as it began to rise.

The rain had increased in intensity, thick drops hitting the roof's flat, tar-papered surface like falling pebbles. Even with the aid of my flashlight, visibility was severely limited from the moment I stepped out of the elevator and heard its doors close behind me, taking its interior's blazing white light with it. The weathered stone gables at the roof's corners appeared merely as blurred, hulking shadows, their majestic peaks indistinguishable in the gloom.

Squinting against the rain and the darkness, aware of my progress across the roof only by the sound of my shoes scraping against loose cinders, I moved with a deliberate slowness. One foot in front of the other, swinging my flashlight beam in an arc before me.

Where was I supposed to go? What was I supposed to find? And what had happened to Noah?

Then, suddenly, something raw and desperate inside me gave voice to my frustration. My growing panic about my friend.

"Maddox!" I shouted over the rain. "Where are you?"

I took another few steps, anger rising.

"Maddox, where the fuck are you? Where's Noah?"

Nothing. No smirking laugh, no mocking retort.

"Where's Noah, Maddox? What have you done to him?"

It was only then that I heard the familiar, arrogant timbre of his voice. Amplified, mechanical. From a speaker.

"What have I done to Noah? Only grant him his fondest wish. His heart's desire."

I whirled, sharpening my ears. Trying to get a bead on where his voice was coming from.

I made another sweep of the roof with my light.

"Where is he? What are you talking about?"

"See for yourself, Danny. See little Noah, happy at last."

Suddenly, some kind of floodlight flared on to my right, illuminating a broad swath of the rooftop to my left. Eyes momentarily stabbed by the light, I staggered back.

Then, turning, I saw what that light revealed.

It was Noah Frye, standing with his back against the wall of a large, box-like structure probably containing the clinic's air and heating system. Rough-bricked, peaked with shingles sluicing rainwater. Squat and ugly.

But all I saw was Noah himself. Though his feet were flat on the tar-papered roof, his arms were outstretched, his face contorted in agony. Head lolling.

Even in the pouring rain, I could see the blood trailing from his hands, mixing with the water pooling at his feet. A swirling eddy of red and black.

The backs of his outstretched hands were each flush with the wall. Cruelly held there by thick nails, driven deep into his palms.

Noah had been crucified.

It took an eternity of seconds to accept the unspeakable reality of what I was seeing. Then, shoving my flashlight into my free pocket, I started running toward him.

I wasn't three feet away when his head rolled up, terror-filled eyes blazing into mine. His voice like grinding glass.

"My God, my God, why hast Thou forsaken me?"

His body had already begun to slump, its weight pulling against the flesh of his hands where they were nailed to the wall. Tearing against tendons, muscles, bone.

With a cry, I threw myself against his body, trying to hoist it up with my own. To relieve the pressure on his ravaged hands, his distended arms.

"Noah! It's me! I'm here!"

Whether he heard me, or even comprehended what I'd said, I'll never know.

With his rain-drenched hair matted in wild ringlets, his eyes streaming tears, he rolled his head up again, face pointing to the heavens. A wild, animal cry of pain, of intolerable agony, exploding from his lips. Primal. Heart-rending.

Half-mad with my own grief, I began frantically looking around the rain-soaked roof for something to pry the nails out. At a loss, I went around the corner of the brick shed and spotted a small wooden access panel. Probably used to enter when the machinery within needed repair. I ran up and kicked at the wood. It was old and splintered, but from the deep thud I could tell it was pretty thick. Good.

Crouching beside the panel, I dug my fingers into the edge of one of its sides and pulled. I heard a dull crack, and, pulling harder, broke off a length of rough, jagged wood. About the size and thickness of a two-by-four.

I ran back to Noah and wedged the piece of wood under the broad head of the thick construction nail buried in his left hand. Bracing my knee against the brick wall, I tried to use the wood as a lever to work the nail out. At first it wouldn't budge, so I began wrenching the wooden stave back and forth, widening the hole, hoping to loosen the nail's bite in the wall. Ignoring Noah's panicked, guttural screams.

Finally, pulling with all my strength, I yanked the bloodied nail free. Which brought another howl of pain from Noah, as I let it fall to the roof's surface. His weakened left arm instantly dropped, dangling uselessly at his side.

Repeating the same agonizing steps, I used the shaft of wood to work the nail out from his other hand. Though by then Noah's only response was a choked whimper. His freed right arm flopping against his side.

Gasping, I tossed the broken piece of wood to the roof, even as Noah began to fall forward. I reached for him.

Wrapping my own arms around his barrel chest, I gently lowered him to the roof's wet surface. Lay his head back against the wall, down which blood and rain drizzled in rivulets.

"Help's coming, Noah. Stay with me, okay?"

But his head fell forward again, chin resting on his chest. He was unconscious.

Hands open, bleeding freely, profusely.

Quickly I snatched the cell from my pocket.

"Lyle! Gloria! Now! The roof. You'll find Noah—"

Those were the last words I remember saying. Suddenly I was aware of a rush of footsteps splashing behind me, and then felt a searing pain at the back of my head.

And then I felt nothing at all.

Chapter Forty

I only knew one thing.

As my eyes became accustomed to the dim, green-tinged light, I realized I was in some kind of cage.

Coming to, I'd found myself lying on my back on something cold and hard. Though my head ached from where Maddox had struck me, I managed to pull myself up to a sitting position, my hand rubbing the raised bump at the back of my skull.

Forcing myself to breathe deeply and slowly, I struggled to understand where I was. The answers came quickly.

I was sitting on the concrete floor of something big and rectangular, a cavernous expanse with smooth walls lit by enclosed globes embedded at regular intervals. It was a swimming pool. The unused, emptied indoor Olympic-sized pool that had been one of the storied features of this turn-of-the-century mansion. It was in a high-ceilinged, below-ground structure whose length and breadth spanned the entire dimensions of the great house above.

When, years later, the building was converted to a private psychiatric clinic, the administration at Ten Oaks maintained the swimming pool to provide exercise for its patients—until one resident, despite being supervised by a staff counselor at the time, managed to drown himself. The pool was immediately drained, and stayed that way ever since.

By now, my head had cleared enough for me to risk standing,

though I was a bit wobbly at first. To maintain my balance, I instinctively grabbed for the wooden sticks that made up the walls of my cage. Smooth, rounded sticks with knobs at their ends, the whole cage reinforced by thick wire mesh with which they were interwoven.

Gripping the bars of my cage with both hands, I swiveled my head around, anxious to get my bearings before Maddox appeared. As I knew he would.

The cage was about six feet by six, enclosing me on all sides except the floor. It had been placed in the far end of the pool, where it gently sloped so that, when filled, it would be the deepest part. Long-empty, the pool was dry and cracked, a huge rectangular space that dwarfed the size of my cage. And made me wonder—

Suddenly, something about the way the rounded sticks felt in my hands made me release my grip. Their smoothness, the pale whiteness, the knobby ends encircled and held by wire mesh…

The cage wasn't formed by wood. These were…bones.

Human bones.

I staggered back, mouth opened in horror.

Because I knew. I finally understood.

Based on what Maddox had called himself. How he'd referred to himself as an "excitable boy." Like the title of the song by Warren Zevon. A song about a disturbed teenager who rapes and kills his prom date. And then, after he's released from a psychiatric facility, he—

The last lyric flickered in my mind.

"He dug up her grave and built a cage with her bones…"

That's what Maddox had done. Now I knew what had happened to Barbara's remains. Those he'd stolen from her grave at Bassmore and replaced with a manikin.

He'd built this cage out of her bones.

Stunned, I stared down at my hands, which moments before had gripped her bones like a prisoner grasping the bars of his cell.

Which is what Maddox had done to me. He'd made me a prisoner in a cell formed by my late wife's exhumed bones. Stripped of whatever flesh had remained, rubbed clean and smooth. Her literal skeleton encasing me.

The horror of it flooded through me, and I doubled over. Bent, heaving, as though to vomit. Tasting the bile in my mouth.

I retched. Cried out. A choked, anguished cry.

I couldn't stand it, couldn't allow it to be true...

But it was. And suddenly the whole world seemed to be tilting on its axis. Spinning. A black, unending vortex, into which I felt myself falling...

My legs gave out from under me and I fell to my knees. My head in my hands, I began to slowly rock. Lips moving, but with no words coming forth. Just a low, sibilant moan.

An acid-like, skin-peeling pain enveloped me. Tears streamed from my eyes. At the same time, a pulsating, convulsive shudder tore through me.

I felt like I was coming apart.

Then, from the deepest part of me, I gave voice to a different, terrible, full-throated cry. An angry howl.

Of resolve. Of defiance.

No...! This is what he wants. To break you...

Gasping, spittle dripping from my lips, limbs quivering, I shook off the nausea. Flattened my palms against the concrete floor. Began pushing myself up to my feet. Slowly, falteringly, as if under a great weight.

Until, finally, I rose. Legs wobbling beneath me.

And saw, standing not a dozen feet away from me on the swimming pool's floor, Sebastian Maddox.

He was still in the black hoodie and jeans, though with the cowl thrown back. His shaved head gleamed under the fluorescent lights hanging from the ceiling far above us. His eyes aglow.

Maddox took a few steps closer, raising his hands. In one, he held a canister of gasoline. Both its label and the pungent smell proclaimed what is was.

In his other hand was a small canvas bag, containing something whose shape was like that of a bowling ball.

He held it up toward me. Smiling.

"You know what this is, don't you, Danny?"

I nodded. I wouldn't say the words.

"But don't worry, you'll get to hold it soon. Lovingly, in sad remembrance. Like Hamlet with Yorick. In fact, I was going to leave it in the cage for you to find, but then I had a better idea. I'll just toss it in with you at the end." He shrugged. "What can I do? I'm a sucker for the dramatic gesture."

Still smiling, he lowered the bag to the floor. Then he began unscrewing the cap on the gasoline canister.

"By the way," he said casually, "in case you're wondering, your friend Noah is still up on the roof. His hands look pretty bad, but I don't think he'll bleed out. Not until I get back up there and help finish the job. I'm thinking maybe I'll stab him in his side. Like that Roman guard did to Christ with his lance. I think Noah'd like that, don't you? Kind of completes the whole crucifixion thing."

I did my best to hide my reaction. Meanwhile, my mind raced. Did Barnes and Gloria even receive my last message to them? To get to the roof and find Noah? All I could do now was hope that they had, and that they were at this very moment coming to his aid.

"Luckily for you," Maddox went on, oblivious, "Noah's unconscious, so he doesn't know that it was *you* who spoiled the fulfillment of his life's desire. If it wasn't for you, he'd have died like he'd wanted. Alone and reviled for his sins. A fitting end that you took away from him."

Maddox started walking backwards, one measured step at a time, pouring the gasoline in a thin stream from the canister, making a zig-zag pattern on the concrete floor.

I stealthily reached into my pocket for my cell.

It was gone.

Maddox stopped what he was doing long enough to give me a knowing smirk.

"Oh, come on. I took your cell from you when you were out cold. And your flashlight. In case you were thinking of throwing it at me. You know, I'm still pretty pissed about that steak knife you threw in your kitchen. Not to mention how you spoiled my chance to get rid of both the old man and the girl."

He went back to spreading the gasoline.

"I suppose I'll get around to them later. Leaving things undone is a sure sign of laziness, and I pride myself on being steadfast when it comes to task-completion."

Maddox shook the last of the gasoline from the canister. After watching the shining liquid swirl and undulate like a living thing on the concrete, he gazed back at me.

"I've waited a long time for this moment, Danny boy. But unlike poor Noah, I *am* getting to fulfill my heart's desire. To see you die in a cage of Barbara's bones. To see you both consumed forever in a lake of fire."

The phrase brought a flicker of recognition to my mind. He must have seen that reflected in my face.

He put down the empty can and folded his arms.

"Well, maybe you're not the cretin I supposed," he said. "Seems you've heard of the lake of fire. Spoken of by Plato in his Phaedo. In reference to Tartarus, where the souls of the wicked are tormented for eternity."

I took a step forward, my face close to the sides of the cage, my own eyes returning Maddox's unwavering stare. While a single thought burned in my mind.

If Barnes and Gloria *had* arrived, and were in the building, there was still a chance for my plan to work. But only if Gloria had managed to find the Clinic Director's office.

For the first time since Maddox had appeared, I spoke.

"So I'm supposed to die in a lake of fire? Here, in a goddam swimming pool?"

"A classic end, don't you think, Danny? Enveloped in flames in your own private hell, in the basement of the building where you and Noah Frye first met. Another circle completed."

"Yeah, I get it, Maddox. Symmetry. But that's only if I stay cooped up in here."

I abruptly backed up, about to kick out at the bones and wire mesh. To break out of my cage.

Until the gun in Maddox's hand stopped me. An automatic.

"You're not going anywhere, Danny. Of course, I'd much rather see you burned alive, screaming in agony, but I'll settle for shooting you and watching your corpse go up in smoke."

He kept the gun aimed at my chest. "It's your torment I want. But it's your death that I *need*."

It was then that I knew I had to risk it. I couldn't afford to wait any longer.

"You got what you wanted, Maddox." My voice low, measured. "The truth is, I've been in torment since this whole thing started. But the worst torment was to come."

He frowned. "What are you talking about?"

"I'm talking about Barbara's private journal. One she'd been keeping in the last years of our marriage. When things were falling apart between us."

"A journal?"

I nodded. "Before having to leave my house, I went through all her things. Hoping I'd find something that might help me. That's when I came upon the journal. I never even knew that she'd been keeping one."

"Vaguely interesting. But so what?"

"I read it last night, and it devastated me. Because it was all about you."

He started. "Me?"

"Yes, Maddox. You. It—"

Suddenly, it came. Through the clinic's extensive P.A. system. Gloria's strong, clear voice, from the wall speakers.

"*Oh, God, what a mistake I've made,*" she said, the words

echoing off the tiled walls of the underground enclosure. "*What a terrible, terrible mistake.*"

Maddox squinted at me in confusion.

"Isn't that—?"

"Yes," I said firmly. "It's Gloria Reese. I gave her the journal. Told her to read it."

"Why, for Christ's sake?" His own voice rising.

"Because I don't want to be the only one in torment, you son of a bitch. I don't want to be the only one suffering."

His face was twisted by sheer incomprehension. Meanwhile, Gloria's words droned on, filling the concrete expanse as though a voice from the grave.

"*I never should have married Danny. It was Sebastian, all along. Right from the beginning. I loved him as much as he loved me, but I was too blind to see it. Too foolish to know my own heart.*"

Maddox blinked furiously. "Wait a minute, this isn't real. It's some kind of—"

"*When I think of the things I said to him, I'm filled with shame. Yelling at him on the street. Calling him 'Mad Maddox' in the school cafeteria. All those spiteful, hurtful things I said. And all he wanted was to declare his love for me.*"

I called to Maddox from within my cage.

"It's no trick, Sebastian. It's her journal, all right. How would I know she called you 'Mad Maddox'?"

"She...she might've told you..." His voice quavering.

"You know that she didn't. Remember, I didn't even know you existed until a week ago, when you showed me the video of you and Joy Steadman. Barbara never once mentioned you when we were together. But now, thanks to this goddam journal—"

"Shut up!!" Maddox had lowered the gun, his head tilted up. Listening to Gloria's slowly rising voice, the bristling of emotion threading through it.

"*Sebastian was everything a woman could want. Handsome,*"

strong, brilliant. And he could have been mine. What a stupid, unthinking bitch I was! How I've ruined my life!"

"It's her…" Maddox's own voice had softened to a harsh whisper. "It's…I can hear her in the words…"

"Instead, I'm married to Danny. My father was so right about him. How unsuited he is for marriage. Stubborn, self-absorbed. Arrogant. That's the irony. Against my father's wishes, I married a man who's exactly like him! And it's a living hell."

Maddox raced up to the cage, eyes ablaze as he smiled at me. Sweat glistening on his forehead.

"See, Rinaldi? She *hated* you! She finally realized she never should have been with you, when she could've been with me. She *did* love me. Me, *not* you!"

"But everything's going to be all right. The way it should have been. I checked, and Sebastian's being released from Buckville in three weeks. I just have to last three more weeks with Danny, until my true love—my real, true love—gets out of prison. Then I can divorce Danny and run back to Sebastian. If he'll even take me back, if he doesn't hate the sight of me. Oh, God, please let him still love me! Like I love him. Then, at last, we can be together. The way it should've been. The way it will be. I know it. I love him! I love him so much—"

Suddenly, her voice fell silent. A silence so stunning and total that it seemed to reverberate off the walls.

I stared at Maddox's wide, crazed eyes through the cage separating us.

"That's it," I said coolly. "The end of the journal."

"But you heard her." A pained, horrified grin. "She loves me! She wants to be with me! You know what this means?"

"Yeah. It means you killed the only woman who loved you."

Grin vanishing, his brow screwed up in agony, eyes burning with intolerable pain at the realization of what he'd done.

As I'd hoped. Instead of challenging Maddox's delusion that Barbara had loved him, I'd used what he thought were her own words to *confirm* it. To hammer into his brain, like the nails he'd driven into Noah, the awful consequences of his actions.

Now I gazed mercilessly at that shattered face, a rictus of mad grief. Each of my words a punishing blow.

"Her *murder*, Maddox. And everything you've done since then. *All a mistake.* A horrible mistake. *Because she loved you and you killed her.* Ending the life you two could have had together."

He stepped back, mouth working, soundless lips trembling.

"With the woman whose head is in that bag at your feet..."

As though in a trance, he peered down at the canvas bag on the concrete floor, encircled by eddies of gasoline. The smell of the liquid now permeating the whole room.

The gun dropped from his grasp.

"No...I...Oh, God, oh no! I..."

He staggered back another few feet, hands clasping the top of his head. As though to keep it from exploding.

That was my chance. I reared back and kicked at the wire mesh. Once, twice. The gate swung open, bits of bone and twisted wire hanging loose from the mesh.

Barbara's bones...

Another wave of nausea convulsed me, as the image seared itself into my brain. Piercing, penetrating. Shattering.

But I fought against it. Pushed it down. To be replaced by an anguished, inchoate rage.

In two strides I was on Maddox, and we collapsed, fiercely grappling each other, to the wet floor. Gasping, I tried to pin him down. But he was as strong as he looked, and managed to push me off. As I fell back, barely staying on my feet, he rushed me, raising his fist.

It was a clumsy blow, but a powerful one, and it sent me reeling. Then he backstepped, hunkering low, eyes filled with a hatred I'd never witnessed before.

I saw something else, too. For Sebastian Maddox, there was nothing to lose now. No turning back.

The same was true for me. As my own hate rose up inside me. Coursing like hot lava through my veins.

Suddenly, propelled by feelings beyond my control, I lunged forward. Tackled him at the knees.

He went down hard, the back of his head thudding against the concrete. I got on top and pummeled him with my fists, my rage now so unmanageable that I was afraid I'd never stop.

For Barbara, for everyone he'd hurt or killed…

His face bloodied, his eyes streaming tears of pain, he tried to wriggle out from under me. Huge hands gripping my shoulders, pushing up. A gasp of intolerable pain issuing from his split lips.

I brought my fist down again, connecting with his jaw.

His eyes rolled up in their sockets. But I kept hitting him.

I couldn't stop. I wanted to kill him.

I was *going* to kill him.

"Doc! No!"

Lyle Barnes' voice cut through the haze of my own madness, my own lust for blood. For revenge.

"Stop, Danny! DANNY!"

It was Gloria this time. Coming from somewhere behind me.

And then, just as suddenly, it was over. I felt the rage ebb out of me, even as I was aware of the pain in my fists. My battered hands, bloody and throbbing.

I reared back, gasping for breath, and rolled off Maddox's prone body. He seemed barely conscious, but breathing. Alive.

Climbing awkwardly to my feet, I turned and saw Barnes and Gloria standing at the edge of the pool. Gaping at me in alarm.

"Are you okay?" Gloria called to me.

I managed a brief nod. "But Noah…"

It was Barnes who answered. "We found him. I stayed with him till the ambulance got here. The EMTs are with him now."

Still trying to catch my breath, I headed toward where the two of them stood at pool's edge, my shoes slipping a bit on the inch-high river of gasoline.

I'd almost made it across the pool floor when Gloria cried out, pointing past me.

"Danny! Watch out!"

I turned and looked behind me, in time to see Sebastian Maddox on his feet. Dazed, stumbling. His own shoes sloshing in gasoline as he veered toward where he'd dropped the automatic.

"The gun!" Barnes shouted.

Maddox scooped it up, then turned toward me. But didn't shoot. Instead, with a look of poisonous rage, he gave me a cool, even smile. Monstrous in its hatred and self-loathing.

I knew then what he was about to do. To both of us.

Smile intact, he lowered the gun and aimed it at the swirling eddies of liquid. And fired.

The gunshot's boom echoed in the cavernous chamber, as the bullet sparked off the concrete. Igniting the gasoline.

In second, flames leapt up, spreading in all directions. Toward Maddox. And me.

"Danny!" Gloria screamed. "Run!"

I turned again and started running to the pool's edge, the heat of the encroaching flames searing my back. Barnes and Gloria were leaning over, hands outstretched, ready to pull me up to the lip of the pool.

Stumbling as I ran, enveloped by the smell of burning gasoline, I somehow made it to the pool's edge before the flames could reach me. Eager hands grabbed at mine, and, together, Barnes and Gloria heaved me up onto safety. I rolled on the concrete lip of the pool, gasping.

Gloria bent over me, both worried and relieved. Behind her, though, Barnes had straightened, and was pointing toward the other end of the pool.

"My God," he said quietly. "Look."

I scrambled to my haunches and followed his gaze.

By now, the pool was entirely engulfed in flames—having literally become a lake of fire.

There, at its end, stood the bone-and-wire cage with tongues of flame licking at its sides.

Inside the cage was Sebastian Maddox, the canvas bag at his feet. Cradled in his arms was a skull. That of my late wife.

I couldn't breathe. Couldn't parse out the jumbled cascade of emotions burbling within me. And doubted I ever would.

Instead, I just stared in disbelief at Maddox, his face unreadable, standing stolidly in the middle of the cage.

And then, in an angry rush, the flames roared up, advancing on the cage. Encircling it. As though they were the manifestation of his own private, unshakable demons. Seeking their due.

The three of us stood, unmoving, spellbound. Unable to speak. Even as the heat from the lake of fire pulsed against us, stinging our eyes, baking our skin.

Within moments, the cage—and the mad creature within it—were swallowed whole by the fiery inferno. If Sebastian Maddox cried out from the heart of this flaming pyre, or made any sound at all, I didn't hear it.

Instead, what I did hear, far in the distance, was the wail of approaching sirens.

Chapter Forty-one

We had, as Sergeant Harry Polk pointed out, a lot of explaining to do.

It was less than an hour later, and he had Barnes, Gloria, and me sequestered in a well-appointed visitor's alcove in the clinic's reception area. Weirdly, it was bright as day. The uniformed cops, called to the scene by Barnes right after he'd summoned the ambulance, had turned on all the lights.

Soon afterwards, Polk and his partner Jerry Banks arrived, followed by two fire trucks that had also been called to the scene. The firefighters extinguished what few flames had yet to burn themselves out in the subterranean pool, and had remained on-scene to assess the situation. They were then joined by CSU techs and a young medico from the coroner's office, tasked with dealing with what was left of Sebastian Maddox.

Now, arrayed on the absurdly luxurious couches, beneath framed plaques displaying awards that Ten Oaks had received from various civic organizations, we watched an incredulous Polk scratch his bristly chin. Midnight was not a good time for him.

"Okay," he began in a weary tone. "Let's get everybody sorted out."

Lyle Barnes explained who he was and the nature of his involvement in the past week's events, and then Gloria Reese did the same. When added to my own report, Polk had enough to get a general sense of what had happened.

"Y'ins all know how fucked-up this is, right?" He flipped his notebook closed. "I mean, each o' ya will have to give more complete statements downtown, but just from what ya told me…"

He shook his head, then turned to me.

"So *you're* the one who pulled Angie Villanova outta the river? And ya didn't say nothin' in the hospital room?"

"I told you, Harry. Maddox threatened to kill a lot of innocent people if we alerted the cops. Or the Feds. To prove it, he even did so…that drive-by shooting in Blawnox…"

He scowled. "Yeah. Well, as an old captain of mine used to say, tell it to the judge. Now, about tonight…"

I explained my plan to use entries from a fake journal that my late wife had supposedly kept to rattle Maddox. My thought was to disabuse him of the rightness of his mission of revenge, forcing him to decompensate. Lose control. Giving me enough leverage to stop, and, with any luck, subdue him.

"I wanted to use his own delusion against him," I said. "Which is what triggered Maddox's guilt. Made him hate himself for killing her. That's why he cracked. When a person's delusions are confirmed, and then a terrible outcome derives from its being true, it can be literally devastating."

"That's where I came in." Gloria stirred. "While Lyle looked after Noah Frye, I found my way to the Clinic Director's office and used the P.A. system's mike to read those words Danny had written. Supposedly revealing to Maddox that Barbara had actually loved him, too, and regretted marrying Danny."

I spoke again. "This way, Maddox would be in extreme internal conflict over the fact that he'd mistakenly killed her. And this would destabilize him. Which, hopefully, we could use to our advantage."

Polk merely glared. "Uh-huh."

Barnes laughed. "Yeah, I know, Sergeant. At first, I felt the same way."

He turned to me. "By the way, Doc, you did a great job making it sound like Barbara thought you were an asshole."

"It wasn't that hard. She often did."

A lame remark, I admit. But I have an excuse.

I was slowly going into shock.

For the next two nights, I woke up gasping, crying out. Disoriented, feverish, drenched in sweat. My fragmented dreams a kaleidoscope of vivid, excoriating images, replaying the horrors of the past week. The loss of life of friends and patients. The recurring, sickening experience of being trapped in a cage made from Barbara's bones.

A cage, in my dreams, from which I never escape.

Of course, I recognized the symptoms. The hallmarks of severe trauma. I also knew that I needed help. So the first morning after the fire, before being picked up at my house and driven downtown to give my formal statement to the cops, I contacted my old therapist, Dr. Ricci. Luckily, he made room in his schedule to see me later that day.

Other than that required trip, I stayed alone in my house. Rarely eating, swallowing pain pills, and doing my best to tend to my physical wounds. These, I knew, would heal pretty quickly.

It was the wounds to my head that concerned me.

Yet, by the second day, after setting up some regular sessions with Dr. Ricci for the foreseeable future, I began to feel more or less all right. Just knowing I was starting toward some kind of equilibrium about what Maddox had wrought provided great solace.

Meanwhile, watching the story unfold on the local and national media, I was grateful for my self-imposed isolation. Every hour, more details about Sebastian Maddox's bizarre reign of terror were revealed. How such seemingly unrelated deaths as those of Stephen Langley and Harvey Blalock were connected. How the kidnapping of young Robbie Palermo figured into Maddox's plans. And what had actually happened to Pittsburgh PD's own Angela Villanova.

Naturally, I was the focus of all these revelations. Which meant my phone rang constantly. Worried calls from colleagues and friends on my home answering machine, and from anxious patients on my office line. Requests for interviews from both local and national reporters.

At least, I recall thinking, there was a silver lining to having my cell phone in pieces and my laptop destroyed at the safe house: no flood of e-mails choking my inbox.

True, I had to contend with the army of media types camped out on my front lawn. On-scene reporters standing next to my Mustang, complaining to viewers about my unwillingness to be interviewed, or to take one step outside my house.

Soon enough, however, they tired of this waiting game and moved on to other stories. And, thankfully, other locations.

The only other piece of good news came at the end of the second day, when Harry Polk left a message about Lieutenant Biegler's desire to get me booted from the Department. In the swirl of publicity about the Maddox affair, and with Chief Logan mentioning during a press conference his gratitude for my help in rescuing Angie, Biegler apparently felt it wise to refrain from going forward with his complaint.

Though relieved to hear it, I also knew that Biegler wouldn't stop trying to damage me in the eyes of the Department brass. Fuck him. After what I'd just been through, I had more to worry about than the machinations of some ambitious creep.

I did, however, make two calls while sequestered at home, both to hospitals. First, I checked in about Noah's condition at Pittsburgh Memorial. Despite his considerable blood loss, he was slowly recovering from his injuries. His hands would require surgery, after which he'd have to begin a regimen of physical therapy. Whether he'd ever regain full use of them was as yet too soon to determine. Especially with his being a pianist. The odds, the surgeon admitted, were markedly against him....

Charlene was in Noah's hospital room, so after speaking with the doctor I asked to talk to her. She was holding up well, it seemed, though I could hear the tremor in her voice. She did report that Noah was once again on medication, and that his mental status was more or less within the acceptable range. Before hanging up, I made plans to come visit him tomorrow.

I got similar conflicted news from Dr. Hilvers regarding Angie's condition. He was happy to report that her speech was improving. But as to the long-term effect of the paralysis on her left side, he once again demurred from making a prognosis. As I had with Charlene, I told him I'd check in on Angie personally the next day.

After finishing that second call, I sat back at my rolltop desk and let my grim thoughts arrange themselves.

Noah and Angie had each paid a heavy cost for Sebastian Maddox's insane war against me. Though not as heavy as that borne by Stephen Langley and Harvey Blalock. And it was only dumb luck that rescued Robbie Palermo from a similar fate.

My last thought, though, was for Joy Steadman, whose vicious murder was the starting point for everything that followed. Her death was an unconscionable loss, and one whose echoes will stay with me for a long time.

The following morning, as I sat out on my rear deck, drinking black coffee and watching the sun break through the last lingering rain clouds, I heard a message being left on my answering machine inside.

It was Eleanor Lowrey, her voice laced with concern, asking how I was doing in the wake of all that had happened. And then saying that we should probably talk soon. About us.

While I was debating whether or not to pick up the phone, her message ended. Just as well. Given my state of mind, it wasn't a conversation I was up to having at the moment.

By mid-morning, showered and dressed, I drove over to where Lyle Barnes and I had agreed to meet. It was a coffee place near his house in Franklin Park. He still owned that weary, sleep-deprived look, though his arm was no longer in a sling.

"Your reporter friend, Sam Weiss, keeps calling." He frowned. "But I keep putting him off. Who needs that crap?"

I nodded. "He'll probably want an exclusive with me, too, but knows me well enough to wait till the dust settles."

"Has it settled?" His eyes found mine. "For you, I mean?"

"Not yet. But it will."

We spoke about the past week's events for a while, and then I asked for the check. I also suggested that Lyle consider resuming therapy with me for his night terrors.

"I'll give it some thought, Doc. Though I've been sleeping pretty well the last couple nights. For me, at least. I knew I would, once we took down Maddox."

When we were about to leave, he reached under his seat and brought up Barbara's bound manuscript. Handed it to me.

"I was damned curious, but I didn't read it," he said. "I figured that the first look belonged to you."

Gloria Reese closed the door of her office in the FBI building downtown and returned to her seat behind her desk.

After a long, welcoming hug when I first entered the room, she'd indicated the single chair facing her desk. I took it.

Like Barnes, Gloria seemed exhausted, her face drawn. Looking especially pale when contrasted with her business jacket and black slacks—the standard FBI outfit for female agents.

"Are things okay here?" I leaned forward. "I mean, with the Bureau. After what you did?"

"You mean, working a serious case off the books? Not informing my superiors about a mad killer at large? Endangering the lives of the public? Yeah, the Director loved all that."

"So what'll happen to you?"

"Could go either way. Given all the press coverage, they might be forced to give me a commendation. On the other hand, I might get sent back to Quantico for re-training."

"I'm sorry you got caught up in all this, Gloria. Grateful for your help, but still sorry."

Her hand reached across the desk to take mine.

"I'm not. Though I'm not sure what happens next. With you and me, I mean."

"Neither am I. But I'm willing to find out."

And I was.

Chapter Forty-two

They held a memorial service for Harvey Blalock the next day at his neighborhood church. I was among the mourners, standing well back from the altar, where one after another of his friends, family members, and colleagues eulogized him. For whatever reason—perhaps out of consideration for Harvey's wife and children—Lily Chen wasn't in attendance.

When I walked outside, I was pleased to see that the skies above the city had cleared. Although it was still fairly cool, there was some comfort in feeling the sun on my face.

I was joined on the sidewalk by Chief Logan, Harry Polk, and District Attorney Leland Sinclair, as well as a number of local luminaries. Sober handshakes all around, and then, predictably, we scattered. As I left, I noticed the Mayor being bundled into a limo by his handlers. But, never one to miss a photo-op, only after he'd smiled for some upraised cameras.

In a matter of minutes, the rest of us left as well.

And life, as it always does, went on.

That night, I found myself where I'd been at the very beginning. Sitting on the sofa in my front room, whiskey in hand, flipping through the pages of the dossier. Scanning the reports, photos, and case notes that had started it all.

I noted, ruefully, that there was a symmetry to this that Sebastian Maddox would appreciate.

I drained my glass. Then got up, went into the bedroom, and opened the closet door. Placing the dossier on the top shelf, I pushed it as far to the back as it would go.

I doubted I'd ever want to open up that dossier again, but somehow I felt the need to keep it.

Returning to the sofa, I poured myself another drink, then picked up Barbara's unfinished manuscript from the coffee table. Her scholarly work on linguistics that she'd dedicated to me.

But I didn't open it. Not just yet. I needed time to let the truth of my feelings speak to me.

And to listen to what they had to say.

From the moment I'd received the dossier, my desire to find out what really happened that deadly night long ago was prompted mostly by a sense of duty. By what I believed was my obligation to Barbara. In honor of our past love.

But what I *couldn't* do then—and still couldn't now—was locate that love in the present, the actual living love that I once had for her. It was as if all that remained was the memory of having loved her. Before. In another life.

I took a deep breath, then let myself lie back against the sofa cushions. Instinctively closing my eyes.

Maybe this was what it meant to be "moving on." Now *there's* a cold, unrepentant phrase. Accurate, perhaps, though something about its self-justification has always bothered me.

Whatever I might call what I was feeling, I couldn't deny that I felt it. No matter what it did or didn't say about me.

And then I recalled something written many years ago by John Fowles, one of my favorite authors: "All pasts are like poems. You can derive a thousand things, but you can't live in them."

I always treasured the wisdom in those words. And I knew that they were true.

So, eyes still closed, I pictured Barbara in my mind. And silently thanked her for our brief, passionate, and complicated life together.

I sat like that for a good long while. And then I opened her manuscript.

It was an academic work deconstructing some conventional wisdom regarding linguistics. Since it wasn't my field, I didn't grasp all of it. But even I could appreciate its subtlety, its profound insight. And wished that she'd been able to finish it.

Then I heard the words echo in my mind. Clear and bittersweet.

Good-bye, Barbara.

I turned the last page.

To see more Poisoned Pen Press titles:

Visit our website:
poisonedpenpress.com
Request a digital catalog:
info@poisonedpenpress.com

CPSIA information can be obtained
at www.ICGtesting.com
Printed in the USA
BVHW080154030119
536941BV00001B/15/P

9 781464 208188